M000209344

HALCYON

"So, how we going play this, Sheppard? You let them bottle us up, and—"

"I'm working on it," Sheppard replied, cutting Ronon off. "We miss our call-in and Atlantis will send out Lorne and a rescue team."

"That's not much of a plan."

"Hey, I'm making this up as I go."

Rodney snorted. "No change from normal there, then."

"I see one," said Bishop. "End of the street, he's scoping us."

"They won't try to wait us out," said Dex, "that's not how they do it. They'll rush us." He sneered. "Wraith like the direct approach."

"Couldn't be more than a dozen of them clowns out there," noted Hill, "even counting those we put down."

Sheppard looked around. "Ammo check. Anyone low?" He got a chorus of negatives from everyone except Teyla. The Athosian woman was stock still, sighting down the length of her gun. "Teyla, you with us?"

She shuddered, and he saw the distant, fearful look in her eyes that he knew meant trouble. "John. There are more Wraith out there. A lot more. They know—"

Teyla's words were drowned out in a howling chorus of blaster bolts as the aliens opened up on the stone building from all sides.

"Return fire!" barked Sheppard. "Targets of opportunity!"

STARGATE
ATLĂNTIS ™

HALCYON

JAMES SWALLOW

FANDEMONIUM BOOKS

An original publication of Fandemonium Ltd, produced under license from MGM Consumer Products.

Fandemonium Books
PO Box 795A
Surbiton
Surrey KT5 8YB
United Kingdom
Visit our website: www.stargatenovels.com

S T A R G A T E
A T L A N T I S ™

METRO-GOLDWYN-MAYER Presents
STARGATE ATLANTIS
JOE FLANIGAN   TORRI HIGGINSON   RACHEL LUTTRELL   JASON MOMOA
with PAUL McGILLION as Dr. Carson Beckett and DAVID HEWLETT as Dr. McKay
Executive Producers BRAD WRIGHT & ROBERT C. COOPER
Created by BRAD WRIGHT & ROBERT C. COOPER

ISBN: 1-905586-01-9   ISBN-13: 978-1-905586-01-1

Printed in the United Kingdom by Bookmarque Ltd, Croydon, Surrey

For Jo and Dave,
for Adam, Sarah, Sam and Emma
— my favorite Goa'ulds.

<u>Acknowledgements</u>

Special thanks to Mum and Dad and Mandy, Barry and Karen and Nicola, Colin and Brenda and Kathy, John and Christine and Vicki and Andrew, Darren and Mandy and Callum and Regan, Sue and Carole, Darren and Emma and Harry and Matthew, Philip and Mary, and Aunt Glad.

Tips of the hat to Steve and Jo, Ming, Ian and Diane, Pete and Mike, Pete and Nicola, Jon and Sophie and Alex, Mark and Suzanne, Paul and Jo, Jackie and Paul, Andy, Rhianna, Ashley and Jane, Adam and Liz and Isabel, Alison and Jeff, Dennis, Karen, Tom and Max, Ave, Jonno, Big Al, Cathy and Paul, Sue, Win and Cat, Sean, Stewart, Kathy and Martin, Gary, John and Jack, Nick, Dave and Vicki, Tony and Jane, Piers, Christine and Ian, Andrew, Tina, Joan and Mike and Alison, Rachel, Paul and Judie, Jim and Chris, Wil and Sue, Viv and many more who know who they are.

Thanks also to Karen Traviss, Dave Bishop and the gang at Novelscribes, to Sally and Tom for coming back, and finally to Keith Topping and David Howe for going Beyond The Gate.

Author's Note:
The events depicted in *Halcyon* take place in the second
season of *Stargate Atlantis*, between the episodes "Runner"
and "The Lost Boys".

CHAPTER ONE

The phenomenon was wholly alien to her. She tried to quantify it, to find an antecedent from her life that could compare. Nothing suggested itself; the sensations churned inside her body, fighting for some form of expression, for a way to get out. They manifested themselves in the motion of her limbs, the powerful pumping of her legs. On some instinctual level, she understood that if she allowed it, the heady rush of these new feelings would overwhelm her, take her beyond rational thought and into a realm of pure, animal reflex. In its own way, it was enticing.

The terrain was difficult and it did not lend itself well to stealthy movement. The rolling gray-white landscape shifted underneath her boots with each footfall, at times putting her off balance and threatening to tip her from her feet. There was little cover from the howling winds that scoured the shallow valley ranged around her. The hard, knobbed growths of stocky trees protruded from the hillside, hunched low against the weather. They were capped with spindly branches in spiked crowns, the thin twigs clattering against each other as the gusts caught them. In the dull light of the planet's sunset, the trees cast strange shadows that jumped and moved. They played tricks on her eyes, suggesting the forms of pursuers when in fact there was nothing there.

She took a moment to rest, her breath panting out of her mouth in chugs of vapor. She pressed herself into the lee of a larger tree and took stock of her situation, desperately ignoring the constant tingle of the new sensations. The chill was nothing to her; she was no stranger to the cold, but the drifts of frozen precipitation were an unpleasant hindrance, dragging at her, slowing her down. Worse still, she left a trail that only the sightless would not have been able to follow. The flakes of snow were falling constantly around her, and she hoped that they would smooth out her footprints before the hunters caught up.

Crouching, she drew her clothing around her, sinking into the shadows. She sniffed the air and attempted to fathom the scents of the planet, sorting them into signals she could understand; but this place was too different, too alien. She would have to rely on other senses to find her way.

She listened for the presence of her fellows and heard nothing. The constant snow coated everything with a layer of heavy silence. She wondered if the stillness was a sign that they had fled; the alternative was something she did not wish to contemplate. In an unconscious gesture of solidarity, she brushed a thin finger over the tribal tattoos visible on the bare skin of her neck; she shared the same pattern there as all of her kindred, and now she touched it as if it were a talisman, a fetish that would keep her safe. The valley snaked away beneath her vantage point, past the blinded windows of the crude township to the north. She knew that salvation lay just beyond that collection of domiciles and sties. If she could just get close enough, then escape was within her grasp. The silver ring was out there, silent and waiting. She knew the symbols for home as well as she knew the faces of her clan. If she could keep one step ahead of the strident, foul hunters, if she could make it to the podium at the foot of the ring — then she could call on the device to transport her away from the frozen wasteland. Perhaps that was what the others had done. Yes, she wanted to believe that, she hoped it would be so. It was hard to hold on to that possibility, however; after they had been separated in the first attack, the keening wind had brought her the sounds of sporadic weapons fire and cries of agony.

Her teeth bared, a little in bravado, a little in anger. There was fury mixed in with the strange new feeling, and she clung on to that. Rage was something she could fully understand, something she could take hold of and make her own. There was already a part of her thoughts spinning ideas of vengeance. Once she was safe, she would come back with a dozen, a hundred—

Movement.

She did not dare to breathe. Yes, she was not mistaken. There, coming out from the tree line, three of them in a wary formation, long rifle-like weapons held at their hips, the blunt maws of the guns sweeping the path before them. They were, as far as she could tell, males; but then these creatures all looked alike to her. Two were identical to her eyes, faces concealed behind the blank shutters of masks, garbed in clothing that might perhaps have had some military rationale in the hunter hierarchy. The one that lead them was clear by the way it moved, a stark arrogance in every step. Even from this far away, she could tell the one in the long dark coat was the leader just from the way the other two showed it deference.

They spoke to one another in guttural, atonal sounds that were hard on her senses. It seemed more like the squealing of animals or the chatter of insects. She felt revulsion at the sight of them, a deep-seated loathing that bubbled up into a snarl in her throat; and there it was once more, the new emotion, coiling at the pit of her stomach. It made her veins sing and her nerves tingle. Her muscles bunched with the need for fight or flight. In that instant she had the measure of it.

Was this... Could this be real *fear*? The roiling flutter in her torso, the pressure against the inside of her ribcage? The novelty of the experience faded like smoke. *No*. She refused to give these creatures such a hold over her, she denied it to them. How dare they have the temerity to strike at her people, what right did they think they had to attack her kindred?

New strength borne of wrath flowed into her, and she rose slowly, keeping the bole of the tree between her body and the three figures. If she kept her silence and let them pass, they would never know she was there, and then she could move on to the ring; but what sort of an epitaph was that for the others, killed— or worse, *captured*— by these freakish beasts?

The weapon tucked into her pocket was only a short-range pistol, its effectiveness reduced in anything but close quarters, and there were three of them, all well armed; but she bared her teeth in a feral smile as she contemplated them. She would leave this frigid world, but before she departed she would pass on a message for these creatures. They were lucky here today, that was all, they had caught her kindred by surprise. She would end the lives of these three in a most bloody manner and do it alone. Then it would be *their* turn to feel fear and jump at the flicker of every shifting shadow.

She drew the gun and coiled her fingers around the knurled grip, taking the weight of it, feeling the warmth as it became active, sensing the threat of imminent violence. She waited until they had drawn past her, listening to them bleat and squawk. Her smile widened as she watched them make a mistake. They were completing the arc of a patrol sweep through the woodlands, and in sight of the village they had relaxed their guard, keeping their eyes off their backs.

You are overconfident, she told them silently, *and you will pay for that conceit with your lifeblood.*

The anticipation of the attack was sweet, but now she threw off her concealment and leapt into the air, spinning into a jump that brought her down right behind them.

The two masked ones reacted, one shoving their leader aside in a gesture of protection, the second spinning the rifle-weapon around to attack. She was too quick for them. Her pistol shrieked and white fire engulfed the second hunter, throwing it back into the snow with a shattering crash of displaced air. The other discharged its weapon with a bark of sound, but she was moving, still moving. With a handful of claws she raked at the leader and tore through layers of clothing, her sharp nails coming away with dark fluid on them. The first hunter tried to club her with the butt of its rifle and she ducked, the blow slipping over her head. She jammed her claws into right side of its ribcage and tore. The hunter howled and liquids frothed from the grille of its mask. The scent of fresh blood bloomed in the cold air as it collapsed into the white drifts and died.

The leader moved, the wound she had inflicted bringing a snarl to its face. This creature had a peculiar weapon of its own, a hybrid of handgun and short sword that came up so quickly she felt the blade point strike home in her stomach. The pain made her furious and she backhanded the weapon from the leader and kicked it to the ground. The flood of aggression fuelled her hunger, and she leapt on the winded creature, her tongue flicking out of her mouth. The pistol forgotten, with one vise-like grip she wrapped her pale fingers around the leader's neck and held tight; and then, with her heart racing in excitement, she opened her palm wide and let the serrated feeding cavity in her hand unfold, shiny with enzymatic fluids. In a single brutal thrust, she plunged her hand through the shredded material of the leader's jacket and felt the warm human flesh underneath. She gave a little shudder as the feeding began, the nourishing torrent of organic energies drawing up into her. The adrenaline in the man's veins made it *delicious*.

But too late she understood that she had been careless, that she had made the same error as her fellow Wraith; she had underestimated the resilience of the prey. The second hunter, the one she had cast aside, shook off the effect of the blaster and leveled its rifle. She had assumed that the weaker-willed human would not attack while she was so close to its leader for fear of striking it. The pitiless look it returned her showed otherwise. It no doubt believed that it was performing a mercy on the other man-prey by ending its life before her feeding could be completed. The second hunter's gun spat puffs of gas and vapor, releasing a volley of razor-edged needles. The scatter-shot blast tore her off her victim and threw her into the snows.

She felt the burning spines deep in her tissue and understood abruptly that this was death. As much as she tried to fight it off, to decry it, the ripple of fear returned tenfold and dragged her down.

The Wraith perished, her fangs bared to the icy sky above.

She made a point, whenever she could, to watch the sun rise. From the high balcony atop the central tower of Atlantis, there was no better view of the pale golden disc as it emerged from below the horizon, the first rays of light turning the dark ocean into a sheet of glittering, beaten copper. The thin cirrus clouds overhead glowed pink underneath, drifting frames around the star as it climbed into the teal blue sky. There was ozone in the air and the strange salt tang of alien seas.

If ever a day comes when I forget why we are out here, I can just walk up and look at this. Elizabeth Weir smiled to herself and turned her head, looking around at the angular minarets and steeples of the floating city. Atlantis was a work of art in many ways, as much an expression of the character of the Ancients who built it as the scientific legacy they had left behind. Seen from the air, it drifted atop the ocean like a silver brooch on a vast indigo cloak. Up close, the city-complex was all glass and steel spires reaching up into the heavens. The shapes of the towers reminded Elizabeth of origami, turned straight edges and seamless folds of brushed metal. It was a metropolis built by cool and studied minds, and while it wasn't a clinical place, she sometimes felt that Atlantis lacked the warmth and the small chaos of cities on Earth. She thought of the senses she had of New York, of London and Paris, Delhi, Moscow or Hong Kong; Atlantis felt lonely in comparison, even after more than a year of human occupation, and she wondered if that would ever change. *The Ancients lived here once upon a time, so why couldn't we?* The smile broadened as she imagined the sights of children going to school on Atlantis's metallic boulevards, dog-walkers, baseball games and couples in the parkland, markets in the great atrium. *Maybe one day.*

It was in moments like this, when she was alone with the city's melancholy quiet, that Weir felt closest to the people who had made this place. Back home, it was something she hadn't really been able to understand, not completely; she'd seen the look in the eyes of astronauts who'd been to the Moon, she'd seen it in people like Samantha Carter and Daniel Jackson when they spoke about other worlds. Now she saw the same look in the mirror, in a wiser face framed with dark hair, a kind of insight about Earth and mankind, about how small and precious they were.

After months of being here, they were still only paddling in the shallows of the great oceans of knowledge left behind by the Ancients, and sometimes Elizabeth wondered if there was still something left of them in these walls, watching silently.

In any other place, such a thought might have been eerie and disturbing, but she found it the opposite. If the Ancients were the progenitors of humankind, then the Pegasus expedition team were the children returning to the birthplace of their parents and making it their own. Perhaps it wouldn't be within her lifetime, but one day Earth's people would know all the secrets of this place; and the bright future that knowledge would bring would make everything they had endured here worthwhile.

That is, if the Wraith don't destroy us first. She frowned at the dissenting voice in the back of her mind. *Or the Genii, or any one of a dozen other threats...* "We never thought it would be easy," she said aloud, and reached for the steel mug at her side to take a sip of tea. Weir looked down; on the lower tiers she could see people moving around, going about their duties. Out by the western atrium, Dr. Kusanagi and her group were setting up an air-monitoring experiment that would give them a better handle on the planet's weather systems. Directly below, she could hear the echoes of barked orders where some of the military contingent were sparring on a lower level; the recent additions of troops from the Russian Federation and the United Kingdom — part of a treaty agreement surrounding the Stargate program — were meshing well with the existing Atlantis Marine Corps garrison. And out on one of the spade-shaped 'petals' that formed the outer districts of the city, a maintenance team were preparing the landing platform for the arrival of the *Daedalus*, the starship that in recent months had become the lifeline for the outpost.

The regular returns of the vessel were now an important part of life on Atlantis, with a palpable rise in the morale of the people here in the days running up to its landing. *Daedalus* brought news and mail from home, supplies and new faces, and most importantly the ship made the Atlantean contingent feel *connected*. A year of isolation and a Stargate they could never use to dial home had taken its toll, but with *Daedalus* Earth was only a hyperspace journey away. Each cargo she brought made that distance seem a little less; out here in the Pegasus Galaxy, even seemingly tiny things like replacement toothbrushes or toilet paper took on a great level of importance — it was the small, mundane details like those that helped keep the human presence in Atlantis on an even keel, helped the people working and living here to forget that they were Earth's most distant outpost of mankind. Despite the friction that seemed a regular part of her interaction with *Daedalus*'s commander, Colonel Caldwell, Weir had to admit that the sight of the ship always raised her spirits. *Daedalus*, with her blunt, aircraft carrier lines, might lack the crystalline beauty of Atlantis, but her mere presence conveyed an important message. *You're not alone out here.*

The data pad at Elizabeth's side chimed and she gathered up the device. The flat screen portable computer terminal seemed never to be more than arm's length away from her, constantly feeding information from the city's heart — and sometimes distracting her with games of Solitaire or Minesweeper. An alarm window was open; Weir had set the prompt to remind her of the morning's departures through the Stargate. Three teams were outbound today on missions to target worlds from the city's vast database of addresses, basic reconnaissance jaunts to search for new allies, Ancient artifacts or to just plain explore. She scanned down the list and saw the name of the commander of the team assigned to the next transit through the Gate; *Lieutenant Colonel John Sheppard.*

Weir tapped the pad with a finger and left the balcony behind.

"So," said Sheppard, rubbing his thumb over his chin, "either of you two got an inkling about this place we're going to?"

Ronon Dex shook his head without looking up from unfolding his greatcoat. "Never been there."

The tawny-skinned woman standing across from Dex cocked her head. "I too have never visited the colony, but there were some of my people who did." Teyla Emmagan paused as she zipped up her uniform tunic. "As I recall, the planet has only a handful of settlements quite close to the Stargate. They trade furs and cured meats harvested from the local wildlife."

"So, kinda low-tech, then?"

"No more than Athos," she said, with a hint of a smile, "but if you are asking if they might have relics of the Ancients, then your question may be in vain."

Off to one side, the fourth member of Sheppard's core team made a comment under his breath about 'wild goose chases' and returned to lacing up his boots. The colonel gave Dr. McKay a sideways look. "Thanks for the input, Rodney." Sheppard turned his attention back to Teyla. "What about any, uh, hostiles?"

"The Wraith are active in that part of the galaxy, but I do not believe the settlement has experienced a culling in many years, certainly not since I was a child."

"Some good news, then. Maybe this place is too far off the beaten track for them to bother with."

Dex pulled on his coat. "Or maybe they're just overdue for a feeding frenzy."

Sheppard gave a tight, humorless smile. "That's what I like about you, Ronon, you're such a ray of sunshine." He crossed the prep room to where the other half of his unit was gathering themselves together. "Sergeant Mason, right?" he asked, picking out the most senior-looking man in the group.

"*Staff* Sergeant Mason, sir," said the soldier, his pug-face creasing.

"Oh yeah," nodded Sheppard, "different ranks for you guys, right?" The four men were relatively new to Atlantis, one of two squads of British Special Air Service troopers brought in to serve in areas of Stargate Command. As part of a rotation that would put the men on front-line duty in the Pegasus Galaxy, it fell to the colonel to take them with him on a few missions, to show them the lay of the land. This was the first time he'd had to deal with the Brits face-to-face; until now he'd only seen them around and about in the city, laughing in rough humor or playing in animated poker games with the Marine Corps contingent. "You've been off world before, right?"

Mason nodded. "Did a tour at Cheyenne Mountain, sir. Dealt with some of them growlers while we were there."

"Growlers?"

"Goa'uld, sir," said one of the other men, a stocky guy with dirty blond hair, "that's what we call them, on account of the way they talk. Y'know, all that *puny humans, you will die* stuff —"

"Clarke, shut it," said Mason, with curt finality.

Sheppard gave a small smile. "Lance Corporal Clarke, right? And these two other gentlemen would be Privates Bishop and Hill?"

"Sir," chorused the men. Both the privates had the watchful look of career soldiers.

"Well, listen, I'm not expecting any trouble but you never can tell. The Wraith aren't like the Goa'uld, they don't waste time bragging, they just go straight for the jugular."

"Actually, it's the heart," McKay chipped in. "That's where they prefer to feed from."

"Whatever," Sheppard met Mason's gaze. "The point is, don't be stingy with your ammo. You got one in range, take it down."

Mason nodded. "That we can do."

The colonel patted him on the arm. "Welcome to the team. We don't have a secret handshake or anything…"

"We'll manage," said the soldier.

Sheppard left Mason's men to their preparations, catching a whispered comment from Clarke as he walked away. "He seems all right for a Rupert."

Rupert? John had a feeling serving with these Brits was going to be a whole new learning experience for him.

The doors to the prep room hummed open before Weir to reveal Sheppard's team in varying states of readiness. McKay appeared to be the least organized person there, in the middle of attempting to don a webbing vest festooned with equipment packs, and trying secure a pistol in his thigh holster at the same time. He was contorting himself in the process, much to the amusement of the military contingent. Ronon, Teyla and the rest of the squad were at their gear racks, making last minute checks and loading their weapons.

Sheppard looked up from the open breech of his P90 sub-machinegun. "Elizabeth. Come to see us off? Don't worry, I remembered to pack my mittens."

Weir raised an eyebrow and gestured with the data pad in her hand. "I'm glad I caught you before you left, John. There was something I meant to query you on." She extended the pad to him and he took it.

An involuntary wince crossed his face as he read the file displayed there. "Oh yeah. Riley." Behind him, she saw McKay make a similarly pinched expression.

As part of the paperwork that was required each time *Daedalus* arrived at Atlantis with supplies and new staff, as the director of the outpost Weir was required to provide full reports for the ship to carry back to Earth, on everything from Ancient archaeological finds and Wraith force intelligence to personnel dispositions and equipment requisition forms. Dealing with the paperwork also meant that it was her ultimate responsibility to handle one of the worst parts of the job — the casualty reports. Every time they lost someone, Elizabeth was required sign off on their death certificate, and if there were remains, it was her responsibility to ensure they were ready to go home on the next hyperspace flight.

But it wasn't always possible to return the dead, however. Sometimes — as was the case with the late Master Sergeant Riley, USAF — there was nothing but a cloud of free atoms left behind. The unlucky soldier had been caught in the nimbus of an Ancient plasma generator, which had shorted out explosively during a venture into the city's lower levels; there one moment, vapor the next.

Sheppard held out the data screen to her. "I signed off on him. What's the problem?"

Weir didn't take the screen back straight away. "I reviewed the Sergeant's records, Colonel. It made for some interesting reading."

"Really?" replied Sheppard warily. "Well, he was an, uh, interesting guy."

"Did you know that during his entire tour on Atlantis, Sergeant Riley never once took part in any hazardous off world excursions? As far as I can determine, he hardly ever left the quartermaster's stores where he worked."

Sheppard's expression turned a little sheepish. "Well. He probably had a lot of... Boxes to move. And stuff."

She tapped the screen with a finger. "It's remarkable. It seems every time Riley's name came up on off world rotation, someone swapped duties with him, or he was otherwise excused. I wonder why that was."

The Colonel said nothing. He gave McKay a sidelong look and the scientist blinked back at him.

Weir leaned closer. "I did a little digging. Do you know what Riley brought with him as his personal gear allocation when we first came through the Stargate from Colorado?"

"No?"

In her diplomatic career, Elizabeth had spent time in the presence of liars of all kinds—including a few non-human ones—and she knew the untruth on Sheppard's lips automatically. "Eleven high-density data storage devices. Capable of storing thousands of hours of video. It says here that they contained 'instructional films'. Is that an accurate description, Colonel?"

Sheppard returned to loading his P90. "I guess so."

"Some of them..." McKay added, a slightly wistful tone in his voice; then he blinked. "I mean. That is, so I was lead to believe."

"They were entertainments," said Ronon, without preamble.

McKay rounded on the bigger man. "You saw them too?"

Weir's eyes narrowed. She hadn't once taken her gaze off Sheppard. "Am I correct in thinking that Master Sergeant Riley was in fact running a video library for the crew aboard Atlantis?"

"I found the romantic comedies to be very informative," offered Teyla.

"And there's also the matter of the floating crap game. And the glassware and medical boiler that went missing from Dr. Beckett's infirmary."

"You couldn't hide a still on Atlantis," blurted McKay, "the internal sensors would register any heat build-up—"

"Rodney," growled Sheppard, silencing the other man.

"If Colonel Caldwell sees this, he won't be happy." Weir took the data screen and weighed it in her hand. "He runs a tight ship, John."

Sheppard met her gaze. "You know, when the Wraith invaded the city last year, Riley put down two of their bruisers and kept them out of the lower levels. Okay, so he bent the rules a little, but we're the farthest men from home out here. Riley was a good guy. I turned a blind eye because I thought people could stand to blow off a little steam. You know I'd never let anything go so far that it would compromise Atlantis."

After a moment, Elizabeth found herself nodding. "That's all I wanted to hear." She leaned in and lowered her voice. "I know people think of me like I'm some kind of school principal, watching everyone from up there in the gallery, but I'm not. I live here too, John. I know what homesickness can feel like."

"Oh, good," he smirked. "No detention then?"

McKay gestured at the air. "What, uh, happened to the data devices?"

Weir eyed him. "Oddly, Dr. McKay, they don't appear to be among the Sergeant's personal effects. I can only assume some enterprising soul has appropriated them."

Rodney gave a solemn nod. "Ah. It's what he would have wanted."

"The rest of his belongings will be loaded on the *Daedalus* when she arrives. Colonel Caldwell is bringing a new rotation of staff and troops."

"Any washouts?" said Sheppard. Generally, the turnover of people on Atlantis was small, with only a few voluntary transfers every now and then. For the most part, psychological evaluations made sure that anyone coming to serve a tour in the Pegasus Galaxy was mentally able to deal with the isolation, but there were still the occasional one or two who found the impossible distance and alien environment just too much.

"A couple of transfers from the civilian contingent. Doctors Walton and Ming. They're both taking reassignments to the *Daedalus* science team."

McKay rolled his eyes. "Ming. That figures. Do you know, he had the nerve to call this assignment boring? Good riddance to him. He's been bleating about getting a posting on the *Battlestar Galactica* ever since we got here..."

"You know Caldwell hates it when you call the *Daedalus* that?" said Sheppard.

Rodney gave an arch sniff. "Yes, I am fully aware of how much it annoys him."

"Well," broke in Weir, "while you're enjoying the crisp sub-zero wonderland of M3Y-465, I'll be sure to give the Colonel your best regards when he arrives." She gave the group a nod and left them to their preparations. "Be safe, people."

"Sure thing, Teach," said Sheppard.

Having finally negotiated the pistol holster, McKay approached Sheppard with a grimace on his face. "One moment. Sub-zero? She said 'sub-zero'?"

Sheppard nodded. "She did."

Rodney shook his head. "No. M3Y-465 is a temperate planet. I saw the MALP reports, cool, a bit cloudy, lots of trees..."

"Nope," Sheppard replied. "You're thinking of M3Y-565. Captain Paterson and his team lit out for there this morning. He got the trees, we get the ice and snow."

"Snow," McKay repeated in a leaden voice. "I don't perform well in the cold, Colonel. I get the, ah—" He pointed at his nose. "The sniffles."

"Then take a scarf."

McKay squinted. "Why don't you take Zelenka? He's from above the Arctic Circle, or something. He'd be in his element."

Sheppard secured his weapon and threw a nod to Staff Sergeant Mason. "Let's move." The other man nodded and barked out orders to his troopers.

"John?" prodded McKay, as they entered the Gate Room, the shimmering disc of blue energy already open before them.

Sheppard halted as the others filed across the atrium. "Rodney, I don't want to appear like I'm uncaring or disinterested in your complaints, but I am, so that's how it comes out."

McKay made a face. "Fine."

The Colonel pointed at the SAS soldiers and as one Mason and his men moved in ahead of them, crossing the event horizon of the wormhole.

Four more figures came through the Circlet after the first group. They seemed different from the men in the uniforms of strange gray-white camouflage who had moved on ahead, all but one wearing heavy-weather gear in mid-blue. They were most definitely not Wraith, and their kit matched no known pattern, not even the most basic element of the sanctioned army standards. They had weapons — it was an assumption, albeit a logical one — but the firearms seemed small and spindly, doubtless of inferior power and range. The eight figures moved away from the Circlet as the shimmering gateway folded in on itself and vanished. These people paid it no mind; clearly, they were seasoned travelers. In a loose spread they walked on, picking their way through the snows.

It was peculiar; some of them moved with the vigilant air of military training, while others — one most notably — stomped across the drifts with little concern for protocol. The two figures that watched them exchanged glances and fingered their rifles, weighing their options.

Then one of the new arrivals looked up, directly at them, the wind flickering long auburn hair out from under her hood.

"Teyla?" Sheppard drew close. "What is it?"

The Athosian woman was silent for a moment. "I... Am not sure, Colonel. I thought I saw a..."

John's gloved fingers tightened around the grip of his P90. "Wraith?"

"No." She shook her head. "I was mistaken. The play of the light from the Stargate on the snow, perhaps."

"You don't sound convinced." He eyed her. "If that spider-sense of yours is tingling, I want to know about it."

Teyla looked away. "I'm sorry, John. My... Gift is not predictable. It is not like a lamp I can simply switch on or off."

Sheppard nodded. The genetic kinks in Teyla's DNA, the dubious donation of years of Wraith experimentation on her bloodline, had left her with a preternatural instinct that the colonel had quickly learned to trust. "Okay. Let's keep our eyes open, huh?"

Corporal Clarke approached them. "Sir? Staff Mason spotted what looks like a village farther down the valley." He jerked a thumb over his shoulder. "No lights, though. Seems dead."

"Feeding frenzy," said Ronon.

Sheppard made a face. "There you go with that upbeat attitude again." He nodded to Clarke. "Let's move in."

Trudging up behind them, McKay's face peered from the woolly oval of an arctic parka. He waved a handheld scanner at them. "I'm not picking up any energy traces." He sniffed wetly. "You know, this would have been a lot easier if we'd taken a Puddle Jumper."

Sheppard ignored him. "Teyla, Ronon, watch our backs. Let's go pay a house call."

"Oh, good," McKay sneered, "and while we're there, we can ask Santa to let us borrow Rudolph and his sled."

The settlement was as silent as the snowy landscape. The highest structure in the hamlet was a watchtower growing from the center, tall enough so an observer atop it could sight out to the Gate and alert the inhabitants to any new arrivals. The buildings clustered around it, fanning off short alleyways in radial spokes. The construction was a mix of stone and heavy, dense wood, the lodge-like domiciles low to the ground like they were drawn tight against the chill. There were no footprints, no signs that there had been any life in this grim little ghost town. No lights burned anywhere, just as Clarke had reported, and the fans of illumination from the torches on the team's guns cast peculiar shadows. The only sounds were the crunch of snow beneath their boots and the thin howls of the bitter breeze.

Ronon chose a house at random and pulled open the door, peering inside. He saw a bed and a stove, desk and chairs. The bed was rumbled, slept in. A book was open on the table. A thin rime of frost covered everything, making it twinkle in the torchlight.

Sheppard glanced at McKay. "Anything on the scanner?"

Rodney shook his head. "Eight thermal blooms inside the settlement boundary and nothing else. I'm not reading anything further out, just static. Might be something in the local rock strata interfering with the scanner."

They drew slowly into the middle of the township, and at the foot of the watchtower lay the largest building they had yet encountered. "Is it a town hall, maybe?" suggested Private Hill.

"Could be," agreed the colonel. "Let's take a look-see."

Mason spoke up. "Sir, we should form a perimeter around the hall, just in case." Off Sheppard's nod of agreement, he snapped out orders to the rest of his unit and they fanned out. "Hill, go with them."

Teyla entered first, holding her weapon close to her chest, the fire select set to three-round bursts. The inside of the hall was open, studded with thick wooden pillars to hold up the roof. There were dead oil lanterns dangling from beams, but faint illumination came from a long, low counter set along one of the walls. "What is that?"

McKay pointed at a series of dull yellow-green bowls made of glass fitted to the walls. Liquid was visible inside, glowing faintly. "It looks like bioluminescence. Probably extracted from plants or insects. Cheap lighting, if a little gloomy-looking."

They spread out through the room, their eyes adjusting to the dimness, and abruptly Teyla realized the function of the building. "This is a tavern." On a round table before her there were a couple of flagons and a discarded clay pipe. The faint whiff of stale beer was still detectable in the air.

Sheppard swept his P90 around the hall. "No bodies anywhere."

Ronon fingered a fan of oval playing cards on a long bench. There were other hands here and there, and a pile of stamped metal rings in a clay bowl before them. "Someone left their winnings behind."

Hill crouched by a larger table. "Look here, sir. These chairs are knocked over, like maybe the person sitting there got up quickly."

"Whatever happened, they had little or no warning," ventured Teyla, "there are no signs they had time to prepare an adequate defense."

The soldier frowned. "But there's no indications of any weapons fire, ma'am, no burns or bullet holes. Did the blokes who lived here just put down their pints and give up without a fight?"

"Okay," said Rodney, folding down his hood. "I'm going to put this out there, just say what we're all thinking. *Culled.* The people here were culled by the Wraith."

Sheppard glanced at the ceiling. "They must have swept in with Darts and just beamed them straight up," he said, turning to Hill.

Teyla suppressed a shudder, thinking back to of the awful screeches of Wraith Dart-ships buzzing through the air of her own village, trawling for human lives.

"No doors are locked," noted Dex. "Must have been panic in the streets."

"Blimey," whispered the Private.

"Question is, how long ago?" Sheppard studied the floor. "There's a little snow in here. It couldn't have been more than a few days."

Ronon sniffed at a discarded tankard. "Maybe less."

"And so we come to the big questions," said McKay, crossing the room. "Are they still here? And why don't we discuss this in greater depth back on Atlantis?"

"This is not the only settlement on the planet, Doctor," said Teyla, "there are several others within a few day's riding."

"The Wraith would have taken this one first," noted Ronon. "It's closest to the Gate. Then moved out in a spiral, looking for any more."

Sheppard frowned. "All right. I'm just about ready to call this one. As much as I hate to admit that Rodney might be right about something, we're gonna head back to Atlantis and come back here after sun-up in a Jumper. We can scope out the other villages and look for survivors."

"There won't be any," said Ronon, with grim finality. "I've seen this before, on dozens of worlds. They don't leave people behind. The Wraith don't waste anything."

McKay was leaning close to a support pillar, shining a penlight at a bony disc halfway up the length. "This doesn't look right…"

"What is it?"

"The design looks different from the other manufactured items here-" Without warning, the disc let out a whirring sound and unfolded like a skeletal flower.

Teyla saw a shock of recognition on Ronon's face; in the next second Dex had his particle magnum in his hand. "Get away!" he snapped.

McKay barely had time to duck before Ronon's pistol barked and a flare of bright energy blew the pillar and the disc into burning fragments.

"You could've killed me!" wailed the scientist.

Dex turned on Sheppard. "That was a Wraith sensor pod. They leave them in places they've harvested in case they miss anyone the first time around."

Hill nodded, getting it. "So any poor sods who came home thinking they'd gone would set it off, and back they come."

"Okay, that's it," said Sheppard. "We're not waiting around here to see if the Wraith want us for a dessert course." He toggled his radio. "Mason,"

"*Sir*," came the reply. "*Heard gunfire, do we have enemy contact, over?*"

"Could be. Get back to the Gate on the double, I'm scrubbing this mission."

"*Roger that,*"

Sheppard looked up. "Let's move."

Teyla heard his order, but it seemed as if the words were coming from a very great distance. She felt dislocated, suddenly unconnected to the cold and ill-lit tavern. She could feel something, out in the ice and the snow, out there in the howling winds. A predatory sensation in the back of her mind, the pale shadow of something cunning and hungry. It wasn't the same glimmer of threat she had felt at the Stargate, there and gone, the very barest touch on her senses. This was different, strong and horribly familiar.

"Teyla!"

She found herself again and turned on Sheppard. "Wraith. They're already here."

The clatter of assault rifles met them as they raced from the tavern. The wind carried the sound from the direction of the Stargate, gunshots joined by the shrieking cracks of Wraith stunner blasts.

"Mason, report!" demanded Sheppard.

"*Heavy contact*," grated the Staff Sergeant, "*they must have flanked us, come back around past the Gate. We got no cover up here!*"

"Fall back to the village and regroup," ordered the colonel. He turned to the others. "Hill, you're with me. Ronon, Teyla, McKay, find something defensible, something with thick walls, and hole up there. If they got Darts and they catch us in the open..." John let the sentence trail off. He didn't need to spell it out.

"If we could just make a run for the Stargate-" began Rodney.

"And let them know Atlantis *isn't* a pile of radioactive rubble?" Sheppard shook his head. "Nope. We gotta deal with this here. Go!"

He sprinted off with Hill at his flank, moving quickly from cover to cover in the lee of deep shadows. McKay's escape plan, while crude and direct—and not without a certain appeal, John had to admit—was out of the question. The Wraith siege of Atlantis, months ago now although it still seemed fresh in his mind, had ended with a magic trick that David Copperfield would have been proud of. The city's defensive shield had been turned into a cloaking device to fool the aliens into thinking

Atlantis had been obliterated, but now each time an off world team ran afoul of a Wraith raiding party they were effectively on their own. They had to operate as if they were isolated survivors who had escaped the city's destruction, lest they tip off the aliens that Atlantis was still intact.

And right now, that meant they had no easy way out of this.

Gingerly, the adjutant ventured a question. "Highness, what would you have us do in this engagement? The troops await your orders."

His commander remained silent for a long moment, observing the unfolding fray in the village through a bulky brass monocular. When the answer came, it was another question. "Who are these people? Their livery and wargear is of no manufacture I can place, not from the homeworld or a vassal planet."

"I suspect they are Genii," offered the adjutant.

The commander made a negative noise. "I know those skulks, and these people do not wage war like them." The exchange of fire became furious, reaching them in the cover of the tree line. "Genii warriors would run. These ones stand and fight. They have zeal."

"Highness," said the man, "if you would forgive my temerity to say so, but their zeal will give them little support against such numbers of Wraith. The second group of the predators we observed even now approach from the far side of the village. These people, whomever they give allegiance to, will perish if we do not intervene. Is that your wish?"

The commander snapped the monocular shut and met his gaze. "That would be poor form, don't you think? It would be impolite of us, to say the least."

"Your will, Highness." The adjutant nodded and turned to his troops. "Charge your guns, gentlemen, and ready the horns."

Sheppard and Hill met Mason and the other men at the edge of the township. White fire from Wraith guns sizzled down after them, flaring off the snow. Private Bishop had Corporal Clarke on his shoulder, helping his comrade scramble away. Mason was low behind them, spraying bullets from his L85 rifle. Sheppard and Hill fell against cover either side of the alleyway and set up corridors of gunfire, covering the retreating men. Bishop and Clarke scrambled past them, and the colonel saw the corporal's face slack and numb along the left-hand side, like a stroke victim.

"He got clipped by a stunner," said Bishop, by way of explanation.

"Bathtahds," lisped Clarke, 'worz thun been drung,"

"Fall back," snapped Sheppard, "we got you covered."

Mason came after them, ducking low. "Reloading!" he shouted, ejecting the clip on the bullpup assault rifle.

Sheppard and Hill kept up the pressure, taking down Wraith warriors with careful aimed shots to the torso. Mason joined in as the colonel's own weapon ran dry. He dropped behind a wooden barrel and levered off the empty magazine.

"*Sheppard*!" Ronon's voice crackled from his radio. "*Teyla found a place we can use as a strongpoint, west of you, a conical building.*"

"Copy that, we're on our way." Sheppard called out to Mason. "You get that, Staff Sergeant?"

"Clear as a bell, sir,"

"Then let's go!"

Moving and firing, the five of them made their way back into the village in an overwatch formation, two men covering the others as they dropped away from the Wraith advance. They turned the corner and sprinted the last few meters to the building Dex had described, half-dragging the injured corporal with them.

Teyla was at the heavy wooden door, her P90 primed and ready. "Did you bring any guests?" she asked dryly.

Sheppard nodded. "Afraid so. And they all want dinner." He cast a look around inside. The building was circular, with only one door but a number of slatted hatches in the walls. The air smelt of mould. "What is this place?"

"A granary," said Teyla. "We are lucky it is summer. In winter this would have been full."

"Summer?" echoed McKay. "That's summer out there?"

Ronon crouched and gave Clarke a look over. "Don't worry, the pain will pass. Can you hold a weapon?"

"Yeh," managed the soldier, his head lolling. "Jus' point me atta door."

Mason directed the other men to firing positions at the slats and Dex approached the colonel. "So, how we going play this, Sheppard? You let them bottle us up, and—"

"I'm working on it," he replied, cutting Ronon off. "We miss our call-in and Atlantis will send out Lorne and a rescue team."

"That's not much of a plan."

"Hey, I'm making this up as I go."

Rodney snorted. "No change from normal there, then."

"I see one," said Bishop. "End of the street, he's scoping us."

"They won't try to wait us out," said Dex, "that's not how they do it. They'll rush us." He sneered. "Wraith like the direct approach."

"Couldn't be more than a dozen of them clowns out there," noted Hill, "even counting those we put down."

Sheppard looked around. "Ammo check. Anyone low?" He got a chorus of negatives from everyone except Teyla. The Athosian woman was stock still, sighting down the length of her gun. "Teyla, you with us?"

She shuddered, and he saw the distant, fearful look in her eyes that he knew meant trouble. "John. There are more Wraith out there. A lot more. They know—"

Teyla's words were drowned out in a howling chorus of blaster bolts as the aliens opened up on the stone building from all sides.

"Return fire!" barked Sheppard. "Targets of opportunity!"

Hot flares of muzzle flash stabbed out into the night, reaching toward the Wraith advance; but they were coming like a snarling tide, shrugging off glancing hits, furious in their attacks.

Rodney unloaded his pistol into the enemy advance, firing

off the whole magazine in what seemed like seconds. He felt a momentary surge of elation as one of the Wraith warriors went down, but then realized that the gun was empty. He fumbled desperately at a fresh clip, ducking behind Ronon as the Satedan ex-soldier sent shot after shot into the enemy attack. *I should get a laser gun, too,* he told himself, *none of this stupid reloading stuff with those space blasters.*

The Wraith shots rang the granary like a bell, sending rains of powdery snow and wood fragments falling from the support beams. The breech of the Beretta pistol finally snapped shut and he brought it up to firing position, fighting off the trembling in his hands. "I am not going to die cold and scared," he whispered. "I am going to die of old age surrounded by nubile graduate students and my many Nobel Prizes." It had become a kind of mantra for McKay, a quiet little prayer he relied upon whenever things took a turn for the worst... And that seemed to be a regular occurrence these days. The first part changed depending on the circumstances; "cold and scared" had previously been "as Wraith snack food", "of suffocation", "in a nuclear fireball" and so on. So far, it seemed to have worked. *So far.*

He started squeezing the trigger; and then he heard the reveille of a brass section. *That's it,* he realized, *I've gone mad with the fear.*

"What the bloody hell is that racket?" shouted Bishop.

Something that sounded like a cross between a set of bagpipes and a trumpet was blaring out a clarion call across the snowbound valley, echoing back and forth over the village; then moments later it was joined by a crashing, thunderous fusillade of gunshots.

"We got fire support," said Hill.

"But from where?" asked Ronon.

McKay craned over Dex's shoulder. "That's not Major Lorne..."

Sheppard's face creased in unease. "Sounds almost like... Muskets, or a blunderbuss."

"There!" Rodney pointed. Figures in heavy black greatcoats were rushing down from the tree line. Brocade and filigree on their clothing glittered in the moonlight, and thin wisps of steam trailed from packs on their backs. They wore high hats with dark face masks. Some carried long rifles, others bright spotlights with stark yellow beams, and a couple — well, a couple of them were playing long brass trombone-like contraptions.

The new arrivals had the Wraith caught unawares, and the aliens broke off their assault on the granary, scrambling to regroup to meet the larger force. Mason and the others took the advantage and pressed forward out of the doorway, striking at the enemy as they disengaged.

"Rodney, stay with Clarke!" Sheppard snapped and vaulted out with Ronon and Teyla behind him.

McKay pressed himself up against the hatch slats and saw the Wraith break under the hammer of the hooded soldiers. There were ten of them that he could count, and they moved in drilled lines like Roman legions, shifting about and taking the Wraith down with quick, efficient moves. Each time one of them fired a shot, the blocky bulk of their rifles spat out a plume of vapor and snarled like a dog. He couldn't smell the acrid tang of cordite; instead he tasted wood smoke and steam.

The hooded troopers made short work of the Wraith, some ripping into them with flights of flashing steel darts, other guns releasing slow-moving shells that stuck to Wraith battle armor and let off crackles of electric discharge. The men with the horns produced pistols with wide, bell-shaped maws and from these they fired expanding nets that enshrouded any Wraith who fled, pinning them to the ground.

Then the aliens were all dead or subdued, and only the Atlantis team remained standing before the soldiers. The sounds of battle died away into the night and silence fell heavily.

Clarke dragged himself to his feet and stumbled painfully outside, and McKay followed warily behind. "I am not going to die on this stupid Lapland planet," he began quietly.

Sheppard could see from the corner of his eye that the P90 still had half a clip remaining, but he had no idea about any of the others in his team. If things were going to turn bad, it would happen in the next few seconds, and with a sinking feeling he realized that the choice would be all down to him.

Two of the hooded figures detached themselves from the main group and took a couple of steps forward. The colonel's first impression was a flash of memory from a history book he'd read during officer training school. The uniforms looked like something from the Napoleonic era, hats like the Prussians wore, big shoulder pads and buttons, panels of etched armor plate and ornamental tabards. With slow and careful motions, Sheppard pulled down the hood of his parka and allowed the P90 to point at the ground, taking care not to let his finger stray too far from the trigger.

One of the figures had more gold leaf and jewels encrusted on their uniform than the others, so it was a safe bet this was the person in charge. John could see lines of pressed metal medals down the right arm of the soldier, twice as many as any of the others.

He gave his best winning smile. "I'm Lieutenant Colonel John Sheppard, United States Air Force. We appreciate the assist."

The lower ranked soldier tensed. "You will not speak until given —"

A raised hand from the commander silenced him, and he gave a contrite nod. With equal care, the highly decorated figure released a series of clasps around the hood-helmet headgear and removed it. The cold wind caught a flurry of striking red hair and pulled it up like a pennant. Sheppard found himself looking at a young woman with a regal, composed air about her. "I am the Lady Erony of the Fourth Dynast. You may consider my intervention a gift."

"I do," said the colonel. "I mean, thanks." John frowned a little. The tension didn't seem to be easing any. "If we trespassed on your village, we're sorry —"

"This?" sniffed Erony, with a faint air of disgust. "This is not our world. Surely you recognize our insignia? We are a hunting party from Halcyon, here seeking a lost splinter of our brethren."

"We're kinda new to this part of the galaxy," Sheppard replied. "We, ah, we're from out of town."

"Indeed?" said the woman. "And yet you have already made an enemy of the Wraith."

"Well, you know them. They make an enemy of just about everybody."

"True." Erony hesitated as her subordinate leaned close.

The other man nodded at Ronon. "Highness, the dark-skinned male. He bares the mark of a Runner."

"So I see. I am intrigued." Erony studied Sheppard's team. "Your soldier is injured?" she asked, indicating Clarke. "I would offer assistance to him, if you wish."

"Very kind of you," said Sheppard.

She cocked her head. "The Wraith are the bane of life. Anyone who hunts them can be an ally of Halcyon."

"My Lady," insisted the soldier, "we know nothing of these people, where they hail from or what they intend. If the Magnate —"

She gave the man a hard look. "You will be silent, Linnian. This is my splinter, and I alone decide the play of the game." Erony looked at Sheppard again. "I grow so jaded with the hunt at times, Lieutenant Colonel, and there are so few new distractions these days. Your party will accompany us back through the Great Circlet to Halcyon."

Sheppard blinked. "Well, that's a very nice offer —"

A loud sneeze from McKay broke through his words. "Sorry," ventured Rodney. "I think I've caught a chill."

Erony gave a small smile. "I'm sure your cohort will enjoy it there. Halcyon is far more temperate than this frigid sphere."

"We have people waiting for us on the other side of the, uh, Circlet. They'll be expecting us to contact them."

"Do so," said the woman. "Inform them that you are now guests of the Fourth Dynast. Make it clear to them that the Lady Erony does not give her invitations lightly, nor does she expect them to be refused." Her eyes flashed. "I trust we understand one another?"

"We certainly do," said Sheppard, eyeing the ranks of hooded troopers outnumbering them.

Weir leaned forward and folded her arms on the gallery rail, staring into the placid vertical pool of the open Stargate. "Halcyon? The name doesn't raise any flags in the database. What's your take on this, John?"

Sheppard's voice was tinny in her radio earpiece. *"Ronon says he's heard of these people, but only a few whispers. They're fighters, apparently, but they keep to their own turf. They sure made a mess of the Wraith out here."*

"Well, any enemy of the Wraith could be a friend of ours."

"That's pretty much what Lady Erony said. They want us to go back with them. I'm thinking we should play along for the moment, just to be gracious."

"They did just save your lives."

"Yeah, and we don't want to get a reputation for rudeness in the Pegasus Galaxy, right?"

"I concur, John. I have my hands full with the preparations for *Daedalus*, so I'm authorizing you to make official diplomatic contact with Halcyon's government on behalf of Earth. I think we're overdue to build some bridges out here."

There was a hiss of static as he paused. *"Elizabeth, I don't know if I'm exactly the right guy for the job..."*

"I'm certainly not going to ask Rodney to do it. You'll be fine, John. I know you can pour on the charm if you need to."

She heard the smile in his voice. *"Flattery will get you everywhere. Okay. I'll report back after we make some progress."*

Weir nodded. "Watch yourself, John. Come back safe."

"Count on it. Sheppard out."

The wormhole vanished into nothingness, the blue chevrons turning dark. It was a long moment before Elizabeth could turn away and return to her duties.

Sheppard looked up as Ronon and Teyla approached him. "We have a go, so I guess we better put on our best shoes."

Ronon threw a look at his footwear. "These *are* my best

shoes."

"How's Clarke doing?"

"The stun blast is wearing off. He will be fine. Colonel, there's something we wanted to bring to your attention," said Teyla, a serious expression on her face. "While you were in communication with Atlantis, Lady Erony's men have been at work on the Wraith."

"Define 'at work'…"

"They left a few of them alive," noted Dex, "they stunned them and trussed them up like cattle."

"I heard some of them talking. They are taking the survivors as prisoners. After we go back to Halcyon with Erony, they will follow us with the captured Wraith."

Sheppard's brow furrowed. "What would they want with live Wraith?"

"Your guess is as good as mine," said Ronon, "but I don't like it."

The colonel's answer died in his throat as Lady Erony walked over to the DHD where they stood. "You have conversed with your friends?" she asked.

Sheppard nodded. "I've been given full diplomatic status, apparently. It's kind of a new string to my bow, but I'm hoping to do well with it."

She began to enter a sequence of symbols on the oval podium. "Excellent. I will furnish you with a formal introduction to Halcyon's ruler after we arrive."

The Gate flared with exotic energies and opened. "You can do that?"

"Of course," said Erony, with a hint of amusement. "He's my father."

CHAPTER TWO

They emerged from the Stargate into the yellow sodium glare of harsh spotlights, and for a moment Sheppard had to fight back the reflexive twitch of his trigger finger. Then the beams turned aside and a set of bells and trumpets struck up a brief fanfare, the flourish echoing around them as Lady Erony walked forward.

"She must be important," McKay said from the side of his mouth, "she's got her own theme music."

Blinking away the afterimage on his retinas, the colonel glanced around and took in the place where they found themselves. The chamber was long and wide, open inside with illumination in tight clusters from the spotlights and thin window slits at the tops of the walls. There were aircraft hangars out at Nellis and Groom Lake that were large enough to hold a B-52 bomber with room to spare, and this place could have swallowed one of those easily. He imagined that a good pilot could have backed the *Daedalus* in here for a touchdown. The Stargate had pride of place, raised up on a wide dais and ringed with skeletal derricks. As he stepped forward, Sheppard heard faint whirring noises coming from the tops of the towers and looked up. He could see ornate horns like something from an old gramophone and huge glass-eyed, wooden-bodied cameras that were the size of a doghouse. Thick cables snaked away from them into the shadows. A broad pavement led down from the dais, marked every few meters by poles topped with elaborate ceremonial banners. Beyond those were indistinct shapes in the dimness past the pools of yellow light, broad cylinders of dull gray metal. More men with the same large rifles as Erony's party stood at attention in a semi-circle before them, heads bowed. The colonel noted that their uniforms, while similar in cut to those of Erony and her men, were of a different color and the tabards were reversed. *Same army, different unit?* he wondered.

There were giant cogwheels on pinions overhead, thick chains big enough to haul battleship anchors, and massive, silent pistons. Sheppard couldn't be sure, but he thought he could see the very slightest knife of daylight coming from a long horizontal join in the roof above. The Gate Hangar — he was already thinking of it as that, as it was way too big to be considered a Gate 'room' — was hissy with steam and there was the unmistakable smell of oil and grease. This was a wrought iron edifice, heavy, boiler-plated and industrial; the absolute antithesis of the clean silver lines of Atlantis.

From the corner of his eye he saw Mason and the SAS troopers, Ronon and Teyla, all of them eyeing the shadows with the same air of wariness.

McKay looked at the ground under his feet and nodded. "Huh. We're standing on a natural stone platform. Looks like this place was built around it, or maybe it was brought here from somewhere else."

"The latter is the correct assumption," said Erony. "You are quite observant."

"I'm a scientist," McKay noted. "Observation is part of what I do."

"Indeed?" The woman gave him an appraising look, as if she were re-evaluating him. "Forgive me, but I do not have your name…"

"Oh yeah, sorry," said the colonel. "I'm terrible with introductions. This is Dr. Rodney McKay."

"Greetings," said Erony, inclining her head.

"Ronon Dex, Teyla Emmagan, Staff Sergeant Mason, Corporal Clarke and —"

"Of course," Erony didn't appear to be paying attention to Sheppard any more, still studying McKay.

"—and, uh, Privates Bishop and Hill…" The colonel concluded.

"It is unusual for a scientist to be part of a hunt splinter on Halcyon," she continued. "Is this the first time you have been allowed to venture from your conclave?"

Rodney straightened. "Absolutely not. I'm a valuable member of a front-line team. In fact, I'd go as far to say that my expertise has often been the key factor in the survival of this, uh, this unit."

"Couldn't imagine life without him," added Ronon.

If Erony noticed the faint sarcasm in Dex's words, she gave no sign of it. "You will all accompany me, then. My adjutant Linnian has summoned a conveyor to take us into the capital." She gestured at the pavement. "This way."

"If I may ask, where did your Stargate come from, if it was not found here?" said Teyla, as they walked.

Erony spoke over her shoulder. "Star-Gate? That is what you call the Great Circlet? What a delightful term." She smiled briefly. "Yes, my ancestors brought our Circlet from an area in our polar regions, many generations ago, long before we had deciphered the sigils on the podium and learned the secrets of the portals it contained. It remains here now, inside the Terminal, held secure so that all on Halcyon understand that they are protected from any intruders it might admit."

Sheppard glanced up past the banners and got a better look at the oval-topped cylinders. Now he could see them for what they were; a cordon of gun turrets, short, stubby barrels of large caliber all pointing inward toward the Stargate. He had no doubt there were just as many on the other side of the Gate from where these stood.

Erony saw where he was looking and threw him a proud nod. "Invaders who come through the Circlet with malice in their hearts are not allowed far, Lieutenant Colonel." She pointed up at one of the flat concrete walls and Sheppard could just make out the discoloration of old blast damage. "The Wraith sent one of their screamer-ships here, when I was a small child. They paid for their impudence."

"So I see."

At the end of the pathway, two more troopers snapped their rifles to arms as a large elevator platform came level with them. Erony's second-in-command from the ice planet had gone on ahead and stood there now, waiting for them. He bowed. "High-

ness, all is prepared. The Lord Magnate has been informed of
your return. He wishes to speak with you."

The group boarded the elevator and it began to ascend. "Just
so," said Erony. "I will see him when we arrive at the High
Palace."

"Forgive me if I correct you, My Lady, but the Lord Magnate
desires otherwise. He wishes you to contact him via telekrypter
prior to leaving the Terminal."

There was a flash of annoyance on Erony's face. Sheppard
gave a wan smile. "Parents, huh?"

The elevator rattled as it rose out through the ceiling of the
Gate Hangar and into bright daylight, past the upper tiers of the
facility. Through the iron mesh of the shaft's walls the layout of
the complex became clearer.

"Military base," said Ronon, noting the dispersed lines of
blockhouses, the parade grounds and ranks of troops. Many of
these wore the colors of the men on the lower levels, but many
more were in different hues of blue, brown, red and purple.

"Cathedral," countered McKay, indicating the ornamental
rows of statuary that studded the site. There were vast arches
and spires more suited to a church, obelisks and what looked
like complex shrines.

"I am not familiar with that word," said Erony. "What does
it mean?"

"A cathedral… It's a place of worship, a building where you
can venerate your religion…"

The woman let out a short laugh. "Oh, Doctor, do you seek to
mock us? Please, Halcyon is not some backwater world of savages where we huddle in caves and pay homage to ephemeral
deities! This is a society of rational, intelligent thinking. You
will not find the delusions of religion here."

"You have no faith on this world?" said Teyla.

"Of course we do," said Erony, "but it is in our fellows, in
our own humanity, our might." She said the words with the
rhythm of a rote recollection. "Our faith is in our swords and
our shields."

They continued upward until the lift halted at a raised plat-

form several stories above the ground level. They followed
Erony out and Sheppard realized that they were standing in an
elevated railway station.

"You will excuse me," said Erony, moving away with Linnian, "this will take but a moment."

When they were out of earshot, Sheppard turned to his
team. "First impressions?"

"Technology level seems comparable with late 19th cen-
tury Earth," began McKay. "Post-industrial revolution, pre-
atomic, at a guess. Electricity, fossil fuels..."

Mason sniffed the air. "Steam engines." The soldier nodded at the single iron rail running off into the distance. "Me
granddad was an engineer on the railway. Worked on the
Pullmans. I'd know the smell anywhere."

"This is an armed people," added Teyla. "Everyone we
have passed, even those down on the ground, they carried
firearms or blades, often both."

Ronon rubbed his chin. "Swords and shields."

"Good eye," said Sheppard. "What else?"

Clarke was standing at the edge of the platform, looking off into the distance, still a little pale from being on
the wrong end of a Wraith weapon. "Rolling hills out there,
lots of farmland. Reminds me a bit of Wales, actually." He
pointed. "Looks like a city over that way."

Sheppard removed his binoculars from his pack and looked
in the direction Clarke indicated. Beyond the valley where
the Terminal complex lay he could see towers in dark red
stone rising behind the hillside, and there were tall chimneys
belching black streamers of smoke. It was hard to tell at this
distance, but there were objects drifting between the buildings, some slow-moving sliver-white ellipses, others quick
glitters of wings as fast as mayflies. "Airships? Helicopters?"
He wondered aloud.

"Something else," added Ronon. "Why haven't they asked
us for our weapons yet?"

Teyla nodded. "Ronon is correct. Erony and her men have
already seen them in action, yet they have not requested we

surrender them."

"Maybe they just haven't got around to it yet."

"Or," said Bishop, "maybe they don't see us a that much of a threat."

"Let's keep it that way," agreed Sheppard, "we're guests, remember? Best behavior."

"They're going to want to know where we're from," said McKay, "the question is going to come up. Are we sticking with the 'Atlantis got all blown up except for us' cover story?"

"They don't know we were talking to Atlantis back on M3Y-465. We'll play the cards we got for the moment. I don't think they know who we are at this stage."

"Of course," scoffed Rodney, poking a finger at the Velcro tab on his sleeve. "Our enemies will *never* recognize us now we've removed our insignia. That's about as good a disguise as a stick-on moustache. Why is it that we have to leave our patches behind every time we go off world, anyhow?"

"Regulations, sir," replied Mason. "Special operations. No identifying markings permitted on active duty."

McKay snorted. "I'd like to remind everyone that this planet is a kajillion light years from anyone who has even heard of Earth, let alone someone who might be able to recognize the flags of all nations."

"How much is a kajillion?" rumbled Ronon. "It sounds like a lot."

McKay ignored the sarcasm and kept talking. "Okay, sure, so we do have a patch that says '*Atlantis*' on it, and maybe we might want to keep where we come from a secret from some people, but who in the Pegasus Galaxy can even read it? I don't see the point."

"You're forgetting one thing, Rodney," said Sheppard.

"And what's that?"

"For all we know, on Halcyon a red maple leaf on a white background could be a symbol for 'please eat me alive' in their native language." He threw a glance over his shoulder. "Why take the risk?"

The two soldiers behind McKay smothered snorts of
amusement and looked away.

Lady Erony returned as their ride arrived at the platform. A
long steel-gray bullet, the monorail train hissed and spat like
a live thing, rolling to a clanking halt. Thick hatches of armor
plate dropped open like drawbridges and men in red tabards
scrambled around the hull of the machine, checking pipes and
valves. The central carriages of the train were detailed with fine
scrollwork etched into the dull metal. The lines and whorls of
engraving were polished to a high sheen; but it was clear where
parts of the conveyor had been panel-beaten back into shape
after some kind of blunt impact, and there were disc-shaped
patches here and there that might have covered bullet holes.

Inside there were lush carpets and crafted furniture of honey-
colored wood. Gas lamps lit the interior, catching gold and silver threading all about them. In each corner of the carriage,
ornamental bell jars contained raptor-like birds that had been
stuffed and mounted. The hatches slammed closed and locked
with a grunt of hydraulics.

"All aboard," muttered Mason, as the monorail launched
away from the station and out over the countryside.

The train picked up speed quickly, the view through the
windows blurring. Erony waved the Atlantis team to seats in
the open carriage and nodded to Linnian. "Refreshments," she
ordered, and the shorter man bowed in obeisance.

She took a device like a ticket dispenser from a nearby desk
and cranked the handle; a tape of paper emerged and she scrib-
bled on it with a stylus. "I would ask each of you to carry one of
these with you while you are in our domain," said the woman,
handing the first voucher to Ronon. "It is a permission from my
Dynast, identifying you as a guest of the High Palace." Erony
set to work on more of them, and handed them out to the group.
Sheppard studied the machine-imprinted paper; the text on it
was a series of bars and blocks. "Looks like Ancient script," he
noted quietly to McKay.

Rodney nodded. "There's some linguistic drift, but I'd say it came from the same root." Then suddenly, as if a thought had occurred to him, the doctor took a seat and removed his laptop from his pack.

Linnian returned with a pair of servants in tow, each carrying trays of cups and small food dishes. Lady Erony helped herself to a few things and then gestured at her guests. "Please, partake. Volla Leaf tea is a personal favorite of mine."

Teyla took a wary drink and smiled. "Quite lovely." Despite the hard look Mason gave to Clarke, the corporal took a handful of bread-like things and ate them.

Erony's mood seemed to have changed; Sheppard could sense a false note of forced jollity there, and he wondered what had been said during her conversation with her father. "Lieutenant Colonel, I must ask. I have been studying your wargear and I find myself wondering. Where are your swords?"

"Ah, well, we don't really do the sword thing very much," he began.

"Speak for yourself," broke in Ronon, pulling his wicked blade from the scabbard on his back. "This is a Satedan battle steel. Each one is unique, tailored for the owner."

"I see," Erony nodded. "Ronon Dex is your blade champion, then?"

"Something like that," smiled the colonel.

Erony approached Dex without hesitation or fear, despite the fact that he towered over her. "I wish to hold it."

Ronon turned the sword in his grip and presented the hilt to her. Erony took it and made a couple of low practice swings. "Heavy, and yet it is finely balanced. Not an ornamental weapon, but a war-blade." She studied the sword closely, looking at the nicks in the edge. "Have you dispatched many Wraith with it?"

"I lost count."

The woman returned Ronon's property, and Dex nodded to Linnian's gear where it hung on a wall rack. "Interesting rifle."

"Show him," ordered the woman, and her adjutant bowed, passing the bulky steam-gun across.

Sheppard watched the interplay carefully. There was an odd kind of bonding going on here, the same sort of macho venera-

tion of gear he'd seen a hundred times among soldiers of every
stripe—and yet it seemed slightly off-kilter to him, almost ritualized. In her own way, Erony was mapping out the hierarchy of
his team against the martial rules of her people. *Not just a pretty
face*, he opined silently.

Ronon had the rifle's chamber open. It had a rotating section
in the middle, like a revolver, with slots for shells of different
diameters. "Variable ammunition," he noted. "Useful."

"The long-lance can project a needle nest cartridge or a solid
round as required," explained Linnian. "Net loads and volter
shells may also be used."

"For stunning and capturing targets?" said Mason, without
weight. Ronon and Teyla exchanged glances.

"Correct." The adjutant took the weapon back. "Perhaps we
could arrange a visit to the Ducal Gun Enclosure for a live dem-
onstration during your stay."

"What fun," murmured Teyla.

The monorail turned slightly and rumbled over a set of points,
making the decking tremble. Sheppard caught movement from
the corner of his eye and his arm shot out to grab one of the
servants who had lost his footing. An ornate cup left the tray in
the youth's hand and shattered against the floor.

The servant—he was just a boy in his mid-teens—cowered
away from the colonel's grip as if he was expecting a blow to
follow. The boy was wearing a necklet, like a Celtic torc, made
from bronze.

Linnian made a harsh hissing noise with his teeth.
"Clumsy!"

The boy looked at Sheppard with real fear in his eyes. "Sir,
begging your pardon."

John let go of him, feeling uncomfortable. "No, it's okay, it
was an accident." He managed a smile. "No harm, no foul."

Erony's adjutant seemed wrong-footed by Sheppard's reaction, but then his eyes turned flinty. "You are *dismissed*," he
growled. The servant boy gathered up the cup fragments and
fled the carriage. The Lady herself seemed to be unconcerned
with the brief moment of drama, as if dealing with the hired

help was beneath her.

"Forgive that dolt's error," said Linnian. "He will be chastised."

"There's no need for that," insisted Sheppard. "It was my fault. I must have startled him."

"We have rules," insisted the adjutant, "and they must be adhered to."

Lady Erony gave Sheppard a long look. "Ah, but now we appear too strict and harsh in the eyes of my guests, Linnian." She settled back in her chair. "We of Halcyon are of a hardy, determined stock, Lieutenant Colonel. You may view our world now and see a verdant and pleasing land but it was not always so. In our old history, Halcyon was a hard mistress, she fought us and made life treacherous. We grew up strong because of it and we learned that life works, not by the edict of some phantom divinity..." The woman glanced at Teyla, then away. "But because of *rules*. That which one can codify, one can master. Do you not agree, Dr. McKay?"

"Hmm?" Rodney looked up from his computer. "What? Oh, yes, I suppose."

"You will see that ours is a civilization based on a skein of regulations, honor codes and strict laws of status and chivalry. Codes that have kept our society in check and flourishing for millennia."

Once again, Sheppard was struck by the cadence of her words, as if they were something she had been taught to say, not something from her heart. Part of him knew that here and now was not the time to get drawn into a debate over politics, but he couldn't stop himself from replying. "We have our rules too, and liberty for all is pretty much the first one on the list."

Erony smiled warmly. "We have *so* much in common."

Teyla found her attention drawn to the landscape as it changed, trees and fields giving way to thickening strands of conurbation. As Colonel Sheppard and the woman Erony talked, the Athosian studied the outskirts of the city flashing by. Spider webs of cables hung over everything from tall poles, and tight

streets of narrow homes ranged away in long, featureless terraces. The train moved so quickly that all she saw were snapshot
images; children engaged in a game with bats and a ball; lines
of washing flapping like flags; a small feline animal coiled over
the warm spot on a rooftop; heavy steam-driven trucks rumbling
along narrow alleys.

It seemed a grim and busy place, with nothing in kind to the
tents and yurts of the village where she had grown up, no forests
or rivers. Teyla fancied that the people of Halcyon saw their
industry and their works as the most impressive thing on the
planet, ignoring the simple beauty of the countryside outside the
conurbations. It was very different from the way of the tribes of
Athos, living close to the land and using their advancements to
enhance that pastoral lifestyle, not supplant it. Teyla knew that
she could never be at home in a place like this; she needed the
sight, the touch and the scents of nature around her.

She saw Lady Erony from the corner of her eye as she took
a sip of the rather bland tea and gave a musical laugh. Teyla's
lips thinned. It was difficult for her to put her finger on the
root cause, but there was something about the noblewoman that
sat poorly with her. It wasn't rudeness or malice she sensed,
not something so blatant as that. No, Erony just seemed to be
a little... *Patronizing*. The Athosians were more than familiar
with such behavior toward them, with people from other worlds
considering them somehow backward because of their agrarian
lifestyle. It was a mistake that even Sheppard's group had made
the first time they met.

Teyla pushed the thought away. Perhaps she was being unfair
in her assessment. After all, she had only just met the woman,
and under less than ideal circumstances; still, it was difficult to
shrug off her first impressions, the 'gut feeling' that she had so
often heard John speak of.

She looked back at the windows and noticed for the first time
that there were mechanical shutters that could be lowered down
over them. *In case the nobles do not wish to look upon the less
fortunate as they travel*, she thought.

McKay suddenly bolted up from his chair and gasped. His computer was making a strident beeping. He threw a look left and right and then pressed up against the windows of the carriage. "I, I need binoculars! Quick, quick!"

"Is something wrong?" asked Linnian.

"You require a magnification device?" said Erony. "Here. You may use mine." She handed him a brass-plated monocular.

"Yes, excellent, thanks!" McKay darted looks at the laptop and then peered through the stubby telescope.

"Rodney?" said Sheppard, with a warning tone in his voice. He followed McKay to the window. The scientist was looking westward.

"Where are you? Come on...." McKay was talking to himself. "Where... Aha! There she blows!"

"Rodney!" Sheppard repeated, and this time with force. "You're acting weird and it's making me look bad in front of the nice Lady."

"Look at this," said McKay by way of an answer, thrusting the laptop into Sheppard's hands. John studied the screen. There were lines like sine waves and shifting bars denoting energy output. The patterns looked vaguely familiar. "You don't see it, do you?" said Rodney. "You got the gene and you don't even know what this is." He shook his head. "The ticket thingy, the text? It got me thinking. Ancient-style writing means exposure to Ancient culture in the past. Ancient culture in the past could mean Ancient artifacts lying around *here and now*."

"It's a power source?"

McKay was becoming more animated by the second. "Very faint, possibly nothing, but rather similar to a ZPM." Grinning, he pointed out the window. "Take a look."

Sheppard accepted the monocular and squinted through it. And there, beyond a ridge, isolated and distant, was a tall monolith in slate-gray stone. He'd seen the same style of construction on a dozen planets in the Pegasus Galaxy. Ancient architecture. A legacy of the people who built the Stargates. The obelisk was already moving out of sight as the monorail pulled away, but the shape of it was unmistakable.

And where there were Ancients once, there might be a Zero Point Module gathering dust. Suddenly, the stakes had changed in this little diplomatic jaunt. The ongoing search for a ZPM unit was one of the top priorities for Atlantis's off world teams, and there were standing orders that even the merest sniff of such a device had to be investigated. The power requirements for the city complex were massive, and only the advanced technologies of the zero point energy devices could keep Atlantis running at full capacity. If the team could get their hands on another one...

"You think they'll let us take a closer look?" McKay's voice took on a conspiratorial hush.

"I think we'll have to play friendly if we're going to get the opportunity," Sheppard noted.

Erony came to them and reclaimed her monocular. "You are interested in the dolmen, yes? It is a remnant of a people known as the Precursors, who pre-date all civilizations in known space."

"Yes, we, ah, we're familiar with them too. We call them the Ancients," said Rodney.

She smiled. "Ancients? You do have such charming names for things. Very... Straightforward. The dolmen is a site of some scientific curiosity, although the study of the past is not of primary interest to our learning council." Erony leaned closer, and Sheppard felt himself being edged out of the sphere of conversation. "I must confess to a fascination with these... Ancients, as you term them. Are you interested in them also?"

McKay grew smug. "Actually, I'm kind of an expert. *The* expert, you might say."

The monorail rocked slightly and began to lose speed. "Highness," said Linnian, "we are a few moments from the Palace platform."

Erony nodded. "Of course." She threw Sheppard and McKay the same bright smile. "We will talk more of these matters later. For now, there is a presentation to undertake."

The steam train deposited them in a glass-roofed station

where another honor guard was waiting. They had a small band with them, who played out a longer version of the recorded fanfare that had announced Erony's return through the Stargate. Ronon flexed his fingers and waited for the caterwauling to stop. All this pomp and circumstance made him itchy.

The group crossed through a stone and steel archway and there before them was the High Palace. Dex tilted his head back to take in the whole height of it. The building was at least as tall as the central tower back on Atlantis, but in a strong, dark red hue and carved from huge blocks of stone. It was thickset in design, crested with minarets and crowned by large domes that ended in sharp spires. Gold and silver detail, too far up to see distinctly, glittered in the pale yellow light of Halcyon's sun. At other levels above and below them, walkways criss-crossed leading in and out of the edifice. Stanchions in the shape of lean warrior statues held them up in the air.

"Blimey," said Hill. "That's a palace, all right."

"Those domes look like the Taj Mahal or the Kremlin," noted McKay. The names meant nothing to Ronon, but the other Earthers nodded in agreement. "Interesting mix of architectural styles. There's some Ancient in there as well."

Dex let his practiced soldier's eye range over the building as they approached it. "Not just impressive," he noted, "good tactical design."

"Yeah," agreed Sheppard. "It's well hidden, but this place is as much a fortress as it is a palace."

"Plenty of locations for hard points. Revetments disguised as gardens. Fire corridors from the gun slits in the walls." Ronon looked up. "Any siege force you threw against this would break apart." He glanced at Sheppard and Mason, and saw the same thoughts in their eyes. This was a culture with its roots in warfare; and yet they had seen no evidence of battle or its aftermath. Dex took a deep breath of the Halcyon air, let it fill his lungs. After Sateda, after visits to dozens of other conflict-scarred worlds, Ronon knew the reek of war intimately; and yet he couldn't sense it here. The disconnect between the martial manner of these people and this planet, with its sky clear of battle-storms, rang a sour note with the ex-soldier.

Lady Erony hadn't been wrong about the warmer weather here. The team had discarded their parkas and Dex unbuttoned his greatcoat, letting the leather swing open. He became aware of Erony's adjutant close at hand, sneaking surreptitious looks at him.

"Ask me," he said, without looking at the man.

Linnian licked his lips. "You... You are a Runner, yes?" With his collar turned down, the Wraith glyph on Ronon's neck was clearly visible. "I have heard of your kind, but I have never seen a live specimen before."

Dex spread his hands. "Take a good look."

"How have you survived against their stalkers?"

With a flick of his wrist, he drew his particle magnum and held it an inch from Linnian's face. "I'm fast," he said simply.

"Ronon," warned Sheppard. "Play nice."

Dex returned the pistol to its holster and Linnian grinned. "Impressive. I understand the Wraith place tracking implants beneath your flesh—"

"Sheppard's man dealt with those for me," he noted, tapping his shoulder. "Now they don't see me coming. They won't follow me here, if that's what you're afraid of."

The adjutant snorted and ran a hand over his neatly trimmed beard. "We don't fear the Wraith on Halcyon, Ronon Dex. The Wraith fear *us*."

Ronon listened to the man's bravado and looked away, wondering. Such a statement either made Linnian a fool, arrogant or both. As they fell under the shadow of the towering palace, something caught his eye. On one of the lower walkways, a unit of six soldiers in identical garb were walking back the other way, with a single man in a uniform like Linnian's leading the march. What held his attention was the battle dress they wore. It wasn't the ornate coats and hats of the other Halcyons, but articulated metal plate armor. Chain mail was evident beneath, but not an inch of bare skin was visible. The faces of the armored troopers were hidden behind ornately worked helmets that had been fashioned after the heads of snarling canines. The only things that gave them an identity were streamer-like scarves around their necks. The low breeze caught them, making them flutter like thin flags. The figures walked in mechanical lock-step behind their commander, away and out of sight.

Dex looked up again as they came to the entrance of the High Palace. Doors wide enough to fit a battalion through lay open before them, and it took a conscious effort on his part to stop his hand from straying the butt of his pistol once again.

"Welcome to the Grand Chamber of Audiences," said Erony with a flourish, as they entered a massive ballroom.

Sheppard blinked. "You get the feeling they're trying to impress us?" he asked McKay.

"With monarchies, it's all about the size of your castle," replied Rodney.

"I'll say. You could dry-dock an ocean liner in here." The hall was as big as the Gate Hangar, but it exchanged the industrial look for something that seemed more like the inside of a chocolate box. The ceiling was a huge mural of proud soldiers and pastoral scenes, suspended on thick marble pillars over a floor of wood so highly polished it could serve as a mirror. Between each pair of pillars there were cabinets made of finely worked iron and brass. Some of them were given over to the preserved pelts of animals that were no doubt long dead or hunted to extinction. Others had weapons laid out like artworks, guns and axes and daggers in lethal array. The one that caught the colonel's eye was filled with skulls of different shapes and sizes. Some were small, like the kind you'd find in a rat or a dog, others more obviously feral. There were a couple of down-right alien looking ones as well, broad curved things, maws with spiky mandibles and something he caught a glimpse of that looked unpleasantly human.

McKay nudged him and surreptitiously indicated the other side of the chamber. Over there were full size hunter's trophies, huge beasts similar to grizzly bears arranged in mid-roar, wild-cats atop fake rocks. "Looks like taxidermy is a popular pastime here," said Rodney quietly. John said nothing. He was looking at the animal heads mounted over the arches. He couldn't see it clearly, but one of them looked a hell of a lot like… Well, like a Wraith.

Dozens of men and women in regal finery and over-decorated military uniforms drifted here and there, pausing to bow as Lady Erony passed them by. A small legion of servants moved among the islands of chattering people, serving food and drink. Sheppard's nose wrinkled with the mingled scents of a hundred cloying perfumes.

The Atlantis team collected arch looks and outright stares from the Halcyon nobles as they followed Erony and Linnian up the long hall. Some of the expressions varied from obvious distaste to guppy-faced surprise. The colonel reminded himself that this was a diplomatic mission now, and he did his best to smile nicely at everyone who turned his way, trying to look pleasant and non-threatening. Still, he couldn't escape the return of a familiar sensation at the back of his mind; the recollection of childhood visits to the house of his elderly Aunt Betsy. A stern and rather unforgiving old lady, every trip to Betsy's house would result in little Johnny Sheppard being paraded in front of his aunt's blue-rinsed sewing circle, who would proceed to criticize everything about the lad and his misbegotten generation. This felt a lot like that.

"My father is the Lord Magnate," Erony was saying, "that means he is the sole authority on Halcyon and her dominions. He will attend momentarily." She swept her hand around. "He sits at the head of a court drawn from the noble families of all the Dynasts."

"And the Dynasts are what, exactly?" said McKay. "Barons and dukes, the holders of fiefdoms, landed gentry, that sort of thing?"

"Quite right," she replied. "Have you a similar manner of governance on your world?"

"Yes and no," said Sheppard.

At the far end of the hall was a raised section with couches and what was unmistakably a throne. Erony stepped up and wandered toward a curtain behind them. "I will return."

"So," Sheppard turned to McKay. "Nice digs, huh?"

"Sure," said the scientist dryly. "I'm just hoping they don't look at me and shout '*Orf wiv 'is 'ead!*'"

"Are you kidding? I think Erony is taking a shine to you."

Rodney colored a little. "Don't be ridiculous!" He paused. "You think so?"

A ripple of raised voices drew Sheppard's attention away. "Trouble..." said Mason in a low tone, drifting closer.

Further down the chamber, two nobles—one in a tan uniform, the other wearing light blue—were degenerating into a shouting match. Both men were stabbing fingers in the air and making angry gestures. Sheppard knew instantly that physical violence was going to kick off between the pair of them in the next few seconds. They each had large swords at their hips and fat revolvers in jeweled holsters; it could turn very ugly very quickly. He stepped forward.

"Colonel," called Mason. "Reckon we shouldn't interfere, sir—"

Ronon gave a humorless smile. "Ten to one he starts a fight with both of them."

Corporal Clarke shrugged. "I'll take those odds."

"Pestilent!" snarled the noble in blue. "You, sir, are a gutless child without the courage of your convictions! I would run you through if I did not think it would dirty the floors of this august place!" He had his hand on the hilt of the sword and it clattered in its scabbard.

I'll be darned, thought Sheppard as he approached, *that's what they mean by 'rattling your saber'*.

The noble wearing the tan uniform bared his teeth in anger. "You dare insult me so under the roof of our Lord Magnate? I will see you dead in the soil and your lands annexed to my fief!" The other man drew a length of bright steel blade from his own weapon.

"Hi there," said Sheppard brightly, interposing himself between the two men. He took their empty hands and pumped them both in a vigorous handshake. "I'm John, and I'm new around here, but I just wanted to tell you two guys what a great planet you've got. I love this palace. It's big, you know?"

"What?" said Blue, nonplussed by this sudden interruption.

Sheppard kept talking, careful to block the path of any potential violence between the nobles. He pointed upward. "And that roof? Wow. Just wow. Honestly, that beats the Sistine Chapel hands down, am I right?"

"Now, see here-" began Tan, struggling to regain control of the situation.

"Hey," Sheppard put his arm around Tan's shoulder. "That guy in the painting, up there? Who is he? I'd love to know, 'cos I'm a bit of a tourist at heart..." Suddenly he was guiding them apart, out of fighting range of each other.

"It... It is the former Lord Magnate Trahvis, leading the victors at the Battle of the Nine Loops..."

"Trahvis, huh? He was a mean-lookin' fella, wasn't he?"

"Stop!" snapped Blue. "There is an issue of honor here, and I will not be denied!"

The colonel made a conciliatory gesture. "Guys, hey. We're getting along so well here. Let's not spoil it."

But then the man in blue had his sword drawn and the blade hung in the air, a dangerous arc of glittering silver. "Step away, outworlder, or I will gut you as well—"

"You will do no such thing," said a smooth, cold voice. A man clad in the same black uniform as Erony approached them. He had olive skin and elfin eyes, and he walked with swiftness and grace. Something about him sent up warning flags in Sheppard's mind. He wasn't like these two poseurs. He moved like he was dangerous.

The reaction of the noblemen confirmed it. Tan bowed his head and Blue's blade drooped. "There is a issue of honor, Baron Vekken," repeated the swordsman.

Vekken nodded. "If that is so, it will be dealt with in a civilized manner, as the codes decree." His voice hardened. "It will *not* be dealt with through wanton bloodshed in the Magnate's residence, in front of the guests of his Highness's daughter."

"Of course," said Blue after a moment, sheathing his sword.

"I beg the court's pardon. In the heat of my ire, I forgot my place."

Vekken inclined his head and looked to Sheppard. "Lieutenant Colonel, yes? I am Baron Aldus Vekken, personal adjutant to the Lord Magnate. Please, attend me so we may make formal introductions."

Sheppard threw a smile at the two cowed nobles. "You guys be cool, okay?"

Vekken lowered his voice as they walked away. "A word of advice, sir. Only the Magnate or his agents may intervene in disputes in the court."

"I just didn't want to see the party ruined," countered the colonel, "but boys will be boys, right?"

Vekken raised a quizzical eyebrow. "Indeed."

Teyla watched the colonel and the Magnate's man, unable to take her eyes off Vekken. The taciturn adjutant did not meet her gaze once, but she was certain he was aware of her scrutiny. He seemed different to the other Halcyons they had encountered up until now, and in some peculiar way she could not fathom, the man was *familiar* to her. The realization was unsettling for the Athosian woman and she flattened the disquiet in her chest, pushing it away. Too many things about this place were distracting her, and that would not do. For all the airs and graces these people displayed, the moment of swordplay just now showed her that violence was bubbling just below the surface of their courtly manners. The group would all have to be on their guard, in case the next burst of hostility was directed at a member of the Atlantis team.

Vekken stepped up on to the lowest of the dais's tiers and cleared his throat. When he spoke, it was with a clear and steady accent that carried to the back of the chamber. "Dukes, Barony and escorts, guests and attendants. Give your salute and your recognition to his Highness, the Lord Magnate Ranavar Daus of the Fourth Dynasty, Peer of Peers, Magister of the Sovereign World of Halcyon and her dominions, Hero of the Tephite Campaign and the Hand that crafted the Lokrist Accord."

The curtain behind the throne parted and Erony's father emerged, smiling broadly. At once Teyla saw both the family resemblance to the young woman, and to the faces of the heroic figures painted on the ceiling. Daus, like so many men and women here, wore clothes of a military cut, but his differed with the addition of a large cloak and elaborate chains of office about his neck. Thickset but not stocky, the Magnate had the look of a man who had been a formidable fighter in his youth, now robbed somewhat of his power and stamina by easy living and the passage of time.

The ruler of Halcyon accepted a scattering of applause from his courtiers and embraced his daughter. Teyla expected him to take the throne, but he did not, walking down the steps of the dais toward the Atlantis team. Vekken moved with him, a constant and watchful shadow, and behind them came Erony and two other men.

"When she was a child, my dear daughter would often bring small animals to me for my attention," Daus smiled, "and to this day she continues to bring me new and fascinating faces." The Magnate made a kind of ritual salute at Sheppard. "Welcome to our world, my friends."

"Thank you kindly," said John. "I, ah, apologize if we're a little underdressed for the occasion. These are just our working clothes, and we wouldn't want to give you the wrong impression." He glanced at Mason and the other SAS troopers, the fragmented camouflage of their uniforms wildly out of place in the huge ballroom.

"Ah," Daus accepted this with a nod. "It is of no consequence. The wargear of a gallant soldier is as dignified as any finery in my eyes." He studied the group before him. "You are the Lieutenant Colonel, yes? Leader of this hunt splinter? Erony has given me your names and told me of your fight with the Wraith on the ice moon."

"Just another day at the office," said Sheppard.

The Magnate gestured to his associates. "You have already had the pleasure of meeting my child and my strong right arm

Vekken. These others are my advisors, First Minister Muruw and Master Scientist Kelfer."

Teyla watched two very different expressions on the faces of the two men. The balding and burly Muruw seemed disappointed with the new arrivals, while the dark-skinned Kelfer showed a flash of clinical interest.

"Master Scientist?" echoed McKay. "We should talk."

"One thing at a time, Rodney," said the colonel. "Let's not get ahead of ourselves."

McKay continued, spotting an opportunity. "Lady Erony mentioned a… a dolmen? I'd very much like to see it."

Kelfer frowned. "The dolmen is a site of historical interest and access is strictly controlled to prevent annexing. But perhaps something could be arranged."

"There is common ground already between us." Daus gave each of them a penetrating look. "It is fascinating to make new acquaintances. I confess, your garb and your wargear are unknown to us. Tell me, where do you hail from?"

Sheppard ignored the *I-told-you-so* expression on McKay's face. "We're originally from a planet called Earth, Teyla and Ronon here are from Athos and Sateda."

"Earth," the Magnate considered the name. "Is that a Genii colony?"

"Hardly," snorted Rodney, without thinking.

"The Genii aren't exactly top of our buddy list," Sheppard admitted. "We've had some disagreements with them."

Daus smiled again. "That pleases me to know, Lieutenant Colonel. Halcyon and Genii have crossed swords in the past, and if you were in their service, I'm afraid your welcome would quickly expire."

"They are a low-born people," added Muruw. "They trade in deceit and secrecy."

"You'll get no argument from me about that," agreed Sheppard.

"You said you were 'originally' from this Earth," Vekken broke in. "Where do you reside now? On the ice moon?"

This is it, John told himself. "No. Up until recently, we were living in Atlantis."

There were gasps. "Atlantis? The lost city?" said Kelfer. "That's just a fiction. A Precursor story for children."

Teyla spoke up. "Not so. The city of the Ancestors, the Ancients, is no fallacy."

Daus tapped his chin. "You are the New Atlanteans... I admit, I have heard second-hand of such rumors from outworlders who trade with our hunters, but I gave them little credence." He shook his head. "Incredible. Today truly is a day for surprises."

Vekken stepped down and closed the distance with Sheppard. "But if this is so, if you are genuinely the ones who reawakened the City of the Precursors, then tell us. What of the dark tales we have heard of late being spread by the Wraith?" John tensed as the man gave him a threatening glare. "Is it true? Have the Wraith destroyed Atlantis?"

Sheppard swallowed hard. "They came in a dozen hive ships," he began, skirting the lie. "If they had taken the city, then they would have had access to all the knowledge of the people who built it."

Genuine shock showed on the faces of all but the Magnate. "You allowed the city to be obliterated?" spat Muruw. "A legend, sacrificed for your own lives?"

"Is it true?" pressed Vekken, never breaking eye contact with Sheppard.

"Enough!" snapped Daus, turning a harsh glare on his minister. "We will not scorn these people, we were not there on that day, and we cannot know what trials they faced. A dozen Wraith hive vessels... I have never heard of them grouping in such numbers." The Magnate stepped down to the floor with Sheppard for the first time, and the mood in the room shifted; clearly the symbolic gesture of coming down to their level carried great weight. Daus placed a firm hand on John's shoulder. "A tragedy." He spoke up so the whole chamber could hear him. "But we speak of the Wraith, the most ancient foe, the dread enemy of life! I would put my own beloved daughter's neck to the blade of my sword and burn this palace about me, if I were pressed to deny them!"

Sheppard flicked a glance at Erony, but her father's bold and gory statement didn't seem to trouble her.

"You are welcome to take respite here, Lieutenant Colonel," said Daus, moving away. "Perhaps this day will mark the start of a strong comradeship between your people of Earth and mine?"

"Sounds good to me, Your Highness," John forced a weak smile, glad to be away from the business of lying to the faces of complete strangers. These people seemed a little supercilious for his liking, but he didn't enjoy misleading them all the same. If there was anything that life had taught him, it was that lies and half-truths had a way of coming back to bite you in the ass when you least expected it.

"You fight the Wraith," began Ronon, "but this planet... It doesn't look like it's ever been culled." Sheppard knew what Dex was getting at; worlds where Wraiths regularly trawled for victims had distinct similarities, with broadly spread settlements or concealed cities to hide them from the alien predators. By contrast, Halcyon would be an open-air buffet for a fleet of Dart ships and cruisers.

Daus nodded. "There has not been a culling on this planet since before the Age of Unification. Such a thing has been unknown here in centuries."

"How have you stayed free of them?" asked Sheppard. "Erony's Wraith-hunting gang, that's not something they'd let go unanswered."

"My daughter's hunt splinter is but one of hundreds," the Magnate replied. "Each of the barony you see here has splinters of their own, to a greater or lesser extent. We stalk the Wraith on many worlds across our segment of the galaxy."

"*You* hunt *them*." Ronon said flatly, skepticism in his tone. "With gas-powered muskets and sabers."

"And steely hearts and unbreakable will," added Erony. "We do indeed."

Muruw gave a harsh chuckle. "My Lord Magnate, I fear our new friends do not understand the Halcyon way. They are too familiar with the terror and cowardice rife on other worlds, where men flee from the mere mention of the Wraith." He sneered at Ronon. "Runner, we of the Dynasts have been fighting the Wraith for hundreds of years and winning. We beat them at every turn. You ask why it is that Halcyon has not been culled? The answer is simple. Because they are afraid of us. They know that if they come to this world they will die."

Sheppard thought of Linnian; he'd overheard the adjutant's similar comment to Dex outside the place. Both he and Muruw seemed utterly convinced they were right. A scattering of brusque laughter and applause rippled out across the chamber in support of the First Minister's assertion.

"But what about the others?" said Teyla quietly. "What about the Wraith that you do not kill in battle?"

The Magnate's face became fixed, and Sheppard knew straight away that the question had tripped some taboo, crossed some kind of line.

Muruw's expression clouded. "Your concubine is an inquisitive one, Lieutenant Colonel," he said mildly.

"Teyla is not... *that*." Sheppard frowned. "She's a member of my team."

"Oh," said the Minister. "Forgive me. In our hunt splinters it is typical that the leader takes their favor from a cohort. Pardon the error of my assumption, if the matter is otherwise..." He gave a pointed glance at Dr. McKay instead.

Rodney blinked as Muruw's insinuation registered with him. "Oh, good grief, no!"

Sheppard's temper flared. "We don't... We're not... That doesn't apply to us, Minister." The balding man smiled thinly, and the colonel's annoyance rose. The guy was deliberately provoking him to deflect attention from Teyla's question.

Daus stepped away, moving up the tiers once more. "You will forgive me, but affairs of state preclude me from continuing this discussion. Erony, you and Duke Kelfer will attend to our guests, see that they have rooms in the visitor's wing. Make them comfortable." The Magnate threw a vague nod at the chamber and then he had turned his back on them, dismissing them completely.

"That's it?" said Bishop. "That's the audience? Huh. I was expecting something, you know, a bit more showy."

"Shut it," warned Staff Sergeant Mason.

Erony summoned a servant, who bowed and gestured for them to follow her. Ronon matched pace with Sheppard as they made their way from the hall. "I don't like this," said the Satedan. "They're hiding something."

"So are we," noted the colonel. "Let's just keep our eyes open, huh?"

CHAPTER THREE

She was running. Always running. Her limbs pistoned as she threw herself forward, heedless and unguided through the monochrome landscape. The hills and the twisted, skeletal trees rose up around her, black shadows falling across the dirty white ice that coated the ground. She sensed the wind on her bare arms, her neck and face; it should have been razor sharp and frigid, but her body was flooded with warmth and she felt clammy with sweat. The snow fell in a steep-angled blizzard, washing over her. *It was wrong.*

She was running. The sky was hollow and dark, the icy rains crossing it like a screen full of static. Where was she going? Did she even know where she was?

Emerging here and there from the snowdrifts were yellowed hummocks of cured hide and canvas, some whole, others ripped open and flapping in the wind. The tents were arranged in a familiar pattern, in the way of the tribes of Athos; but this was a dead village, torn into shreds and murdered in the frozen gloom. There were no bodies. There never were.

She hurtled through the encampment, unable to stop, her pumping legs refusing to give up the headlong pace. In the black out there she could hear the murmur of alien voices, growls and shrieks, animalistic noises. *It was wrong.* They encircled her even as she fled them, distant and echoing.

She was running. The ground around her spilt and splashed beneath her boots, the snows disintegrating into puddles, melt water pools shrinking and retreating into the dark. Where the ice withdrew she saw that the things that looked like tents, trees, hills, were nothing of the kind. They changed without changing, the earthen ground they clung to turning hard and obdurate. Faded grasses merged into hard stone cobbles, and streets grew up around her. Tall tenements that vanished into the night sky, high chimneys throwing clotted gray ashes from their mouths.

She stumbled and fell, striking the rough-hewn paving stones, scarring her hands; but there was no pain. *It was wrong.*

With effort she propelled herself to her feet and saw the children there beneath the sickly, sputtering light of a yellowed street lamp, dancing and laughing around the crooked iron pillar. The shrieking, screaming chorus was getting closer, looming along the pitch-black alleys that radiated away from where she stood.

She called to them, but her throat went tight and rebelled against her, stopped her from making a single sound. The children turned their backs, bats and ball in their hands, making play against a red brick wall, jostling one another.

The tremor of the silenced cry shot through her body in a shocking electric wave. Did they not hear? Could they not see to the shadows, the pale-faced things loping and stumbling, closer and closer?

She faced the darkness, the uncountable snarling horrors, ready to fight them; but her training failed her. As if a dam had breached and the reservoir of all her warrior skill had been drained away, she could bring up nothing to battle the beasts with.

It was wrong. She saw them now, the straggle-haired and corpse-pallor killers shambling into the halo of weak lamplight. They were different; the monstrous arrogance in their eyes was gone, replaced by a bestial, brutish manner. They howled like graywolves.

She spun in place, desperate to try one last time to warn the children. The players turned and altered as they finally heard the faint cry that she pressed from her throat. The children were Wraiths, hands distending into claws of black nails, hair fading white, faces crinkling as new features emerged and orchards of fangs split from red mouths. They advanced on her, snapping and purring at one another, and suddenly she understood that they were not in danger.

I am.

And then she was running, running and fleeing, but nothing

moved, the road sucked her down, and the Wraith came close, hands extending, each of them desperate for a taste of her.

John heard the scream, and the sound jolted him instantly to wakefulness from the light doze he had slipped into. Before he could properly register it, the reflexive actions of his training had propelled him out of the bedroom with his Beretta pistol in his hand. He was across the anteroom in ten quick paces, bisecting the circular chamber and rushing headlong for the guest quarters provided for Teyla Emmagan. He was dimly aware of movement behind him as Mason and the others were alerted.

Sheppard saw the splintering around the brass handle and the gap where the door was hanging ajar. Leading with the gun, safety off and hammer back, the colonel shouldered the door open and moved swiftly inside.

It was stuffy; he smelled human sweat, feverish and clammy. In the center of the bedroom, identical in layout to each of the chambers off the anteroom, there was a wide bed with a net of gossamer muslin thrown over it. The sleeping pallet was in utter disarray and the silken sheets were a coiled snarl, dangling off the bed and heaped on the wooden floor. John came around the side of the muslin mesh and there was Ronon, also armed, low down in a crouch next to the tangle of sheets. Teyla lay there, shivering.

"Oh," managed Sheppard, a sudden and unexplained dart of resentment rising in him. He pushed it away. "You, uh, were—"

"I was outside. Heard her cry out," explained Dex. He jerked a thumb at the door. "She locked it," Sheppard thought he caught a note of awkwardness in the other man's voice. "Came running."

"Yeah, me too." The colonel made his weapon safe, holstered it and bent down to help the Athosian woman extricate herself from the sheets.

"Forgive me, John," she mumbled. "I… It was…"

"Problem, sir?" called Mason from the doorway. "She need a doc, sir?"

"We'll handle this," Ronon told him firmly.

Mason said nothing and backed away.

Teyla took a long draught from a carafe of water beside the bed. As Sheppard watched, her breathing eased. "That was most disturbing."

Dex eyed her. "Bad dream? Is that all it was?"

"It was vivid. I felt something."

"Felt something as in a nightmare something, or…" Sheppard made a winding-up motion near his temple. "Or a Wraith kinda something?"

"I cannot make sense of it," she said, her brow furrowing in concentration. "The recall fades. It is like trying to catch smoke in my hands." She licked dry lips. "Before, when the Wraith touched my mind, my dreams, it was different. There was intelligence there, malicious but with clear intent. This was not like that."

"Go on," said John. He was the first to admit he didn't fully understand the workings of Teyla's Wraith-altered physiology, but what he did know was that she could touch the edges of the telepathic network the aliens used to communicate. If that was bleeding into her dreams, then he had to give it his complete attention.

"They were more…" Sheppard could see Teyla was struggling to hold on to the dream images, trying hard to articulate them. "Vicious. Primitive. Like wild animals."

"The Wraith have always been animals," said Ronon, with feeling.

"But not like this. Not literally." She sipped more water. "Colonel, I am certain of one thing. This dream was not just the creation of my mind. There are many Wraith here, on Halcyon."

"How many?" Sheppard felt ice forming in the pit of his stomach.

"Hundreds. Perhaps more."

Ronon and John exchanged a loaded glance. "Are you okay now?" Sheppard asked.

Teyla gave him a shaky smile. "Yes, thank you. If I could

have a moment alone to gather myself."

The two men left the room. "We'll be right outside if you need us," added Dex. "Sorry about the door."

Mason and the other SAS soldiers straightened as they walked back into the antechamber. Sheppard saw right away that they had a wary look about them, as if they'd been caught discussing something they shouldn't have. Mason returned a level gaze, but the question was clear in Corporal Clarke's eyes.

"Let's hear it," said the colonel. "Who's going to say what you're all thinking?"

Private Hill found an interesting piece of carpet to occupy his attention. After a moment, Clarke gave a slight frown. "Lieutenant Colonel, sir," he began, pronouncing the rank as *Left-tenant* in the way the Brits always did. "Your lass there, Tina…"

"Teyla,"

"Yeah. There was talk back in the city about her. Some of your Marine Corps lads said the bozos did something to her, when she was a nipper, like."

Sheppard noticed that Mason wasn't doing anything to stop Clarke from speaking his mind; clearly the senior non-com wanted to know the same thing as his subordinate. "She's not a danger to the unit, if that's where you're going with this," he broke in, steel in his tone. "Teyla Emmagan is a vital part of this team and you will respect that, Corporal."

"I don't doubt it, sir. It's just that… Well, are we going to have to jump every time she talks in her sleep?"

Sheppard gave Clarke a penetrating look. "Just so we're clear on this. Teyla's 'gift' may be the very thing that keeps us alive when the Wraith come calling. If she has something to say, you listen. Get me?"

Clarke stiffened. "Sir, yes sir. Didn't mean to cast aspersions, sir."

John sighed. "Look, I know it's not conventional intel, but nothing out here is conventional." He smiled a little. "That ought to be the motto of Stargate Command."

"You're telling us," said Hill in a low voice.

Mason threw a nod at the door that led out of the guest quarters. "I've set up a two-point watch rotation, sir. If anything else... *unconventional* happens, we'll be ready."

Sheppard nodded. "I'll take the first shift, Staff Sergeant. Now I'm awake, might as well make the most of it."

"I'll join you," said Ronon. "Can't sleep on beds that soft anyhow."

John shrugged as they walked away. "If we ask the Magnate nicely, I'm sure he'd find a big rock for you, or something."

Dex was silent for a moment. "Clarke had a point. About Teyla."

"Yeah," agreed the colonel, "but I trust her. We know the locals planned to bring the Wraith they captured on M3Y-465 back through the Gate. Could be them she's sensing."

"What if there's more to it?"

"Now that..." Sheppard frowned. "That's a different question."

McKay leaned back from the eyepiece of the massive telescope and a glimmer of amazement crossed his expression. "I apologize," he said, half-turning to look at Kelfer and Lady Erony. "Obviously, it was impolite of me to suggest that you didn't know how to take the lens cap off your own telescope. I see that now..." Down below on the lower level, McKay could see Private Bishop, nibbling from a ration bar and generally looking a bit bored. Sheppard had, of course, insisted he take an escort with him; not that he thought he couldn't handle someone so clearly as stolid as the Magnate's chief scientist.

"It was an honest mistake," said Kelfer, wearing a forced smile. "An error that any new visitor to our planet could have made."

"Yes..." Rodney looked along the length of the device, out through the oval portal in the observatory's dome to the night sky beyond. The firmament up there was black as coal, and of course, naturally he had just assumed that it was due to light pollution from the city masking out all of the weaker stars. But when he peered through the optics and saw the same flat blackness, McKay's first reaction was to suggest the telescope was broken. *I mean, no stars at all? How likely was that?*

In fact there were some faint suns out there, but hardly any. The sights that hove into view as they swung the observatory dome around were mostly the planets in the stellar shallows orbiting Halcyon's yellow star, gas giants and lifeless balls of ice and rock.

"In the southern hemisphere," Erony was saying, "the sky looks very different. There is a band of stars crossing the sky from horizon to horizon. Our forefathers called the constellation the White River."

McKay stepped down from the observation chair and worked at the portable computer he had brought with him. "We must be right out on the edge," he said, thinking aloud. Before visiting the observatory, Erony had taken him on a walk through a library in the heart of the palace, past racks of scrolls veiled in cobwebs. He'd only had time to look over a few of them, a handful of historical tracts and yellowed charts of the skies. "If those stellar maps you showed me were accurate, then we can deduce the location of Halcyon in physical space and its relative distance from Atlantis..."

"To what end?" said Kelfer.

McKay hesitated. "To, uh, gain an idea of how the Pegasus Galaxy is structured..." The device beeped and presented a wire frame graphic of the galactic disc. "Do you see here?" He pointed as the image zoomed in toward the very tip of a feathery limb of star-stuff. "This solar system is on the end of a spiral arm. You're in the interstellar equivalent of the boondocks!" Rodney smirked at his own joke.

"Boohn-dox?" repeated the scientist. "I don't know this term."

McKay's gag fell flat and he moved on. "Halcyon is on the very edge of the Stargate network built by the Ancients... The, ah, Precursors. That place where you keep the Gate? When someone named it the Terminal, they weren't far wrong. If you think of the Stargates in the same terms as your monorails, then this planet is at the end of the line!"

"Are you making light of us?" said Erony gently. "I assure you, Dr. McKay, Halcyon is anything but a parochial outpost."

"No, no," Rodney insisted, back-pedaling a little. "I was just using a metaphor. Bad choice. Sorry." He tapped a finger on his lips. "This opens up a lot of possibilities about Gate travel here, the pattern of the network. A portal this far out from the main concentration of inhabited worlds could mean we'd see a similar spread of Stargates to those in our own galaxy... I mean, my galaxy, Earth's galaxy..."

Kelfer gave a derisive snort. "Your Earth is in another galaxy? Impossible. The power to translate across extragalactic distances would be incalculable!"

McKay gave the other man a sideways look. "You think so?"

"Of course!" Kelfer replied hotly. "The magnitude of energy would be greater than the detonation of an exploding star! No science could create a mechanism to contain such intensity."

It dawned on Rodney that Kelfer, for all his high title and impressive clothes, was narrow-minded and not in the market for challenging viewpoints. Moreover, his statement made it clear that the Halcyon scientist had never even conceived of something like a Zero Point Module.

"No science?" McKay repeated. "Not even that of the Precursors?"

Kelfer snorted again. "I admit the Great Circlet is a masterpiece of technology, but not even the builders of that device could do such a thing. They were mortal beings, after all, not gods."

"Depends on your definition..." said Rodney, half to himself.

"It pleases me that you have found such food for thought here, Doctor," said Erony with a smile. Her eyes flashed as she met his gaze and something in her look make him swallow hard. She continued; "I must admit, I find this intellectual discussion to be most stimulating. Sadly, there is precious little opportunity for the scientific disciplines that do not directly impact upon Halcyon's martial or industrial might."

"No doubt," McKay nodded. He had noted on the way in to the observatory that the facility was dusty with age and showed little signs of regular use. "Astronomy isn't much help when you're building weapons, I suppose."

"Quite so," agreed Kelfer, completely missing the irony. "It is the duty of every learned person in our society to work toward keeping our planet strong and maintaining our superiority over the Wraith."

"Hmm. Well, your 'superiority'?" Rodney made quote marks with his fingers. "I think that may have more to do with your astro-geographical location than how big your guns are."

Kelfer sneered. "This is another one of your theories, out-worlder?"

McKay gave a thin smile. "Trust me, Kelfer, after a while most people catch up to the fact that my theories and the truth are the same thing..." He paused, the smile faltering. "Well, most of the time they are. But anyway. I'm willing to bet that the reason your planet has been free of Wraith attacks is because of its remoteness, galactically speaking, in relation to Wraith territory."

"Pah!" spat the scientist, his ire building. "I will not hear you disparage our military in such a fashion! The Halcyons are for-midable warriors with a reputation that strides the stars! We are the ones who give *them* nightmares!" Kelfer stalked away, out on to the balcony around the dome, fuming and muttering.

"It's always nice to meet someone with an open mind," said McKay.

"I could not agree more." The silky tone in Erony's words made Rodney's mouth turn arid. "You are a most interesting man, Dr. Rodney McKay. I wonder, is there anything else you might like to observe this evening?"

"Oh," He was suddenly at a loss for words. "Um." But that was hardly surprising. It wasn't every day a princess came on to him. "The dolmen?" The question came out in a squeak.

Erony seemed crestfallen for an instant, but then the flash of disappointment was gone. "Of course. I have petitioned my father on your behalf. As the site is of great significance to our people, he must personally approve your request to visit it. I imagine he will give you an answer in a few days."

"Great," Rodney replied. "Phew. Well. It's been a long day. Perhaps we should get to bed." He blinked. "I mean, *I* should get to bed. To the quarters. To rest."

She gave a gracious nod. "Of course. Please, follow me. I'll show you back to your associates."

Private Bishop rolled his eyes as he caught up with McKay. "Smooth, Rodders. Very smooth."

"Shut up," he hissed, and kept walking.

Sheppard leaned against the stone balustrade and took in the view. The air out here had turned chilly after sunset, so he had put his jacket back on. The P90 and the rest of his gear were back in his room, but he had his service pistol on him, just in case. The colonel couldn't shake the cautious feeling that was gathering at the nape of his neck, the slight warning tingle that made his fingers drum on the carved marble.

Hell, who am I kidding? He asked himself. *I am way outside my comfort zone here.* Sheppard was too much a soldier to ever get used to the mix of outward smiles and inward suspicions that this whole diplomatic, first contact thing involved.

A figure emerged through the heavy curtains from the ante-room. Teyla nodded to him as she approached. "Colonel."

She looked better and he was pleased to see it. The sallow, frightened expression on her face in the bedroom was so at odds with the casual confidence the Athosian woman usually displayed, it had concerned him. "How're you feeling?"

Teyla frowned. "Sleep eludes me for the moment. Perhaps it is for the best." She paused. "I have not sensed the Wraith again, Colonel."

"I wasn't asking as your commanding officer, I was asking as your friend," he replied. "I know it's hard on you."

She nodded. "Yes. Thank you, John. I appreciate your concern." Teyla gave him an appraising look. "And how do you feel?"

Sheppard gave a half-smile. "Just peachy."

"I do not envy your role in this," Teyla admitted. "The direct-ness of battle is far more desirable to me than the courtly word-games of these aristocrats."

"Ah, you know how it is. Rich folks are different to ordinary Joes like you and me."

"They are polite, but... I think they may privately see us as their inferiors."

Sheppard nodded. "You got that too, huh? Well, this is their planet, and they do have a big huge palace. I guess if you're going to throw your weight around, a palace would be the place to do it in."

"But their arrogance towards the Wraith concerns me, John. And there is also the issue of the prisoners we saw them take on M3Y-465. Lord Daus never answered my question."

John tapped the stones. "Could be they're going to interro-gate them, but then we know from experience that kinda thing yields mixed results at best."

"There is another possibility. The Halcyons may be harvest-ing the enzymes in their feeding sacs."

Sheppard's eyes narrowed as he considered that. Unbidden, thoughts of his friend Aiden Ford rose to the front of his mind; he recalled the young Lieutenant when they embarked from Stargate Command on the first trip to Atlantis, the eagerness in his face — and then he remembered the changes in him after the Wraith assault that nearly cost Aiden his life, the single dark eye that now disfigured him, the legacy of the changes the alien forced upon the young man. He was convinced Ford was still out there somewhere, too cunning to die easily, his heart pump-ing with doses of the mutagenic Wraith biochemical. Stronger, wilder, out of control. The idea that people might willingly be harvesting the narcotic fluids of the Wraith filled him with dread. "The thought had crossed my mind. We're going to have to find out what's up with that before we open any real dealings between Halcyon and Atlantis."

They were both quiet for a moment. Teyla looked out over the cityscape beneath them. "This citadel is built on the tallest part of the landscape in this area. The Magnate has made sure that everyone below in the city understands who rules them. They only need to look upward."

Sheppard followed her gaze. "I get the feeling they're only showing us what they think we need to see." He nodded at the city sprawl radiating away from the palace, the lights in the streets far below and the grim clusters of buildings. "I'd like to peek behind the curtain..." The colonel broke off. He heard a voice from the anteroom and realized that McKay had returned.

"Thanks again," said Rodney, ignoring the smirk on Bishop's face, and he gave Erony a small wave, unsure if it was correct protocol to bow or shake hands. For her part, the noblewoman inclined her head. They had left Kelfer behind, the scientist making excuses about 'vital work' requiring his attention, but in truth McKay suspected it was the building dislike between them that drove the other man away; which was fine. Rodney wouldn't miss him.

Sheppard and Teyla crossed the room, and the colonel threw a nod to the SAS soldier. Bishop responded in kind, and McKay found himself wondering how it was that military types could communicate so much with just a non-verbal twitch of the head. *Must be something they teach them in boot camp*, he thought.

"Colonel, Teyla," said Erony. "I trust you find your accommodations to your satisfaction?"

"Sure do," said Sheppard. "I trust Dr. McKay was on his best behavior?"

"He was a consummate gentleman," she replied. Erony did the little bobbing-head thing again and made to leave. "If there is anything you require—"

"There is," Teyla broke in on an impulse. "A question." The Athosian woman glanced at Sheppard, who did nothing to halt her. "In the hall today. I asked after the fate of the Wraith we saw your hunt splinter take captive in the abandoned village. I did not receive a reply."

Erony's face tightened. "That matter is of no consequence to you."

"Pardon me," Teyla pressed, "but I would insist otherwise. Any Wraith, even those held in chains, are a dangerous prospect."

"What you *insist* is irrelevant!" snapped the other woman, suddenly fierce. McKay blinked, wondering where the demure princess who had made advances on him had gone. The change in her manner was as swift as it was surprising; but then Erony's face softened and her flash of anger was gone again. "Please understand, Teyla Emmagan. You are all outworlders and unfamiliar with the ways of our society. Trust me when I tell you that the Wraith we took pose no threat."

A thought struck McKay with such abruptness that he was speaking it aloud before he could stop himself. "Was that where Kelfer was going? Are you... Oh no, are you draining that enzyme super-freak juice from them?"

"What are you implying?" Erony showed genuine shock.

"The Wraith feeding enzyme," said Sheppard. "Are you harvesting it to use on yourselves?"

The woman's face turned ashen. "What... What kind of people do you think we are?" She looked for a moment as if she were going to be ill, the color draining from her face. "The mere idea of such a thing! That we would take the filth that runs in the veins of those animals and put it into the body of a Halcyon? The thought disgusts me!" Erony shook her head, her voice rising. "We do not need to taint ourselves with their base blood! Our will to fight is more than enough to defeat them!"

"No one would willingly allow themselves to be marked by the Wraith," said a new voice. Vekken emerged from the shadow of the corridor, watching Teyla carefully. "Such things are anathema to the Halcyon character."

Rodney gulped. "Lady Erony, I'm sorry, we didn't mean to insult you..."

The woman became calm again, shooting a sideways look at her father's adjutant. "Of... Of course. You will pardon my outburst. You are outworlders and you knew no better than to suggest such a thing. Clearly, you have much more to learn about the temperament of my people than I thought."

"My Lady," said Vekken. "Your father asks that you attend him at your earliest convenience."

"Yes, thank you." Erony gave a small bow and walked swiftly away, her boots clacking on the wooden tiles. She never once met the steely gaze of the adjutant.

"Dodged the question again," said Sheppard in a low voice. "That's two-for-two."

"The affairs of the Wraith are not something that is spoken of in polite society, Lieutenant Colonel," Vekken noted. "Her Highness's outburst was a mild admonition compared to the rebuke you might have received had you asked the same question to one of the barony. Indeed, blood might have been shed because of it."

"But you were all for bragging about how many of them you'd killed!" snapped McKay.

"That is a different matter, Dr. McKay. A warrior's battle record is something to be celebrated."

Sheppard's brow furrowed. "Y'know, I'm having a hard time following the way you people think."

"That much is certain," noted Vekken dryly. "Then, in the interests of smoothing the path of your future parlays with my Lord Magnate, let me explain this to you. There is among the nation of Halcyon a great abhorrence for the Wraith, coupled with an innate knowledge of our superiority over them."

Rodney snorted in derision, but if Vekken noticed he didn't acknowledge it.

"But this is matched by a loathing of what they represent. Their bestial, vampiric nature is the very antithesis of ours," he tapped his chest, "and the thought of being alike to them in any way fills other souls with cold horror."

"Well, there's something we got in common, then," said Sheppard. "Now, do I have to ask again? What's going on with the prisoners?"

Vekken gave a small smile. "You'll learn that soon enough."

Since the adjutant's arrival, Teyla had remained silent; but now she spoke. "You said 'other souls'. Do you not include yourself among them?"

He studied her. "No, Teyla Emmagan, I do not. And I would imagine you already know the reason why."

Teyla hesitated for a long moment. "This man... He is like me. His bloodline was once changed by the Wraith. I can sense it..."

Vekken nodded. "I knew it to be true when I first saw you, Teyla. Our kind is very rare on Halcyon. Many of the families who suffered the machinations of the Wraith were wiped out in the Age of Unification, once the Circlet's portals were opened. Those of us who remain are feared."

"Erony," considered McKay, "she was spooked by you the moment you arrived."

"That is why her father made me his adjutant. There is no better guardian and warmaster than a Wraithkin. The fable is as sharp as any blade."

"*Wraithkin...*" Teyla repeated the word, weighing the meaning of it.

"I saw that term in some of the historical scrolls I glanced through," said Rodney. "I wasn't sure of the translation, but that fits." He turned to Sheppard. "Basically, the Halcyons think of people with Teyla's, ah, gift, like people on Earth used to think of witches."

The colonel blinked. "You're kidding me."

"Nope. And when I say witches, I don't mean the mead-drinking, naked-dancing Wiccan kind. I'm talking the baby-eating, broomstick-riding, turn-you-into-a-frog kind."

Sheppard looked at Vekken. "Thanks for the heads-up. Anything else you want to share with us?"

"Tread carefully, Lieutenant Colonel. Everything you do here is under close scrutiny. You are being judged, and if you are found wanting..." He showed that thin smile again. "Halcyon has never been tolerant of weakness." Vekken turned to leave and then hesitated on the threshold. "Oh. How remiss of me. Our conversation was so engaging, I almost overlooked the purpose of my visit. I have an invitation from the Lord Magnate for you and your associates. His Highness requires your presence tomorrow at an event in the Relia Lowlands."

"A party?" said Sheppard hopefully.

Vekken walked away, throwing a last comment over his shoulder. "He's hosting a war."

Rodney's jaw dropped. "A *what*?"

The rotorplane flew fast and level over the countryside at treetop level, gently rising and falling in and out of the nap of the earth. Through the oval portholes in the main cabin, Sheppard saw flashes of greenery and the odd cluster of lonesome buildings. They'd been airborne for an hour or two now, and except for a brief fuelling stop, the aircraft had been racing at what appeared to be full throttle all the way.

"I must admit, I do not understand your curiosity," Linnian was saying as Sheppard moved up the metal deck to the front of the rotorplane. "Do you find the passenger cabin to be uncomfortable?"

"Nope," John replied. "I'm just interested, that's all. I've never ridden in a steam-age helicopter before, and I'd like to see how it works."

"Actually, our gyro-flyers are powered by electrochemical batteries and powdered fuel volatiles," replied the adjutant. He frowned, clearly caught between his orders to obey Sheppard, and his Halcyonite ideas of decorum. But his mistress wasn't here, so he had to go with the colonel's demands. Linnian opened the hatch and ushered John into the wide cockpit.

The pilot and co-pilot both started as they realized they had company. Like Linnian, they wore the black of the Fourth Dynast, but their uniforms were cut differently, with less in the way of medals and sigils. Sheppard threw them an easy grin. "Hey guys, don't mind us. Just looking around."

The pilot gave Linnian a confused look and the adjutant returned him a shrug.

John leaned forward. The design and structure of the cockpit reminded him of the pressed-steel interiors of old warbirds from the 1940s, but more ornate. Etched brass and turned wood detail was on everything. Bright sunlight filled the cockpit from curved greenhouse windows. Back along the streamlined fuse-

lage he could see the sweeping arc of two interlocked, coun-
ter-rotating helicopter blades on stubby winglets. "Hell of a lot
different from a Huey or a Pave Hawk…"

The co-pilot blinked at him. "You… You are an aviator?" The
very idea appeared to be absurd to him.

"Lieutenant Colonel John Sheppard, United States Air Force.
If you can catch sky with it, I'll fly it."

"But we were informed that you are officer nobility on your
own world. Do you not have subordinates for the work of pilot-
ing?"

"Some do. Frankly, though, the day I don't get to take the
stick anymore is the day I'll retire."

Linnian frowned again. He was doing a lot of that. "Our command cadres do not sully themselves with such labor, Lieutenant
Colonel. Frankly, I am surprised your people do otherwise."

Sheppard threw the co-pilot a wink. "Well, I guess I can
understand you boys not wanting to let the senior ranks fly this
baby. They'd find out how much fun it was and then you'd be
out of a job, right?"

The other man smiled briefly, and John knew that he'd connected with him; they shared a moment of mutual respect, and a
flyer's passion for the open skies. "Perhaps… You might like to
take the controls for a moment, sir?"

"Oh yeah," Before Linnian could complain, Sheppard had
swapped places with the co-pilot and gave a nod to the aircraft
commander. "Thanks."

The pilot seemed wary and somewhat alarmed at being spoken to directly. Sheppard ran his eyes over the console. Most
of the usual dials and controls were there, but labeled in the
Halcyon semi-Ancient-style text. Still, he picked out the artificial horizon, what looked like airspeed and engine temperature.
There were foot pedals for the rudders and a complex set of gear
and throttle levers behind a butterfly-shaped yoke. He'd seen
something similar on the wheels of formula one racing cars. "I
have the aircraft," he announced.

The pilot nervously relinquished control, and there was a
slight flutter as Sheppard settled in; but then he got it, leaning

into the motion of the gyro-flyer and letting the craft tell him how it wanted to move. "Sweet," he said. "She handles real well."

"This flyer has been in service to His Highness for nine cycles," said the co-pilot, a hint of pride in his voice. "We've ferried the Lord Magnate himself on no less than four sojourns."

His eyes locked on the horizon, Sheppard kept his voice level. "Seen any combat? She's pretty nimble, I bet."

"Not in this vessel. I was once a Shrike pilot," said the other man. "They are rocketplanes with gun capacity. I served under Lord Daus's cousin Kalyn before his holdings were annexed."

"Rocket, huh? If we get the chance, I'll show you something that could leave that in the dust. We call it a Puddle Jumper —" Sheppard's words died in his throat as he caught sight of something in the distance. His seasoned aviator's situational awareness took his eye to it immediately. Sunlight glittered on metallic white spheres and a large silver cylinder was moving ponderously over a hillside; but what made him alert were the flickers of cannon fire and the plumes of black smoke rising from the valley. The distant rumble of shell detonations reached them seconds after a string of orange flares.

"Take the controls!" snapped Linnian, and Sheppard found himself jostled out of the seat by the apologetic co-pilot. "Lieutenant Colonel, I think we should return to the passenger cabin."

"In a second," John said firmly, placing himself behind the pilot's chair. Blinks of white from a spotlight atop the cylinder — which was quickly resolving into the shape of a huge airship — reflected off the windows. The co-pilot used a device like a flashlight to return another series of blinks, Morse-code style.

The gyro-flyer climbed as they crossed a stand of high trees and then abruptly they were over a war zone. The pilots guided the aircraft around thick tethers holding the fat balloons in place at the borders of the valley. Sheppard saw ringed decks dangling from the gasbags as they passed them by. He looked down.

There were no trees or brush of any kind on the ground, the

space beneath them just acres and acres of cracked and broken earth, marred by impact craters and the broad, long scars of trenches. He spotted the stone domes of pillboxes, snarls of barbed wire and shallow bunkers. Wrecked ground vehicles were dotted randomly, mired in the rust-colored mud. Here and there were pillars that were strangely untouched by the battle, with large wooden placards hanging off them on chains. The flyer turned away and then back toward the airship in a long loop, coming in toward the far side of it. Through streams of smoke he saw a column of men in tan-colored uniforms rise up in a wave from a trench and surge out across the no-man's land, rifles barking and spitting vapor.

"We won't be fired upon," said Linnian, pre-empting the question forming in Sheppard's mind. "The combatants know that their exercise would be forfeit if even a single shot were to strike a neutral unit."

The rotordyne slowed to a hover over the spine of the airship and settled on to a flat landing platform across its back.

The opulent design of the monorail carriage was repeated inside the massive zeppelin. The design of the airship, even down to the scrollwork on the iron girders, made the craft look more like a flying basilica than a vehicle for transport.

"His Highness has several of these ships for duties of state," explained Linnian as they walked down through the wood-paneled decks. John led the group with Teyla, Ronon, McKay and Hill following. Despite Staff Sergeant Mason's misgivings, Sheppard had ordered him to remain in the city with Bishop and Clarke.

Linnian was still speaking. "This vessel serves as his personal air-yacht."

"More like air-battleship," murmured Rodney. "It's got gun turrets all over it. All it needs is *Hindenburg* written on the side..."

Hill went a little pale. "You saying this blimp is full of hydrogen gas?"

"Yes," sniffed McKay, "that would be the faint fart smell in

the air." He shot Sheppard a lethal stare. "How I let you talk me
in to coming aboard this death-trap —"

"Stop talking," grated Ronon. "Or you can get off."

"Believe me, I'd love to, but we're a hundred feet above the
ground!"

"That's right."

McKay fell silent for the moment.

The adjutant nodded to a pair of soldiers as they approached,
and the men opened a wide oval hatchway. Linnian directed
them through, and they emerged into a broad observation gallery with a low ceiling, situated at the bottom of the main gondola below the airship. Sheppard had wondered about leaving
his weapons behind in the palace before coming here, and in the
end he had opted not to take the P90, but kept the pistol. Now
he felt positively under-armed, as everyone in the gallery, from
the officers in their over-decorated uniforms to the gossamer-
dressed companions on their arms, had some kind of weapon
on them.

Erony was waiting for them. She had changed her hunt
clothes for something less masculine, although the tunic and
skirt still had the look of a soldier about them. "Lieutenant Colonel, everyone, welcome. Please, come with me."

The gallery was an inverted fishbowl that looked down on the
battlefield, the shadow of the airship casting a dark ellipse upon
the earth. Gunfire and war cries reached them through the windows. It was clear straight away that the assembled observers
were clumped into three distinct cliques. On a raised platform in
the middle of the room were Daus and his group, Vekken at his
shoulder watching Sheppard's team with an unveiled stare. The
Magnate, Kelfer and Muruw were engaged in an animated conversation, and now and then Daus would pause to look at a sheaf
of paper offered up from a brown-hooded servant. The servant
shuttled back and forth between large teletype machines that
clattered and hummed, spitting out more paper at regular inter-
vals. The other two groups were as far from each other as they
could get, each against the opposite side of the gallery, crowding the windows. The closest was composed largely of men in

tan uniforms the same shade as the soldiers Sheppard had seen on the ground. Among them he saw one of the noblemen whose disagreement he'd curtailed in the Chamber of Audiences. There was a crash of explosive noise from outside and the baron and his party clapped and gave harsh laughter. Over their heads, a board with glowing valve-digits hissed and changed, although Sheppard couldn't read the meaning in them.

"Oh, hard luck for Palfrun!" said one of the tan officers to his commander. "I do feel so sorry for him!" The tone of the man's voice made it quite clear that the reverse was true.

An angry snarl drew John's attention to the other group, who were a similar mix of nobles, except there the predominant uniform color was light blue. Another familiar face pushed his way to the front of the group; it was the hot-headed swordsman that Vekken had faced down in the palace. "*Baron* Palfrun, lackey!" spat the man. "You will show me the respect of my rank! Or are your men short of even the most common decency, my esteemed Baron Noryn?"

Noryn—the tan nobleman—inclined his head. "High spirits, comrade. Nothing more. Do not let it distract you from the fighting at hand."

Palfrun saw Sheppard and shot him an acidic glare, then turned to one of his own men and spoke urgently into his ear. The blue-clothed officer moved to one of the teletypes and began to work it.

"What is all this?" said Teyla. "I do not understand."

But Sheppard was already putting it together, and he didn't like where it was taking him. Erony led them up to Daus's podium and the Lord Magnate gave them a jaunty salute. "Ah, our guests! Welcome, welcome! You missed the opening salvoes and a few most entertaining sorties by Palfrun's hussars, but there's still plenty of cut in the blade yet!"

Another explosion sounded and McKay gaped as the illuminated boards above their heads changed. "These are casualty tallies. You're keeping score."

Kelfer looked up from a scrap of paper. "Yes, although I must say I've not seen so poor an opening gambit since the days of old Lord Loegis. Noryn should learn to be should be more dynamic and less reactive."

"Slow and steady has its advantages," noted Muruw. "The Great Trahvis once made an engagement last for six days. He starved his competitor into surrender."

Sheppard shook his head in disbelief. "You're talking about this like it's a football game."

"Foot-ball?" asked Vekken. "That sounds like it might be painful."

Kelfer gestured with the paper. "Noryn has left his base thinly defended. A risky gambit, if Palfrun's sappers take the baron's standard."

"But then Palfrun's men must take it clear across the field to their base," the minister replied, "and there is much to challenge them on the return journey."

The scientist sniffed. "I predict the tan banner will fall first."

Hill's lip curled. "They're playing 'capture the flag' out there."

Daus waved a hand, securing a flute of wine from a passing servant. "This is an honor engagement, Lieutenant Colonel. I wanted you to witness it first-hand, considering that you had some degree of involvement in the events that led up to it. And you may also learn something of our culture along the way."

Erony explained. "The Barons Palfrun and Noryn have had a disagreement that cannot be resolved by any civil means, as we saw in the palace. Despite Lieutenant Colonel Sheppard's attempt to forestall any bloodletting, Palfrun made petition for a duel between their Dynasts."

"Where I come from, duels were usually fought by the men with the dispute," said the colonel. "You know the kind of thing, back to back, pistols at dawn? Two men enter, one man leaves?"

Muruw laughed. "You're not suggesting...? Great blades, you are! You actually suggest that the nobles should fight *each other*?" He chuckled.

"I'm not encouraging anyone to go killing anyone else. I just think that staging a mock war for the purpose of settling an argument is a little over the top."

Muruw's incredulity turned to confusion. "This is not a 'mock' engagement, Lieutenant Colonel. Where would the honor be in that?"

Another rattling fusillade of rifle-fire sounded below them and Sheppard and the others turned toward the sound. They saw a unit of bluecoats gun down a handful of tans and charge on, to the hoots and cheers of Palfrun and his group.

"Those men are dead," said Ronon, in an icy voice.

"With honor," noted the Magnate. "When the battle is at an end, they will be interred as heroes deserve."

Sheppard's blood ran cold as Teyla spoke in a brittle tone, voicing the disbelief that all the Atlantis team felt. "The soldiers below us are using live weapons."

"You are shocked?" said the Magnate, smiling outwardly but with a hard glint in his eye, daring them to react. "Halcyon is not a world for the squeamish, my friends. We embrace might and fortitude, we reject cowardice and frailty. Only through strength can we remain dominant in a galaxy that would take us as prey if we showed an instant of weakness." He sipped his wine. "We hunt the Wraith to make us strong and to keep us sharp. No other world can say that. Strength, Lieutenant Colonel, force of arms. That is the marrow in Halcyon's bones, it is the law by which we live." Daus gave a fatherly nod to Erony. "My Dynast is the strongest, our army is undefeated, and that is why my kindred have ruled as Magnates over this world for centuries."

"Might makes right, huh?" said Sheppard, matching gazes with the nobleman.

Daus clapped his hands together, as if the colonel was a student who had just solved a difficult problem. "Exactly! You understand perfectly!"

"And what if the people wish otherwise, if they do not want your rule?" asked Teyla. "What then?"

"Any Dynast can challenge another, in matters of honor or dominion," he said nonchalantly, "as we see here today. Some have dared to challenge me. As to their success..." He spread his hands and smiled again.

Ronon took a step closer to the Magnate and Sheppard saw the tension in him, the anger in the corded muscles of his neck. Vekken saw it too, and moved casually to a position where he could intercept the Satedan, if he needed to. "This is how you fight your battles?" he said in a low snarl. "This is what you call honorable? You fence in your soldiers and count them like points in a card game? You make them die for a piece of cloth?"

Muruw raised an eyebrow. "You would do well not be so high-handed, Ronon Dex. We keep our warfare well mannered and equitable. It does not spill out into the streets and fields, it does not consume our society and claim the lives of the inno-cent. Our codes of conduct keep these engagements regimented. See, here. In this battle today, the use of aerial warfare is pro-hibited, as is that of gaseous or disease weapons, and explo-sives beyond an agreed yield. Our referees ensure these rules are adhered to. To be a victor today, a faction need only hold the banners of both sides. No cities will be bombed, no villages or farmland razed to ashes. There are no wars on Halcyon as you would know them, that is true, because we control them. We ensure no heedless massacres or wholesale destruction." He nodded in agreement to his own argument. "Surely you would agree that ours is the more civilized form of warfare?"

"I've never been what you'd consider civilized," growled Dex, before turning away. "I need some air." He stalked away and out of the gallery.

"Teyla," said Sheppard. "Go after him. Make sure he doesn't break anything." The Athosian woman moved away, clearly content to be free of the company of Daus and his nobles.

"I think I have upset him," Muruw's words were arch and dismissive.

"Oh trust me, you'll know when he's upset," said McKay. "He'll leave a trail of destruction and everything."

Daus gave a sage nod. "Ah, a thought occurs to me. I think I understand the root of Ronon Dex's choler." The Magnate glanced at Sheppard. "He is a Runner, yes? Perhaps his experi-

ences as quarry in the cruel games played by the Wraith clouds
his impressions of us. I assure you, we are very different to
those creatures."

Sheppard watched the other man carefully. "I have no doubt
you believe that."

Teyla's concern became an outright, fully blown worry when she
found a third member of the airship's crew lying unconscious on
the decking. She followed the path of open hatchways and insensate
soldiers to an open bay in the belly of the ship, a few frames down
the hull from the observation gallery.

The bay was open to the air along its length, and through it she
could see the continual melee of the little war raging back and forth.
Ronon was at the far end, strapping himself into a leather webbing
rig attached to a fat drum of steel cable. He was quite furious.

"Ronon, what are you doing?"

He threw her a quick glance. "What does it look like? I'm going
to put a stop to their damn game."

"I dislike this as much as you do, but if you go down there, you
will be killed! What do you expect to accomplish?"

Dex kicked at a switch and the cable brake released. "You heard
him in there. Fighting stops when victory is declared. The victor is
the man with both flags." He drew his particle magnum and his short
sword from inside his greatcoat, and stepped to the edge. "I'll see
you in the winner's circle."

Before she could stop him, Ronon stepped out into thin air and
fell away from the airship. The cables played out, dropping him
down with a screech of cogs. Teyla saw him fall free of the rig and
land in a tuck-and-roll. He came up fighting, stunning two men with
gun blasts and knocking another down with the flat of his sword.
Then he vanished into the battle smoke, toward the pole where the
tan pennant was snapping in the wind.

In the observation gallery, cries of alarm and shouts of anger
warred with a grating alert siren.

"Someone has descended into the engagement!" snapped
Baron Noryn. "This is a gross breach of the rules!"

"It's the Runner!" called another man, peering through a tele-scope. "He's violated the field of conflict!"

All eyes turned to Sheppard, and he could have sworn there was amusement on Vekken's lips. "What is the meaning of this?" demanded Daus.

"Ah," said John.

CHAPTER FOUR

Ronon kept low, dodging between what little cover he could find on the battlefield, doing his best to avoid the combatants and taking them out from range when they left him with no choice. He halted in the shade of an overturned steam truck to catch his breath, checking the charge on his pistol.

Dex's anger enveloped him with a steady, drumming fury. His dislike of these self-styled 'nobles' had gradually ramped up from the moment they had crossed paths with them on M3Y-465, little by little their contemptuous and faintly mocking manners grating more and more on his patience. He might have been able to tolerate their foppish conduct and the way they played at being soldiers, if they hadn't brought them to see this pathetic game that masqueraded as a real war.

Honor and duty, those were ideals that Ronon understood. Once upon a time, he might have even been willing to die for them; but things were not the same now. Years of fleeing from arrogant hunters had taught him differently. The Satedan had learned the hard way that true battle brought no glory, no favor. It was nothing but blood cost after blood cost, and no amount of accolades or pieces of shiny metal pinned to a man's chest could balance the butcher's bill. That lesson had been a harsh one, harsh enough to end all life on his homeworld.

He cast a cold-eyed glance up at the airship overhead. These aristocrats, floating over the carnage in all their finery, heavy with hollow decorations and toy weapons, they understood nothing. He imagined them stripped of their privileges, without bodyguards to defend them, facing a true enemy, facing Wraith. Dex doubted if more than a handful of them would have the spirit to fight for their lives. They were nothing but spoilt, arrogant children, and he was sick of their little games.

The Runner burst from cover as a trio of tancoats marched

past him. With a blow from the curved pommel of his short sword, Ronon felled the first man and shot another at point-blank range with his pistol, the red flash of the stun bolt knocking his target down. The third tancoat was on his guard, and fired his lance-rifle. Dex twitched away as a volley of needle-shot cut through the air where he had been standing, and he threw himself at the soldier. The last man cried out as Ronon bunched a fistful of his uniform and pulled him off-balance. He took a head-butt across the nose and his eyes rolled back, insensate. By the time he hit the mud, Dex was already sprinting through the thin haze of smoke, zigzagging around tumbleweed clumps of razor wire and rusted tank traps.

Ronon hopped over trenches, ignoring shouts of alarm and sporadic flashes of gunfire. The soldiers saw him and their first reaction was uncertainty; he could read the question on their mud-stained, smoke-dirty faces. *Who is that man? Whose side is he on?* With no sigils or sashes, no uniform as they understood it, the troopers didn't know what to make of him. Their enemy today wore powder blue, and Dex's clothes of tawny leather matched no uniform they had ever seen.

His greatcoat flapped open like the wings of a raptor bird as he threw himself over a revetment and on to the foot of the hill where the tan banner was based. Ronon saw the thin gun slits of a low bunker, and emerging from a vent in the roof, a white-painted flagpole from which the Baron Noryn's battle standard hung.

"Hoi!" shouted a voice. A concealed trapdoor in the hillside flapped open, revealing a tancoat wearing a forage cap laden with officer braid. "Blade's sake, who are you? Name and unit, man, or I'll take you apart!" He had a bell-mouthed blunderbuss in his grip.

"Specialist Ronon Dex, Satedan Regulars." He gave a grim salute with his particle magnum.

The tancoat officer blinked in confusion. "Eh? I've never heard of that division. What's your Dynast, whose side are you on—"

From nowhere, a mortar shell exploded nearby and the concussion made the soldier flinch. Dex took the opportunity and struck the man with a snap shot, grabbing him and dragging his body out of the foxhole. "Mine," he told the unconscious officer. "I'm on *my* side."

Ronon dropped through the open hatch; as he guessed, the inside of the hilltop was lined with tunnels leading up to the bunker at the crown. Holstering the pistol, he fished in the deep pockets of his coat and retrieved a trio of stubby black cylinders. *What was it that Sheppard's people called them? Flash-bangs.* He smiled coldly. The directness of the name appealed to him. Dex pulled the pins on the stun grenades and threw the cylinders hard down the tunnel, into the heart of the bunker, then ducked down and pulled his coat flap over his face.

There was a crashing screech of detonation and a blast of white light. Ronon shook off the whining from his ears and moved forward quickly, through tancoats lying on the floor, rocking and clawing at their eyes.

He emerged in the pillbox where the flagpole stood and punched out the single rifleman there who tried to oppose him. Ronon's blood was up, and on some level he realized he was enjoying this. It wasn't often he had to fight without killing his foes outright, and the challenge of beating these men using non-lethal methods was novel to him. He liked the way it was testing his skills in new and interesting ways.

Dex swung his short sword in a shallow arc and severed the cords holding the tan pennant to the mast. The banner fell to earth, dropping through the hole in the bunker roof and into his open palm. He tied the cloth around his shoulder and knotted it, then scrambled out of the bunker and on to the hill. "One down," Ronon announced to the air, saluting the airship with his sword, "one to go."

Rodney looked away from the gallery's gimbal-mounted telescope and grinned incredulously. "He's taken one of the flags. On his own."

Sheppard caught a glimpse of the running figure through the haze and then he was gone again, sprinting out of sight toward the opposite end of the battle zone. He fought to keep a smile off his face. Yeah, sure he was pissed at Ronon right now for getting in the middle of this, but there was a part of him that wanted to cheer him on as well.

"This is an outrage!" thundered Baron Noryn. "A clear and undeniable violation of the codes of engagement! I demand a cessation in hostilities immediately! This cannot stand!"

Across the observation gallery, Palfrun and his men were animated and bellicose. "You know the rules, Noryn!" said the other nobleman. "An engagement can only be closed when victory conditions are met, or by appeal to the Lord Magnate's veto... And I feel no such need to ask for it."

Noryn stalked toward the other man. "Rule breaker!" He stabbed a finger at Palfrun, and the gasps the declaration brought with it made it clear that on Halcyon, the insult carried an awful lot of weight. "Did you conspire with the outworlders in this? What did you grant them in order to employ that primitive thug?"

"Hey, now, watch it with the name-calling-" began Sheppard, but his voice was lost in a chorus of recriminations.

"I have no influence over this Runner. Perhaps you ought to address his master? Or better yet, why not improve the training of your riflemen so that one single attacker cannot so easily cut thought their lines?"

"I want this match stopped!" Noryn stamped his foot in impotent rage, his cheeks turning crimson. "I demand it! I insist that the Lord Magnate halt this cheating immediately!"

"You insist?" Daus's words were mild, but his voice silenced everyone. "You insist that I obey your demands, Baron?"

Noryn's bluster disintegrated. "I... My Lord, I spoke out of turn..."

Palfrun grinned at his opponent. "Play the game with good humor, old warrior. Try to lose like a gentleman."

Up on the dais, Kelfer and Muruw chuckled at the insult, amused by the sport.

Erony's father glanced at the other baron. "Ah, Palfrun. Always so quick to declare victory, yes? Should you not wait until the outcome of the day is clear?"

Hesitation showed on the bluecoat noble's face. "But... I had assumed... The Runner, I assumed he clearly intended to ally himself to me."

"Think so?" said Sheppard. "You can't be that good a judge of character, then."

"But what else would he hope to achieve? What..." Palfrun's words dried up as understanding crossed his pinched face. He went pale and faced Daus. "My lord! Perhaps I was, ah, hasty in my words to Baron Noryn. I feel now that, with your permission, a cessation of battle would serve us best."

"Indeed?" said the Magnate. "I do not grant it." Daus ignored the scattering of surprise. "Lieutenant Colonel Sheppard's man has violated the field of conflict and therefore, I deem that it falls to him to deal with this. *Immediately.*" Daus laid a heavy, threatening gaze on Sheppard, masking nothing.

"He's kinda free-willed," said John. "I don't think I'd be able to talk him around."

"I do not expect you to," replied the Magnate. "I expect you to stop him by whatever means you wish to employ. Of course, if you decline, I will be forced to order my gunners to deploy sheetfire against the ground. It is an indiscriminate weapon, but quite effective on living targets."

"Father —" began Erony, but he silenced her with a wave of his hand.

"Fine," said Sheppard, "but I'm not guaranteeing anything."

Daus nodded. "Vekken, accompany the Lieutenant Colonel and ensure his safety as best you can. Sadly, the battle will continue around you, so do be careful."

Teyla stepped forward. "I will come with you."

"No," said the Magnate. "Three intruders on the field are quite enough."

Hill took his L85 off his shoulder, handing the assault rifle and an ammunition pack to Sheppard. "You might need this, boss."

"Thanks."

"You're not really going down there?" McKay's eyes wid-

ened. "I'm sure you haven't missed the whole bullets-explo-
sions-warfare thing."

Sheppard took the rifle and shook his head. "I'm going. And
this time, when I say I want the rest of you to keep out of trouble, I really, *really* mean it."

The cable rig dropped them at the edge of a shell crater, and
the colonel shook off the rush of the descent. "Whoa. Like bun-
gee jumping, but without the kick."

Vekken landed like a cat and gestured sharply at him. In
his other hand, Daus's adjutant carried a compact version of
the lance-rifles used by the rank-and-file soldiers, twin-barreled with a sickle-shaped magazine protruding from the top.
Sheppard fingered the safety catch on the British-made rifle.
He didn't want to shoot anyone if he could help it, but a hollow
feeling in his stomach was telling him that he probably wouldn't
have the choice. "Aim to wound, then." he said aloud.

"This way." Vekken broke into a run and John had to scramble to keep up. Smoke bombs were popping overhead, white
fronds of mist settling over the ruddy-colored mud in lines,
obscuring everything more than twenty feet away. Vekken's
black coat bobbed out there, moving and weaving. Sheppard's
pace was more cautious. This place looked like something from
the Battle of the Somme, and the last thing the colonel wanted
was to run straight into a minefield or a flooded crater. And
who knew what other kind of weird weapons these people might
have lying around?

"Damn it, Ronon. What the hell were you thinking?" But the
question was irrelevant. Sheppard knew precisely what Ronon
had been thinking. He'd known Dex long enough now to have
the measure of the man; and it irked him to admit that under
other circumstances, he too might have tried something just as
reckless to short-circuit this cruel blood sport.

The clattering rattle of lance-fire reached his ears and he
turned. Two tancoat troopers rushed forward, firing as they
moved. Both men saw Sheppard in a crouch and turned their
guns on him, bracketing him with shot.

"I'm not your enemy!" he shouted, but they ignored him. The Atlantis uniform jacket John wore wasn't the same shade of blue as the uniforms of Palfrun's men, but these two clearly thought it was near enough as made no odds. Needle rounds hissed past his head and Sheppard raised the L85. "Ah, damn it." Selecting single round fire, the colonel put one bullet apiece into the legs of both tancoats, sending them down in wailing heaps. He'd barely dealt with that when the high-pitched keening of a mortar round sounded. Sheppard glimpsed a foxhole from the corner of his eye and threw himself into it, yelling as he went. "Incoming!"

He landed hard and winced as a rain of muddy gobbets followed him into the dugout. Blinking away the shock, he glanced up—and into the barrel of another lance-rifle, hovering an inch from the tip of his nose.

At the other end of the gun was a kid in a powder blue long coat, his high hat at a cocked angle and lines of blood issuing from a cut on his cheek. His eyes were hollow and full of terror. Behind him were four more of Palfrun's troopers, clustered around the body of another of their number. The corpse didn't appear to have a head.

"Easy, son," Sheppard said, gently pushing the barrel away from his face. "I'm not your enemy." This time around, the words seemed to work and the young bluecoat let his rifle drop. "Where's your commanding officer?"

One of the other soldiers, a girl with ragged red hair, threw him a confused look. "Aren't you?"

"Our brigade marshal is gone," said the boy with the rifle. "Haven't seen him since the order came down to advance." He gestured up at the airship.

"Advance to what?" demanded Sheppard. "What's your objective?"

The boy blinked. "Kill the enemy?"

John shook his head, disgusted. "What's your name, son?"

"Bryor."

"How old are you?"

"Seventeen cycles, sir. Indentured straight from the orphanage."

"Bryor, you're brigade marshal now, understand me? I'm field-promoting you."

The girl gaped. "That's against the rules—"

"New revisions, just in," Sheppard said over her. "I'm letting everyone know." He had an edge here, however tenuous, over these conscripts; all that officer training school stuff was paying off as these kids paid attention to him, sold on the idea he was of senior rank to them. "Bryor's in command here. He's going to keep you all safe until the battle's over." John blew out a breath. "Which shouldn't be much longer, I hope."

Sheppard peered up over the lip of the dugout. The fighting had moved on for the moment. He made ready to vault up and over.

"Sir!" said Bryor, his voice cracking. "I… Don't know what to do! I need orders!"

"No, you don't." Sheppard said flatly. "You're the leader now. Your only mission from now on is to keep your unit alive, get it? You want orders? Stay down, don't attract fire. *Survive*."

John heard a voice shouting his name and the sound of hoof beats getting closer. "But we're supposed to fight for the banner," said the boy.

The colonel ran his gaze over the cluster of soldiers and saw nothing but a group of frightened children. "Not today."

"Sheppard!" It was Vekken, and he emerged from the smoke on the back of a riding animal. He spotted John and beckoned with his weapon. "I secured transport! Quickly! Climb up!"

He ran over. The animal looked something like a shaggy-coated horse, but with a head that was more lupine than equine. It hissed through a bridle at him. Sheppard noticed that the mount had blue detail on its saddle. "Where'd you rustle up this thing from?"

Vekken jerked his head. "The previous owner had a fall."

"I'll bet he did." John hauled himself up on the back of the beast. The animal was longer than a horse, and there was more than enough room for both men to ride easily. Vekken swatted the neck of the animal with a stubby riding crop and it launched away into a gallop.

Daus's man rode hard and fast; it was clear that he was an expert horseman. Sheppard hung on for dear life, clutching the rifle to him as they threaded through the battlefield. They re-entered the zone of densest fighting and the wolf-horse snarled at the gunfire, spitting out foam from its lips.

"What does your Runner hope to achieve, Sheppard?"

John noticed that now it was just the two of them, Vekken didn't feel the need to address him by his rank. "My guess is he's angling for a draw."

"And what then? Will he invade every other honor engagement and contest? Battles bigger than this one are waged in skirmish enclosures every week on Halcyon. Our people welcome them. They give our society structure and an example to follow. Your Runner's interference will alter nothing."

"Haven't you ever heard of the phrase 'Give peace a chance'? You might wanna try it sometime."

Vekken laughed. "You dress like a soldier, you carry yourself like one, but I see now that it ends there. Are all you Earthkin so shy of bloodshed?"

"Sadly, not nearly enough," replied Sheppard.

Ahead, the blue bunker was becoming visible, the soldiers defending it mired in a sea of advancing tancoats. More shells shrieked down from the air and a chain of yellow fireballs erupted around them. The animal balked and reared back, throwing the two men off and into the mud. Sheppard got to his feet and hauled Vekken up.

The adjutant glanced at the wolf-horse. A shrapnel wound on its thigh was pink with new blood, and it gave off a pitiful mew. Without hesitation, without even a flicker of concern, Vekken shot the animal dead.

"What the hell did you do that for?" Sheppard exploded.

"It was useless to anyone in that state. Better to finish it quickly." He moved away, toward the sound of gunfire. "This way."

Sheppard's face hardened. On the wind, he heard the familiar crackling snap of Ronon's pistol.

Dex's path wasn't hard to find. Injured bluecoats and tancoats alike were scattered about like fallen trees. Vekken grinned. "It seems your scientist McKay was correct about the Runner. He has indeed left a trail of destruction for us to follow." Shells and guns crashed across the landscape in a constant rumbling chorus. The adjutant bent, pausing for a moment to study the face of a comatose bluecoat rifleman. "Good economy of use in his blows. He fights well for a man who dresses like a low-born."

Sheppard snorted. "Could you be any more arrogant? I mean, really, I'd like to know. Every time I think you can't be more snobbish and patronizing, I'm proven wrong. I'm just wondering if there's some kind of upper limit."

"There is no shame in acknowledging one's own superiority, Lieutenant Colonel. A man who knows his place in the world is content."

John's lip curled. "I bet you have a whole book of those little homilies, don't you?"

They entered the tunnel network at the foot of the hill; shots came from up above them, and Sheppard heard Ronon's voice in a wordless snarl of pain and anger.

Vekken continued, unconcerned. "If you find Halcyon unpalatable, then I am sure you could take your leave to the Great Circlet and go..." He smiled to himself. "Oh, but that's right, I am remiss. You have no home to go to, do you? After you surrendered the City of the Precursors to the Wraith."

"We didn't surrender it," Sheppard retorted it. "We..." He swallowed, catching himself. "They saw it destroyed and then they left."

The adjutant gave him a quick look. "The Wraith can be easily fooled, if one knows how to do it." He looked away. "But I suspect you stay here for another reason. The Magnate spoke to me of Dr. McKay's interest in the dolmen. I wonder, you think us so objectionable, and yet you would tolerate us just to take a look at an old, crumbling stone obelisk? The Lady Erony has always suggested that our scientists should give it closer scrutiny. Perhaps she is correct."

John realized he was on unsteady ground here, and he trusted this man about as far as he could throw him. "McKay is interested in the Ancients." It was the truth, in a manner of speaking—just not the whole truth. "It's scientific curiosity, which

I guess might be hard for you to get a handle on, seeing as you people seem to think you know everything already."

Vekken laughed again. "You amuse me, Lieutenant Colonel. For that alone, I think you should not yet leave Halcyon."

Sheppard bit his lip and refused the urge to retort to the man's comments; instead, he shifted carefully into the flag bunker, his nose wrinkling at the smell of burnt metal and ozone.

Ronon Dex was sitting atop an ammunition crate with his pistol laid across his lap. The snub barrel of the gun was cherry-red with heat from its discharges. The Satedan had the powder blue pennant of Baron Palfrun's Dynast in his hand and he was tearing a strip from it. He gave Sheppard a weary nod, and returned to shredding the flag into a makeshift bandage. Dex had a line of puncture wounds on his upper left arm where needle rounds had struck him. His coat was dotted with dark smears of blood and mud.

He lifted his other arm to show the tan pennant hanging there. "Game over. Tell the Magnate, I have both flags. I claim victory."

"Most impressive," Vekken allowed, "even though Palfrun and Noryn's conscripts lack the skills of the higher Dynasts, for one man to take them all on... You have exemplary skills." Then he sighed. "However, as I tried to explain to the Lieutenant Colonel, your ignorance of our rules has led you to a sadly mistaken conclusion. Yes, the codes of engagement do state that he who holds both pennants is the victor, but the letter of the law requires that person to be a duly sanctioned soldier in the service to a noble Dynast, or an operative of the Magnate's will. And you, Ronon Dex, are neither of those. The battle continues."

Ronon came to his feet, snarling, the gun in his grip. "I *won*!" he spat. "Call it off!"

"I do not have that authority," Vekken said coolly. "All you have done, Runner, is ensure that there will be *more* bloodshed, not less."

The mood of belligerent amusement that had filled the observation gallery was gone now, replaced by cold fury and righteous consternation from the two opposing cliques of noblemen. Minister Muruw and the scientist Kelfer were watching and talking quietly; it seemed like they were setting up a private wager on the outcome of the day's events. Rodney saw the tension in the stances of Private Hill and Teyla, the two of them drawing closer around him, ready to fight if things turned the wrong way. McKay's fingers twitched nervously, and he gripped a mounted telescope to give them something to do; something other than stray to the holstered pistol on his belt.

Violence was ready to ignite here at the drop of an ornate hat. "One wrong word and these guys will be at each other's throats," he whispered. "It's like being in the stands at a hockey game."

"More like Rangers versus Celtic," said Hill. "Stick close if it kicks off."

Linnian accepted a teleprint from one of the servants and studied it gravely. "Observers in the north quadrant report that the Runner appears to have secured the second pennant." He blinked, as if he wasn't sure of what he'd just said aloud.

The Magnate gave a small smile but said nothing. The turn of events appeared to be entertaining him.

A chorus of denials and angry retorts came from Noryn's group, although the baron himself said nothing, kneading the grip of his sword.

Palfrun stepped forward, and drew a cluster of metal rods from inside his coat. "My Lord Magnate, I petition you."

"No!" cried Noryn, eyes wide with shock, "Do not say it!"

Palfrun ignored his adversary. "This tender represents a group of my holdings. I bid them in request to engage your favor."

Linnian took the rods and counted through them; Rodney suddenly understood that these were the Halcyon equivalent of coins or paper money, perhaps even deeds or tokens of ownership. Erony's adjutant nodded at the Magnate and the rods vanished into his tunic.

Noryn was shaking his head. "This... This is not fair!"

"You may make a counter-offer, if you wish," said Linnian.

"Speak now, Baron, if that is your intention."

"You know I cannot!" Noryn thundered. "The poor harvest after the storms in Gethil Province, the loss of my hunt splinters in the last sojourn... I have no resources to spare!"

"Then you should not have sought to engage me!" replied Palfrun. "I am willing to take this to the certain conclusion... Unless you will concede?"

"To you? Never!" Noryn went for his sword, but a nod from Linnian made sure that the Baron's own cohorts stayed his hand. The man's face fell. "Please, I beg of you..."

"Do not be so weak," Palfrun was disgusted. "Accept the inevitable."

"What are they on about?" said Hill quietly. "I can't follow this posh twaddle."

"I believe he is paying Daus to intervene in the battle." Teyla replied.

"Bribing the referee? That's a bit rough," said the soldier.

Baron Palfrun bowed to Daus. "I humbly ask that I might call upon my Hounds to deliver the final blow in this honor engagement."

The Magnate considered the request. "The codes do not allow Hounds in a skirmish of this size, Palfrun; but then, the play of today's events has made this anything but a common battle. I will endorse this petition. You may deploy your Hounds."

Palfrun bowed again and gestured to one of his men, who ran off to give the order. Rodney saw that Baron Noryn had gone pale, shrinking against the glass windows. The handful of other nobles who didn't wear the same colors as his men detached themselves from his group and drifted away. Even though McKay didn't understand the full dynamics of the situation, the meaning was clear; Noryn was finished.

Moments after Palfrun's adjutant had relayed his master's command, Rodney saw the shape of a large gyro-flyer rattle over the tree line and drop into the combat zone. He scrutinized it through the telescope. Powder blue insignia lined the sides of the aircraft. The flyer dropped into the middle of the fighting and ramps fell open from it. Figures emerged; they wore glittering armor plates of silver metal, with full helmets designed after the shape of a wolf's head. Light blue scarves hung from their necks. Most of them were unarmed, but those that were only carried melee weapons; curved, cutlass-style swords or battle axes with diamond-shaped heads. They waded into the fight like berserkers, attacking anything that moved with feral intensity. McKay looked away, sickened.

Hill kept watching. "That must be their heavy mob."

"We have to get Sheppard and Ronon out of there," began Rodney, turning to Teyla. "We —" McKay's words died in his throat as he saw the look on the Athosian woman's face. Her eyes were distant, locked on some horror that only she could see. "Teyla?"

"Oh no," she whispered.

Dex's attack on the second bunker had caused a momentary lull in the battle, as troopers on both sides hesitated while news of the Runner's interference spread across the lines. Sheppard and the others emerged from a trapdoor on the hillside to an odd quiet broken only by the sporadic crack of shot and the lazy murmur of the engines on Daus's airship. Ronon was the first to see the gyro-flyer deploying the new arrivals.

"What's this?" he demanded, still holding both pennants in his fist.

Vekken's entire posture shifted the moment he saw what Dex was pointing at. "It would seem that the Magnate wishes to bring this engagement to a swift conclusion. He's given Palfrun leave to release the Hounds."

"Dogs?" said Sheppard. "What, are we supposed to make like foxes now?"

Sunlight glinted off metal plate armor. "I saw them when we arrived at the palace," said Ronon, "a squad of armored warriors."

Vekken shook his head. "No, those were Hounds from the Lord Magnate's personal kennel. The Fourth Dynast wields the largest pack on Halcyon. Those who join us now are from Palfrun's paltry stock. I imagine that may be all he has."

Sheppard squinted through his field binoculars. "They're wearing Palfrun's colors, and—" The colonel gasped as he saw one of the Hounds kill two tancoats in as many seconds with brutal attacks. The others were fighting with wild abandon, shredding flesh with iron claws fixed to their chain mail. "They're slaughtering those kids out there!" He turned on Ronon. "Give him the flags. Vekken, take them! You win, just tell Daus to call them off!"

The adjutant gave Sheppard a pitying look. "It does not matter, Lieutenant Colonel. The Hounds are wild animals. They are simply set loose with one order in mind, and they kill and kill until it is achieved, or until they are beaten back."

"You're down here, too," snapped Ronon. "Doesn't your lord and master care if they kill you?"

Vekken smiled. "Lord Daus clearly has great faith in my will to survive."

Dex turned to Sheppard. "Looks like that leaves us with only one option, then." He drew his gun and his sword.

"Ah hell," grated John, checking the ammo on Hill's rifle. "This mission is getting worse by the second."

"Think of it this way," said Vekken, hoisting his twin-barreled weapon, "if nothing else, today you have gained a rare insight into the Halcyon personality."

Sheppard's radio crackled. "*Colonel!*" cried McKay. "*They're sending in reinforcements!*"

"Thanks for the update, Rodney," John replied dryly, "but we're a little busy right now. We'll talk later, if we don't die horribly first."

The Hounds were coming toward the hill in a silver wave, laying down everyone who stood against them. Sheppard started firing, moving forward with the L85 at his shoulder, advancing down to meet the attackers.

Ronon took a second to draw a bead on one of the armored warriors as it loped up the shallow hill toward him. Truth be told, there was a part of the Satedan soldier that had wondered about the figures in silver plate when he'd first laid eyes on them, a part that measured himself against them and wondered what they might be like in a fight. So far, he hadn't been very

impressed with the quality of Halcyon's fighters; the bluecoats
and tancoats were a poor match for a seasoned veteran like him,
badly trained recruits who seemed to fight more with numbers
and scattershot fire than they did with anything like skill. But
these ones, these Hounds, they were something different. Just
from the way they moved, he could see they were dangerous.
The name was a good one, because these warriors sprinted
across the ground like attack dogs let off a leash; and they didn't
kill with the cold detachment of a career soldier. The Hounds
were savage, and they liked shedding blood.

The lead Hound bobbed and he fired at it. The energy bolt
clipped the warrior and he stumbled, but kept coming. Dex grimaced, for a second wondering if he had neglected to switch
the particle magnum's beam setting from low-level stun intensity to the higher killing force. The second shot hit home and a
red glow flashed over the metal chest plate as the Hound went
down, a final snarl echoing from inside its helmet.

Sheppard was having similar difficulty, the ballistic projec-
tile weapon in his hands barking as he fired bullet after bullet
into the advancing enemy. "Next time, I'll bring armor-pierc-
ing," he quipped.

Vekken worked the muzzle of his weapon and twisted the
choke on the gun to narrow the cone of fire. Steam clouds spat
as the rifle ejected a swarm of steel needles and Ronon saw one
of the Hounds blown back off its feet to tumble back down the
hill.

The three of them kept up the firefight, but the Hounds were too
fast. They came into hand-to-hand range and threw themselves at
the three men, clawed hands out. Ronon had his sword at arms and
beat back a warrior who went for his throat with a vicious downward slash. Armor plate distorted and the blade tore a rent in the
chain mail beneath. Dex had a momentary impression of dark, oily
blood, but then he was moving on to his next challenger, dispatching it with a point-blank pistol blast. On they came, storms of claws
and spitting fury, mad with bloodlust. He could taste a harsh metallic scent in the air from the aggressors, and it flashed a warning in
his memory; but he was too deep into the fight to dwell on it, mov-

ing from second to second, trading sword blows for kicks, punches for claw strikes. It was all instinct now, all down to one simple equation. *Fight or Die.*

He heard Sheppard snarl as a Hound came at him; a ripping discharge of bullets from the colonel's rifle slammed into the torso of the warrior and it spun away, trailing blood. For his part, Vekken had reversed his grip on his gun and was fighting off a pair of growling Hounds with the spiked butt of the stubby weapon.

Claws raked his back and Ronon roared in pain, turning away from the blow and swinging the short sword. The Hound that struck him dodged backward, unwittingly falling into Sheppard's field of fire. The colonel saw Dex's situation and took the sliver-armored attacker down with a burst of shots.

Ronon returned the favor as another Hound reared up behind Sheppard, ready to tear his head from his neck. Dex threw his sword and the blade buried itself in the warrior's stomach. The Hound stumbled to the ground and lay still.

"Runner!" shouted Vekken. "Clear my way!" He barely had time to duck as the adjutant fired both barrels at once, blasting solid slug rounds as thick as a hammer's head into the enemy.

The ex-soldier knew that only minutes had passed, but in the fury of the fight it had seem far, far longer. The Hounds lay ruined across the hillside around them, their pristine armor and powder blue scarves dirty with thick, black blood. A couple were still alive, but not for much longer.

Vekken, bleeding, crossed to one of the still-twitching corpses and shot it in the head. He spat out a stream of pink spittle and wiped his mouth. For a brief moment, the arch, aristocratic mask he wore slipped and Ronon saw him for what he really was; a cold-eyed killer.

Sheppard was breathing hard. His jacket had claw marks across the arm and he bore a shallow cut on his forehead. "That all you got?" he shouted defiantly to the air. "I'm barely breaking a sweat here!" He met Ronon's gaze and Dex knew that the opposite was true. The brief, vicious confrontation had staggered all three of them in its intensity, and it wasn't something the Satedan wanted to go through again any time soon.

Ronon stepped to the corpse of the Hound he had dispatched with his short sword and recovered his weapon with a sickly sucking pop. The blood on the blade glittered darkly, and he smelt the rough metallic scent again. Despite the heat he felt from the exertion of fighting, Dex went cold. "Sheppard," he said in a quiet voice. "You had better take a look at this."

The colonel was beside him, rifle stowed, bending at the knees. Sheppard leaned over the body of the dead Hound and ran his hands over the enclosed steel helmet. There were latches at the neck ring, and they came open easily even though the metal was wet with fluids. The halves of the wolf-head helm fell away on to the mud underfoot, and Ronon felt his gut twist in a reflexive churn of hatred and disgust.

The head beneath the helmet was all too recognizable. Where he would have expected to see thin tresses of white hair there was a forehead shorn down to bare gray fuzz, but everything else was familiar. Ashen, pallid skin lay slack and waxy in death, a tracery of blue-green capillaries visible around a heavy brow and two scar-like pits on the cheekbones. A mouth flecked with dots of foam was gaping, revealing lines of jutting, serrated teeth. And the eyes; black, doll-like eyes stared up at them, still hateful and feral in lifelessness.

Vekken chuckled. "Was I not correct, gentlemen, when I told you in the palace that you would learn the fate of our prisoners soon enough?"

Ronon saw hard anger flare in Sheppard's eyes. "These Hounds of yours... They're all *Wraiths*!" He spat the last word like a curse. "Are you people insane?"

"Far from it," Vekken seemed unconcerned by the colonel's anger. "We have taken our greatest enemy and made them our slaves."

Teyla tried to push the word from her mouth, but she couldn't. The sheer folly of the thought stopped her dead — *that someone dared to think they could tame the Wraith like a man might domesticate a canine?* It was inviting chaos and destruction!

Daus tipped a wineglass to her in a coy salute. "Ah, the girl has it, at last. I see the understanding in her eyes." He threw a languid look at his daughter, and Erony nodded awkwardly.

McKay had watched the unfolding battle on the hillside through the telescope, hissing in sympathetic pain as Sheppard and Ronon fought off the Hounds, and now he was pacing, flapping his hands in distress. "Let me see if I have this right," he said, his voice high and strident. "Those iron-clad psychos out there are… are…" He blinked. "Good grief, I can barely wrap my head around it… Those things are Wraiths?"

Kelfer tittered. "Bravo, Dr. McKay. Your insight does you credit."

"Don't mock me, you lab hack," Rodney snapped back, angry and afraid all at once, "at least I'm smart enough to know that letting Wraith run wild on your homeworld is a recipe for annihilation!"

"They do not run wild," said Erony, trying to calm the tense atmosphere, "we have tamed them. They are completely under our control."

"Tame?" McKay spluttered. "I'm sorry, but are we talking about the same beings here? Pale faces, teeth and claws, sucking the life out of you through their hands, living off human misery? And you expect us to believe you've taught them to roll over, play dead, and do back-flips?"

Daus shifted in his seat. "Calm yourself, Dr. McKay. You're disturbing the other guests. My dear Erony is quite correct. The Hounds that you see down there, in my palace, or elsewhere… Teyla Emmagan was so eager to know what befell the Wraith taken on the ice moon, and now she does. This is the fate of the Wraith captured alive by our hunt splinters, on dozens of worlds beyond the Great Circlet. We bring them back to Halcyon and teach them discipline, we break them of their free will."

"How can you control them?" asked Teyla.

Minister Muruw touched a finger to his neck. "The Hounds wear a torc about their throat, a choke-collar. It can be adjusted by a trainer to starve them of air and cause them pain. We prevent them from feeding, and instill a service-reward regimen. They obey, and they live. They disobey, and they die. They soon learn to submit."

"And you use them like, what, shock troops?" said Rodney.

"That's so twisted its almost clever. No one would ever want to fight hungry, mad Wraith, would they?"

The next question formed in Teyla's mind, and she was almost too afraid to ask it, for fear of what the answer might be. "What do they feed upon?"

"Enemy soldiers on the battlefield, prisoners of war or criminals. Sometimes each other, if they are desperate enough." Kelfer sniffed. "Admittedly, their ongoing well-being is not of great concern to us. They are considered as a military resource, and those that die are regularly replaced by captures from our hunt sorties."

McKay advanced on Daus, but Linnian blocked his path. "Listen to me, you can't treat these things like pet Dobermans, pretending they're house-trained! They are intelligent, ruthless beings! They were smart enough to wipe out the Ancients and you can bet they are smarter than you!"

The Magnate's eyes narrowed. "We have owned Hounds for hundreds of years, Dr. McKay. In all that time, we have remained their masters. Believe me, you have nothing to fear." He smiled again and stifled a mock yawn. "But now, I grow weary and I feel this day's war has become a poor amusement for all. I rule that this match is null. The honor debt of both parties is satisfied, and the battle is at an end." Mingled gasps of disbelief and relief rose in the gallery.

"All that for no result?" said Hill quietly. "Bloody hell."

Daus continued speaking. "Kelfer, we must see to our guest's request to view the dolmen in the coming days, yes? You will liaise with my daughter to see this comes to pass." The Magnate rose, and the assembled nobles bowed. Daus left the room, never seeing that the Atlantis team stayed standing, fighting down the churn of emotions that each of them felt.

The return journey to the capital city took place in grim silence. Sheppard made a curt throat-cutting gesture to the rest of the team as they boarded the gyro-flyer to take them back. Despite a few attempts to start small-talk conversations with them, Erony's adjutant Linnian got nothing but monosyllabic answers. It was only when they were back in the guest quarters that they spoke freely—and even then, only after the colonel had ordered them to check every shady corner for spy holes or possible listening devices.

The Atlantis team sat in a tight circle, heads bowed and voices low. Sheppard briefed Mason and the others in blunt, quick terms, outlining what had taken place out at the war zone. Now and then, Teyla would add a point. Mason said nothing, but once or twice he sucked air in through his teeth. It was the most animated Sheppard had ever seen the dour SAS soldier.

"These toffs are off their heads if they think they can keep the bozos on a chain," said Corporal Clarke. "I mean, you've seen that bunch of chinless wonders. They'll get eaten alive when the Wraith turn up looking for their mates."

"The question is," said Mason, "why hasn't that happened already? His lordship said they they've been at this for what, hundreds of years?"

"True, but you have to remember that the majority of the Wraith have been dormant," noted McKay, flicking a look at Sheppard, "although that's changed recently thanks to *certain people*."

"Are you ever gonna let me forget about that?" said the colonel tersely. "I don't keep reminding you about that planet you blew up." He puffed out a breath. "Mason's right, though. You have to wonder why the Wraith haven't culled this place into the dirt, and I'm pretty damn sure it's not because the Halcyons are the great warriors they brag they are."

"Location," said Rodney. "Halcyon is a long way off the galactic axis. I'm willing to bet that only reason the Wraith aren't here is because they haven't got around to it yet. There are plenty of rich, cull-able planets much closer to the main concentrations of Wraith activity in the Pegasus Galaxy. But it's only a matter of time. Could be weeks, years, decades... But sooner or later, they'll pop in for a snack."

"So what do we do in the meantime?" said Ronon. "Daus and his nobles are treating us like something to amuse themselves with. I don't think we're going to get anything out of them Atlantis can use."

Mason spoke again. "They may have a rod up their backsides and be in love with the sound of their own voices, but let's not forget, if this city is anything to go by, then Halcyon must have a huge standing army. If we did have a treaty with 'em, they could end up as a strong ally..."

Teyla nodded. "That is true, but could we ever find common ground with them? We share the fight against the Wraith, yes, but their morality is callous and ruthless. I find it difficult to believe that Dr. Weir would be willing to make a pact with someone like Daus."

"There's no getting around it, Staff," added Hill, "the big man, he's a dictator. I joined up to put blokes like him out of a job, not to make friends with them."

Bishop chimed in. "Isn't there anyone else on this planet we could talk to? Get a different point of view?"

"Nice idea, if Daus would let us," said Rodney. "I get the impression he's a bit of a control freak, don't you?"

"Lord Daus rules Halcyon through superior military might," Teyla noted. "Lady Erony's adjutant Linnian took great pains to emphasize this point to me. His clan, the Fourth Dynast, has the largest number of Hounds of all the noble houses on Halcyon. This is how his family have stayed in power for so long."

Ronon snorted derisively. "No wonder he didn't like hearing what McKay wanted to tell him."

Sheppard glanced at his watch, studying the display that showed what the Stargate teams had taken to calling AMT — Atlantis Mean Time. "Look, we're due to touch base with Atlantis soon for our regular sit-rep. Before I talk to Weir, I want to have a handle on this place, from all sides."

"What are you proposing?" asked Teyla.

John got up and walked toward the balcony. He pointed at the streets and buildings beyond the walls of the High Palace. "There's a whole city out there that we haven't seen yet. Everyone we've talked to so far has been rich folks, or the people in their pockets. I think we should hear what the man on the street has to say about life on Halcyon, don't you?"

"Daus will never let you out unescorted," said McKay. "I had three riflemen trailing me the whole time I was with Erony and Kelfer, and we never even left the palace."

"I wasn't thinking about asking permission." Sheppard gave Ronon a crooked smile. "You up for walk?"

Hill frowned. "Boss, you won't get ten feet dressed in our gear. You're gonna need some sort of cover."

As the soldier spoke, a knock sounded at the door and two brown-hooded servants entered, delivering a trolley of food and drink for the evening meal. Ronon gave the servants a measuring stare and smiled. "I don't think that will be a problem."

CHAPTER FIVE

The setting sun threw a golden glow through the hexagonal windows of the Sword Gallery. The light glittered off the aged steel of a hundred ceremonial blades where they hung in glass cabinets, suspended on spun wires so thin that from a distance the weapons appeared to be floating in the air.

The Magnate glanced up at the sound of Erony's footsteps on the marble flooring and he gave her the slightest of frowns. Her father was taking a schooner of blackbrandy and a pipe while Vekken and one of the senior generals talked him through the day's conflict results. The Magnate liked to have his briefings held here, in the museum quiet of the colonnade. Erony imagined her father thought it a subtle way of reinforcing his own reputation with a blade; but in all honesty, he hadn't used a weapon in anger for years. She recalled the last time with exact clarity; Lord Daus had run through an assassin disguised as a wine waiter. Vekken's agents later determined the interloper was some sort of dissident from the farmlands. She didn't remember the details of the dead man, just the slam of the falling body echoing through the Chamber of Audiences. Vekken stepped back to allow her to approach her parent. Yes, with Vekken never beyond arm's reach, she doubted the Magnate would ever need to touch the hilt of his sword again. The Wraithkin adjutant was as swift as he was disquieting.

Despite herself, Erony's gaze flicked to the largest of the cabinets, just behind her father, just for an instant. Inside there was a curved scimitar broken around two thirds of the way down the length of the blade. She knew the runes and tracery along it like she knew the lines across her own palm. Her mother had perished with that sword in her hand, cut down in some nameless forest on some nameless planet. The body that had returned was of an elderly, frail lady, not the vibrant and imposing woman

that had left her daughter waving goodbye at the lip of the Circlet. In darker moments, Erony wondered what manner of death
her mother had delivered to the Wraith that took her life force.
She hoped it had been a painful one.

"Daughter," Daus inclined his head.

"Father," she returned. "A moment, if you please?"

The Magnate nodded, the implied order sending Vekken and
the general away, off toward the windows and out of earshot.
"What is it, child? Speak to me."

"Today's display..." Erony began haltingly, "the outcome
raises conflicts in my thoughts."

"You doubt my wisdom in this matter?" Her father's voice
held a faint note of reproach.

"I question the presence of the Atlanteans there. Was it nec-
essary? It brought only discontent, among our own cadres as
well as in theirs. The incident with the Runner... It might have
been avoided."

Daus drew on the pipe. "You are your mother's daughter,
Erony. You have so little artifice." He chuckled. "It pleases and
saddens me in equal measure to see her reflected in you."

Her lips thinned at the attempt to deflect her. "Father," she
said again, "I would know your thoughts if I am to understand
the reasoning behind today's events."

He placed the pipe on a stand and sipped the blackbrandy.
"To rule, one must know the color of a man's heart, one must
understand the truth behind the pretty words that would-be
allies bring to our table. These outworlders take the measure of
us and we must do the same. I brought Sheppard and his party to
the war to watch their reactions. How they view us shades how
we will deal with them."

"What did you learn?"

Another dry chuckle. "That the gallant Lieutenant Colonel
is, under all his weapons and wargear, just a commoner at heart.
And too, that he and his splinter think us too harsh and ruthless."

"What value is there in that? Surely we should court them,
make Sheppard think well of us."

Daus waved her into silence. "No. We are Halcyons, we do not hide what we are. Let them understand the truth of our society. There is no point in obfuscation."

Erony was silent for a moment. When she spoke again, it was difficult to keep the taint of accusation from her words. "Is that why you sanctioned Palfrun's petition for the Hounds?"

"He made the request in good order. What would you have had me do?"

"Deny it," she retorted. "In such a small skirmish, over so trivial a matter as an argument over, what was it? A gambling debt, or some such? In other conflicts, on other days you would have dismissed Palfrun's petition out of hand. Why not today?" She shook her head. "It was unwarranted."

"So you challenge my interpretation of the codes of conduct, is that it? You wonder if allowing the use of the Hounds was a fair ruling?" He shifted and sipped more drink from the schooner. "I am Lord Magnate, my dear. The codes are mine to direct as I see fit. I make the rules, Erony. Never forget that."

She colored. "I have not. But I must ask you why. Please explain it to me."

"If any other made that demand of me, I would have them dispossessed on the spot and flogged in the square." Daus put down the glass. "But to you, I will give an answer. It is simply this; today it was my desire to test the mettle of these Atlanteans, to cut to the core of them. Are they worthy of Halcyon's friendship? Have they the same steel in their bones as we do?" He looked away. "I believe I found them wanting."

"If that is so, then why are they still here?"

The Magnate gave his daughter a heavy-lidded glare. "Because they may be of some use to us. Kelfer has searched his records for any scraps of intelligence on these men from Atlantis. He has found reports to corroborate their claims about the Precursor City, of conflicts with the Genii and their many battles against the Wraith. It is possible they have knowledge that can be of use to the Fourth Dynast."

"Knowledge," Erony repeated bleakly. "You refer to..."

"Our 'problem'," said Daus. "Sheppard's people may be able

to assist us."

She frowned. "Why not simply ask them, father? Sheppard spoke of making formal treaty between us, would not this be a firm step toward such a partnership?"

"Halcyon has no partners, my dear, only equals or lessers, and these Atlanteans do not appear to be the former. I will not reveal our dilemma openly! That would be tantamount to bearing an open throat to a wildcat. No." He shook his head. "For now we watch and appraise them. I expect you to be most prudent in this." The Magnate took her hand and held it. "Our Dynast keeps Halcyon stable, Erony, it always has. We must maintain our dominion for the good of our world, our people. You know that to be true."

"I do," she replied.

Her father smiled. "Good. Your mother would be so proud to see you now, strong and regal, doing what is right for our planet. It fills me with joy to know you stand at my side in this."

"I do," Erony repeated the words, her eyes focused on the broken sword.

"Can we discard these cloaks yet?" said Ronon. "This cloth irritates me."

Sheppard resisted the urge to scratch his neck where the rough-hewn robes rubbed at his skin. "Just drop the hood. We can't chance being seen by one of the nobles or their men. Not yet, anyhow."

Ronon looked around. "I don't think we're going to run into any high class types down here, do you?"

The colonel followed Dex's gaze. He had a point, Sheppard had to admit. The narrow streets of the lower city were grim and more than a little stinky. It was a far cry from the perfumed halls and elaborate décor of the High Palace. John glanced up over his shoulder and saw the tall towers and minarets of the Magnate's complex rising over the roof slates of the tumble-down apartment blocks and factory shacks of the metropolis. The palace looked even larger from down here, and he didn't doubt that was the way the nobles wanted it, casting a subtle oppression on the common folk just through the size and shape of the massive building.

Sheppard had expected it to be a lot harder to get down to the lower levels than it actually was; in fact, there were several poorly-guarded funicular railways leading into the wide city sprawl, and it had been relatively easy for Dex and the colonel to sneak aboard a carriage full of soiled laundry on its way downward. Ronon noted that the defenses on the outer walls of the palace were more geared toward keeping people from getting in, than they were for keeping people getting out. The return trip would be a tougher prospect, but for now Sheppard wasn't thinking about that. He pulled the brown robes closer as a gust of cold wind fluttered past them. The two servants they'd encouraged to lend them the garments were currently guests of Mason and his men, and would remain so until this little covert operation was dealt with. John patted the Beretta pistol concealed in his hip holster in an unconscious gesture of self-protection. To Ronon's displeasure, he had insisted they go lightly armed, and Sheppard had made doubly sure that both of them were carrying the paper dockets Erony had provided on the monorail, just in case things went south and they had to reveal themselves to someone in authority. He hoped it wouldn't come to that, though.

They kept walking, leaving the district where they had disembarked behind, moving on the edges of crowds, keeping to the shadows. Sputtering gas lamps with oily flames were popping on all along the streets, and now and then raucous hooters sounded as heavy steam trucks growled past over the cobbled road.

The lower city was busy with people moving back and forth, and it had the cold and impersonal edge that John remembered from some urban centers back on Earth. It was similar enough to make him uncomfortable, different enough to make him realize how far from home he was. The city was a mixture of shantytown barrios, red stone buildings and archaic industrial constructions that were better suited as the backdrop to a lurid, turn-of-the-century Jack the Ripper movie than a modern metropolis.

Ronon looked up as a wide blimp droned overhead, low enough that they could see the shapes of men moving around inside the control gondola. "Bigger than Daus's warship," noted the Satedan, "slower too. Cargo carrier, maybe?"

"Could be." John's gaze shifted as they passed an alleyway. He caught sight of a huddled group of figures, sheltering in doorways or under old, torn awnings. They were dirty and hollow-faced, eyes blank. He caught the scent of sickness from them.

Another truck rolled past in the direction of the funicular railway station, laden with tones of oval, greenish fruits. Sheppard had seen the same things on the dinner plates of noblemen in the palace. "Food for the Dynast," Dex opined. "Daus likes to live big."

Sheppard jerked a thumb at the vagrants in the alley. "They don't live so big down here."

Ronon nodded. "Ghettos are ghettos, no matter where you go."

"Yeah." The two men kept in the flow of people, and ahead of them the crowds grew thicker as the radial streets fed out into a wide-open plaza, walled on all sides by more sheer-faced tenements. Many of the buildings were covered with scaffolds or giant billboards dominated by artwork of Halcyon soldiers or portraits of a smiling Lord Daus. Sheppard's lip curled at one particular image, which showed the Magnate rendered in heroic proportions, dispatching a horde of demonic Wraith. He didn't need McKay to read the accompanying banners for him; he knew propaganda when he saw it.

"Look there." Dex tapped him on the shoulder and pointed. Across the plaza, past the thronging crowds, one billboard-sized panel shifted and stuttered as black-and-white images rolled over it. Immediately, John realized they were looking at a massive film screen being fed from a concealed projector. Whoops and cheers went up across the people in a wave of noise as crackly organ music played from speaker horns arranged on towers dotted across the square. A broad regimental crest appeared on the screen and martial music blared. The image changed to scenes of battle, men with steam-rifles rushing over trenches, rolling tanks, biplanes and blimps.

"It's a newsreel," said Sheppard. "Hey, maybe we'll get a cartoon as well."

"*Halcyon on the March!*" A cultured voice brayed from the speakers. "*In battle against the Wraith, our brave soldiers lead the fight!*" More cheers greeted footage of Fourth Dynast troopers milling around a downed Dart on an arid sand dune, and then a slow pan over a dozen dead Wraiths piled like cordwood. "*Halcyon's supremacy remains unassailed! Forward to victory, says the Lord Magnate, and forward to glory!*"

Sheppard watched as footage unfurled of Daus, heavy with his regalia, advancing down the steps of the High Palace with Vekken and his other adjutants behind. The camera lingered for a second on Erony, who forced a smile for the lens. A few young men standing close by made lecherous catcalls and whistled.

"She's popular," noted Ronon.

Daus's voice boomed from the speakers, a speech made up of platitudes and belligerent rhetoric; but Sheppard wasn't paying attention. He was watching a gangly youth with a red headband shouting to be heard over the sounds of the speakers. The agitator was thrusting pamphlets into the hands of anyone who looked his way. The colonel caught the odd word here and there, something about "Magnate", "unfair", "traitor". When Daus's face filled the screen again, the youth booed and spat. As Sheppard looked, he saw a few other figures with the headbands dotted amongst the crowd, reds moving in the tide of gray.

John thought about Dex's comment. "Guess we can't say the same for her dad, though."

The tone of the newsreel changed; the propagandist opening segued to something that reminded Sheppard of Sunday night NFL score round-ups on ESPN. The narrator was calling out kill tallies and battle reports. Blocky strings of text marched up across the bottom of the screen in a teletype.

A bearded, middle-aged man in a leather jerkin next to John patted his pockets frantically and cursed. He turned to Sheppard and thrust the bag in his hand at him. "Here, be a gentleman and hold on to this for me a trice, would you? I can't find me slip!"

"Uh, okay." John took the bag. It was full of ugly-looking vegetables, dark red like sweet potatoes. They smelled a little off and his nose wrinkled.

The man produced a piece of paper from a pocket and held it up, comparing the numbers on it to those on the screen. Sheppard saw other people doing the same. The man's face twisted in annoyance. "Ah, for wound's sake!" He tore the slip into confetti and brushed it from his hands. "Never the score, hey? Never the blade-forsaken score for old Rifko!"

The colonel had seen enough horse races to recognize the face of a losing bettor when he saw one. "Bad luck?"

"Bad? *Bad*? Ah, laddie, it's been a dozen cycles since I've had a win, if it's a day. I'm in for a change of fate, I know it, but when it will strike me, that's unknown." He blew out a breath and sighed. "Ah well. There's always a war tomorrow."

"Yeah..." Sheppard noted. "So you bet on the outcome of the skirmishes, then?" He handed back the bag.

The man gave him an odd look. "Well, don't everyone?" He studied Sheppard and Dex. "Ah, but you're from the country, are you? I seen the way you looked about, like your necks are on a swivel. Don't get the tickers out there in the fields, right?" He gestured at the film screen.

"That's right," nodded John. "We're both from out of town."

The other man smirked and spread his hands. "Well, then. Welcome to the capital, lads. Don't let the tall buildings scare you!"

"We'll try not to," said Ronon.

"I'm Rifko Tenk," he said, "a kitesmith."

"He's Ronon Dex, I'm John Sheppard."

Rifko laughed. "John the Shepherd, you say? Sorry to tell you, you won't get much work hereabouts! No herd beasts in these neighborhoods! Men would eat them soon as look at them!"

"Food's in short supply here, then?" asked Dex.

Tenk shrugged. "When isn't it? Ah, you scoff what you can." He hugged the bag closer to him. "Bit o' meat when you can find it."

Sheppard smiled, trying to keep the man at his ease. "That right? We thought that things in the, ah, capital would be different. Plenty of food and wine, servants and shiny silverware..."

Rifko laughed even harder than before. "What's that you say? Oh, maybe that's so up yonder in the palace, but down here..." He pointed at the cobbled street. "Down here, laddie, a man is lucky if he sees clean water and a fruit without a speck of mould on it once a month!"

"And that's no wonder!" came a new voice, high and strident with agitation. Sheppard turned to see the gangly youth with the headband coming closer, stabbing a fistful of papers at Rifko's chest. "Nobles take it all, every fig from our lips! What they throw to the pigs after a feast could feed a downcity family for a week!"

"Here, now!" snapped Rifko. "We don't want none o' your red-talk!"

"How many have to die from the bone-rot before we stand up and say no more?" The youth thrust a leaflet at Sheppard and John took it on reflex. The paper was rough and poorly cut, printed with bright red ink that came off on his fingers. The Ancient text was a mystery to him, but the presentation was clearly angry about something. The kid's fierce demeanor made it clear what that was. "Poverty and disease run in our streets! Daus is a traitor to Halcyon who feathers his nest while we all starve —"

"Enough of that!" snarled the older man, shoving the agitator away. "Be off with you, before the peace officers come and strip us all for just being near you!" Rifko shook his head, turning away. "Blathering fool!"

Ronon watched the youth stumble away, a thunderous look on his face. "Does that happen a lot?"

"Too much these days," noted Rifko. "Fair gives me a headache it does." He nodded in the direction of a doorway. "I feel the need for an ale to settle my nerves. Care to join me, country lads?"

"Sure," said Sheppard, "lead the way."

They found a table in the corner of the room where they could get a good look at the comings and goings inside the decrepit pub. Rifko was clearly a regular, evidenced by the way the barkeep greeted him and the nods that came from other drinkers as they wandered through.

"Bet this is a new sight to you, eh?" said the man, pointing at the gas lamps dangling from a ceiling brown with tobacco smoke. "I hear there's only candles and lanterns to be had in the country."

"Nice place," said Sheppard, surveying the room. "The last tavern we went to was kinda dead."

"Literally," said Ronon, taking a seat.

Rifko brought a battered steel jug and three metal mugs to the table and poured out a dark, bitter brew. "On me," he grinned. "Consider that a proper greeting from the Magnate himself."

Sheppard contented himself with a sip, but Dex downed the tankard in one. "It's good," noted the Satedan, pouring out some more.

Rifko blinked, and studied Ronon as if noticing him for the first time. "They breed you lads big out on the farms, don't they?"

John took in the men and women around them. They had the look about them of people who were used to a life of hardship, the kind of beaten-down faces that accepted their lot with grim determination and dogged tolerance; but beneath it all there was a faint, directionless tension, the ghost of unspent anger. The same expression was reflected in the kitesmith's eyes. "Rifko," he began, "let me ask you something. These battles that the nobles are always fighting. Do you think it's right?"

"Right?" The man sipped from his mug. "War is war. If we didn't put up a fight, the Wraith would cull us all, wouldn't they?"

"I'm not talking about fighting the Wraith. I'm talking about the Dynasts fighting each other."

Rifko eyed him. "What do you mean?"

"Wouldn't life be better if the nobles didn't spend all that time killing each other's troopers? I mean, how much does it cost to feed and arm all those soldiers? Wouldn't it be better if they spent some of that money on keeping people housed, or with food on their tables?"

Sheppard saw a moment of indecision in Rifko's eyes, but he covered it with another swig of beer. "Look, that's how it goes. It's the way it's always been. The nobles have their little tussles and men like thee and me are always open for paid service to 'em, should we want it. Keeps things stable."

"Peace is more stable than war," said Ronon in a low, intense voice. "The Magnate could have that if he wanted it."

"Aye, well..." Rifko gave a mirthless chuckle. "His Lordship likes to keep the little pups nipping at each other, so they say. Stops them from biting the big dog, if you catch my meaning."

"Daus makes the barons fight among themselves so they can't threaten him. Yeah, we've seen that," noted Sheppard.

"What was all that about 'bone-rot'?" added Ronon.

The man frowned. "You not have the bane out in the hills, eh? Count yourself lucky, then. I don't reckon there's a single family in the city that hasn't lost one of their number to that accursed sickness. Comes up on the weak, it does. Not a fair way to die, oh no."

"And your government doesn't do anything about it?"

Rifko leaned closer and spoke quietly. "See here. Now there's barely a man who wouldn't want a better life... What kind of fool would say no to that? But there's not a jot a kitesmith or a countryman can do about the set of things. I hear talk now and then of lower echelon barons with thoughts turned to moderate ways, of elections, public works and democratic votary, but nothing comes of it!" He shook his head. "And I doubt anything ever will. So we live our lives, try to make the best of it."

"One thing is certain," said Dex, "there'll be no change while Daus is on the throne."

"Aye." Rifko looked into his beer.

Sheppard produced the leaflet the youth had forced upon him. "But what about all this? Someone's clearly not taking things lying down."

The other man's face went pale and he snatched at the paper, tearing it from the colonel's hands and knocking over his beer mug. "You shouldn't be showing that in a place like this!" He crumpled the leaflet in his fist, squeezing it into a roll and jerked a thumb at a grand portrait of the Magnate over the bar. "This isn't a basement smoke-den for mouthy kids and fire starters! Them noisy red-bands out there just make things worse for all of us!" Rifko's face colored and his voice rose. "Maybe you two oughta head back to the countryside—"

"What's all this ruckus?" said the barkeep, approaching with a hard glint in his eye. "Rifko Tenk, what is that you've got in your greasy mitt there?"

"It's nothing," began Sheppard, but the burly tavern owner slammed a fat hand down on the table and trapped the errant pamphlet beneath it.

"Red paper." His voice was a growl. "In all my years, Rifko, after you've been warned not to talk out of turn about his Lordship, you brought a red paper into my pub?"

"It's not like that," said the kitesmith.

The barkeep stabbed a thick finger at Rifko's face. "I let you off the other times, seeing as how you had a skin-full then. But you're sober now and you're bringing this *filth* into my establishment!" Before anyone could react, the tavern owner back-handed Rifko on to the floor.

Sheppard and Ronon were on their feet in an instant. "Hey!" snarled the colonel, "there's no need for that! The paper is mine, I didn't know what it was."

"I don't recognize you!" barked the barkeep. "You got the look of a troublemaker on you, though! Betcha both bomb chuckers and sneak thieves too!"

"No, no…" Rifko was saying thickly, struggling to get up. "No trouble…"

But they were past the point of no return now. In his peripheral vision, Sheppard saw other figures moving from their tables, ready violence in their tense poses. Voices were rising around them

"So what if he's a red-band? They're right, what they say—"

"Scum! The Magnate's made this planet what it is—"

"Unseat the lot of them snobs if we could—"

"Children on the streets begging and starving—"

"You oughta be grateful for them—"

"Dying of the rot and no-one cares—"

"Saved us all from the Wraith, and for that alone they—"

Something glass shattered, and the fight erupted. The barkeep swung a ponderous haymaker that narrowly missed Sheppard's head, the wind of its passing tickling his cheek. Ronon belted the big man with the beer jug and sent him reeling backward, but the tavern owner did not go down. On other tables, shouts and punches were flying thick and fast as quietly-held viewpoints that had long been silent now came alive.

Ronon's hand went for his particle magnum, but the colonel stopped him. "No guns," he snapped, "let's just get the hell out of here."

Sheppard pulled Rifko to his feet amid the melee. "Sorry about all this."

"Woulda happened sooner or later," he mumbled through swelling lips.

Dex batted away a thrown mug with one hand and pushed a chair aside. "Sheppard, come on!"

They were making for the door when it slammed open and four figures entered. The first three wore uniforms similar to the soldiers of the Dynasts, but these were dark green and accented with silver badges. They had high hats with a bronze shield upon them. Something in the back of John Sheppard's mind instantly threw the word *Police* to the front of his thoughts.

But it was the fourth member of the group that made the brawl in the tavern die away. The colonel's gut tightened as a Hound followed the men into the pub, and in the sudden silence following their arrival, he found he could hear the enslaved Wraith panting inside the canine mask of its helmet.

"Peace Officer," said the leading greencoat. "You people know the punishment for affray." He looked to the barkeep. "I want an explanation."

Here it comes, Sheppard thought, glancing at Ronon. He was starting to regret not drawing his pistol while he'd had the chance.

The tavern owner thrust the leaflet at the officer and pointed at Rifko. "He brought this trash into my establishment." Not a single soul was moving now, all of them staring at the Wraith with naked fear. For all intents and purposes, it was as if the fight had never broken out.

"That's not true," said Sheppard.

"You'll get your chance." The peace officer didn't look at the colonel as he approached Rifko. "You there, show me your hands."

"He has nothing to do with this," Ronon growled.

One of the other greencoats produced a blunderbuss-pistol and brandished it at Dex. "Shut up, vassal. You'll speak when you're told to, or else."

"Your hands, man," repeated the first officer. Rifko reluctantly turned his palms upward; and there on his skin were smears of red ink. "Well, well. Why don't you dissidents ever think about wearing gloves, eh?"

"I..." Rifko blinked. "S'not what it looks like."

"It never is," said the peace officer. He turned to address the tavern. "We live in a society of rules and codes, thanks to the honorable leadership of our great Magnate. But there are always some who think they know better than he does. My job is to show them the error of their ways." He turned back toward Rifko. "The best means for that is an object lesson."

"You're not going to kill him," snarled Sheppard.

"Of course not," said the greencoat, and he drew a thin whistle from a chain around his neck. He blew into it, and on the very edge of hearing, there was a reedy squeal of noise.

It happened so fast; the Hound threw itself forward, the swiftness of its movement raising cries of surprise and fear from the other people in the pub. The Wraith snatched at Rifko and pulled him into an embrace, one hand ripping through his jerkin.

"No!" Sheppard and Ronon went after him, but the armed officer had the gun at the ready, blocking them. John watched, sickened, as the Wraith fed on the kitesmith, dragging years off his life. Rifko's cheeks became sunken and hollow, his hair thinning and turning white. Sheppard felt ill, for one moment recalling the face of Colonel Sumner trapped in the belly of a Wraith Hive Ship, the look of pleading on the Marine's face as his life force was drawn out of him.

After a moment, the lead peace officer tugged on a dangling lanyard from a collar around the Hound's neck and metallic cogs in the mechanism whirred. The Wraith choked and stumbled backward, releasing Rifko. The kitesmith sagged, holding his newly wrinkled hands up before his face.

"The Lord Magnate does not tolerate dissent. Halcyon is a society of laws." The peace officer pointed at Rifko. "If any of you doubt that, look to this man. His punishment is your warning."

"He was innocent!" spat the colonel, advancing, daring the man with the gun to shoot him. "You took twenty years off him for nothing!"

The greencoat nodded. "And now I'm wondering how much I should take from you."

"You can't!" The voice came from the corner of the room, and Sheppard turned to see a young boy in a brown cloak similar in cut to the ones he and Ronon had appropriated. With a start he recognized the youth; it was the servant boy from the monorail conveyor who had stumbled and broken a cup. John hadn't seen him there, hidden in a corner. "Those men are guests of the Lady Erony."

"Really?" The peace officer nodded to one of his men. "Search them."

Sheppard and Ronon grudgingly allowed the rough checking. He took a moment of dark satisfaction from the look of surprise when the greencoat discovered their guns. Finally, the search turned up the dockets that Erony had given them on their arrival.

The senior officer studied the papers in silence, his expression rigid. "These appear to be in order," he said, after a long moment. "You shouldn't be down in the lower city. Lucky for you the boy was here."

"Lucky for *you*," retorted Ronon.

"Come with us," continued the greencoat officer, "you may consider yourself now within our protective custody."

"I'm not done sightseeing yet," said Sheppard.

"You *are*," said the other man, "unless you'd like to stay a while and watch the Hound dispense another lesson?"

The peace officers took them to a special funicular tram that in turn had them back in the grounds of the High Palace in a few minutes. Sheppard half-expected to be clapped in irons or slammed in some dingy stone dungeon, but the greencoated men simply handed them over to a cohort of the Magnate's soldiers, weapons and all, and descended back into the city with their Hound trailing at their heels. The troopers escorted them to one of the citadel's larger terraces where a garden was open to the night sky. The contrast of the garden's elegant fragrance to the sour taint of the smoggy lower city was stark and jarring.

Daus was waiting for them, with First Minister Muruw and Vekken. The Magnate had a conflicted expression on his face. He was trying to pretend he was amused, but Sheppard could see the annoyance just beneath the surface in the way he gestured with his smoking pipe. "Lieutenant Colonel. I must apologize. I had thought that the quarters we provided to you and your party were more than adequate. Imagine my surprise when the telekrypter brought us a report that you had been seen in the lower city." He tapped the bowl of the pipe on a stone pot, emptying spent ashes into an ornamental fishpond. "If you wished something a little more coarse and unrefined, you had but to ask. I could have placed you in the cellars."

"I'm not much for taking the package tour," said Sheppard. "I like to get my own view of things."

"What were you doing down there?" demanded Muruw. "We would be within our laws to have shot you!"

"From what I've seen, you've got worse punishments than that," Sheppard replied, working to keep his voice level.

Daus nodded. "Hmph. It is regrettable that you had to witness such a thing, but our justice must always be swift and terrible to behold, or else it has no power."

"Your thugs attacked an innocent man," growled Ronon. "What kind of justice is there in that?"

"Innocent?" Daus said lightly. "How can you hope to know that, Ronon Dex? How long were you in the man's company for? Have you known him all his life? Were you aware of his numerous transgressions against the nobility?" The Magnate shook his head. "I understand your indignation, but you must trust that my peace officers did what was right for the people."

Sheppard's hands were tightening into fists. "So, no trial, then? No due process or appeal, just step up and let a Wraith suck the life outta you? I guess it saves on building prisons, huh? Why lock up a man for ten years when you can just drain the time from him on the spot?" He resisted the urge to spit. "Bad enough you use those creatures on the battlefield, but on the streets of your own city? As a deterrent? Is life that cheap to you people?" John shot an acidic glare at Vekken, but the adjutant remained silent, content to hover like a shadow at the Magnate's side.

"Life is nothing if not lived in strength," retorted Muruw. "The Hounds remind us all that to survive we must be strong."

"What is it with this 'only the strong survive' stuff you keep spouting?" John's mouth twisted in a humorless sneer. "You live a life of luxury up here but you talk like you're an inch away from death — and meanwhile, all the poor saps who really *are* living on the poverty line are barely holding on! Destitution and disease... I bet it's the same in every damn city on this planet!"

Daus smirked. "You are a conundrum, Lieutenant Colonel Sheppard. You and your Atlanteans, you show courage, strength and martial prowess, and yet, you are so *weak* inside. You gnash and cry at the wounding of inferiors, you encourage vulnerability and you glory in your failings. You look like soldiers but you

talk like commoners. I cannot even begin to understand the kind
of society that breeds a man like you."

"Yeah, well, we're complicated that way."

"The bone-rot only strikes the infirm or the frail," noted the
nobleman, "people whose contribution to our culture is negli-
gible at best. They are not missed."

"Have you even tried to find a cure?" snapped Ronon.

"We have other, more important endeavors to occupy our scientists."

"You think you are better than us because you show *compassion*," broke in Muruw, making the last word a mocking insult.
"But what has your empathy earned you? The Precursor City
obliterated, your people scattered and so desperate for help that
it takes a mere slip of a woman and her cadre to rescue you from
the Wraith?"

Daus stepped closer to the colonel. "Our hearts are harder
than yours, Atlantean, because Halcyon is cruel." He spread his
hands. "You do not see it now, but in the time before my Dynast
came to rule this world, the hardest winters and the worst fam-
ines in our recorded history swept the planet. Millions perished.
Wars raged out of control. Life here was pitiless and brutal.
Only though sacrifice, through determination and spirit, were
my forefathers able to bring Halcyon under control and into this
golden age. Our people are colored by that experience, Lieutenant Colonel. Perhaps if we had lived on a world no doubt as soft
and pleasant as your distant Earth, then we too might share your
flaws of character."

"Compassion isn't a flaw," Sheppard locked gazes with the
Magnate, "cruelty is."

The other man ignored his interruption. "We are not afraid
to take the hard road. We do not shy away from making choices
that you might consider to be ruthless or callous. Until the last
Wraith dies, we are at war!" Daus's voice became a snarl. "Like
every living human in this galaxy, we are fighting for our lives
each day. One moment of inattention, one instant of weakness
and the Wraith will strike at us! Halcyon must be ever strong,
always ready!"

Ronon snorted. "And what happens along the way? You give up what it is to be a human being? You become killers and predators, you become like *them*?"

Daus turned and walked away, refilling his pipe. His moment of ire faded, his calm and condescending demeanor returning. "It has come to me now," he said, "I think I see the root of your problem, Lieutenant Colonel. You Atlanteans, you are naïve. Oh, yes, you fight hard when your backs are to the wall, and in those moments perhaps you touch the iron will that hides deep inside you... But I warrant there is a part of you that hopes one day to end the war without bloodshed, yes? Peace. You want peace."

"Every soldier wants peace," said Sheppard, "it's why we fight."

"Perhaps. But we have been fighting the Wraith for centuries, and we know them better than you ever could. And one day — perhaps within your lifetime, I truly hope — one day you will understand that to defeat them you will have to take the hard road." He gave the colonel a level, flinty stare. "You hate the Wraith as much as I do, I see it in your eyes... But how far are you willing to go to vanquish them?"

Sheppard found his throat turning dry. "Not as far as you," he managed, after a moment.

Daus smiled and lit the pipe, the flare of the match giving his face a brief demonic cast in the twilight. "Mark those words well, my friend, because you will remember them. On the day the Wraith swarm across your Earth, you will remember them, and you will know that I am right." The Magnate turned, dismissing them, and walked away into the darkness with Muruw.

When the other men were out of earshot, Vekken spoke for the first time since they had arrived in the garden. "Ah, Sheppard, you would be wise not to test the Magnate's munificence any further. Muruw counseled him to have you put to the Hounds for daring to leave the palace environs. His Highness may not be so quick to disagree the next time you try him."

"I'll take that under advisement." The colonel frowned. "It's been a big day. I think we've had enough excitement for now."

Sheppard and Ronon began to walk off in the direction of the guest quarters.

"I've doubled the guard," Vekken called after them. "Do not attempt any unescorted sojourns again. I have left orders to have any man who allows you to escape to be executed."

Sheppard froze and threw Vekken a hard glare. "You wouldn't do that."

"I would," said the adjutant. "Cruelty has its uses, Sheppard, and right now I am using it on you."

John turned on his heel and walked away.

Ronon gave Sheppard a sideways look. He hadn't often seen the man angry, but he was seeing it now, the cold fury burning in the colonel's eyes and the set of his jaw. "Where do we go from here?" he asked, watching Sheppard's expression.

"If I had to call it, I'd scrub this whole mess right now, Zero Point Module or no Zero Point Module. Everything's a game to these people, us included, and I'm getting pretty damn sick of it."

Dex's head bobbed in agreement. "You'll get no argument from me."

Sheppard blew out a breath. "But McKay's champing at the bit to take a peek inside that dolmen, and if there is a ZPM…"

"…It might serve them right if we just helped ourselves to it." Ronon finished.

"The thought had crossed my mind." Sheppard hesitated. "But I'm not going to shut this down without talking to Weir first. Like it or not, this is still technically a diplomatic mission, and she gets the last word on those."

The two men walked in silence for a few moments before Dex spoke again. "Sheppard. I hate to give him any credit, but Daus was right about something. One day we might have to go places we don't want to… to beat the Wraith."

John didn't look at him. "We'll cross that bridge if we come to it. But not before."

CHAPTER SIX

The open wormhole lit the Gate Room with soft, silvery light.

"I'm receiving Colonel Sheppard's IDC," said the technician.

Dr. Weir patted him on the shoulder. "Thank you, Keith. Go ahead and lower the force field. Have the guards stand down."

The invisible energy barrier enveloping the Stargate flashed as it fell, allowing unfettered egress through the metal ring. Weir was halfway down the broad staircase from the control room when John Sheppard marched through the Gate, his face unreadable. With a whoosh of displaced energy, the wormhole evaporated behind him. Elizabeth saw it instantly; the man's body language rang a warning bell in her mind. Questions crowded her thoughts. Why was he here in person, instead of just sending a radio message? Where were the rest of the squad?

"John?"

Sheppard threw her a weary nod. "The others are still on Halcyon, as guests of our gracious hosts." He said, anticipating her thoughts. The word 'guests' was laden with heavy sarcasm. "McKay asked me to pass this on to you, it's his preliminary field report." John offered her a data screen and she took it.

"Diplomacy taking its toll on you?" She managed a weak smile, trying to lighten the mood.

"And then some." Sheppard frowned. "I've learned a few things about these people, Elizabeth, and it's not promising."

She was paging quickly through McKay's report, scanning the gist of it. "Ancient constructions... Possible presence of a ZPM..." Weir paused. "Is this a good news, bad news thing?"

"Not so much of the good," John noted. "I wouldn't trust these people as far as I could throw 'em."

She returned a wry grin. "Welcome to my world, Colonel."

They walked away from the silent Gate. "Let's adjourn to the briefing room, and you can bring me up to speed."

A nod. "I think Beckett should sit in on this as well. His input could be useful."

Weir tapped her communicator headset. "Carson?"

A Scots brogue sounded in her ear. "*Beckett here.*"

"Can you come up to the central tower?"

"*Aye, I'm on my way.*"

Weir looked back at Sheppard and saw the hollow, troubled look in his eyes. "John? What did you see out there?"

"It's a long story."

Elizabeth steepled her fingers and remained silent throughout all of the colonel's report, now and then scrolling through the data screen's collection of digital images captured by Rodney McKay's camera, but content to let Sheppard find his way and tell them his impressions of Halcyon without interruption. A veteran of hundreds of conferences where a taciturn poker face was a basic requirement, Weir kept her own emotional reactions under tight rein, retaining a neutral aspect. Throughout her diplomatic career, in the days before the Stargate Program took over her life, Elizabeth had made a skill of listening to troubling discussions without revealing her own opinions. By contrast, Dr. Carson Beckett, the resident chief medical officer on Atlantis, bore his reactions with no artifice at all. The soft-spoken Scotsman cursed under his breath at some of Sheppard's descriptions of life on the other planet, shaking his head in disbelief.

"How can they exist like that?" Beckett asked. "Blood sports, and warfare as an organized team game? It's barbaric, that's what it is."

"There are several tribal cultures on Earth that used ritualized combat as a form of entertainment or to solve disputes," offered Weir, "but nothing on the scale you described, John."

Sheppard laid his hands flat on the table. "And from what I was told, the battle we witnessed was just a small-scale skirmish. A minor disagreement."

"It's not just that," added the doctor, "it's this racial ruthlessness that I can't stomach. I can't see how a culture so callous could survive for long."

"Cossacks, Romans, Vikings... All of those peoples had societies with customs that would seem horrible to us today," continued Elizabeth. "Of course, none of them had the level of technology present on Halcyon."

"Yeah. If there was ever a planet in line for a regime change, it's this one." Sheppard rubbed his face wearily.

"What about the Wraith issue, these 'Hounds'?" Weir looked at a still photo of the aliens in battle armor. "Can we be sure that the Halcyons aren't just working with the Wraith? We've seen that before."

John shook his head. "No, you know the Wraith. They'd never accept a subordinate position to humans. I don't know how they've done it, but the Wraiths on Halcyon have been stripped back to a feral state. They're not much more than savages, kept on leash with those collars." He pointed at the picture. "It's the only explanation as to why the Hounds haven't risen up and torn them all to shreds."

"Do you think the Wraith know about Halcyon?" she asked.

"McKay seems to think not. The planet's way off in the sticks, a long hike from any Wraith territory we know of."

Elizabeth studied the data screen again. "Quite frankly, John, there's a part of me that wants to recall the team right now and lock the Halcyon address out of the dialing computer."

"Me too. But..."

"But indeed." She tapped the panel. "The fact is, as objectionable as we might find Lord Daus and his people, if there's even the very faintest chance that we could locate a zero point energy module on this planet, we have to investigate. Atlantis is running on one ZPM right now and it's designed for three. If we could get our hands on another..."

"And you think the Halcyons will just hand over a piece of Ancient technology to us, no questions asked?" Beckett shook his head. "They'll probably want to fight us for it, or something."

"They don't care about the Precursors... The Ancients," said

Sheppard. "McKay told me their top egghead Kelfer dismissed the whole thing out of hand. It's likely they don't have the first clue about Ancient science. If they have a ZPM, they'd be more likely to use it as a paperweight. I get the feeling Daus and his gang wouldn't be too comfortable with the idea of someone being smarter than them."

"Egotistical *and* in denial, then? Sounds like a case for Dr. Heightmeyer."

"We should be thankful for small mercies. A society like this with access to Ancient science... I dread to think what could happen." Elizabeth considered the situation for a moment. "These people are arrogant, so we should use that. You said Daus accused you of being weak?"

"Several times. Hurt my feelings something terrible."

"Then let's play to that. If the Halcyons want to underestimate us, we should let them. If we don't disabuse them of that belief, we might be able to convince them to part with the ZPM—"

"*If* they have one," Carson broke in.

"—If they have one, and they'll be none the wiser. Daus will have us in his debt, and there's nothing people like him enjoy more than having someone owe them a marker."

Carson considered this for a moment. "Of course, if they realize we're trying to pull a fast one, they won't be nice about it."

Sheppard sighed. "Okay. So I'll Gate back and we'll bite our lips until McKay gets his look-see inside this dolmen. If there's a ZPM, we bag it, if not, we smile politely and go home."

"That's the gist of it, yes," said Elizabeth. "But I don't want another Genii situation with these people, John. If Daus starts demanding weapons or technology in exchange, tell him no. Food or medicine they can have, but nothing military in nature."

"Way ahead of you on that one."

Beckett tapped the table. "On the subject of medical aid, I'd like to add something."

"Go on."

The doctor sighed. "I'm going back to Halcyon with Colonel

Sheppard."

John shook his head. "Uh-uh, no way. Remember the organized war and blood sport thing? I've got too many people on that planet as it is, I'm not taking another one."

"Another three, actually," continued Beckett. "I'm going to turn over the Atlantis infirmary to Dr. Cullen for the duration and take Holroyd and Kenealy with me. This illness you mentioned in your report, the 'bone-rot'. The symptoms sound like something connected to malnutrition, maybe toxins in the water supply. If I'm right, it would be simple enough to address."

"Carson —" began the colonel.

"I'm not going to stand by if there are sick people out there and I can do something about it. It's my job, John. I have to try to help." He looked away. "Besides, saving the lives of their workers might make these nabobs a little more well-disposed towards us when the time comes."

Weir nodded. "I agree. Colonel Sheppard is right that there's a risk, but Carson is correct. The commoners are not Daus and his barons. If we can help them, we must."

John frowned again. "Fine, but I want to take a little extra insurance with me. A Puddle Jumper."

"I though we wanted these people to underestimate us," said Beckett. "Won't an invisible Ancient spaceship raise a few eyebrows?"

Sheppard gave him an arch look. "I'm not gonna do the 'invisible' thing. Not unless we need to, anyhow."

"Permission granted," said Weir. "Carson, gather your team and whatever supplies you need. John, Jumper Three is in the hangar and prepped for launch." Beckett left them alone, and Elizabeth touched Sheppard's jacket where a series of ragged rips were visible. "You might want to get a change of uniform while you have the chance."

"Oh yeah. Right." He blinked. "Sorry. I've kinda been in the moment for the last couple of days." John sighed. "How do you do it, Elizabeth? How do you look a scumbag in the eye and make nice, when all along you just want to deck him?"

"Thinking happy thoughts helps," she noted, "that, and having a punching bag you can take out your annoyance on."

That raised the first smile Weir had seen from Sheppard since he came back through the Stargate. "Good advice. I'll keep it in mind."

She hesitated. "John, I know I don't have to say it, but I'm going to anyway, just for my own peace of mind. Tread carefully out there."

"Wanna go in my place?"

"What, and let Caldwell turn up on the *Daedalus* to find me gone?" Weir said lightly. "He'd be moving into my office in a hot minute." She smiled again, but it faded quickly. Elizabeth felt conflicted, and for once she knew it was showing on her face. "I think Daus has another agenda. Call it diplomatic instinct, but from what I hear from you and Rodney, I think you need to be prepared for another play from him."

Sheppard met her gaze and held it. "Don't worry. We'll be ready."

Advance. Parry. Lunge. Turn. Block. Strike. Strike. Parry. Strike once again.

Teyla moved through the training regimen with a flowing grace, her moves seamless and swift. Years of practice on Athos had turned the routine into something she could do by sheer reflex, the motions coming from memory ingrained in her muscles and nerves. The two short sticks in her hands hummed as they moved through the air of the courtyard, assailing invisible foes.

Sheppard had a name for these kinds of exercises; he told her they were called *kata* on his world, a word from the native language of the scientist Dr. Kusanagi back on Atlantis. Kusanagi's people, so John had explained, were known on Earth for a martial art called *kar-ah-tey*, although Teyla had never seen the bookish woman exhibit any prowess in it. Sheppard had shown her recordings, these dramatic presentations the Earthers called "movies", where men and women demonstrated this *kar-ah-tey* and other fighting styles called *kung-foo* and *bok-sing*, often in battles where they were hugely outnumbered or were forced to use eclectic common objects as weapons.

Many of the soldiers from Earth were also trained in these techniques, although none of them seemed to have the ability to balance on the tips of sword blades or skip across rooftops, like the fighters in the films. Teyla enjoyed sparring with them; the way they fought was fresh and it challenged her own skills. Similarly, she liked the occasional match against Ronon Dex. Where Teyla's stick fighting was all about grace and accuracy, the Satedan fought with power and speed. John Sheppard, by contrast, was a wary and careful opponent, looking for the swiftest way to bring the fight to a conclusion. Sheppard didn't glory in combat the way Ronon did; the colonel fought to win, not for the thrill of it. They were both very different men...

Parry. Back-fist. Turn and sweep. Block. Advance. Cross and strike.

The clean, pure flow of the *kata* helped her clear her mind of distraction, of all the fears and concerns that had crowded her since they arrived on Halcyon. This was the first real moment of peace she had felt in days, the distant psychic murmur of the Wraith retreating as she found her focus. The woman let herself draw in, become centered.

She pivoted as she moved, her eye line crossing the cloistered corridors running around the edges of the quad. Teyla knew the palace guards were there, watching her without trying to be obvious about it. When she had asked a young trooper where she could take an hour of exercise, the look on the soldier's face was one half of shock, half of fascination. She heard him whisper to his comrades as she walked away, one word spoken like a prayer to ward off evil. *Wraithkin.*

The trooper had directed her here, to this training square. The large open courtyard itself was deserted; part of it was a short weapons range with steel target silhouettes in the shape of a man, and at the other points of the square were racks of wooden training swords, a jointed practice dummy and something like a climbing frame. Teyla moved in tight circles on a broad rectangle of yellow flagstones worn smooth by hundreds of years of sparring.

And rest.

She completed the exercise by bringing the sticks to her chest with a *clack* of wood on wood. Teyla panted, the air cool on her bare arms; and then there was a tingle at the back of her mind.

"Interesting," began Vekken, emerging from the shady side of the quad. "Your method has some similarities to the Halcyon two-dagger school from the Rekil Era. You seem very proficient."

Teyla watched him approach. "I led a large community on my homeworld. It is important to have the skills to back my leadership with force, if matters require it."

Vekken accepted this with a nod, pausing to examine the training weapons. "But you are no longer a leader? You serve Lieutenant Colonel Sheppard."

"We are colleagues," she corrected. "We work in unison." Teyla sensed the adjutant's verbal feint and parried it. "We have common goals."

The other man selected something resembling a quarterstaff, but with a curved hook at one end, like a herdsman's crook. "I often use this place to take exercise myself," he explained, removing his tunic. Beneath, Vekken wore light cotton clothing better suited to melee combat than his usual brocade jacket. He produced two glass bottles of water and offered her one.

Teyla took it and sipped warily.

"Still suspicious?" Vekken took a long draught from his bottle. "I would think you have nothing to fear from us now the Magnate has decided to be open with your commander."

"Would you give your trust easily in my place?" she replied.

Vekken gave a brief, rueful smile. "I would not." He weighed the staff in his hands. "You and I, Teyla Emmagan, we share an understanding that few others do. The touch of the Wraith upon us... It gives one a unique viewpoint, do you not agree?"

"That is one way to consider it." She moved to leave. "If you will excuse me —"

Vekken held out the staff to bar her way. "Ah, but there is a minor question of rules to address. You see, this square was allocated to me this morning, and you have used it without my permission."

"The soldier did not mention this."

"I imagine so. Normally, I would let the matter pass, but the soldiers are watching and it does not serve discipline for me to allow an infraction. You are on the quad," he tapped the flagstones with the staff, "and so I must take it from you. By force."

"Your rules?" Teyla sniffed. "I do not wish to fight you."

Vekken brought the staff up to a guard position. "Just a little friendly sparring, Teyla. Enough to satisfy protocol. Unless you wish to concede to me?"

She raised her sticks. "Very well. First to yield, then?"

He nodded. "First to yield." The staff flashed out at her and Teyla knocked it up and away, sidestepping and taking distance.

Vekken flipped the weapon around his hand and thrust it like a pike. Teyla dropped low and made a foot-sweep; she did it with little art, throwing an easy attack at the adjutant to see how he would react. Vekken dodged without effort and stabbed out again. The staff nearly caught the tip of her ear as the Athosian moved into a parry-strike-parry combination.

"Heh." The man pivoted and twirled his weapon overhead. "You are quick. More a warrior than a leader, I would warrant."

"And you are more a soldier than a royal aide."

Teyla tapped her sticks against one another and gestured for him to try again. From the corner of her eye she glimpsed movement; some of the guardsmen were gathering near one of the cloister pillars to observe them. She imagined they would be taking bets on the outcome.

The next attack came with frightening speed, and Teyla understood that Vekken had been toying with her at the start. She took a blow on her right forearm that sent jolts of fire up her nerves, and by impulse she hit back with a double strike that met Vekken's ribcage on either side. He grunted and dropped back, an instant of surprise on his face, then gone.

"I'm curious," said Teyla, licking her lips. "The men in

Daus's court, the barons like Noryn and Palfrun; you clearly have a greater martial skill than they, yet you seem to have no fiefdom of your own. Am I wrong?"

Vekken shook his head, shifting his stance. "No, you are correct. But I serve the Lord Magnate willingly. It is my place." He struck and Teyla parried again. "My family has always been tied to the fortunes of the Fourth Dynast."

She shifted and caught the staff in a tight grip, locking the two of them together. The muscles in her arms bunched as Vekken pulled against her. "Because you are Wraithkin, yes?" Teyla panted. "Does that forbid you from being a lord yourself?"

And there she saw a moment of unguarded truth from Vekken, the briefest flash of what was beneath his studied mask. Teyla took the distraction and hit him, scoring three quick blows. He struck back, the curve of the hook clipping her chin. Vekken tried to snag her with the hooked end and she barely skipped away.

"My clan has served as the protectors of the Magnate's line on Halcyon for generations," he hissed, "and I gladly continue that tradition, as will my children, and their children."

Teyla shook off the shock of the impact. "How… How can you be so sure that the Fourth Dynast will reign in the future? In a society like this, there will come a time when they will be unseated. It is inevitable."

"Lord Daus's authority will not be overcome. No-one on Halcyon can match his power."

She went back to a guard stance. "His army, you mean? How does he have so many Hounds at his command, Vekken?"

The adjutant did not answer; instead he came at her leading a storm of blows, and it was all Teyla could do to parry them away. She felt herself pushing back toward the walls, losing ground to the furious assault. He brought the staff down hard and she caught it in the cross of her sticks. "Yield!" he spat.

"No…"

"*Yield*!"

"*I will not*!"

There was a commotion at the cloister, and then Ronon darted from the shadows, his pistol in his hand. "Didn't you hear her? She said no!" Mason and Bishop trailed behind him.

Vekken stepped away and gave Teyla a gracious bow. The glint of anger in his eyes was gone. "Of course. Forgive me. I sometimes become too caught up in the moment." He smiled at Dex. "Just a little good-natured sparring, Runner, nothing else. I did not intend to cause you undue concern."

Ronon gave Vekken a hard look, and then with exaggerated care, he holstered his particle magnum. "You okay?" he asked.

Teyla collected herself. "I am uninjured." Although that wasn't precisely true; she would have some interesting bruises by tomorrow.

Vekken replaced the staff on the rack. "Perhaps you might also consider a match of skills, Ronon Dex." He was casual with the offer. "I would be interested to see if you are as quick to defend yourself as you are the honor of Teyla Emmagan."

Ronon took a warning step toward the adjutant. "Any time you like—"

She put a hand on the Satedan's arm. "Ronon," she said firmly, "did you want something?"

Dex threw Vekken one last glare and then nodded. "Sheppard's back."

"Oh," noted the adjutant. "I shall have the conveyor station notified to have a train ready for him."

Ronon shook his head. "He's brought his own ride."

Teyla looked up as a familiar high-pitched whine reached her ears. Bishop pointed into the morning sky. "There he is, two o'clock high."

From out of the blue came the drum-shaped form of the Atlantean shuttlecraft. It circled overhead and then came to a halt before dropping gently to a landing in the middle of the training square. Teyla's mouth curled in amusement at the obvious surprise on Vekken's face.

Sheppard left Beckett to his people and stepped from the back of the ship. He instantly caught the vibe of dissipating tension in the air and glanced at Staff Sergeant Mason. The SAS soldier made a small gesture with his hand, and the look on his face said *no problem, everything's cool.*

Vekken was peering at the striated hull of the craft. "I've never seen an aerodyne like this. It has no rotors or engine intakes." He considered the ship for a moment. "This is Precursor technology, yes? Rescued from the ruins of Atlantis, no doubt?"

"Something like that," Sheppard replied, refusing to be drawn. "We call it a Puddle Jumper. We use it to travel through the Stargate when we don't feel like walking."

"Puddle... Jumper?" repeated Vekken. "That seems a curious appellation. For a vessel that travels through your Stargate, would not Gate-Ship be a more fitting name?"

"Have you been talking to McKay?"

Teyla looked over at him. "How did you get the Jumper out of the Gate Hangar?"

"I asked nicely," said Sheppard. "We had a little moment when they pointed all those gun turrets at us, but eventually they retracted the roof and let us go."

Ronon nodded at Beckett and his medical team. "What are they doing here?"

"A fine question indeed," said Muruw, approaching with a pair of guardsmen at his flanks. "I receive word via telekrypter that you have brought your own warship into our territory, and then discover it here, inside the very walls of the Magnate's home!"

"It's not a combat vessel," the colonel replied, "not exactly, anyhow."

"I see no weapons clusters," admitted Vekken, "and I am sure Lieutenant Colonel Sheppard would not be so foolish as to return to Halcyon with violence in mind."

"And yet he brings more soldiers with him," snapped Muruw.

"We're not military!" said Carson, stepping down from the Jumper. "Far from it! I'm Dr. Beckett, chief medical officer of... Of our team."

The minister's face crinkled in bewilderment. "Healers? Why

have you brought healers? Is someone unwell? I assure you that the Fourth Dynast has excellent apothecaries in service to its courtiers."

"I'm sure that's true," said Beckett, "but we're not here for you and the rest of the lords of the manor."

Sheppard stepped forward. "What Dr. Beckett is trying to say is, we'd like to offer some help to your people. The folks down in the lower city."

"The commoners?" Muruw blinked.

"That's right. Carson here is about the best, uh, healer, this side of the Pegasus Galaxy. He might be able to assist with this 'bone-rot' problem of yours."

'That aliment is no problem of mine," retorted the minister. "Only the dissolute, the lower orders suffer from it."

"Aye, well," broke in Beckett, "perhaps I can do something about that."

Muruw was about to protest further when Vekken spoke out. "What a generous offer, Lieutenant Colonel. I'm sure the Magnate would see the value in such an altruistic gesture. Don't you agree, First Minister?"

Something in Vekken's tone brought Muruw's protests to heel. "Yes. Yes, of course. The Magnate has the best interests of the common folk at heart."

Beckett looked to Sheppard. "I'd like to take the Jumper down into the lower city, then? Set up a temporary clinic, do some tests?" He shot a glare at Muruw. "If that's okay with your lordship here?"

"I will allow it," said the minister haughtily, and prodded the soldier standing next to him. "You men, go with them. See that nothing *untoward* occurs."

"Great," Sheppard replied. "Staff Sergeant Mason, why don't you and Private Bishop tag along too?"

"The military skills of your troopers will not be required," said Vekken.

John fixed a rigid smile on his face. "I don't doubt it, but Mason and Bishop here are, uh, fully qualified medical...guys. They're going to help Beckett."

"Indeed?" The adjutant seemed unconvinced.

Mason directed Bishop into the back of the Jumper. "Oh, yes, sir," said the gruff sergeant. "I'm well known for my sensitive bedside manner."

Beckett threw the colonel a nod. "I'll check in with you once we're set up."

"Sure you're okay flyin' that thing?" Sheppard called, as the drawbridge hatch began to close.

"Nae problem," said Carson, his face pale as he took the pilot's chair.

Teyla beckoned the assembled group. "We should stand back."

With a sudden trill of noise, the Jumper leapt up into the air, rising like an express elevator. It wobbled for a second, and then drifted away, out of sight.

"He breaks it, he bought it," said Sheppard from the side of his mouth. John looked around to see Vekken and Muruw both eyeing him with unmasked suspicion. "Thank you. Lord Daus won't regret this."

"Not unless Beckett crashes into a building," muttered Ronon.

"You may tell him that in person," said Muruw. "I came to inform you that His Highness has called you to an audience aboard his air-yacht. He is touring the enclosure forests at Carras over luncheon."

"Another war game?" Dex snorted. "I'll pass."

"Far from it. The Lord Magnate wishes to speak with you on issues of trade and treaty. He has decided that matters between your people and ours must be decided once and for all."

Vekken nodded. "I will have a gyro-flyer prepared immediately."

Sheppard hesitated. Suddenly, everything was going in the direction he wanted it to; so why was his gut telling him something different? *Diplomacy*, he told himself, *it's a different kind of battlefield, John. Adapt to it*. "I'll need to let the rest of my team know —"

"If you are referring to Dr. McKay, there is no need," Muruw interrupted. "While you were on the other side of the Great Circlet, he accepted the Lady Erony's invitation to view the site of the dolmen. Duke Kelfer is conducting him personally."

John looked at Teyla. "You know about this?"

She nodded. "Rodney was eager to go, so I agreed in your absence. Corporal Clarke and Private Hill went with him."

Sheppard clapped his hands together. "Okay. I guess we got a lunch date, then."

"Yeah," said Ronon in a voice that only John could hear, "but what's on the menu?"

"Oh, my." Rodney McKay blinked and ambled to a halt, his head tilted back to sight up along the length of the tall stone obelisk. Abruptly a thought occurred to him. "Ah! Pictures!" He fumbled in a pocket on his gear vest and removed his compact digital video camera, snapping open the viewfinder to shoot footage of the site.

Erony studied the device. "That... That is a kinescope?"

"A camera? Yes," McKay said, distracted. "This is interesting."

From behind them came Kelfer's voice; a bored drawl. "Really? It clearly takes little to hold your attention then, Doctor."

Rodney ignored him, using the camera to get close-ups of the text that patterned the sides of the memorial. The script was Ancient, all right, thousands of words of it, going all the way up to the top.

"How big you reckon it is, Doc?" said Clarke, resting his hands on his rifle's frame where it hung on its webbing. "Looks like that monument you Yanks got in Washington."

McKay gave him an irked look and pointed at his own face. "Canadian," he said, "not 'Yank'."

Clarke didn't seem to hear him. "Wrong color, though. This one looks like its made of slate."

"Washington Monument," offered Hill. "My sister sent me a postcard of it once."

Rodney turned on them both. "Yes, thank you both for that

astute piece of architectural analysis. Perhaps you'd both like to assist me further by shutting the hell up? I'm trying to concentrate here."

"Sorry, Doctor," said Clarke, and then added *sotto voce*; "Plonker."

"It really is quite breathtaking in its own way," said Erony. "I confess, I have visited here before and walked the circumference of the grounds and still found nothing to express its purpose." She took in the wide circular stage of gray stone on which the dolmen stood. "My father once spoke to me of records from the chaotic years, which spoke of the pillar's function, but I have never seen them."

"It is a burial marker, nothing more," insisted Kelfer. "Some remnant of the primitive people who came before Halcyon's current civilization, doubtless their vain attempt to signal some mythical sky-gods for salvation."

"Primitive? Not likely." Rodney gestured with his free hand. "Look closely at the cut of those stones, the precision of the inscriptions. Some caveman didn't carve those with a flint chisel. Whoever built this had to be an engineering genius just to make it that tall in the first place." He pocketed the camera and replaced it with a hand-held scanner, similar to the kind found aboard the Atlantean Puddle Jumpers. Wreathes of exotic radiation shimmered on the small screen, shifting and changing as McKay panned it over the landscape. "I was right..." He whispered. "The energy readings are so much clearer here. I'm detecting a power source, but there's more. I think this thing..." He paused and glanced up at the top of the monument. "I think this obelisk is actually broadcasting some kind of radiation."

Clarke's face paled. "Please don't tell me my hair's gonna start falling out."

"Not like that," said Rodney. "The pattern looks familiar, but I can't place it." McKay moved to where a low stone wall created an inner barrier around the dolmen and pulled his laptop from his backpack. "Let me hook this up."

"What are you doing?" asked Erony, but he waved her into silence. The scientist felt it; that old, familiar tingle of something coming together in his mind, the giddy little rush of pre-discovery. There was nothing like it, that unexpected head-swim that came when you cracked a thorny conundrum, when all the pieces of a problem suddenly went *click* and slotted into place. He'd tried to explain it to other people, to non-genius people like Sheppard and Weir. They didn't really get it, not like McKay did. Maybe Zelenka understood. Maybe. Just a little bit. But this sort of thing was what Rodney lived for, the days when science was better than sex.

Or so he liked to believe.

The laptop had an encrypted copy of much of McKay's own personal research database, terabytes of data stored on a mod-ified hard drive, packed with every last bit of information it could hold about the Ancients, the Pegasus Galaxy, everything. He'd created an interface program that let the human tech of the computer talk to the comparatively godlike tech of the Atlantean scanner device, and as they communicated, he saw the answer a split second before the laptop found it as well.

"Yeah, that's it!"

"What's what?" said Hill.

"I knew I'd seen the energy waveform being transmitted from the dolmen somewhere else, so I cross-referenced the sig-nal with the records database from Atlantis, and I was right," The words spilled out of him with barely a pause for breath. "There's a low-level interference pattern emitting from this thing, it's on a shallow band but the power output behind it is enough that its radiating out across most of the planet."

"Interference? You talking like electronic countermeasures, or something?"

McKay snapped his fingers. "Exactly, go to the top of the class. It's a jamming field. A dampening effect." He grinned. "And this is the cool part. The frequency it's operating at? It's only a hair's breadth from these readings Carson took of Wraith brain activity!"

"So, what, it's like a Wraith dog whistle, or something?"

"No, no, wrong wrong, dunce's hat for the corporal. If you want a bad analogy, it's more like a… A white noise generator, creating static on their psychic network."

"Dr. McKay, you really are the limit!" huffed Kelfer. "These wild theorizations you spout have no basis in fact!"

"That's why the Wraith you have here are docile...." Rodney gulped, looking at the Halcyon scientist. "Well, relatively speaking. The Ancients obviously made this and left it here as a passive defense system for the planet. It affects the functioning of the telepathic ability of Wraiths." He halted, thinking it through. "It must work on their higher brain functions, which explains why your pet Hounds are so animalistic in nature." McKay glanced at Erony. "But it doesn't seem to effect humans, or people with Wraith DNA like Teyla or Vekken."

"I am so glad we have had this time to let you indulge your flights of fancy," grated Kelfer, gesturing to their armed escorts. "But now, I think the day is done. Take your kinescope images and make an end to it, McKay. Your tour is concluded."

"Oh no," Rodney waggled a finger in the scientist's face. "I didn't come this far just to take some stills and get a brass rubbing. We're going *inside*." He strode quickly to the dolmen and ran his fingers over the carvings.

Kelfer threw up his hands. "Inside? It is a solid stone pillar, you fool! How do you possibly expect us to get inside it?" The man broke off as he realized what McKay was doing.

Rodney found the right glyphs exactly where he expected them to be. Trust the Ancients to be precise and thorough in everything they created. It was a simple enough matter to push *here*, press *here* and *there*...

"For blade's sake, what—" The rest of Kelfer's words died in his throat as stone ground on stone, and a thick slab at McKay's feet shifted back into the structure of the dolmen. Puffs of age-old rock dust gusted into the air.

The look of utter smugness on Rodney's face was total and complete. "Oh look," he said condescendingly, "there's a doorway."

The entrance led down a shallow incline to an open area beneath the dolmen's base. It was a hexagonal room, lit by soft glows from consoles that still operated, thousands of years after they had been activated. McKay noted how Kelfer's face had taken on the shocked cast of a man utterly out of his depth. *Hear that, Mister Chief Scientist? That's the sound of your preconceptions coming crashing down around you!*

Lights in hidden recesses came on as they approached them. Clarke took point, having left Private Hill and the other Halcyon troopers outside. Rodney had seen the expressions of the riflemen; the dark tunnel into the obelisk frightened them. He glanced at Erony; her face was quite the opposite, lit from within by wonder and awe.

"The Precursors made this…" she husked.

McKay nodded. "Yup."

Corporal Clarke trained around the flashlight clipped to the muzzle of his assault rifle. "Looks just like Atlantis down here," he said quietly as Rodney came closer. "Built from the same kit."

He nodded again. "A lot of Ancient technology seems to be modular in nature. My guess is they could re-purpose hardware for whatever task they had at hand." There were dust covers of plastic-like fabric over a central podium in the room, and he pulled them aside. On the far wall, a glass screen reacted by illuminating a display of power curves and energy output gradients. The waveforms shown there matched the scans Rodney had taken outside. He touched a few controls experimentally and called up pages of blocky Ancient hieroglyphics. "Huh. These are Wraith biometrics. A full physiological work-up, it looks like."

"You were right, Dr. McKay," said Erony, from the far side of the room. She was examining a metallic pillar that included a bubbling liquid component. "You did not exaggerate that day in the Terminal."

Kelfer finally managed a huff of derision. "How is it that you are such an expert on the Wraith, then?"

"I've been inside their ships, I've been zapped by one of their culling beams," he said off-handedly. "I know more about the Wraith than any sane man should." Rodney bent over the console. "Believe me, it's not by choice."

The Halcyon scientist made the same noise again. "The... The dust in this chamber is clogging my breath. I will wait for you outside, after you have completed your little diversion, My Lady."

"Yeah, 'bye," McKay spoke without turning. The hand-held scanner was drawing in streams of data from the dolmen's control system. He touched a combination of glassy keys and crossed to where Clarke was standing. "Step away from the panel." He threw a glance at Erony; she was entranced by a scrolling computer screen.

At a touch, a cylindrical compartment in the far wall grew a seam down its length and parted. Inside there was something that looked like a large g-clamp and nestled in its jaws was a roughly conical construction of rough-hewn crystalline rods. The object bathed the two men in a warm orange glow.

"Pay dirt," whispered Rodney. "A Zero Point Module. I love it when I'm right."

Clarke squinted at the ZPM. "So that's a space-alien super-battery then, is it? Oh."

"Oh?" McKay repeated. "You're looking at a controlled bubble of space-time feeding vacuum fluctuation energy from m-brane differential states, a device containing the power of a minor sun. What did you expect? Something with a copper-colored top?"

The soldier shrugged, unruffled. "I dunno. I thought it might have electricity sparking off it, maybe." He fluttered his free hand. "You know. *Bzzzt!*"

Rodney made a face. "You watch too many movies, Corporal. Back off a little." He touched a control pad next to the ZPM.

"Wait. You're not going to unplug it, are you?"

McKay blinked. "Well. Yeah."

"Would that not be a bad idea, Doc? If you're on the money about this Wraith brain-jammer, then switching it off is going to make every one of those bozos on this planet go out of their heads, right?"

He had a point; in his excitement, Rodney hadn't stopped to

consider the consequences. Certainly, if the dolmen was anything like Atlantis's systems, it would have enough juice in the
system to run for a short while without a ZPM, but once it ran
down... What then? "Ah, nuts." For all the hateful things he
had seen on Halcyon since they arrived, McKay couldn't even
begin to contemplate the thought of turning the Wraith loose on
the planet.

Clarke frowned. "You reckon his lordship back in the palace
knows how this thing works?"

"If he does, then even if I disconnected the ZPM, he'd never
let us take it. I was hoping we might find more than one here,
but..."

Erony came toward them. "Rodney? What are you doing?"

He pressed the control to close the compartment. "Nothing.
Just checking." He paused, and then looked the woman in the
eye. "Erony, I need you to be honest with me about something.
Don't give me any of that Jane Austen circumlocution. Does
your father understand how the dolmen works, yes or no?"

She opened her mouth to speak, but a sharp crackle of noise
threaded into the chamber, silencing her.

McKay's gut twisted in sudden fear. "That sounded like..."

Clarke raised his rifle. "Gunfire."

Linnian was there to greet them as Vekken's pilots docked
the chattering gyro-flyer down with the Magnate's air-yacht.
Sheppard felt a nasty little kick of *déjà vu* as they made their
way across the landing pad. He glanced out over the canopy of
green that stretched out for miles either side of the huge airship.
It was shades away from the barren, broken ground of the war
zone where the blues and tans had gone at it; the forest below
was rich and lush, and were it not for a couple of barrage balloons tethered out in the distance, he might have been forgiven
for thinking this was a wilderness untouched by human hands.
John peered into the trees, looking for signs of movement and
saw none. Was there another little war going on down there
somewhere? He found himself thinking of Bryor and the other
bluecoat conscripts he met on the battlefield. Had they survived

to the end of the game, were they now somewhere else, dying in an equally pointless skirmish?

Linnian saw the look on Sheppard's face. "This is a nature preserve, Lieutenant Colonel. The ecology is tightly controlled so that our hunters may venture into an environment as close to the wild as possible."

"On my planet, preserves are where wildlife are put to keep them alive, not for people to hunt."

"But your planet is very far away," noted Vekken. "Come. The Lord Magnate awaits us in the solarium."

Sheppard threw a look at his people; the expressions on the faces of Teyla and Ronon were the same, both of them wary and uncomfortable with the recent memories the airship brought up. He noticed the Satedan giving long looks at the guards posted in the corridors as they moved through the hull spaces. The number of men on duty had clearly been doubled since Dex's unauthorized venture through the ship.

Linnian took them up along the spine of the air-yacht to a wide glass dome on the prow of the vessel. It was open to the blue sky, a frame of green steel and smoked windows to lessen the glare of Halcyon's pale sun.

Daus rose from a heavy velvet-covered chair as they entered. "Ah. Here we are."

Sheppard forced a brittle smile. "Yeah, we have you right where you want us."

The Magnate grinned. "Very droll, Lieutenant Colonel."

John hesitated, and in that moment he felt something solidify in the back of his mind, the sudden crystallization of a thought that had been forming for days. He couldn't say how, but Sheppard instantly knew. *He's playing us. Right now, to our faces.* Ronon and Teyla seemed to sense it too; they knew their commanding officer well enough to take the cue from his body language. *To hell with diplomacy. I'm not Weir, I shouldn't be trying to handle this like she would. Time for the John Sheppard approach.*

"Yeah, I'm a funny guy." The tone of his words killed Daus's insouciant smile dead. "You called, we came, so let's cut to the chase, your lordship. What do you have to say to me?"

Linnian actually gasped; Daus's face was neutral. "Such bluntness. How refreshing." He helped himself to a drink. "Very well, Lieutenant Colonel, I'll match your directness, for the sake of expedience. As we speak, your Dr. McKay is doubtless venturing inside the structure we call the dolmen. Inside, he will learn that it is a device of great age, constructed by the Precursors to aid Halcyon in her battles against the Wraith."

"A weapon?" said Teyla.

"A shield," replied the Magnate. "A mechanism that operates on some higher science, fogging the minds any Wraith that venture here."

"So that's how you keep the Hounds in line," Ronon said.

"The dolmen's power is key, yes, but our choke-collars and the punishment training we submit the Hounds to plays a role as well. Unfettered by us they would merely be savage animals. We give them purpose, turn them to good use."

"That's debatable," retorted Sheppard. "Why tell us this now?"

Daus drained his wineglass. "I want there to be no falsehoods between us, Atlantean. I want you to understand me, understand Halcyon. To respect what we have to offer."

Sheppard and Teyla exchanged glances. "And what is that?" she asked.

The Magnate went to the dome, edging Linnian out of his path. "Some Wraiths, the ones we cannot break through our training regimens, are brought here to this enclosure. We set them free inside, and when our noblemen wish to sharpen their skills, this is where they come to hunt."

Dex snorted. "More games. More blood sport."

Daus continued. "There is one Wraith that lives in the preserve. I named him Scar." He smiled and tapped his face on the right side. "I once took his eye, you see. I was the only one to come close to catching him, and that was long ago. He has been out there for years, killing hunters and his own kind, surviving by sheer hate alone." The noble nodded to his adjutant. "Vekken has a theory that Scar might be some superior breed of Wraith, able to better resist the effects of the dolmen than his brethren. But I disagree. I think that Scar is merely stronger than all the others. And only the strong can survive. The weak and the powerless, those without allies like you, Sheppard. They are only prey for the hunters."

"Was that a threat?" Ronon drew himself up, but Vekken was there in an instant, blocking his path.

"Only a truth, Runner," said Daus, "only a truth."

The colonel's radio gave a chirp of sound, and John reached for it. "Sheppard here."

"It's me, Carson," came the reply. *"Can you talk?"*

"Yeah," said Sheppard. "We're all friends here. Tell us what you got, Doctor."

There was tension in Beckett's voice. *"I set up a temporary clinic here in an old warehouse near the quays. We pulled in about fifty people at random, all age groups, both sexes. This 'bone-rot', John, it's everywhere. These commoners, as they call them, they all have osteomalacia."*

"Sounds nasty."

"Aye, it is. You'd know it better by another name — Rickets. I'm guessing that we're looking at the long-term effects of vitamin deficiencies, carcinogens in the atmosphere, lack of calcium..."

"Can you help them?"

"That's the good news. Fabricating vitamin shots won't be hard. The tough part will be distribution, but yes, we can make these people better."

Sheppard threw Daus a level stare. "Good work, Doctor. I'll check back with you later."

"One last thing," said Beckett. *"You should know that I'm pretty sure what the root cause of this aliment is, Colonel. No one down here in the lower city is getting clean water or uncontaminated food. From what I can determine, these people are living off the scraps from the nobles. It's a outrage."* He sighed. *"Beckett out."*

Linnian drummed his fingers on a brass rail. "Your healer is very candid in his views."

"Yeah, that's what I like about him." Sheppard kept his eyes on Daus. "We could do something about that for you. We could show you how to make that problem go away overnight."

"And what would you want in return?" Daus put down his glass. "I know your man McKay covets the secrets of the dolmen. Or would you try to de-fang our Hounds and our armies?" He sniffed. "Ask yourself this, Lieutenant Colonel; do you think that I would jeopardize the superiority of the Halcyon nation-state for the lives of a few commoners?"

"Then what do you want to trade? Because you can be damn sure we're not parting with weapons or Jumpers!"

Daus smiled at him, and it was like watching a knife draw out of its sheath. "Halcyon offers you her safety, Lieutenant Colonel Sheppard. She offers you and your poor, lost Atlantean brethren a place to call home. All she asks is that you come under my dominion in return for such protection."

"You're joking," snapped Ronon. "Us join you?"

"Why not?" said the Magnate. "After all, your city is in ruins, is it not? You have no place to go, nowhere to call home. If Atlantis is no more, I would think that you would welcome a safe haven!" His voice rose as he spoke.

"Unless, of course, the tales of the Precursor City's demise are not entirely accurate," ventured Vekken. "Imagine if that were true. Imagine what might transpire if the Wraith learnt of it."

For one long second, John Sheppard balanced on the edge of his first diplomatic incident, his fist cocked and ready to knock the High Lord Magnate on his High and Lordly ass; but then he reeled it in and shook his head. "Thanks for everything, but you know what? We're through talking with you people." He turned his back on Daus and beckoned the others to his side. "Let's go."

The Magnate called after him. "Think on my offer, Sheppard. I am a better friend to you than an enemy."

The words were ringing in his ears as they reached the landing pad with Linnian panting to keep up. The colonel paused as the gyro-flyer's rotors began to spin up to speed and he toggled his radio. "McKay, this is Sheppard, you read me?" Static answered him. "Rodney? Can you hear me? Clarke, Hill, anyone, respond!"

"What is wrong?" asked Teyla.

"I'm not getting anything from McKay..."

Dex sneered. "More damn games?"

Sheppard grabbed Linnian. "You. That thing is fast, right? Go tell your pilot I want him to firewall it. Take us to the dolmen, double-time!"

They were in the air in moments and on the way; but despite their repeated calls, McKay's team remained silent.

CHAPTER SEVEN

Teyla's throat tightened as the gyro-flyer crested the ridge-line ringing the site of the dolmen. A sooty stream of black smoke extended from the stone arena and into the sky, a dark jagged arrow pointing down at the Ancient obelisk. The smoke issued from the smoldering remains of another flyer, the sleek lines and silvery rotor blades now nothing more than a crushed fist of metal. Even from the air, she could see the bodies of men in Fourth Dynast uniforms scattered about.

She heard Linnian let out a small cry of shock. "My... My Lady?"

Their aircraft rocked as the landing skis touched the ground and Sheppard was already at the hatch, flinging it open. "Fan out!" he shouted over the thrum of the slowing rotors. "Look for survivors!"

Teyla had her P90 in her grip as she disembarked close behind Ronon. In turn, Vekken, Linnian and a couple of other riflemen trailed the Atlantis team. Vekken was snapping out orders to his own men as Sheppard moved forward, ducking to avoid the downwash from the flyer. Ronon had his pistol out, swinging it back and forth, searching for targets. She watched the Satedan pause to check the crumpled form of a fallen trooper. He looked up and caught her eye, making a throat-cutting gesture with the blade of his hand.

"Who could have done this?" spat Linnian. "Who would *dare*? The dolmen is a prohibited zone, the rules of engagement disallow any actions here!"

Ronon nudged the dead man's lance-rifle with his boot. "Clip's almost full. Whoever took these soldiers down was quick about it. He barely got a couple of shots off."

"Hounds?" said Teyla, the word hard in her throat.

"No," offered Vekken, "the wounds are from needle shot.

Hounds carry melee weapons only." The adjutant moved away as the whole group spread out into a semi-circle.

Teyla moved low, watching for any signs of movement. The area around the dolmen was largely open, what little cover there was coming from a low wall and stubby stone cubes dotted here and there. Her seasoned warrior's sense told her that what ever had happened had already passed them by, and they had arrived in the aftermath; but it never hurt to be cautious, and on too many occasions she had encountered scenes that appeared unthreatening on the surface, only to be proven otherwise.

From the periphery of her vision she caught sight of a familiar blue uniform jacket and the khaki frame of an L85 rifle. Teyla's mouth went dry as she rounded a squat divider to find Corporal Clarke hunched over, his head lolling forward. His right shoulder was wet and dark with blood.

She slung her P90 and knelt by his side. "Clarke? Clarke, can you hear me?" Relief flooded into her as she touched her fingers to his neck and found a thready but definite pulse.

The soldier mumbled something and shifted, groaning.

"Colonel," she shouted. "Over here!"

Clarke blinked slowly and gave her an unfocussed look. "Think. I took one."

Sheppard bounded over, tearing open the Velcro pocket of his medical pack. "Corporal, what the hell happened?"

"Ambush," said the British soldier, his words thick and slow. "Blokes in. Grey fatigues. Put some of the buggers down, but... But there were too many..." His head lolled forward.

"He's lost a lot of blood," Teyla noted, helping John bandage the man's wounds. She peeled back the slick material of the jacket and found ragged tears underneath.

"We need to get him back to the helo, back to Beckett."

Ronon came over at a run, his face grim. "I found Hill." He shook his head. "He didn't make it."

Sheppard shot to his feet and swore. "Where's McKay?" he demanded.

"Not here," continued Dex, "no sign of his gear, either."

Teyla glanced up as Linnian approached. He had Lady Erony

with him, and she was pale with shock, walking with her adjutant supporting each stumbling footstep. "Lieutenant Colonel," she called, her voice trembling.

"Highness, please," Linnian was saying, "you must come with me..."

She pushed away from the man. "Sheppard! They took him!"

"Rodney?"

"Yes!" Erony wobbled unsteadily. "It was an assault splinter. I don't know how they got through the cordon. They gunned down our escorts, then they turned Wraith weapons upon us." She had tears of anger in her eyes. "Dr. McKay thought they were here for me! He tried to defend me. They shot him with a beam pistol..."

"A stunner," said Teyla.

"But why him and not you?" Sheppard demanded.

"Not just your doctor," said Vekken as he drew near. "Master Scientist Kelfer has also been abducted." He looked at Erony. "My Lady, did they attackers wear the gray?"

She nodded. "As the codes decree. No tabards or identifying sigils."

"So which of your lords or earls has gray coats?" said the colonel. "I don't take kindly to sneak attacks on my people!"

"You misunderstand," said Vekken. "No barony or Dynast sports gray uniforms. Only when a clan wishes to make a covert play against another will soldiers don that color, so their identity remains hidden."

Ronon snorted. "You've even got rules for that?"

"Of course. It is uncommon, but not unknown for a minor noble house to take prisoners of war in order to exert leverage over another Dynast. Although it is quite audacious to strike at a guest of the Magnate."

"You expect us to believe that this is some kind of power play? That doesn't track!"

They finished bandaging Clarke's injuries and Teyla stood. "The colonel is right. Would not Lady Erony have been a more valuable hostage than Dr. McKay?" She still had the corporal's blood on her fingers, and the coppery tang of it made her blanch.

Vekken gestured to his men to carry Clarke back to the gyro-flyer. "You will pardon me for saying, but it is most likely McKay and Kelfer were taken *because* of their lesser value, not in spite of it. Erony's kidnapping, the capture of a Magnate heir, would have meant that Lord Daus would have had no choice but to declare a pogrom and eradicate the guilty parties involved. The two scientists do not warrant that scale of reprisal. A more equitable resolution may be found."

"How genteel," Teyla replied, "and along the way one of our men is killed and another badly wounded!"

"Halcyon soldiers have lost their lives here as well," said Vekken mildly.

Teyla's eyes narrowed. "I wonder how keenly you feel for their sacrifice."

Sheppard nodded. "For all we know, it was Daus who ordered this! Maybe that's why your boss wanted us out of the way for a while!"

"You Atlanteans should be careful of making accusations while your fury is up," Vekken's jaw hardened. "I would advise you keep such ill-founded suspicions to yourself. If you give voice to that dishonorable slander within my earshot again, I will call you to answer for it at the tip of my sword."

"Yeah, whatever," The colonel angrily turned away. "Get Hill's body. We're going back."

Staff Sergeant Mason's face turned to a stony mask after hearing of Private Hill's death. Carson Beckett heard the SAS soldier's growled response to Sheppard when the colonel broke the news.

"You find us the bastards who did it, boss," Mason said, "and we'll see they pay the bill."

The intent behind the words went against everything that Carson stood for, but there was still the smallest part of him that empathized with the dour man. He knew military types like Mason of old, and he understood that the bonds between the soldiers of Special Forces units were particularly strong.

Within the hour the Magnate had called a 'court of greatest import', bringing together all the chattering noblemen and women that the Atlantis team had seen on their first arrival at the High Palace, filling the Chamber of Audiences once more. The ruler of Halcyon had grudgingly allowed Dr. Kenealy to accompany Hill's corpse back through the Stargate, before sealing the Gate Hangar; to prevent, in his words, "the escape of the culprits of this war crime".

The immediate fall-out from the attack on the dolmen meant that Sheppard was no longer willing to leave anyone in a position where they could suffer the same fate as McKay; as such, Beckett and Nurse Holroyd had been ordered—against Carson's appeals—back to the palace grounds where the Atlanteans could stick together. Only Corporal Clarke wasn't here, and even he was safely at rest inside the Puddle Jumper. Beckett appreciated the colonel's regard for his safety, but at the same time he was chafing at this inactivity. Every minute they stayed cooped up in this overblown castle was one less he could spend on helping the sickly commoners.

Lord Daus was in the midst of a portentous monologue about the events of the day, shifting back and forth between veiled allegations and fierce rhetoric. The assembled nobility looked on, whispering among themselves, the barons and baronesses in brash uniforms, the concubines in all their gauzy wedding-cake clothes. The doctor had the distinct impression that these people were just playing a role, paying lip service to something they took little or no real interest in.

At his side, Holroyd's eyes widened as she took in the parade of finery. "Look at those frocks. I'd bet the price of one of those would keep those families we saw in the lower city fed for months."

Carson nodded. "How the other half live, eh?" His gaze scanned the room and found Lady Erony, her adjutant Linnian not far from her side. She looked tired and unwell, staying close to the glass doors that led to the broad balcony outside the chamber.

The Magnate banged his fist on the arm of his throne, drawing Beckett's attention to him. It appeared that some of the higher-ranking noblemen were arguing, some blaming others for the events at the dolmen, accusing each other of conspiracy against the High Lord. Daus's voice rose. "Silence! We shall not have such harsh words spoken in the presence of our honored guests from Atlantis!" He gestured to Sheppard's party. "I will not have petty storms of blame tossed back and forth while our learned Duke Kelfer and the esteemed Dr. McKay are missing! No, we shall find them and recover them!" He threw a hard look at his subjects. "And then, only then, will I turn to questions of culpability and reproach."

"Honored guests?" repeated Teyla dryly. "If we are so honored, then why is it that Vekken's personal guard are watching our every move?"

"They're not there to protect us, that's for sure," noted Private Bishop. "I know minders when I see them."

On the raised platform, Daus drew himself up to his full height. "Mark this well. Those who are responsible for this heinous violation of territorial statutes will know the full weight of our laws."

Carson heard Ronon snort. "He's more annoyed that they broke the cordon around the dolmen than he is they blasted his daughter."

As Daus rumbled on, Beckett glanced back at Erony and he saw her shiver and grow pale. Abruptly, she turned and pushed her way out on to the balcony, leaving Linnian in surprise. The doctor frowned and walked purposefully across the chamber, moving past the adjutant.

"You cannot go out there," he began, trying to block his path. "Her Highness is taking some air and—"

Carson didn't allow Linnian to stop him. "Out of my way, wee fella," he snapped, in the commanding tone he used on children and troublesome patients. "I'm on duty." He went after Erony on to the open balcony and found her at the stone balustrade, breathing hard and sweating.

She turned. "What? Dr. Beckett?" Erony held up a hand.

"Please, I would be alone—"

"Don't worry love, I'm not one of your hoity-toity pals who'd stick a knife in your back if they see you looking sickly. I'm a doctor, so you don't have to hide your weakness around me." He took her hand in a matter-of-fact way and checked her pulse. "You took a Wraith blast, is that right?"

"Yes," she gulped. "It was at quite close range."

"Aye, I've seen this sort of delayed reaction before. Sometimes the neural shock those things project takes a while to get out of your system." He examined her pale eyes. "You should be fine, though. You need to get some rest."

Erony sighed. "Your concern is most appreciated, Dr. Beckett. I am not accustomed to feelings of this sort." She looked away. "I pride myself on my fortitude, as all Halcyonites do."

Carson sensed an opportunity here and decided to pursue it. "Is that so? That's funny, because I've seen some people on this planet who have anything but fortitude. What they do have is a sickness that stems from neglect and pollution."

The woman eyed him. "You speak of the bone-rot and the commoners."

"Those people wake up sick every day, and so do their children. And unlike that Wraith blast, your so-called bone-rot won't wear off after a few hours."

"What is your point, Doctor?"

He pointed over the balcony, down at the city. "Those people keep your society alive, miss. But your fellows in there are letting them die by inches. I could help, if you'd agree to it. I can help the commoners set up vaccination stations, provide them with vitamin boosters, for starters."

Erony sighed again. "In the past, I have tried to bring the plight of the people to my father's ears, but he does not wish to dwell on it. He is like all nobles, Doctor, he despises weakness in all its forms. That is how the commoners are seen, as feeble and worthless. My father is only interested in strength."

Carson frowned. "I'm not talking to him, I'm talking to you. I'm sure that the Lady Erony has enough influence to do what I'm asking."

She was silent for a long moment; then she gave him a firm nod, as the color returned to her cheeks. "Very well," she said. "I will do this. I confess your comrade Dr. McKay has impressed upon me the need for directness above all else. Since the arrival of your party on my world, I find myself thinking... Differently."

"Aye, that's Rodney's influence all right." Beckett gave her a smile. "Thank you, miss. You won't regret it."

Erony paused for a moment. "Doctor, before you go, there is something I must tell you. My father will be searching for your friend as he promised, but he has not been entirely forthcoming about the manner in which it will take place."

"What do you mean?"

"Our codes of conduct are complex. In matters such as this where a prisoner has been taken in order to gain leverage over another, if the abductee is recovered then he who performed the rescue can legally hold the prisoner themselves."

Carson took this in. "You mean like a 'finders, keepers' sort of rule?"

"If I follow your meaning, yes."

"Then I guess we'd better find him first."

The court was dissipating as Beckett caught up with Sheppard. John listened intently as the doctor relayed the content of his conversation with Daus's daughter.

"That changes things," said Teyla.

"Not really," said Ronon. "I was going to suggest we go find him ourselves anyway. Think about it; do we want to trust these people to bring back McKay in one piece?"

Sheppard nodded. "Rodney's part of our team and we don't ever let someone else go after one of ours. Teyla, Carson." He turned to them. "Get Clarke into the guest quarters and settle him there. Mason, you and Bishop make sure you keep them secure."

"What are you planning, John?" said Beckett.

"When those men in gray took McKay, they also took his gear. If we assume they're keeping them together, then there's a possibility we can track the power signature of Rodney's scanner unit from the Puddle Jumper. We find it, we find him."

"Assuming they haven't just tossed it in a ditch somewhere," said Carson, "assuming you pass over the right area. Assuming it's still switched on."

Sheppard shrugged. "Well, I never said it was going to be a cakewalk."

As they began to move away, Beckett halted the colonel. "John. I know you have immediate problems to deal with, but I have to say something. The bigger picture here on Halcyon is never going to alter unless there's some serious changes on this planet."

"So what are you asking, Doc? You want me to go all *Braveheart* and start a revolution? Can't wait to hear what Weir would think of that…"

"All I'm saying colonel, is that I don't think there's going to be an easy solution to all this."

Sheppard gave him a rueful look. "On that, Carson, you and I are in total agreement."

He took the Puddle Jumper up and out of the city sprawl at a deliberately low velocity, ignoring the shouts of alarm from the sentries on the battlements as the drum-shaped shuttle-craft whined past them. Once they were a few miles away, and Sheppard was satisfied that they weren't being observed, he opened up the throttle on the Ancient ship and turned the vessel on its tail. The drive outriggers glowed blue-white and the Jumper described a ballistic trajectory, rising rapidly up through the atmosphere of Halcyon.

Even in moments like these, when they were on dangerous ground, John found it easy to lose himself in the sheer thrill of flying the ship. He could manage most of the Jumper's flight profile without removing his grip from the two-part yoke that extended from the pilot's console; it was an Ancient version of something the military back home called a HOTAS — Hands On Throttle And Stick — a control mechanism that made sure a pilot never had to flail about searching for the right switch when a split-second decision was needed. But the Jumper was more than that. Each time Sheppard took the left-hand seat in this bird, he could feel the craft like it was a presence in his head. It was faint, the gentlest of touches somewhere in the depths of his gray matter, but on some level the genetic heritage that John shared with the Ancients connected him to the vessel in a way that nothing else could.

The Jumpers handled smoothly, too. They flew like a heli-copter at low speeds, moving into a mode similar to a jet fighter at high velocity, and then to something akin to an F-302 in the vacuum of space. At least, that's what Sheppard thought. In the past, the colonel had compared notes on the Jumpers with Marine Corps pilots who'd flown Harriers, guys who had trained with the Navy on F/A-18A Hornets, even former Space Shuttle crew; each of them had a different take on the ships. He wondered if the control systems in the craft were smart enough to read his memories of flying Pave Hawks and F-15s and configure them-selves to match. He wouldn't have put it past the Ancients to build these things that way.

The sky outside the canopy darkened from teal blue to black, and with a slight shudder, they transitioned from the atmosphere and into space. Sheppard slowed the ship's forward velocity to nothing and let them hang there in a geo-stationary orbit high over the capital city. He glanced over his shoulder. Ronon was hunched over a console at what was usually McKay's station, picking at keys on the panel.

"Give me a moment," said Dex, aware of his scrutiny. "I've watched him work these sensor arrays enough times, I can run them."

Sheppard flexed his fingers around the flight yoke. "Let's assume that the gray guys had a gyro-flyer for their egress," he said, thinking aloud. "Based on the top speed of the helos we've seen since we got here and the location of the dolmen, we should be able to narrow down a search area..."

Obediently, the Jumper's internal systems anticipated his requests and threw a display on to the inside of the canopy glass. It sketched a map in wire frame form, drawing a wide circle across Halcyon's central continent. "I love this ship," said John. He patted the console as if it was a well-trained dog. "Good girl."

A strident tone sounded from Ronon's seat and another layer of detail dropped in over the map. "Sensors are on-line," said the Satedan, "scanning for energy traces."

A couple of emerald green blips immediately appeared on the display, one dead center in the search pattern, the other in the heart of the capital city. "That's gotta be the Ancient tech inside the dolmen," Sheppard pointed at the first, "and that's Teyla. I left my hand-held scanner with her." His heart sank as the rest of the map remained barren. "Come on, Rodney, where are you?"

"Something could blocking the sensors," offered Dex. "They might be holding him underground, or they might have just destroyed his kit."

John shook his head. "Nah, unless they had him at the bottom of a mineshaft, we'd read it." He blew out a breath. "I'm going to take her up into a higher orbit. We may have to do this the hard way and run the sensors over the whole damn planet."

"You think they took him off world?"

"No, that's against their codes, remember? It's all about the rules."

The other man grimaced. "Their honor codes didn't stop them threatening us. You think they know that Atlantis is still in one piece?"

"Vekken is smart, I'll give him that, but he's just fishing. There's no way they could know that Atlantis survived the Wraith siege. I made sure I Gated to a neutral planet before I went back for the Jumper, and Kenealy did the same thing when he went with Hill's body. Our people know not to dial direct unless it's a matter of life or death."

Ronon looked away, his face creasing in annoyance. "This is a planet full of liars."

Sheppard chuckled. "You sound like my dad watching C-SPAN."

The colonel worked the controls, and the Jumper drew further away from the surface, the pale blue of Halcyon's oceans and the green-brown of its landmasses turning beneath the ship's hull.

"There is another way we could do this," said Ronon, after a moment.

"At this point, I'm open to any suggestions," noted Sheppard.

"We should play these people at their own game."

John threw him a look. "What, we call in troops from Atlantis and fight one of their private little wars? I don't think so."

"That's not what I meant. Daus and his nobles think they're superior here, but we're the ones with the real edge. We could cloak the Jumper, go in and snatch his lordship... Or better yet, call in Caldwell and get the *Daedalus* to beam him up right in the middle of one of his pompous speeches. If he doesn't tell us what we want to know, we toss him out an airlock."

"That would be regicide. I'm not quite ready to go killing kings yet."

"I didn't say kill him," Ronon continued. "Throw him into space for a couple of seconds, then beam him back in. That'll make anyone talk. Might have to do it a few times, though. He looks like a sturdy guy."

Sheppard sighed. "We don't even know if Daus is behind it." But in all honesty, the colonel knew how lame his denial sounded.

"That's how we would find out."

John turned in his chair. "We are not doing the airlock thing, okay? End of discussion."

"Just trying to be helpful."

On the canopy display, a glowing red dot emerged from the far side of Halcyon's day-night terminator. "Wait a second. What is that?"

"A satellite?" Ronon glanced at the sensor console. "Daus's people put something in orbit?"

The colonel shook his head. "They don't have the technology to build rockets that would get up this far..." He studied the display. "It's smaller than the Jumper. It's definitely something artificial." Sheppard changed their heading and eased the throttle forward. "Let's go take a closer look."

The object grew from a glittering dot and began to take on a clear shape and form. Ronon rose from his chair to stand at Sheppard's shoulder as the colonel brought the Puddle Jumper up into a matching orbit. Dex studied the vaguely ovoid shape of the thing, his mind racing to place it. He had seen things like it before, a long time ago, in the skies over other worlds.

A pair of spindly solar panels turned as he watched it grow larger, catching a glimmer of pale light from Halcyon's star. Ronon could make out detail now, the fluted curvature of the object's structure, the peculiar asymmetrical contours like carved bone.

A shock of icy cold flooded his veins. "Wraith!" he snapped. "It's a Wraith satellite!"

Sheppard was already reacting, veering away as the readings on the Jumper's sensors changed. The Satedan had the fleeting impression of a flower blossoming as the alien machine opened to reveal a cluster of gun muzzles. Energy flashed and abruptly the blackness around them was bright with a deadly storm of photons.

The pilot threw the ship hard over, then back again, and the inertial dampers struggled to compensate. Ronon lost his footing and fell heavily into McKay's chair, grabbing the sensor console to steady himself. Dex had left the scanners running in full spectrum mode, and they were dutifully gathering data, rains of information trickling down the screen as the satellite re-oriented itself and fired again.

Glancing shots sent electrical surges through the glowing panels either side of the cabin, and an emerald pane spat sparks and went dead. Sheppard brought the Jumper around in a tight arc and the Wraith construct loomed large. Targeting cues bracketed the object on the heads-up display and John grinned. "I got tone." He squeezed a trigger bar and Ronon heard the *snap-hiss* of a drone launch. A pair of glowing missiles looped away toward the satellite, their odd squid-like profiles cutting an unerring course through the black.

Puffs of thruster gas jetted from the satellite as the machine attempted to dodge the incoming fire, but the drones split apart and came in at the Wraith device from two different points on the axis. The satellite was caught between them and shattered in an explosion of light and fragments. Pieces of bony matter and warped twists of metal clattered off the hull as the Jumper swerved away from the blast.

"Nice shot," noted Dex.

Sheppard accepted the compliment with a nod. "I thought so."

Ronon blew out a breath, the adrenaline rush of the brief battle waning. He studied the sensor screen. The data there was dense and largely beyond his understanding, but there were parts of the readings that he could decipher.

"That was a close call," said the colonel. "Lucky for us you recognized that thing."

"It's a marker beacon," he noted, "a bigger version of that device we found in the tavern on M3Y-465."

"That doesn't sound promising. What's it doing here?"

"The Wraith use them to tag a planet. Their scout craft scope out systems where there might be large populations and then leave one of those behind. Hive ships come in later and do the actual culling."

Sheppard turned the Jumper's sensors to run a wide scan of the surrounding space. "No sign of any other vessels in the system. It can't have been put there recently."

Ronon frowned at the console. "Might be able to get a reading..." He hissed a particularly nasty Satedan curse under his breath. "Why couldn't he have made working this thing simpler?"

"You got something?"

"Wait!" snapped Dex. "I'm not as smart as McKay, I can't figure this out as quickly!" He was silent for a few moments, working through the data. At last, the console gave an answering beep. "Here. Radiation scan indicates that thing was at least ten thousand years old."

"It must have been dropped here when the Ancients and the Wraith were still duking it out for the galaxy," Sheppard opined. "Question is, has it been talking to any of its friends in the meantime?"

Ronon shrugged. It annoyed him that this was beyond his skills. "I don't know, I can't decipher this. Maybe Teyla..."

The colonel was silent for a moment. "All right, we're going back down. Daus will have to be told what we found. We can't detect Rodney from up here anyhow." The Jumper's engines rose in pitch as the spacecraft turned about and dipped back into Halcyon's gravity well. "We're going to have to find another way to get to him."

"One thing," rumbled Dex, "when we find McKay, don't tell him I said he was smarter than me. If you do, I'll break your legs."

Sheppard rolled his eyes. "Whatever you say."

Dr. Rodney McKay rolled awake and sneezed violently, his entire body contorting in a sharp spasm. His hands came up to his chest in claws and he gagged; the entire effect was as if he was attempting the comical impersonation of a rat. It was this unfortunate physical tic that had earned him the nickname 'Rodent' from some of the more unpleasant pupils who had shared his time at junior high school.

Of course, that was in the days before he had left them all behind, before his teachers had finally had the intelligence to move him from the category of 'bright' to 'child prodigy' and then to 'quite staggeringly clever'. So what if they said it had stunted his social skills, so what? He was smarter than them. The jocks and popular girls who had called him names, what were they doing with their lives now, huh? Living in some dreary suburban nowheresville with their stupid gas-guzzling SUVs, their drink problems, their spiraling debts and their two-point-three ugly children, while Rodent—*no, damn it, my name is Rodney!*—got to make world-changing science, travel through wormholes, visit strange new worlds and get shot—

Get. Shot.

It all came thundering back to him and he blinked out of his half-aware daze. He remembered the heavy metal weight of the pistol in his hand, the way it bucked and snapped when he fired blindly at the men in gray fatigues. He remembered Erony screaming, calling out his name. And most of all, he remembered the blunt prow of the stunner pistol tracking toward him, the sliver weapon lit by the sullen green glow of its power cell.

Rodney went tense as his muscles recalled the horrific, heart-stopping shock as the energy blast took him, consciousness flooding out as the unblemished floor of the dolmen's control room rose up to meet him. Then darkness, black and cold. And now here.

He blinked; his vision was blurry but it was improving with every passing second. Feeling with his hands, McKay found a wall and used it to get to his feet, fighting down the woozy after-shock as he dragged himself up it. The wall was cold and clammy, and it gave a little in the way that something organic might.

A deep breath; and then another. The air was chilly too, and there were mingled scents on it. Dust, eons and eons of dust beneath something appallingly familiar. A metallic stench, like battery acid.

The room he was in took on solidity as his eyes focused, and the blue-black walls of chitinous matter gave him the answer as to where he was. The most terrible, awful answer that he could have had. "No," he muttered, "no no no No *NO*!" Rodney threw himself at the narrow entrance to the dim little cell, his fingers digging into the web of thick, fibrous ropes that blocked the doorway. He pulled and shouted, fear rolling up inside him in a dark tide; at that moment he would have given anything to be in nowheresville, in junior high, anywhere but here.

McKay's cries echoed out along the corridors of the Wraith Hive Ship, ignored and unanswered.

CHAPTER EIGHT

Colonel Sheppard looked out through the Jumper's canopy at the Fourth Dynast blackcoats milling around outside the ship. They had emerged from the cloisters around the open plaza within moments of the ship landing there. John wasted no time getting Teyla inside and closing the hatch behind her. He wanted this conversation to be just between the three of them.

She was nodding as Ronon replayed the events of their short venture into orbit and back. The Athosian woman's expression hardened when Dex spoke about the Wraith machine they'd obliterated. John knew that look of old; he could read Teyla's feelings, the same thoughts that had clouded his mood now forming in her. He opened his mouth to speak and realized there was a Halcyonite rifleman standing just a meter or so away on the other side of the canopy glass. The trooper was staring directly at him, blankly intimidating with his lance-rifle held at arms.

Sheppard very deliberately turned his back on the soldier before he started speaking. The movie of the week on Atlantis last month had been *2001: A Space Odyssey*, and John suddenly recalled the scene in the pod bay where the Hal computer had lip-read the plans of the human astronauts. He didn't want to chance that Daus trained his men with the same kind of skills. "With that satellite in pieces, any immediate danger is over," he began, "but clearly the bigger problem we've got to consider is if that thing has been broadcasting. There could already be Wraith Hive Ships in hyperspace and on their way here as we speak."

"That all depends on how long the satellite had been transmitting for," noted Ronon, "and we don't know for sure if it was. But given our usual fortunes, I wouldn't count on us being that lucky."

"Upbeat as ever," said Sheppard. "Teyla, you wanna chime

in here?"

The woman took McKay's station and scrutinized the data captured from the Wraith device. "I have an idea how we might determine if it was in communication with other craft. From what I know of these marker beacons, they operate in a dormant mode, often for centuries, until triggered by a command from a Wraith vessel." She paged through the reams of information, searching for something. "Interstellar communications require a lot of power, John. These beacons run on solar batteries."

Sheppard got it. "Right, so transmitting a message would take a lot of energy. If the batteries are low, it's likely it sent out a dinner call." He smiled with gallows humor. "Like a Wraith equivalent of those neon signs by the highway — Good Eats, Next Exit…"

"Here," said Teyla, halting the flow of text. She pointed at a string of computer code. The tension in her shoulders visibly lessened as she read through the data. "I think you may be wrong about our luck, Ronon. According to this, the power reserves on the satellite were barely depleted. It was still in an information gathering mode when you happened upon it."

"If you're right, then it must have been activated recently," added Dex, "but why now, after thousands of years of drifting up there in silence? It doesn't make sense."

"We're missing a piece of the puzzle here," said Sheppard, "a big piece, and you gotta know that McKay's connected to it."

Teyla looked away. "If he still lives."

"If they wanted him dead, we'd be looking at his corpse," Ronon said flatly, "we know the nobles aren't squeamish about bloodshed and murder."

Sheppard sat and worked it through, thinking aloud. "If they just wanted a hostage, why take him?"

Ronon shrugged "He's the weak link, he can barely handle a weapon. He's the one I'd choose if I wanted a captive."

"I don't buy that. If they just wanted non-combatants, they could have tagged Beckett and the medical team. No, they took Rodney for what he knows. Or what he found out at the dolmen."

"We can't rule out that it was Erony who set him up," added Dex. "I don't buy Vekken's explanation as to why they left her behind."

Teyla shook her head in disgust. "The more I learn about these people, the less I understand them. Making false glory out of warfare and taking innocents for barter. On Athos, no tribe would ever be allowed to do such things."

"Hostage-taking is just another weapon."

A sharp tap on the Jumper's canopy drew John's attention. Vekken stood at the prow of the ship, peering in at them. The adjutant made no attempt to hide the lingering, appraising look he gave the interior of the Ancient craft. "Lieutenant Colonel Sheppard," he called. "I bring good news. Dr. McKay's whereabouts have been located."

"What? Where?"

Vekken inclined his head. "His Highness the Lord Magnate will provide you with the specifics, if you would accompany me."

The Magnate met them in the gardens where they had spoken before. Sheppard had to admit he was getting royally sick of being 'summoned' every five minutes and submitting to 'audiences' at Daus's whim. He toyed for a moment with the idea of ordering Vekken to bring the ruler to them, just to throw a wrench in the works, but relented. It was their planet, and they expected the Atlantis team to play by their rules. He thought of Weir's advice about letting Daus remain convinced he had the stronger position, and chewed his lip. With each passing moment, it was getting harder and harder to play that role. As ever, First Minister Muruw was hovering at his leader's side, open contempt on his face.

John didn't wait for the usual florid phrase of greeting to spill from Daus's lips; he went straight for the jugular instead. "Where's McKay?"

The Magnate's eyes flashed with irritation at this breach in protocol. "Safe, for the moment. One of my most trusted hunt splinters has located him and determined that he is unharmed and in good spirits."

That's a lie if ever I heard it, thought Sheppard. 'Good spirits' would be the last thing Rodney would exhibit if he'd been held prisoner. "We want our team mate back, right now."

"That is in hand," Daus replied, ignoring the implied *or else* in Sheppard's statement, "but in keeping with the codes of conduct, I am afraid that it would not be proper to merely hand him over to you without... Recompense."

"Proper?" grated Ronon. "You think just because you make war with a rulebook at your back that you can play games with men's lives?"

It was as if Dex had never spoken. "There must be a balance, Lieutenant Colonel. Give and take."

Sheppard folded his arms. "Fine. You want something in return for McKay's rescue, then how about this? I just shot down a Wraith marker satellite in orbit around your planet, thus saving your entire world from the arrival of a culling fleet. I figure that's a fair trade."

Muruw made an explosive snort of scorn. "Is that so? Then, pray tell, where is the proof of such a daring exploit? Please, do show us the evidence of your kill!"

Ronon pointed into the sky. "It's burning up in your atmosphere right now."

"Oh," the minister continued in an arch tone, "so then you have no trophy? Nothing that corroborates this wild claim? I am afraid that with empty palms you have no stock with which to trade."

John's hands contracted into fists. The man's patronizing tone was like nails down a chalkboard. "I could take you for a look, if you'd like," he retorted, "you might find it a little chilly up there, though." Ronon's suggestion about the airlock was starting to seem like a good idea.

Daus gave a languid nod of his head. "The people of Halcyon thank you for your bravery in their defense," he noted, "but I am afraid that this matter requires a different solution."

Inwardly, Sheppard sagged. "Let's hear it. What do you want?" *This is going to be the Genii thing all over again...*

"You recall the rogue Wraith I spoke of? The one we call Scar?"

"Yeah…"

"It is to my eternal disappointment that I have never been able to kill that creature, and our recent venture to the forest of Carras rekindled my hate for the beast. My proposal is a modest one, Lieutenant Colonel. Bring me Scar, dead or alive, and in return my men will see that Dr. McKay is safely returned to your company."

Sheppard blinked. "You want us to hunt the Wraith for you?"

"If you think you are capable," sniffed Muruw.

"That's all?" Ronon asked. "What's the catch?"

Daus smiled, showing teeth. "Ah, such bravery! But be warned, Runner. Scar is a deadly adversary. He has the blood of many hunters on his hands."

Sheppard exchanged looks with Teyla and Ronon. Each of them knew that there was more to this than the Magnate was letting on, but they had little choice. Once more, they were being forced to play along. "All right. We get you something you can have stuffed and mounted, you deliver Dr. McKay."

The Magnate clapped his hands. "Splendid! Muruw will provide you with charts of Scar's known feeding grounds. Best of luck, Lieutenant Colonel!"

Vekken watched the Atlanteans depart, letting the dagger-like glares from the Runner and the Athosian woman roll off him. He considered them both; the Runner was unapologetic about what he was, and in a way, he was to be admired for such honesty. But the man was crude and artless, and for all his prowess he lacked an understanding of combat's true grace and glory. Vekken understood that no amount of instruction would ever change Ronon Dex's mind. He was like the wild Wraith that way, too unstable to ever be made into Hounds, to be domesticated. On the other hand, the woman Teyla Emmagan was a contradiction. He found her attractive on the most visceral level and the adjutant had to admit that her skills were good; and yet, even though they shared the bond of the Wraithkin, he could not help but think of her as inferior. After all, she came from a planet of tribals who still participated in ridiculous deity worship rituals. Even though her master Sheppard had tried to dress her up in his people's uniform, she was still a primitive underneath. Vekken had hoped at the beginning that he might have been able to barter something to Sheppard in return for her indenture, but he saw now that this was unlikely. Sheppard was the strangest of them all, a peculiar mixture of the strong and the weak who had no right to call himself a soldier... And yet here he was, against all odds. Vekken looked up and the Lord Magnate beckoned him closer. He wondered if his master would order him to kill these Atlanteans today. The adjutant sensed that such a decision was very close at hand, and it surprised Vekken how contemplation of it troubled him. But then, he was not a man to challenge his master's commands; Vekken was, above all things, a weapon in the hands of the Magnate. He did not have the luxury of questions, of guilt, of hesitation.

He bowed low. "Your Highness?"

"Have a gyro-flyer track the Atlantean vessel's movements. I want you to keep yourself informed via telekrypter of all that transpires during their hunt."

"Your will, My Lord."

Daus considered him for a moment. "Tell me, Vekken. Do you think the Atlanteans will be able to fulfill my mandate? As a warrior, how do you estimate their chances of taking Scar?"

"A difficult question, Highness," admitted the adjutant. "They fight with competence, their weapons are formidable... But they find it hard to kill. The purity of that instinct is lacking in them, their leader most of all."

The Magnate bent close to Vekken, his voice falling to a low murmur. "Just so," he agreed. "I find myself hoping that the beast Scar will serve me today. I imagine that the Wraith will kill them all, and rid me of these outworlders."

Vekken felt a thrill of shock but did not show it. "If I may beg to say, Highness, but what will you do if they succeed in the hunt?"

"Ah," said Daus, sounding out the word. "In that event, it would be better that Sheppard's people never live to tell of it. After all, it would be detrimental to the well being of our society if our people believe that outworlders made so important a kill. Better that the nobility be seen to have done such a thing. Don't you agree?"

"As you command," Vekken replied.

The Magnate nodded again. "I do indeed."

The Puddle Jumper made it across the countryside in half the time of the fast helo that had taken them to the forest enclosure the previous day. Sheppard concentrated on flying the ship at tree top level while Ronon, Teyla and Private Bishop went through weapons checks in the back of the cabin. With poor grace, Staff Sergeant Mason accepted Sheppard's orders to remain with the injured Corporal Clarke and Beckett's team. He had insisted the senior man stay behind, putting his trust in the SAS soldier to keep the others safe while John's team went on their hunter's outing.

There was one other command Sheppard had given, this time to Carson, and it wasn't an order that sat well with him. Things were moving fast now, and despite Teyla's suggestion that the Wraith orbiter hadn't been broadcasting, the colonel didn't want to take that for fact. He gave Beckett the full story and reluctantly told him to get in contact with Atlantis. Weir had to be told what was going on here, and if that meant risking a radio signal through an open wormhole to the ocean planet, then so be it. He knew that Carson had the ear of Daus's daughter, and he trusted the doctor to use his influence to get a message through the Gate even if he didn't trust Erony. After all, the Magnate had decreed that nobody was allowed to travel through the Stargate; he hadn't said anything about beaming communications through it.

"Any sign of that chopper that was following us, boss?" asked Bishop, slamming an ammunition clip into his assault rifle.

The colonel glanced at a sensor-scope on the head-up display. "He's still out there behind us, runnin' his throttle at maximum in a vain attempt to keep up."

"Maybe you should cloak us," said Ronon, "give them a real fright."

Sheppard shook his head. "Nah, I'm saving that surprise in case we need it. Never hurts to keep an ace up your sleeve."

They made a quick circuit of the enclosure as Teyla pored over the paper map that Muruw had grudgingly given to them. "This document shows several locations where the Wraith Scar was sited." She pointed to the west. "That is the most recent."

"I'll look for somewhere to put us down." He slowed the Jumper, searching for a clearing.

Behind him, Bishop was peering at the hand-held scanner. "Red dots mean Wraiths, right?"

"Yup,"

"That's not good, sir. This thing looks like it's got the measles." The soldier held up the device; the small screen was speckled with shifting red symbols spread out over the entire area.

Ronon stroked his chin. "We could hit them from the air with the drones. That might thin them out a little."

Sheppard nodded. "Nice idea, but we have to bring this creep back intact, remember? Somehow I'm guessing Daus won't accept a bunch of Wraith cold cuts instead." A clearing appeared to port and he put the ship into a hover. "Here we go. I want a quick dispersal when we hit the dirt. Two fire teams; Ronon's with me, Teyla goes with Bishop."

He heard the noise and it brought him up short. The nerves in limbs went tight with anticipation, a reaction so ingrained in his physiology that it happened without conscious thought. The others with him snarled and yowled at one another, spooked by their pack leader's sudden change in manner. He turned his face to them and showed a mouth full of fangs, hissing sibilantly. They quieted, retreating, cowed into submission like the animals that they had become.

He looked up; yes, his senses had not deceived him. The sound that reached through the forest canopy was not the rhythmic thrum of a propeller, not the noise from the human air vessels that came and went, dropping off fresh prey. This sound touched a chord inside him, it flashed on a memory from before. *From the war. Before the long sleep.*

Movement above. It appeared and disappeared through a gap in the trees, just the quickest flash of dark green metal, antigravity drives whining like insects to keep it up in the sky. Feral hate ran hot through him in a wave of recognition. An enemy ship. It was one of *their* craft, undoubtedly. A machine that belonged to the old adversary, the prey-race that had dared to defy the mastery of his species. *So long ago.*

Thoughts wheeled and turned in his mind, base desires to kill and feed warring with higher questions of how and why. He dismissed them all with a wave of his clawed hand, as if he were swatting at a nagging insect. *Focus.* He had to have focus.

His iron hard self-control flexed but did not break; on days such as these it was difficult to drive the haze from his mind, to concentrate on keeping his thoughts whole and alert. It would be easy to slip into the madness of the beast, just like these pitiful wretches around him. Not all of his kindred had the strength of will to fight off the static in their psyche for hour after hour, every single day. Many fell quickly, subsumed by their own animal natures, some too crazed even to recognize him for what he was, as their superior. Those they fed upon, as they were fit for nothing else. They kept his pack alive when the human prey was thin on the ground.

The ache of hunger came upon him. This was the hardest call to resist, the most basic desire of his species. He felt the tremble of the need in his arm, the fleshy gray petals of the feeding maw in his palm opening on their own.

The others backed away, whimpering. They were afraid that he would take one of them to sate himself. Instead he cocked his head, letting the white tails of his mane fall forward.

The Wraith blinked his one good eye and ran a casual finger over the ruined socket of the other, tracing a broad line of ruined tissue down his cheek. His kind healed fast, but the sword cut that had left that mark upon him had been deep and nearly fatal. He sometimes imagined that it was only his hate that had allowed him to survive such an injury; and now the same emotion propelled him forward, into the trees and after the noise of the aerial vessel.

His pack snarled and spat, loping after their scar-faced leader, picking up on his eagerness for a new kill.

The Jumper sealed behind them, the two teams split off from the landing site and made their way into the trees. Ronon's last glimpse of Teyla Emmagan was a curt nod of her head before she followed Private Bishop into the foliage. Dex gripped his particle magnum firmly in one hand, the hilt of his short sword in the other. Ahead of him, Sheppard made himself a compact silhouette, moving quickly but carefully with his P90 at his shoulder.

"Is there some kind of plan I should know about?" asked the Satedan. "Or are we just going to wander around aimlessly until we trip over some Wraith?"

"That *is* the plan," said the colonel, "although without the 'aimless' part. We find the mark, we bag him. Simple."

"Simple," repeated Ronon, in a tone that make it clear he thought this was anything but. "I don't like following that fat aristo's orders."

"Oh, and I do?" Sheppard shook his head. "Believe me, this wasn't my first choice for getting McKay rescued either. Putting more people in harm's way…"

"Say we do this thing. What if Daus doesn't turn McKay over to us? What do we do then?"

The other man halted. "If that happens, I might revise my opinion on that airlock suggestion of yours. Until then, though, we play the hand we got."

Dex dropped into a crouch and fingered a broken plant stem protruding from the forest floor. He moved windblown leaves to uncover prints in the earth. "Wraith. These are recent. Less than a day old." Ronon pointed with his pistol. "Four of them, moving that way."

Sheppard toggled his radio. "Teyla, Bishop. We got tracks

here. Four Wraith, heading in a northerly direction."

The Athosian woman halted in the shade of a tree. "I hear you, Colonel. Private Bishop has also discovered traces of Wraith activity. There are human bones here." She glanced at the ditch where the SAS soldier was standing. "It appears to be a midden."

"*Copy that,*" came the reply. "*Are you, uh, sensing anything?*"

Teyla gave a slight shudder. "Yes," she said, at length. In truth, the buzz of Wraith telepathy had been slowly strengthening in her mind as they approached the enclosure, and now they were here on the ground, her preternatural sense of the predatory creatures was a constant companion. "I... I think he's watching us. There are several of them out there, but one... Just one..." She shook the thoughts away. "Be on your guard, Colonel. Scar must be close."

"*Same goes for you. Shoot first if you make contact. Remember, we don't need this creep alive. Sheppard out.*"

Bishop moved forward. "You all right, miss?"

She nodded and set off again. "I will be."

The soldier gave her a wary look. "Can you, like, turn that off?" He tapped a finger on his temple. "I'm just thinking that if you can hear the bozos, they maybe they can hear you too."

Teyla shook her head. "I control it as best I can. Believe me, it is a 'gift' I wish I was not forced to endure." She threw him a questioning look. "What is the meaning of that word you use for the Wraith?"

"What, you mean *Bozo*?" Teyla nodded and Bishop smirked. "Well, y'know, it's 'cos of their faces. They're all pasty and white, aren't they? Like clowns." The smirk faded. "Never liked clowns, even when I was a nipper."

She was none the wiser. "The men in your cadre seem to have their own names for many things."

Bishop shrugged. "Well, it's tradition, isn't it? Psychological, yeah? Helps you to keep detached, eyes on the ball, that sorta thing. We got slang for lots of stuff."

Teyla eyed him. "Do you have names for people from Athos or Sateda? For Ronon and myself?"

"Uh." The way the soldier blinked told Teyla that the answer was yes. "It, uh. It's a gesture of respect, miss. We all got nicknames."

"What do you call us?"

Bishop looked sheepish. "Tina. And, uh, Bob. On account of how you look a bit like the singers, see." He gave a weak smile. "I'm not a big fan of the reggae bloke, but I do like that song she does, the one about the dancer—" He broke off.

Teyla heard it too; something moving in the undergrowth.

"Target," growled the soldier, all humor forgotten, bringing his L85 up to sight down the barrel. A gray shape detached itself from the shadow of a fallen tree trunk and threw itself at them. Bishop's rifle snarled and his shots caught the Wraith at the start of a leap, slamming it back down into the dirt.

"More!" snapped the woman, as other aliens burst from cover and came at them. Teyla had her P90 set in burst-fire mode and she unleashed ripping discharges of bullets into the Wraiths that raced at them. Glancing hits twisted one about and she was forced to hit him again just to put the creature out for good. She sensed Bishop draw closer to her, bringing their corridors of fire together.

Almost as quickly as they attacked, the Wraith were either dead or retreating.

"What the hell was that all about?" said the Private.

Teyla's brow furrowed as the sense of the feral minds brushed against her psyche. "He's out there… Watching. He's testing us. Measuring our skills."

"Contact!" cried Sheppard, as the first three Wraiths dropped from the trees overhead. On full automatic, he tore a fist-sized wound in the killer that went for his chest, blasting the alien around into a lethal pirouette.

The crackling howl of Ronon's energy pistol sounded through the air, two shots in as many heartbeats killing a second Wraith attacker before the beast's corpse could strike the forest floor.

The third was already sweeping in and went at the colonel with a massive club cut from a rough-hewn section of tree branch. Sheppard ducked and dodged a blow that could have caved in his skull, but the strike caught his P90 and the sub-machinegun spun from his grip and away. John went low as the alien reversed his attack and threw out two quick kicks to the knee, hard and accurate blows that would have shattered the bones of a normal human being. The Wraith gave a cursory grunt and threw itself at him, striking the colonel with a body-check that slammed the wind from his lungs. Sheppard cried out as the creature flattened him into the ground. Its face was just inches away from his, and the monstrous aspect of the Wraith was mad with wild hunger, strings of drool looping from its wicked snaggle teeth.

He fought back with the only weapon he could reach. Sheppard's combat knife came up in a blur and he buried the black carbon steel blade in the Wraith's eye socket, down to the hilt. The alien screamed and rolled away, clawing at its face. Dex threw him his P90 and John caught it, delivering the coup de grace to the howling creature with a single squeeze of the trigger.

Sheppard rocked back on his haunches. "Dang. That was a close one."

Ronon bent to recover the colonel's knife just as the staccato rattle of gunfire filtered through the trees. "Teyla!" snapped Dex.

"More of them, six o'clock!" shouted Bishop, pivoting on one knee to unleash another burst of fire at the advancing foe. His assault rifle's breech snapped open on an empty chamber and he tore out the ammunition clip. "Reloading!"

Teyla heard the call and turned to cover the soldier as the next wave of Wraiths ran at them. She lay down an arc of punishing fire, killing another and knocking back two more; but they were being hard pressed now, the pale-skinned creatures shifting to get behind them, blocking the route back to the clearing and the parked Puddle Jumper. Bishop slammed a new magazine into his weapon and continued shooting.

The Athosian felt her own gun run dry and quickly swapped out a fresh magazine of transparent plastic, the bullets inside rattling against one another. If these Wraiths had been armed with energy weapons, then this fight would have already been over, she realized. All they had were primitive clubs and axes with flint heads; but even those would be deadly if the aliens got close enough.

"What the hell?" She heard a note of panic in the soldier's voice and to her alarm, Bishop aimed away into the trees and fired shots at nothing. "Shadows!" he shouted. "Bloody shadows!"

"Private!" she shouted, "it's the Wraith, they're trying to deceive you! Playing tricks on your mind!" Teyla pulled him to his feet. "Concentrate!"

"Y-yeah," Bishop blinked, like he was waking from a doze. "I got it."

"Teyla! What's your situation?"

She grimaced at the voice from the radio, firing again. "Heavy Wraith contact, Colonel! We're cut off from the Jumper!"

"Find cover and dig in," replied Sheppard, *"we'll come get you once we deal with our own pest problem."*

Bishop jabbed a finger. "That way! Trees are thicker, it'll slow the buggers down!"

She let the soldier lead the way, sending out pulses of gunfire as the Wraiths came running after them, clambering along the branches of trees over their heads, shrieking and throwing stones. Teyla had never seen such behavior from the aliens before; the orderly and coldly vicious manner they usually displayed in combat was gone, replaced with wild and brutish attacks that bordered on frenzy.

The Athosian woman dispatched another Wraith, sending it wailing to the earth from a perch above; and then she felt it again. The pressure of one mind, hard and invasive inside her skull. Teyla could taste the raw need, and through the alien's senses it was almost as if she could hear the rapid hammering of her own heart. The Wraith the Halcyons called Scar was in her head, taunting her, and with abrupt shock she realized that he was laughing.

Alarm flooded her with adrenaline. "Bishop, no!" she cried, too late to stop him. The soldier took one step too far and stumbled. Beneath them the leaf-strewn ground gave way and disintegrated, a false trapdoor of weak wood and woven grasses yawing open. Teyla and Bishop fell into the concealed pit, tumbling against one another to land hard in the black, choking mud. She struck a half-buried stone and the light behind her eyes dimmed. Teyla's vision went to gray haze, then to blackness and silence.

"Back!" snapped Ronon, sending red streaks of energy past Sheppard and into the advancing rank of feral Wraith. Most of these creatures were barely equipped, their usual armor of chain mail and nacreous hides missing or stripped. That meant that logically they'd go down easier; the reverse seemed to be true, however. Sheppard gritted his teeth and fired on another. These untamed creatures were uncontrollable, moving without the first thought toward their personal safety, driven only by an insane hunger. Already, the colonel had seen some of the Wraith dropping back from their chase in order to savage their own fallen comrades, fighting amongst themselves to feed on their dead. John took the opportunity to introduce them to a couple of fragmentation grenades that he lobbed into the middle of the squabbling pack.

The diversion was enough to get them away, and back toward the safe ground of the Jumper. Without energy weapons, there was no way the marauding wild Wraith would be able to inflict damage on the Ancient ship. He sprinted into the clearing as Ronon cracked off shot after shot at the enemy. The Satedan's pistol was glowing hot at the muzzle. Sheppard tore the handheld from his pocket and stabbed at a pre-set code key string. In return, the Puddle Jumper's rear hatch dropped open to admit them.

"Teyla!" he shouted into his radio. "Teyla, Bishop, do you read me? We're at the Jumper!" Nothing but dead air answered him. He swore under his breath as Dex rounded the back of the shuttlecraft.

"Nothing else is moving out there," said Ronon, "at least not for the moment."

"Get in," snapped Sheppard. "I need to re-arm. Those creeps will be back."

Dex followed him inside as the hatch closed again. He stopped dead as he realized they were alone in the ship. "Where are the others?"

Grim-faced, the colonel threw a nod at the dense tree line.

The sudden silver-white flash of the wormhole's formation made Carson flinch back a little in surprise. The strange cloud of energy the Stargates emitted on activation reminded him of a plume of water, a geyser-like spring of light and color that seemed to unfold from the very air itself. Beckett had heard veterans of the SGC refer to the effect as a 'kawoosh', as a nod to the sound it made as it crashed through molecules of stressed oxygen; try as he might, though, the doctor couldn't hang such a playful name on a discharge of exotic radiation that could engulf anything it came into contact with.

He fingered the combat walkie-talkie in his hand, switching the device to the pre-arranged channel for the mission, and in return he heard the hiss of static in his wireless earpiece that told him it was working. Nearby, Staff Sergeant Mason, his face impassive, approached the event horizon of the Gate as close as he dared. With each footstep, the mechanical turrets surrounding the Stargate whined and moved, steadily tracking Mason, ready to open fire if he flaunted Daus's commands and ran for the wormhole. The doctor counted at least a half-dozen cannons trained on them. Mason recovered a radio from his belt and weighed it in his grip. At last, he met Beckett's gaze.

"Go ahead," said Carson.

The soldier raised the radio to his lips. "Atlantis, are you receiving, over?"

Beckett half-turned as Lady Erony stepped up to the Gate Hangar's stone dais, her adjutant Linnian trailing two steps behind.

She gave a shallow nod. "I engaged the cipher on the podium personally. No record of this opening will be kept, as you requested."

From the corner of his eye, the doctor saw Mason give Erony the slightest of looks at her words. The SAS trooper's distrust of her statement could not have been plainer. In truth, Carson didn't like it any more than he did, dialing direct to Atlantis from Halcyon, but circumstances now meant that they had no other choice; and on the other side of that glimmering disc, Elizabeth Weir was waiting to hear from them.

He sighed and returned the nod. "Thank you, miss. Your discretion is appreciated."

"I have done this in defiance of my father's standing orders. He would be sorely displeased to learn of it." Erony studied him. "But then trust is a very rare commodity on Halcyon, Dr. Beckett, and I do not wish to lose what little I have already accrued with your people." She bowed a little and moved away. "Attend me when your communications are concluded."

Mason gave a small sniff of disdain. He had already made it clear to Carson that he laid the blame for McKay's abduction at Erony's feet, convinced that the girl was working for her father's ends. The doctor wanted the reverse to be true, but as she had said herself, trust was hard to find on this planet. He took a deep breath. By now, the duty officers in Atlantis's Gate Room would have alerted Elizabeth of Mason's signal, so at any second—

"This is Dr. Weir acknowledging receipt of transmission. We're ready to lower the shield at your discretion."

"Elizabeth, it's Carson here," he began, "don't drop the force field. This is just an update."

When she spoke again, Beckett heard the wary tone in her voice. *"Okay, Carson, I understand. What's your status over there? We're at Condition Blue, over."*

Beckett nodded to himself. After Kenealy had Gated back with Hill's body, the other doctor had been under orders to give Weir the full story on what had taken place on Halcyon since Sheppard had left with the Puddle Jumper, and that included

Rodney's kidnapping. As part of new security protocols introduced on Atlantis, they had created a series of seemingly innocuous code phrases that could be inserted into radio communications to allow off world teams to send a warning that they were operating under duress. *Condition Blue* meant that Weir understood that Carson was on unfriendly ground, and she was ready to assist. The doctor searched his memory for a moment for the correct counter-sign. "It's, ah, Condition Yellow," he said. "We're okay here, for the moment."

Elizabeth relaxed a little — but only a little. She stared at the open Stargate, visualizing Carson on the other side, his expression taut with concern. Weir had gone over Kenealy's report a dozen times, scouring it for anything she could use. Other duties vital to the running of Atlantis had slipped as the situation on Halcyon had gotten worse, and she had to admit she was finding it hard to keep her mind on the job at hand while her friends were in harm's way out in the Pegasus Galaxy.

"Can you speak freely?"

"*Aye, go ahead.*"

"I'm ready to come through myself to take up a role as negotiator. Perhaps I might be able to secure Rodney's release if I spoke directly with the Lord Magnate."

There was a pause. "*Staff Sergeant Mason is firmly against that idea, Elizabeth, and I'm sure Colonel Sheppard would be to, if he were here. We don't want to bring another senior member of Atlantis staff in where they can take a shot at them. They might decide you're a better bet than McKay and go for you instead.*"

Weir glanced down from the control room to where a squad of men armed with heavy machine guns and assault rifles stood at the ready, poised to advance through the Stargate on her word. She hated playing the military card, but at this stage her options were very limited. "In that case, Carson, we can go for the more direct approach. Major Lorne and his unit are standing by." Elizabeth left that offer hanging, fully aware that Beckett would understand what she was hinting at.

A different voice broke in on the radio channel. "*Mason here, ma'am. As much as I'd like to agree to that, it's my estimation that a show of greater force would be very bad for your Dr. McKay. We need to deal with this at our end.*"

"I hear you, Staff Sergeant." Elizabeth glanced at the Gate Technician to her right. "Keith, tell Lorne and his team to stand down. For the moment."

Beckett was speaking again. "*Things are moving quickly here. Lord Daus has given us notice that his men have apparently located Rodney, although he hasn't shown any proof yet.*"

Weir frowned. "Apparently? If they found him, why isn't he back with you? Where's Colonel Sheppard?"

"*On a hunting expedition.*" She listened carefully as Carson outlined the content of Sheppard's discussion with the Magnate and the trade of the rogue Wraith for the Atlantis team's scientist.

"And John went along with this?"

"*Aye, although he was nae very happy about it.*" She heard the doctor sigh heavily over the radio link. "*But that's not the worst of it. We potentially have a much bigger problem than McKay's capture. Sheppard detected and destroyed a marker drone in orbit over Halcyon. It was of Wraith origin, Elizabeth. They tagged this planet as a food source thousands of years ago.*"

Weir felt her breath catch in her throat. Beckett's statement hung in the air, and everyone in the control room who heard it felt the same jagged little dagger of fear the word 'Wraith' engendered. They had all been there, watching the storms of weapons fire against the city's shield dome when the aliens had laid siege to Atlantis, and all of them understood the ruthless threat the Wraith posed. She heard a soft, muttered curse from over her shoulder. Dr. Radek Zelenka had entered the control room without her noticing, and now stood there, his face pale behind his glasses.

Elizabeth clamped down on her own concerns and moved past them. "Do you know if the beacon was transmitting? Are there Wraith on the way to you?"

"We can't be sure. It's possible."

She tapped her hand on the console. "Then I want you back here. If Halcyon is under threat of Wraith attack, I don't want my people there a second longer than they need to be."

"That's not going to happen," he replied wearily. *"Gate travel to or from this planet has been suspended, under penalty of being shot to pieces. Until that changes, we're stuck here. And even if we could go, I've still got work to do here. Elizabeth, a lot of these people here are dying."*

"They'll all be dying if the Wraith come for them," muttered Zelenka.

She hated to admit it, but the scientist had a point.

"Carson, making those people healthy isn't going to count for anything if a Hive Ship drops out of hyperspace over their planet!" Weir's voice sounded in Beckett's ear and he looked at Mason once again. The SAS trooper was watching the gun turrets. *"If we want to help the Halcyons, we need to think about evacuating them to another world! Let me come through and I can talk to Daus —"*

"No, Dr. Weir," snapped Mason. "I can't allow that. I'm the ranking military authority here in the Lieutenant Colonel's absence, and I'm telling you this. Anyone who comes through that Gate will be a red smear ten seconds later."

"Staff Sergeant, do I have to remind you who is in command of this expedition?"

Beckett swallowed hard at the soldier's gruesome description, but he saw the sense in it. "Elizabeth, listen. He's right. They'll shoot you down and not even blink."

When Weir spoke again, it was with firm resolve. *"Then in that case, Staff Sergeant Mason, I expect you to make sure Dr. Beckett and the rest of the team are kept safe until we can get all of you home."*

"Orders received and understood, ma'am," replied the soldier.

"Carson?"

"Go ahead."

"*Try to keep out of trouble. In the meantime, I'm going to see if I can get you another ride, understood?*"

Beckett and Mason exchanged glances, an unspoken communication passing between them. There were some things that Weir wasn't willing to discuss on an open channel, but her meaning was clear.

"Understood," replied the doctor, the stress of the last few hours abruptly settling on him. "Halcyon out."

Elizabeth turned to Zelenka, to find the scientist already working at a control console, his hands flying over the glassy Atlantean keypad, then to a laptop, then back again. "Radek, can you pinpoint the —"

"Location of the *Daedalus*?" A semi-transparent screen shimmered and solidified into a display of the Pegasus Galaxy's interstellar region. Zelenka touched a control and three cursors illuminated. "This is us, Atlantis. This is *Daedalus*. This is the Halcyon star system."

Weir gave a small smile at the man's ability to anticipate her request; but then he was a genius, like so many of the experts that had come with her from Cheyenne Mountain. "It's within their hyperspace transit range. We may have another option after all." She gestured to the duty technician. "Get sub-space communications on line for me. Send a priority one flash message to Colonel Caldwell."

"On it," came the reply.

"How long do you think it would take them to make the journey?"

Zelenka licked his lips. "That all depends on the energy flux curve they've been operating on during this voyage. You see, if it's a high co-efficient, then there could be a ten to twenty percent variation in the muon —"

"A ballpark figure, Radek," she broke in. "I don't need the decimal places."

"Oh. Of course. Ball-park." He hesitated, considering. "Thirty, perhaps thirty-five hours."

Weir studied the screen. "Is there nothing they could do to

shave some time off that?"

Zelenka shook his head. "Even if they run the drives hot, it still wouldn't make more than a couple of hours difference. Hyperspace travel doesn't work like conventional rockets. It is all gravity curvatures and boson intersections." He gave her a weak grin. "As a famous engineer once said, 'you cannot change the laws of physics.'"

"A famous engineer?"

"Yes. I believe he was from Moscow."

"Dr. Weir?" The technician called out. "I have *Daedalus* on the comm."

She tapped her headset. "Colonel Caldwell?"

The voice of the starship's commander crackled from a hidden speaker. "*Doctor. You're lucky you caught us. We've been conducting experiments on the edge of a Jovian planet's atmosphere, using the hydrogen ram scoop array developed by Colonel Carter.*"

Even though she couldn't see him, Weir held up her hand for quiet. "Colonel, as much as I would usually be fascinated by such an interesting scientific endeavor, I'm afraid I have to ask you to cut it short. We have a situation in the Halcyon system, a few parsecs from your current location." She entered a data string on her computer. "I'm sending you galactic co-ordinates for the system on a side channel, along with everything we have up until now on the mission there."

"*Let me guess,*" Caldwell said dryly. "*Sheppard's team is in trouble?*"

"For starters."

At another time, Caldwell might have argued the matter with her or made an issue of Sheppard's involvement; but the professional relationship between Weir and the captain of the *Daedalus* had now grown to the point where each had a level of respect for the other, and to Caldwell's credit he accepted her orders without question. "*Tell me what I need to know, Doctor, and we'll be on our way.*"

"There's a good possibility that the planet Halcyon is under imminent threat of Wraith attack, and right now our people can't

Gate off world. You are to proceed to Halcyon at full military speed and offer all assistance needed to Colonel Sheppard and his team... And be prepared to engage the Wraith in force when you get there."

She heard Caldwell take a deep breath. "*All right. Daedalus concurs.*" After a moment, the colonel spoke again, quietly so that only Weir could hear him. "*Elizabeth, that planet's a day and a half away even at full throttle. If the Wraith are heading there, we may already be too late.*"

"I know, Colonel," she admitted. "Good hunting, *Daedalus*. Atlantis out."

CHAPTER NINE

The cavern was dank and smelled faintly of rotting meat. No human hunter had ever dared to venture this deep into the core of the enclosure; or at least if they did, they never returned to speak of it.

The Wraith that the Halcyons had christened 'Scar' toyed with some of the items his pack mates had stripped from the prey, picking them up and sniffing them, moving them about with a clawed finger. Presently, he gathered up a pistol made of black steel and turned it in his hand. The weapon was interesting. Scar recognized the shape and form of a primitive ballistic firearm, but at the same time he could see that this was far more advanced than the guns carried by the hunters they usually culled. He licked the frame, tasting sweat and the smallest remnants of flesh-scent there. Scar had always been fascinated by the machinery of lesser species, the way that they forced metals from the ground into hard shapes instead of fashioning organics, bone and bio-matter as the Wraith did. It was a peculiarity of his, an affectation his kindred rarely shared.

One of the pack spat angrily as it came upon something in the pile, and Scar snatched it from his grip. The Wraith growled; the device was a small screen with buttons about its frame, made from some sort of crystalline material that glowed with an inner light. Scar knew the origin of it immediately. The old enemy, his kind's most ancient foe, had fabricated this. With a sudden jerk of motion, the Wraith threw the device into the air and fired the human weapon at it. Sharp retorts of sound echoed around the cave with yellow flashes of discharge from the barrel. The pack snarled at the noise, but Scar grinned widely as the Ancient scanner struck the rock in a rain of broken fragments.

The gunfire jerked Teyla from her painful slumber and she

twitched against gooey bonds that held her hands behind her back. The Athosian blinked and tried to make sense of where she was, remembering the trapdoor and the black pit beneath it. She looked around. *A cave. No way to know how much time has passed.* She caught sight of Bishop, similarly secured a few feet away. He was wavering on the edge of alertness, his head lolling. Teyla tried to work her wrists free, but she had no success. The thick, gelatinous matter that ensnared them was some kind of secreted web, pliant but impossible to break.

Then she shivered, and not through the cold. In her head there were growls and snarls, a wild animal chorus of base, blood-hungry minds. She saw the Wraith, clustered around each other, and before them the single male in ragged clothes with her handgun in his fist. The alien's garb was similar to the coats and battle gear she had seen before on other high-ranking Wraith, but it was ripped and torn, ravaged by combat and years of life as a fugitive. He came closer to her, and in the dimness Teyla saw his scarred and ruined cheek, his single blinded eye.

"What," husked the alien, working at the word. "What are. You?" He spoke haltingly, as if he had not had to form proper speech in a long time and the manner of it had become unfamiliar to him. "What are you?" repeated Scar. "Not the hunters. Not... Not the Enemy. You have their machines... But you are not one of them."

Once, when she was a girl, Teyla had seen her father put a whitehorn to death because it had escaped from the corral and gorged itself on poisonous fruit. In the moments before he had put the animal out of its misery, it had looked directly at her and the Athosian had seen the light of bestial madness in its gaze. She saw the same thing now on the face of the Wraith that confronted her.

Teyla marshaled her resolve and stared him in the eye, refusing to give the Wraith anything. Scar brandished the Beretta pistol under her nose, and she flinched from the stink of hot cordite. "You... Are different from that male." He jerked his head at Bishop, and she could feel him in her thoughts again, the same black slick of consciousness that had caressed her psyche out in the forest. "You are touched by us." Scar rocked back on his haunches and made a clicking noise in his throat, what must have been the Wraith equivalent of a chuckle. "How lucky you are."

She couldn't stop herself. Teyla pulled hard against her bonds, slamming forward a few inches before the sticky ropes went tight and reined her in. Still, she took a little reward in the momentary recoil on the Wraith's face. Scar sneered and composed himself. "I know you. Sensed you." She felt him pushing at her mind and fought to hold him out; fought and failed.

"Tey-lah," said Scar, drawing the word from her. He sounded out the syllables of her name, savoring the resonance of them. "You are far from home, prey." Hate washed over her from him, thick and oily, cold as the kiss of space itself. She gagged.

"Why don' you pick a fight with a bloke, bozo?" Bishop said thickly. "Ought to get yourself a new haircut while you're at it. Th' metal band look went out with Bon Jovi."

The Wraith gave the soldier a sideways look but didn't respond to him. "They want to feed," he told Teyla, jerking his head at the rest of his kindred. "Soon I will let them."

"I do not fear you, creature." The words came up of their own accord.

Scar made the clicking noise again. "Lie."

"If I perish, it will be knowing that a hundred thousand Wraith corpses line my way to the afterlife, all of them dead by my hand!"

He cocked his head. "Oh. A warrior, then, Tey-lah? Proud and strong." He sniffed. "Still prey, at the end."

She watched the glitter of intelligence in Scar's eyes. Daus had been right when he said this Wraith was not like the others on Halcyon. Where his pack mates loped and snapped at each other like primitive simians, Scar was cogent and clever. But there was something else in there, a peculiar need that went beyond his desire to feed off them. The fragmented psionic connection Teyla shared with the Wraith was a two-way street, and she could feel a churn of conflict in the alien's mind. Something akin to loneliness, a sad little streak of arrogance that boiled away just below the surface. She saw broken pieces of thought, there and gone like reflections in shards of a shattered mirror, and an abrupt realization came to her. Scar was concealing something, an old and dark hatred buried deep in his psyche. He was nursing it, cupping the flame of a rage that had been burning for countless years. He had a plan.

The Wraith sniffed at the air and toyed with the pistol. "Brutal and direct," he said, considering the gun. "The simplicity of it amuses me." Scar leaned closer and she caught a whiff of his alien odor. "You are not of the Enemy, but you have their devices. Tell me now. Are they dead? Are the Gatebuilders dead?" When Teyla did not answer, he gave a guttural chug and one of the other Wraiths scrambled over to Bishop, brandishing its feeding maw. The pack mate hovered over the soldier, raw desire bright in its dead eyes. "Answer, or the male is ash."

"Don't tell him nothing," spat the soldier.

Teyla licked dry lips. There was no doubt in her mind that Scar would have Bishop killed if she did not answer him. "The Ancients are gone. We don't know where. They abandoned their cities, vanished."

"Gone." Scar considered this for a moment. "It is fitting. The Enemy died while I slept..."

There was another blink of his memory there in her brain, hard and brittle, of a cold sleep in the chambers of a Hive Ship. The aftermath of a battle, many lives lost and great destruction wrought. She was seeing into him.

Scar glanced at her. "Yes," His words were a gentle hiss. "We came to cull these worlds and found the Enemy here, lying in wait for us. They poisoned the air with their device. Shielded the prey with it. We could not land, could not feed."

"The dolmen," Teyla spoke without meaning to. "The Ancients placed it on Halcyon to protect the natives from you."

The Wraith's head bobbed. "At the height of its power, it drove us mad to be near it. So we remained in space."

Teyla heard noises, half-whispers that came across an impossible distance, across thousands of years. Weapons fire, the roars of combatants and the screams of the dying. Scar was showing her flashes of his past, of a great conflict.

"Our hive, our home, was crippled," he husked, looking inward, "the interstellar translation drives were damaged beyond repair. The Enemy fared little better, fleeing. They vowed to return with reinforcements to finish us. But they never came back."

And then it was all there in her mind, as if she had lived through it herself. Teyla retched, bringing up thin, watery bile, her body rebelling as the shape of the alien memories tried to impose themselves on her recall. "You... Went into hibernation, where the dolmen's power could not affect your minds. Waiting." The woman shook her head, trying to rid herself of the cascade of horrific sensations.

Scar showed all his serrated teeth in a malicious smile. "Ah. You understand. But with each passing year the Enemy's defense wanes in strength. Enough that we can rise against it. *Enough.*"

"Teyla..." called Bishop, a warning in his tone. He'd seen the flare of anger in her eyes.

"You will fail," she spat. "A handful of mindless beasts are all you have! The Halcyons will gun you down the instant you show your ruined face to them!"

The Wraith growled and ran a finger over the scar on his cheek.

"The Ancients beat you ten thousand years ago!" Teyla snarled. "You ran like wounded quarry! You will fare no better today!"

Scar chuckled. "Mistake. We were not beaten, Tey-lah. We merely took our rest." He rose, tucking the gun into his tunic. "That time has passed." At his gesture, one of the other Wraiths came out of the shadows with a metallic ring in its hands. Scar turned the hoop of discolored silver and with a click it split open. He brought it back to Teyla and offered it to her, like a suitor giving a gift.

She saw the intricate cogs and metal spars on the inner face of the ring and understood at once what it was. Teyla tried to back away, but there was nowhere she could go. Scar fastened the metal collar around her neck and it made a clicking sound as the mechanism inside constricted to fit her. The woman coughed as it tightened, settling to a diameter that lay uncomfortably on her throat.

"Ah," Scar said, amusement in his tone. "Now you can be my Hound, human."

Bishop barked out a string of invective that would have earned him a week in the glasshouse if he had said it in earshot of an officer. Scar turned indolently toward him and gave a hollow yowl to the other Wraith in his pack. All of them sprang at the bound soldier with sudden, appalling speed, falling on the man and ripping into him.

"No!" Teyla screamed, but she was powerless to save him. The trooper shuddered and wailed as the Wraiths fed, each of them fighting to draw his living energy from him. She found she could not look away from the horrific display as Bishop's hand snatched at the air, with each second the skin becoming papery, the muscles losing definition, the color draining from him.

After a moment, Scar made another sound and the Wraith pack reluctantly withdrew. Tears spiked Teyla's eyes as she realized that Bishop was still alive, his face sunken and skeletal, each breath a rattling gasp of air. He looked like an old man, decrepit and feeble. Scar bent across the soldier and carefully placed his palm over Bishop's heart. Then, with his tongue flicking out between his pallid lips, the Wraith fed greedily on the last moments of the man's life, taking the sweetest and most succulent nourishment for himself.

"I am not going to die on a Wraith Hive Ship," Rodney managed, trying very hard to keep his voice from turning into a whimper. "I am going to die of old age surrounded by... by... nubile graduate students. Nobel Prizes!" His skin crawled and he bunched his fists, hugging himself in a desperate attempt to stave off panic-induced shivers. "I am *not* going to die," he insisted to the empty cell. "I am going to die on a Wraith Hive Ship-" McKay halted and shouted out loud, abruptly angry with himself. "Not! *Not!* Not going to die! I am *not* going to die on a Wraith Hive Ship, you can't make me, I don't want to, so there!

So there—"

He heard the ringing clatter of footsteps approaching along the corridor beyond the webbed doorway of his confinement, and Rodney shrank back into the corner of the cramped space, frantically trying to fight down the rising wave of abject terror building inside him. He wanted so much to hold on the rational and intelligent part of himself, the piece of Rodney McKay that was smart and clinical, capable of cutting through scientific conundrums like a laser; but that bit of him had gone bye-bye and all that was left was the panicking idiot portion who hit like a girl and barely knew one end of a gun from the other. Not that he had a gun, anyway.

The cell wall hit him in the back and McKay stiffened. He was staring death in the face again, any moment now. Why was he still terrified? This had happened to him so many times, surely by now he should have been used to it?

Two Wraiths halted outside the doorway and one of them did something to a control surface. The spider web of cords blocking him in twitched and retracted into the walls. The other came into the cell and grabbed Rodney, dragging him out into the corridor.

"Please don't suck the life out of me," he managed, and the denial sounded totally pathetic in his ears. *As if they were suddenly going to say 'Oh, okay then,' and shove me back in there.*

The aliens didn't acknowledge his words, and simply propelled him forward, pushing McKay away and down the twisting tunnels of bone. The Wraith guards marched him quickly through open spaces and atriums, some lit with dim bioluminescence, others black and dead. Rodney's mind was running at full tilt, his thoughts racing thanks to the surge of terror-induced adrenaline in his bloodstream. Something felt different about this ship. He tried to put his finger on it.

The usual sense of motion, the slight giddiness of acceleration, wasn't there. Perhaps they were in orbit, or drifting in space? But as he stumbled onward, he felt strangely heavier than he expected to. Every other time McKay had been inside a Wraith vessel, the gravity had been just a shade less than the

Earth-equivalent of habitable, Stargated worlds. He remembered that Zelenka had posited that the Wraith liked a low-gee environment. If he felt heavy—that was to say, normal weight—here, maybe this ship wasn't actually in space but grounded *on a planet*? What the hell did that imply? Why was he even here? The men who had attacked the dolmen, who shot him, they wore gray battledress and they certainly hadn't been Wraiths. Had they?

However, that train of thought went totally off the rails as the guards shoved him through another doorway and along a narrow catwalk over a vast open space in the alien craft's interior. Ranged up above and down below him along the curved inner surface of the chamber there were hundreds, if not thousands of individual cells. Not the same kind of cell as the holding area where he'd been confined, but roughly hexagonal compartments that looked like something from inside of a hornet's nest. Many of them were dark, but a lot—an awful lot—were aglow with pale light, and through the thick matter of their translucent walls McKay could see the humanoid forms of quiescent Wraith. Now and then, the occasional one would twitch in its hibernative sleep. But what caught Rodney's attention was where the cells were marked, where they had been cut open with what must have been blowtorches. *Good grief, why would anyone actually want to deliberately decant a dormant Wraith?*

He turned to look at the alien guards and saw a glitter of light at their necks. Each of the Wraiths had dull, lifeless eyes, and heavy steel torcs that were the twin to those worn by Daus's indentured servants. "Hounds?" The word tumbled from McKay's lips.

Another hatch dilated before them and with one final shove, Rodney's Wraith chaperones pushed him through it. He recovered from a near stumble and came to a halt, his jaw hanging open in shocked surprise.

McKay had never seen the interior of a Wraith Hive Ship's control nexus before, but based on the experience of several Atlantean off world teams, he'd built up a picture of what they had to look like. He was pleased on some level that he'd been so close to the mark, but unhappy on another that he had to make that judgment in person. Standing in the chamber was like being inside a hollowed-out skull, a large bone enclosure with two open orbits that peered out from the dorsal surface of the vessel like eye sockets. As he had surmised, the view from the ports wasn't the black void of space or the shimmering blue of a hyperspatial tunnel, but a pale sky and a lightly forested hillside. The now-familiar yellow-white sun visible in the clouds told him that he was still on Halcyon. *And if that's the closest thing I've had to good news all day, then I really am in trouble.*

There were multiple levels inside the nexus with steep ramps leading up and down to them. Skeletal formations here and there had grown around the glossy shapes of control consoles and the quivering organic lenses of monitor screens. It was all seamless and quite unpleasant in its design, like the folds of natural armor on a scorpion's thorax or the shiny bones of some dead deep-ocean predator. But what shocked him more than the alien lines of the Hive Ship's command center were the chunks of brazen, blocky metal retrofitted into the walls. Festoons of fat, sparking cables trailed back and forth across the deck, and there were puddles of yellowy organic fluid collecting where arrays of glass valves and other primitive electronics had been surgically inserted into the consoles. Hardware better suited to the laboratory of Dr. Frankenstein had been rammed brutally into the slick, inhuman forms of the Wraith consoles.

Men in work tunics were busy at the controls, or in tight groups at wooden benches set up in the avenues between the alien hardware. They all wore the black flash on their tabards marking them as standing in the service of the Lord Magnate.

A familiar and utterly unwelcome face emerged from one of the groups, beaming a supercilious grin. "Kelfer," sneered Rodney, turning the man's name into an insult. "What. Are. You. Doing?"

"Dr. McKay. Welcome." The chief scientist clapped his hands. "Firstly, I must apologize for your mode of arrival here. I trust you did not find it too... Dramatic?"

Rodney waggled a finger at him. "You kidnapped me!" It

came to him in a rush. "That's why you left Erony and me inside the dolmen! You went outside to, what, send a signal to your goon squad? Where is she? Did you hurt her?"

Kelfer rolled his eyes. "As if I would dare to leave a mark upon the daughter of the most powerful man on the planet. The Lady Erony is uninjured."

"Scumbag!" It was the first insult that came to mind, and although it wasn't as nasty as he would have liked, McKay put plenty of venom behind it.

"Doctor, please calm yourself. You were struck by a Wraith Stunner. The effects can be quite troubling."

"Don't patronize me!" he barked. "When your lordship finds out that you're working with the Wraith —"

It was Kelfer's turn to butt in. "Working with the Wraith?" he laughed harshly. "Great blades, man, have you learned nothing while you have been on Halcyon? We despise those beasts!" He nodded at the two Hounds. "*They* serve *us*! Never the reverse! That is the whole point of this endeavor." He opened his hands, taking in the ship around them. "And be certain that the Lord Magnate would hardly be uninformed about what transpires here, on land that has been a part of his ancestral holdings since the Age of Unification!"

Rodney took that nugget of information in, his fingers fluttering at the air. "I return to my original point, then. What are you doing here, *you moron*?"

Kelfer's face hardened at the insult, but he answered nonetheless. "We are learning the secrets of the Wraith," he bit out, "decoding their language, turning their technology to our own ends, examining their physiology to find new ways to condition them and kill them." He puffed out his chest. "It is the single most important undertaking of our race."

But McKay wasn't listening to him preen. The Atlantean scientist's analytical mind was racing ten steps ahead of what Kelfer was telling him, putting together everything he had seen and heard, and following it toward the inevitable conclusion. "Wait. Wait wait. Linnian told Teyla that Daus's rule of Halcyon was unchallenged."

"*Lord* Daus!" snapped Kelfer.

McKay's thoughts spilled out, raw and unfiltered. "His rule was unchallenged because he had the biggest army of tame Wraith in his doghouse, and no one would ever dare to go up against someone who could send in so many Hounds, right? And I couldn't help wondering where he got his fresh recruits from, and now you show me this —" Rodney's brain finally caught up with his mouth and stumbled over the words. "Oh no. No, no, no-no." He took a warning step toward Kelfer, indignation and anger building as he realized the depths of trouble they were in. "Please tell me that you were not so completely, so unreservedly, entirely downright mind-bogglingly dim-witted, that you have actually been waking up those Wraith *on purpose*?"

The control room fell silent as McKay's tirade rose in volume. The Halcyon chief scientist just blinked.

"That's how the Fourth Dynast have kept themselves in power for so long, isn't it? Not by hunting Wraith on other planets and bringing them back like the other clans do, but by decanting them from this Hive Ship, like it's some kind of private wine cellar!" The arrogance of such a thing drained the ire from him in a second. "Do you realize that your ham-fisted efforts tinkering around in here may very well have doomed your entire planet to being the main course at a Wraith barbecue?"

Kelfer composed himself and straightened his tunic with a self-conscious cough. "Dr. McKay, you have been brought here on the direct instruction of His Highness the Lord Magnate to assist me in my work on the Hive Ship's mechanisms. By your own admission, you have stated that you possess some knowledge of these craft and their technologies."

"It's a lot more than just *some*, okay?" Although he probably should have kept quiet about it, Rodney couldn't resist the chance to get in another dig at the pompous man. "The biggest expert on the Wraith this side of an Ascended Being," he pointed at his chest with both hands, "right here!"

"Indeed," continued Kelfer, and it was clear that for the scientist, admitting McKay's superiority in any matter was like chewing on broken glass. "And with that in mind, you will immediately address yourself to the functioning of the Wraith hibernation chambers aboard this vessel."

"Why?" McKay knew the moment the question left his lips that the answer would not be a good one.

Kelfer's lips thinned. "In centuries past, the Fourth Dynast's scientists were able to remove docile Wraith from their capsules and put them to the collar with only minimal incident. However, in recent cycles, more and more of the sleeping Wraith have been emerging on their own, despite our best efforts to contain them. Every attempt to stem this chain of events has failed. We cannot stop them awakening. We do not know why this is."

Rodney knew, but he wasn't about to tell Kelfer. He wasn't willing to admit that it had been Colonel Sheppard's ill-fated venture into the heart of a Wraith Hive Ship just like this one that started a ripple effect, waking up the dormant aliens all across the Pegasus Galaxy. "And you want me to do something about it, is that it? Clean up your, uh, mess for you?"

The scientist sighed. "You will find a way to put the Wraith back to sleep, McKay. If you do not, then your associates will suffer."

"Suffer?" Rodney blinked. "What do you mean by that, exactly?"

"I mean *die*, exactly. At the hands of my Lord's Hounds."

"I don't see anything," said Ronon, peering through the binoculars, "not that I've got a wide field of view out the canopy."

"Uh-huh," Sheppard replied, his attention on the screen in front of him. "Damn."

"You have something?"

The colonel shook his head. "For a second, I thought I did. I tried using the Jumper's sensors to track that Ancient hand-held doohickey I gave to Teyla, but I'm getting *nada*. There was the ghost of return for a moment, but then it faded."

Ronon leaned closer. "Where?"

Sheppard grabbed the paper map of the hunt enclosure and tapped it. "Here, I think. Sensors didn't get enough time to lock down an exact location."

"That's a start. At least we have somewhere to look for them."

"Yeah." John touched controls on the ship's console. "Activating cloak. I'm going to take us up to tree-top level and start running a search pattern."

Dex nodded and attended to his weapons. "Daus didn't give us the whole story about the Wraith here," he noted.

"I think we're way past expecting the truth from that guy, don't you? 'A planet full of liars', right?"

"I don't think he sent us here for Scar. He sent us here to get killed. You saw how those Wraiths were moving. They were feral, but they weren't stupid."

Sheppard turned the yoke as the Puddle Jumper rose above the forest canopy. "The Wraith are a lot of things, but dumb has never been one of them."

"You don't follow me," said Ronon. "They were working in a coordinated pattern. Attack, retreat, feint, attack. That's not how a mind-blanked animal would do it." He pointed into the trees. "They went for our team and Teyla's at the same time. They had a plan. A leader."

"Scar."

"No doubt."

"Well, that's great. So he's not only a super-tough Wraith, he's super-smart as well, out here in the trees with his private militia like some kinda alien Marlon Brando. And I get to be Martin Sheen." He glanced at Dex. "You could be Dennis Hopper, if you like."

The other man made a face. "That psychic jamming device in the dolmen is supposed to fog their brains, but I don't think it's as powerful as the Halcyons think it is. Maybe the ZPM powering it has run down, and those Wraith are just playing along. Waiting for the right moment to strike."

The possibility that Dex could be right about that sent an icy shiver down the colonel's spine. Sheppard shot him a hard look. "One problem at a time, Ronon. One damn problem at a time."

The gyro-flyer rocked as the aircraft caught a sharp updraft, and Lady Erony put out a hand to steady herself. She craned her neck to peer out of the window-slit by her chair and saw the smokestacks and tenement towers of the lower city flash by.

Linnian's fingers knotted and unknotted as he hovered beside her. At length, he gave a theatrical sigh. "Highness, would not it have been simpler to dispatch a messenger to carry your news to Dr. Beckett? Such a method would have much greater alacrity." He forced a smile. "See here, if we return to the High Palace, a courier could reach him in only a few minutes from your word of dispatch—"

"Must you continue to chatter on the same issue over and over again?" she snapped, silencing the adjutant. "I do not wish it!"

Linnian took a breath. "But, My Lady, your father has made it quite clear to me on many occasions that he does not look with favor on any ventures into the common quarters."

Erony made a show of looking around. "Is my dear father here on this vessel?"

"Ah, well, no, Highness."

"And is his adjutant Baron Vekken here, carrying his word and authority in the Magnate's stead?"

The man looked at the deck. "No, Highness. He has joined the Lord Daus on a errand of state in the Great Ward."

"Then by your own admission, it appears that I am the noble of highest rank on board this aircraft, and as such my word is the law."

Linnian bowed, suitably intimidated. "I meant no disrespect, My Lady. It is merely that I am confused by your sudden desire to visit so base and squalid a place as the environs of the lower city." He sniffed archly. "It is beneath one of your great standing."

The flyer was banking over the dockside district now, circling as the pilot searched for somewhere suitable to put down. Erony returned to the view through the window-slit as the sunlight shifted around the cabin. Although she would never admit it to him, her adjutant's words were correct, and she had no doubt that if her father were to discover that she had set out

on this jaunt, his anger would be great indeed. Many was the
time that Lord Daus had imposed his beliefs on his daughter,
that the commoners be left to live their lives and that the nobles
were not to walk freely among them. The people, he had often
told her, should only be able to lay their eyes on the scions
of the Fourth Dynast on annual occasions such as Unification
Eve or when a funeral or betrothal was enacted. He stressed the
importance of the places Halcyon's society had for them, and
for Erony. To ignore the barrier between them, he said, was to
invite chaos and confusion among the simple folk of the cities.
It was for their own good.

And yet... Since she was a youth, Erony had observed the
lower city second hand, through telescopes and the overheard
chatter of her servants. In her more private moments, she had
wondered if it were fair that she should live elevated above
them, while the common folk endured fresh hardships with each
new dawn.

But it grew easy to ignore those voices that prickled her conscience. Erony's life was a world where she wanted for nothing,
insulated and safe. But the arrival of these people from Atlantis had stirred up long-forgotten feelings. They were so close
to the surface, these Atlanteans, so direct in thought and deed.
They could not stand to see an injustice go unanswered, even
if it would put them in harm's way to challenge it. These were
men and women who saw no class or boundary, they worked as
a team despite their diverse backgrounds. Educated men like
Rodney McKay and the good Dr. Beckett side by side with
rough soldiers, tribals even like the Runner and the huntress
from Athos. She admired the easy bond they so clearly shared,
and she felt jealous of it.

Erony glanced at Linnian. He had been her adjutant since she
was a child, and yet she had never once felt in all those years
that they were friends, that she might be able to trust him. On
Halcyon, the children of noble families were taught the rules
of their society from the earliest age, learning the manners of
polite intrigue and courteous back-stabbings. They were taught
that they were superior, and that their wealth and power was not

just deserved, but their birthright.

The gyro-flyer dipped towards the rooftops, and Erony caught sight of figures huddling in doorways to shield themselves from the aircraft's prop wash. *But what birthright do these people have?* she asked herself.

The rotors were still chopping at the air as Linnian dropped the hatch and fairly bounded out of the flyer with two armed riflemen at his sides. Immediately he began shouting warnings to the commoners, the braver ones who had dared to approach the grounded aircraft. Erony pulled the ornate shawl about her shoulders and kept the half-veil of her traveling hood over her eyes as she followed him out. Deliberately, she had left her clan sword in her chambers and carried nothing but a compact gold revolver on her hip. The gasps of the citizens at the sight of her made Erony feel suddenly vulnerable and afraid. *Perhaps Linnian is right, perhaps I should go back, it's not safe here...*

"Lady Erony?" From the open doors of a wide, low ware-house came Dr. Beckett, his sand-colored jacket standing out among the darker hues of the people around him. The soldier who had been injured at the dolmen followed him cautiously. "I'm, ah, surprised to see you here."

"I have brought news..." Her words dried up in her mouth as she caught sight of the commoners milling around the entrance to the warehouse. This place was one of the locations where Beckett had set up a treatment center for the victims of the bone-rot, and Erony found her fright rising as she realized that these poor, hobbled souls were all suffering from the terrible malaise.

The doctor saw the question in her eyes. "Oh aye, that's your bone-rot, right there. We call it 'rickets' on my planet. It used to be quite widespread hundreds of years ago, but now it only turns up in places where there's contaminated food and water."

"Contaminated," she echoed, unable to take her eyes from the twisted limbs of the people around her. She felt a sudden jab of shame as a few of the younger ones bent and shivered. They were trying to bow to her, to show the proper obeisance to a noble, even though it must have pained them severely to do so. Erony shook her head. "No. Tell them, they do not need to do that."

"My Lady," began Linnian, "protocol demands—"

"It is all right," she continued, addressing the commoners directly. "You do not need to bow."

Beckett came closer. "Why don't you come and see what we're doing here? These people have you to thank, after all." He offered his hand to her.

Linnian interposed himself between them. "You will not touch the person of a noble."

The doctor gave the adjutant a withering stare. "I've told you once already, wee fella, don't get in my way, not when I'm doing my job."

"Linnian," said Erony, and he stood aside. "Doctor, please continue."

A pregnant hush moved before them as Beckett led her into the dank interior if the warehouse, inside the sharp tang of the nearby river waters mingling with medicinal odors and human sweat. She saw another Atlantean soldier opening crates of supplies. Beds made of canvas squares and metal rods had been set up here and there, and the doctor's female assistant was hard at work moving between them. Erony watched her smile warmly at a worried young boy as she applied a gun-shaped device to his bare shoulder. The apparatus coughed and the boy rubbed at a red mark where the gun's nozzle had touched him.

"The nurse is giving him a booster shot of vitamins and calcium enhancers," explained the doctor. "It's a stop-gap measure but it will hopefully be enough to reverse the spread of the ailment in most patients. Others... Well, it's already too late for a lot of folk here."

She saw a youth in the brown robes of a palace servant helping an older man secure a brace to his twisted leg. "Who is that?" Erony didn't know his name, but she'd seen the young man before, engaged in servitude on board the royal conveyor.

"We asked around for some volunteers," noted Beckett. "Corporal Clarke organized a few locals to help us set things up."

"Very impressive," offered Linnian in a bored tone.

Erony ignored him and lent closer to Beckett. "And once you are finished here, this bone-rot will no longer trouble them, yes?"

The doctor frowned. "Well, *no*, lass. What we're doing here is holding things back a little. But it's not a cure. For that, you need to seriously re-think your city's food, water and medical infrastructure."

She watched the man with the brace struggle to get back to his feet. With his deformed bones, he looked like a wire doll that had been twisted about by a petulant child. Cold certainty flooded her veins, the shocking realization coming at once that she was responsible for this. Erony, her father, her Dynast, all of the nobles. The pain of these commoners was the product of their arrogance. Her earlier thought returned to her. *What birthright do these people have?*

"My Lady," said the adjutant with a sniff. "I think this visit is at an end. We should return to the palace."

Erony blinked hard, and pulled back her veil, giving Beckett her full attention. In her distraction, she had almost forgotten the very excuse that she had used to journey down here. "Doctor, forgive me, I am remiss. I came here to give you urgent news of Lieutenant Colonel Sheppard and your friends."

Beckett's face paled. "What's wrong?"

"My father has observers following their hunting venture from the enclosure's observation towers. Gunfire was reported in several locations, after which the group was lost to sight. The observers also reported increased Wraith activity in the area." Her lips thinned. "I fear for the safety of your comrades."

The older soldier, the one called Mason, spoke into the communications device on his tunic. "Jumper Three, this is Mason, respond. Colonel Sheppard? Do you copy my transmission?" The communicator hissed back at him.

"They're out of range," said the trooper with the bandaged arm. "Could be in trouble, Staff."

Beckett looked at her. "Erony, this has gone far enough. We cannae stand by and do nothing. You have to help us put a stop to all this."

She answered without stopping to consider it. "I will."

"Highness!" protested Linnian, but she ignored his outburst.

"You," she said, pointing at one of the blackcoat riflemen. "Disarm yourself and take Dr. Beckett's place here. You will do whatever his nurse tells you to, and render whatever assistance she demands, as if the words came from my lips. Is that clear?"

The rifleman bowed. "By your command, Milady."

Erony turned to Beckett. "Come with me, Doctor. Bring one of your warriors, if you wish. My gyro-flyer is a racing model, and with it we can reach the enclosure with great speed."

Her adjutant spluttered. "My Lady, I must protest! This is most irregular!"

"Linnian," replied the woman, putting every ounce of her noble will behind the word, "relay my instructions to the pilot and do not tarry."

"But—"

"*Now.*"

The man threw Beckett an acid stare, bowed, and then scuttled away.

"Clarke," snapped Mason, "keep watch here, got it? You don't hear back from us by nightfall, you evac the civvies and get your arse through the Stargate."

The soldier saluted. "Yes, Staff."

"Thank you, Erony," said the doctor.

She gave her sick and ailing subjects a last look and then nodded. "Follow me."

CHAPTER TEN

The Puddle Jumper moved quickly over the treetops, the gravity drive whining. To an outside observer, all that would have been visible was a sudden glimmer, there and then gone, a swift disturbance in the air as the cloaked spacecraft tracked back and forth in a grid pattern.

Sheppard kept his eyes firmly on the ship's head-up display, frowning at the flickering dots that showed Wraith life signs. "They keep appearing and disappearing..." He shifted uncomfortably; the tension and exertion of the day was taking its toll on him, his black uniform t-shirt damp with sweat beneath his ballistic body armor and webbing vest. John toggled a control to set the sensors to a deep penetration mode, and the display changed, showing a faint network of channels under the surface. "There are tunnels and caverns all over this part of the enclosure."

Ronon weighed a hand-held Ancient scanner in his grip. "That figures. This Wraith they call Scar, he wouldn't have lasted long in here if he didn't have some kind of safe haven."

The colonel's eyes narrowed. "They could have a nest down there, like termites, or something." He shuddered. "That whole Wraith-Bug thing makes my skin crawl."

Suddenly, Ronon gave a shout. "There!" He stabbed a finger at the trees. "Bring us around, there's a clearing! I saw something!"

Sheppard slowed the Jumper and drifted it gently around in an arc, keeping the blunt nose of the craft aimed forward where Dex had indicated. The Satedan had been right. "Good eye," noted John, spotting a figure in the dark blue of an Atlantis combat uniform sprawled on the ground. "Can't make out who it is, though..."

Ronon stuffed the scanner in the pocket of his coat and drew his particle magnum. "Drop the ramp, I'm going down there."

"Wait, I gotta land us first," The pilot put the ship into a hover, carefully rotating it as he gradually descended below the level of the leafy canopy. The open copse was small and setting the ship down in it would be like threading a needle.

"No time," snapped Dex, "she could be hurt." He reached past Sheppard's shoulder, slapping the glassine control that opened the Jumper's rear hatch. Before John could stop him, the other man vaulted out of the craft and threw himself down into the clearing.

Ronon landed hard and rolled to absorb the impact, the shock of it singing up through the bones in his legs. From the corner of his eye he had a moment of optical illusion, where the open portal of the Jumper seemed to be hanging in the air like a door in the sky; then Sheppard dropped the cloak and the drum-shaped ship was there, dithering like a hawk unsure where to settle.

He sprinted across the grassy clearing, vaulting over rocks and brush, towards the slack form he'd spotted from the air. The body was lying face down and curled away from him, head tucked beneath the crook of an arm. In split seconds, impressions crowded Dex's mind. It definitely wasn't a male, the body was too slim and the proportions were off. But the blue Atlantis jacket seemed too big, and it hung wrongly.

"Teyla!" he called, crouching low, moving to the slumped shape. Ronon grabbed the body's shoulder and turned it over. "Teyla?"

The Wraith female wearing Private Bishop's uniform screeched and threw herself at the Satedan, the shock of the corpse-white face and the sudden movement catching him unawares. Ronon snarled as the alien struck him, knocking his pistol from his grip. They rolled into one another and tumbled down a shallow incline, punching and clawing. Dex felt hot and fetid breath as the Wraith tried to bite him and he snatched at her crimson flood of hair, grabbing a handful and jerking it backward. Black claws raked his side, slicing into the material of his jacket, reaching through layers of cloth to his torso.

He struggled to hold off the wild creature's feeding arm, the Wraith howling and shrieking. Ronon brought his head forward and butted the alien on the nose, hearing the satisfying crack of breaking cartilage. In return, the Wraith tore at him with fresh rage, mad and hungry for his life energy. At last, Dex managed to bring his free hand up and flicked it out. A concealed mechanism in his leather wrist guard clicked, releasing a spring-loaded knife, keen and wide with a petal-shaped blade. With a snarl of effort, Ronon punched the weapon into the flesh beneath the Wraith's jawbone and up into its skull. The female gurgled and died.

Dex let the body fall and drew his short sword. More Wraiths were streaming out of the woods and dropping from the upper branches of the trees.

"Whoa!" shouted Sheppard, the Jumper gaining new and unwelcome passengers as it descended toward the ground. No sooner had Ronon jumped ship, so to speak, than there were Wraith throwing themselves from the tops of the forest canopy and on to the floating ship. A singularly ugly-looking male landed squarely on the bow and bellowed at him, banging a blunt-bladed halberd on the cockpit canopy. More thuds and bangs along the outside of the hull told the colonel that this Wraith bruiser wasn't alone. Gripping the throttle and yoke, Sheppard reversed the Jumper's fall and took her up again.

"Sorry to disappoint you," he told the creature, "but I don't pick up hitchhikers!" With a flick of his wrist the colonel shifted the output of the gravity drives, putting the port outrigger up to full reverse and the starboard to full forward velocity. The instant effect was to spin the Puddle Jumper around like a top. The forest and sky became a green and blue blur, and for one brief moment, the Wraith on the bow hung on before centrifugal force tore him away and flung the creature into the trees. Sheppard felt a moment of giddiness as he came back into a hover, but it passed. Without the powerful inertial dampeners the Ancients built into their ships, the maneuver he'd just pulled would have spread him along the inside of the Jumper like chunky salsa.

There was a flicker of motion on the canopy glass, and the colonel saw the monstrous grin of a hungry Wraith reflected there. One of them had got inside. He twisted in his seat as the alien went for him, claws out. *The hatch, John,* his mind screamed, *you left the damn hatch down!*

Sheppard stabbed at the on-off controller for the dampener, then slammed the throttle forward, instantly canceling out the gravity-neutral bubble inside the Jumper. The quick burst of velocity threw the Wraith intruder off its feet and sent it tumbling back down the length of the ship, sparks flying where it clawed at the decking, out the open hatch and away. The colonel felt the g-forces press into him, a suffocating leaden pressure all across his chest, compacting him into the pilot's chair. He managed to tap the dampener circuit again and the pressure evaporated.

"Whew." John blinked sweat away from his lashes, and after a quick check to make sure he was flying solo again, he brought the Jumper back around for a combat landing.

The frenzied Wraith came at Ronon in a hooting wave of teeth and claws, and he met them with energy bolts and the edge of his blade. With one single strike he took an attacker at the throat and the Satedan battle sword parted head from torso in a jet of black blood. He fell into the red haze of his rage, tapping into the hate that had carried him through all the years of his life on the run. The fury of it burned hot, a livid brand like the Wraith glyph etched into the flesh of his throat.

In the thick of the fight, Ronon was dimly aware of the Jumper landing, of Sheppard's cries and the chattering of his machinegun, but it was all second to his anger, which he turned on the Wraith in its full force. He had lost so much at the talons of these repellent freaks of nature, friends and family, a whole world, a life without battle. And perhaps now Teyla Emmagan, the only person among these Atlanteans with whom he had felt any real kinship.

But as abruptly as the ambush had begun, it ended. "Enough!"

roared a voice, and the Wraith spat and disengaged, leaving Dex and Sheppard panting hard with adrenaline and exertion.

And there was Teyla, stumbling on shaky feet ahead of a hard-faced Wraith overlord, clutching at her neck where a heavy silver collar ringed it. Ronon bared his teeth in fury. There was a thick cable snaking away from the device to the Wraith's clawed hand, a steel leash of the sort one might use on an attack dog. "Drop your weapons," hissed the alien, "or the female dies."

The barrel of Sheppard's P90 sank a little but he held on to the gun. Ronon still had his particle magnum pistol in his grip, ready to use it. Dex locked eyes with the Wraith, measuring the ways in which he might kill it.

"You must be Scar," said the colonel, and pointed at his face. "The one eye is a dead giveaway. It's a cool name. I bet the lady Wraiths love it. Let me ask you, though. Have you ever seen *The Lion King*?"

"Drop your weapons," repeated Scar, "or Tey-lah will choke to death on her own blood." He did something to a control on the leash and Ronon heard cogwheels clicking. Teyla coughed and sank to her knees, pulling at the necklet.

"Let her go!" snapped Dex, taking aim at Scar's face.

"I can increase the pressure with a single touch of the dial I hold in my hand." The Wraith licked its lips. "Only you can save her. You know how."

The Athosian woman gasped as she tried to suck in air. Ronon heard Sheppard curse and saw the colonel unclip his gun and let it fall.

"And you," Scar told Dex.

Ronon's thumb moved toward the stun/kill stud on the magnum's grip. He was furious that this creature would try and use a warrior like Teyla as some kind of bargaining chip. He let the gun drop to aim at the woman. "You think you have an advantage. Maybe I'll take it away, shoot her myself. What would you do then?"

"Ronon!" said Sheppard in a horrified voice.

The Wraith studied him for a moment, and then laughed. The sound was a hollow rattle. "Humans. You are so entertaining.

It is almost a pity that you are prey." Scar's eyes flashed with anger. "You cannot deceive me. You are different from the hunters, who care only for their idiotic games and status. You won't kill one of your own."

"*Specialist*!" Sheppard snarled, spitting out Ronon's former rank like a command. "Drop your weapons! That's an order!"

And the truth of it was, the Wraith was right. "Fine." He opened his hands, letting the pistol and the sword go. This alien was smarter than he had expected.

Scar laughed once more and touched the collar controller, letting Teyla breathe properly again.

She choked and wheezed, gulping in breaths. "I... Am sorry, colonel..."

"It's okay," said Sheppard. "Where's Bishop?"

Teyla threw Scar a venomous glare. "He is dead. They fed upon him."

The Wraith leader barked out guttural instructions in its own language, and the rest of its pack gathered up the Atlantis team's gear, bundling it into the parked Jumper. Scar plucked Ronon's heavy pistol from the hands of another Wraith and ran his fingers along the length of the breech, sniffing it.

"Why don't you take a look down the barrel while you're at it?" rumbled Dex. "I'll even hold it for you."

Scar came closer. "You are a Runner. A lucky survivor. Tell me, were you the only one we spared when my kindred culled your planet?"

His muscles tensed with a sudden violent impulse. "I'll kill you for that!"

The Wraith continued to stroke the gun, completely unconcerned. "No," it replied, "you will not."

The last thing the Satedan saw was the muzzle snap up to face him and a crippling blast of blazing red fire.

"*Ronon*!" cried Teyla, scrambling forward. Scar jerked her leash and she gagged, tripping over again.

The Wraith grimaced at the particle magnum and made a negative noise. "A brash and crude tool, much like its owner," he purred, tossing the pistol away to land near Dex's body.

"You son of a bitch," spat Sheppard. One of the other Wraith hit him in the back of the knees and he fell. The alien held him there with an iron grip. "You got what you wanted, you didn't have to shoot him!"

Scar whipped the stolen Beretta pistol from his belt and held it at Sheppard's head. "Energy weapons are so inelegant, do you not agree, human? A single bolt and your target is dispatched. Where is the sport in that?" He weighed the handgun in his grip. "But this… A ballistic firearm, yes? Chemical reactions projecting small metal warheads. You strike your prey with this, and they will not perish straight away." The pistol barrel dropped to Sheppard's chest, to his stomach. "Such ugly wounds left behind, plentiful with pain and suffering. The prey might take hours to die… And the taste is so much richer."

John tensed, waiting for the bullet to come; but instead he was dragged to his feet and thrust toward the Puddle Jumper. Scar came after him, pulling at Teyla. "What kinda mind-games are you playing?"

"No games," replied Scar, "only rules. Obey and the female lives. Disobey and you will watch her suffocate, before I turn you over to my pack."

"What do you want from us?" husked Teyla.

"The blood of the Enemy runs in your veins," he told the colonel, licking at the air. "I smell it on you. You will pilot this craft for me, and take us to the device the Ancients built on this planet."

"The dolmen?"

Scar smiled widely. "The dolmen, yes."

"John, you can't do it —"

Sheppard silenced Teyla with a morose look. "What choice do I have?"

"Go away!" snapped McKay, waving his hand in the face of the Halcyon technician hovering beside him. "Stop lurking around me, it's really very distracting!"

"Doctor," warned Kelfer, "he is merely there to render assistance to you."

"Really?" Rodney turned from the console and made a face. "Well, how about he renders assistance by going away. Do something useful, get me coffee or something, but don't keep spying over my shoulder!"

Kelfer nodded to the technician, who said something rude under his breath and walked away. "We are merely keeping an eye on your progress, nothing more."

"Is that so?" He tap-tapped the silver Atlantis laptop that Kelfer's men had produced just after his arrival. "And were you 'keeping an eye' on this when your monkeys tried to break my computer?"

The other scientist colored a little. "We were interested in your cogitator device."

Rodney's laptop had been taken along with the rest of his gear when Lord Daus's covert squad of soldiers had abducted him from the dolmen, but there were clear knife marks around the hinges where someone had manhandled it in a vain attempt to boot up the machine. "Yeah, well you almost broke it completely." He sneered, and pantomimed an idea occurring to him. "Kelfer, here's a thought. Try to stay with me on this one, I know you find it hard to deal with sentences that have a lot of words in them — but how about, in future, you people just *leave stuff alone that you're too dumb to understand*?" He pointed at the laptop and then the controls in the Hive Ship's nexus chamber. "That goes for anything, Earth tech, Wraith or Ancient! If you'd had that in mind, we wouldn't be in this mess today!"

"Forgive us," Kelfer bit out, sarcasm boiling from his words, "we poor fools on Halcyon do not have the breadth of experience of such a genius as you. Please do take pity on us, oh wise one, and grant us some your magnificent knowledge." The man came closer, his fists balling. "Or perhaps I will have you struck about the head until your disrespect for my high office is beaten from you!"

Rodney managed a weak grin, a little afraid that he might have gone a bit too far. "I don't disrespect your rank, Kelfer," he replied, "it's just you I can't abide." McKay turned his back on the Halcyon chief scientist and frowned at the read outs on his computer. Under other circumstances, he might have been enthused by the chance to tap directly into the core systems of a Wraith Hive Ship, with the chance to learn more about the aliens and their technology from the very source itself. Not so today, however; through the patchy interface he'd forged via the crude Halcyonite electronics to the Wraith organic matrix, Rodney had already passed by whole storehouses of data on weapons, drive systems and bio-ware. He was concentrating on the matter of the Hive Ship's complex hibernation systems, and with every keystroke the thought of his teammates was there in the back of his mind. McKay was sure that Daus would have Sheppard and the others killed if he decided it would motivate Rodney's efforts, and he didn't want to have that on his conscience.

The detached, clinical element of McKay's analytical mind found the Wraith fascinating in their own way. A lethal merging of the human organism with the malleable DNA of the predatory Iratus insect, they were formidable. The accelerated regenerative abilities they showed and the basic toughness of the Wraith were factored directly into the hibernation systems of the ship. It was highly unlikely a regular person could have survived for long in the torpid cold-sleep of the hive, but the Wraith on this craft had been dormant for millennia. These guys had been settling in for a nap around the same time that Rodney's distant ancestors were living in mud huts and trying to perfect that wheel thing.

But not any more. They were waking up, here and now, and not for the first time in the last eighteen months McKay was wishing the whole Atlantis expedition had never even happened. *But*, he reflected, *the Wraith would have woken up again one day, especially with idiots like Kelfer poking sticks into their nests*. It was better that they were here in the Pegasus Galaxy to do something about it, than being none the wiser back on Earth until the day the sky turned black with Hive fleets. If only he could do something about *this* ship, right here and right now. The other, bigger, fate-of-the-human-race stuff he could get to later on.

Data streamed past his eyes, each line of dense Wraith code revealing more than the next, gradually compounding and confirming McKay's worst speculations. He had never wanted to be so wrong in all his life, and yet there it was. "Oh. Crap." The awakening Wraith were just the tip of the iceberg.

A wet hiss drew Rodney from his work and he turned at the sound of the nexus chamber's main hatch. He didn't think he could feel any worse about the situation, but as Vekken and Daus entered the control center, he realized that wasn't true at all. Suddenly his worries contracted to surviving the next few minutes without being shot or skewered with a sword.

The Lord Magnate said something low and fierce to Kelfer and then strode across the room, homing in on McKay. Other robed scientists and lackeys scattered to get out of their ruler's path, obviously afraid to be anywhere near him.

"Doctor," began the Magnate, with chilly, false humor, "please forgive the manner in which you were brought here. It was for your own protection, and for the good of the Halcyon nation."

For a moment, Rodney found himself thinking of someone else's well being instead of his own. "You ordered the raid on the dolmen. Those men in the gray were yours, and you let them shoot at your own daughter." The words had no weight. They were just a bald, hard statement of fact. McKay searched Daus's eyes and saw one tiny glimmer of emotion, but then it was gone so fast he thought he might have imagined it.

"Affairs of state often compel a man to do things that he might otherwise wish to avoid," offered the ruler, "as you now understand I must compel you."

"Why..." He shook his head. "Why didn't you just *ask* us for help? We would have come here freely, with dozens of people, we would have helped you deal with this! You didn't have to shoot me and threaten the lives of my friends!"

Vekken inclined his head. "What must your world be like, Doctor? Is it so open that no man must conceal his strengths from another? On Halcyon we cannot be so naked before the enemies of our clan."

"None must know of this vessel," said Daus. "It has been the most closely guarded secret of the Fourth Dynast. It is the root of our power."

"Does Erony know about it?" Rodney demanded.

Daus frowned. "Not the whole truth."

McKay felt disgust rising inside him. "You even lie to her."

A nerve in the Magnate's jaw twitched with repressed annoyance. "Do not dare judge me, outworlder. I hold your life in my grip." He pushed forward to peer at the computer. "What progress have you made in suspending the Wraith's awakenings?"

When the scientist didn't speak, Vekken made a show of revealing the hilt of his sword. "The Magnate asked you a question. You will respond to it. What progress have you made?"

The answer burst from him in an exasperated rush. "None! Okay? None at all, not a bloody bit!"

Kelfer gritted his teeth. "So much for your superior knowledge."

"Oh yeah, like you could do any better —" Rodney's words were choked off as Daus's arm came up in a flash of motion, and the Magnate's thick fingers gripped his throat. "Ack!"

"You dare to defy my will?" he roared. "Weakling, intellectual fool! I demand that you put the Wraith back to their slumber, and by the blades, you will do it!"

McKay coughed and wrenched himself free. He gave a ragged-throated cry. "I can't! Don't you understand, it's already *too late*!" Rodney turned to the laptop and drew a series of windows on to the screen. In turn, the largest of the glassy Wraith monitor panels illuminated with strings of alien text. "The hibernation system runs from a central command cluster, and once it reaches a point of, uh, critical mass, the hive cells start a total shutdown. We are too far along in the process to halt it." Rodney threw up his hands. "The truth is, you were too far along a year ago! Now there's no way to stop them all defrosting!"

Kelfer's face drained of color. "How... How long until they are all conscious?"

"It's a matter of weeks," he said bleakly. "By then, every single one of the hundred thousand or so Wraiths on board this ship will be awake and hungry."

There was silence in the chamber at Rodney's pronounce-
ment. "Impossible," began Daus, and he turned to glare at Kelfer,
searching for support to his denial.

The Halcyon scientist sat heavily on a makeshift chair and
ran a trembling hand through his thinning hair. "Great blades,"
whispered Kelfer, "we are truly doomed."

"I'm not done talking yet," McKay said carefully. "There's
more."

"More?" Kelfer yelped. "This nightmare grows worse?"

The main screen flickered and scrolled through a sequence of
complex graphics. "I was running a search program I designed
through the ship's logs, looking for information, stuff from the
last entries before the Wraith crew went into cold-sleep and set
the ship down on automatic. I found this." The display showed
an image of an ovoid object, clearly of Wraith manufacture,
drifting in orbit between two dragonfly-wing solar panels. "This
is a beacon, I think. The Hive Ship left it in orbit before it made
planetfall on Halcyon however many centuries ago. It went
active recently."

"The Lieutenant Colonel was telling the truth," murmured
Vekken, "there was a Wraith device circling our world."

Daus gave a curt nod. "Your leader Sheppard claims he
destroyed this thing. If he did not lie, then of what import is
it?"

McKay grimaced. "Quite a lot, if it sent out any signals to
other Wraith Hives!" He pointed at the screen. "If that rang the
dinner gong loud enough, then there's likely to be more ships on
their way here, other Hive Fleets with thousands *more* Wraith."
The scientist paused for breath. "You are, to put it very mildly,
quite screwed."

"*Scar!*" spat the Magnate, wheeling around in an angry turn.
"That filthy alien whoreson! He did this!" Daus advanced menacingly on Kelfer. "You allowed it to happen! It was your fault!"

Vekken saw the question on Rodney's face. "A Wraith, the
one we named 'Scar', we believe it was the commander of this
vessel. There was an accident some time ago and it escaped from

its hibernation capsule…"

"It was your blind tampering!" Daus thundered at the scientist. "We never did determine what havoc he wrought while he was loose on this ship! You assured me he did nothing!"

"I… I believed so…" Kelfer managed. The man was collapsing before McKay's eyes, his arrogance vanishing like vapor. "How could I have known?"

"Scar must have set a stealth program running," said Rodney, "we've seen that sort of thing before. It works very slowly, in the background. It can stay undetected for years. He must have set up a protocol to activate the beacon, and it took all this time just to get around to it."

"We captured the Wraith attempting to activate one of their screamer-ships," noted Vekken. "It could not be broken, so we deposited it in the hunt enclosure to become a training target."

"I should have killed him!" snarled Daus. "Killed him and coated his bones in gold for the trophy hall, then hung you from the gibbet, Kelfer!"

"There's no guarantee a signal was sent," Rodney broke in, trying to calm the situation, "the odds are fifty-fifty the beacon was even transmitting!"

Vekken was the only one who remained cool and emotionless throughout the whole display, never once taking his eyes from McKay. "What can we do to protect ourselves, Doctor? You are as much at risk as we."

Sheppard's words echoed in Rodney's mind. They were an off-world team, on terra incognita, and they were not, under any circumstances, to let it get out that the city of Atlantis was intact. But did that apply here? A moment ago McKay told these men that the Atlanteans would have helped them if only they had asked, and now the adjutant was doing just that. He swallowed hard. "First we have to deal with the Hive Ship here." Rodney gestured at the walls. "Back on Atlantis we have access to powerful explosive devices—"

"*Back on Atlantis*?" Vekken pounced on his words. "You said the city was destroyed. You lied to us."

Rodney shook his head. "Does that matter now? Listen to me,

we have atomic weapons that produce destructive force through nuclear fission, bigger than anything you could create."

Kelfer gave a distracted nod. "I am aware of the theoretical science behind such munitions."

"We can detonate a nuclear device inside this ship and destroy it. You won't be able to live nearby for a few hundred years, but I'm guessing we're somewhere pretty remote right now, and it's a better option than a global culling."

Daus became very still. "What you suggest would mean obliterating a hoard of the most advanced technologies on our planet. Your plan would kill every potential Hound on this vessel."

Vekken nodded at his master's evaluation. "Overnight, the Fourth Dynast's military power would be reduced to nothing. Our clan would be inundated with challenges for the throne from every quarter, and we would not be able to answer them with superior force."

"Listen to me," said Rodney, forcing his voice steady. "If you do not destroy this ship, then your throne won't matter. The Wraith will cut across your planet like a plague of locusts and consume everything. You talked to me about compulsion, well, compel *this*." He advanced a step, and Vekken immediately blocked his way. "You don't have a choice, man! Give up this ship and your Hounds, or watch Halcyon die. You have no other option!"

"You are wrong," said Daus, the practiced conceit of a hundred generations returning to him, denying everything that he did not wish to hear. "I have you. And you'll find another way, or I will order you to be tortured until you die."

The Magnate swept out of the chamber with Vekken trailing behind him.

Rodney's hands contracted into fists and he shouted at the man's back in impotent, incredulous fury. "No! Don't turn away from me, damn it! Can't you understand? *You're signing this planet's death warrant!*"

"Keep the craft at a higher altitude," demanded Scar, watching Sheppard closely from the co-pilot's seat of the Puddle

Jumper. "Do not deliberately attempt to alert the locals to our presence."

John said nothing but inwardly he frowned. "Whatever you say. It's your fare, I'm just the cab driver." Sheppard had been hoping there was an outside chance that a Halcyon defense gunner with and itchy trigger finger might spot the cruising ship and throw a little flak at it, but once they climbed to a couple of thousand feet, the guns the Dynasts used wouldn't even reach the fast-moving vessel. He had successfully deceived the alien about the functionality of the Jumper's cloaking device, claiming that it had been damaged by the shots from the Wraith beacon in orbit. Scar had shown a flicker of concern when Sheppard mentioned that the marker satellite was now nothing more than space dust, but the alien hadn't let it change his plans. On his orders, they were still flying northwards, describing a course that took them toward the site of the Ancient dolmen. John kept the throttle set at the middle detent, trying to lengthen the time of the flight while he worked out a plan of action.

So far, so bad, he told himself. Sheppard gave Scar a sideways glance. Something about a Wraith sitting there as comfortable as anything inside an Ancient ship was just... Well, *wrong.* It lay badly with the colonel on a bone-deep, instinctual level, and he wondered if there wasn't something in the ATA gene he carried, the genetic connection to the Ancient bloodline, that made him dislike being in such close proximity to a Wraith. For his part, Scar seemed quite unruffled by the whole experience. If anything, he was fascinated by the soft glow of the Jumper's control console, studying it closely like a human would scrutinize a bug under a magnifying glass.

Still, for all his apparent distraction, the Wraith never once slackened his grip on the controller box attached to Teyla's steel leash. The Athosian woman sat behind Scar, her shoulders hunched forward and her hands supporting the metal collar at her neck. Sheppard chewed down a surge of anger at the sight of his friend's mistreatment. For a moment, Teyla caught his eye and she forced a weak nod. *Hang in there,* he thought, *I'll get you out of this.*

And yet he hadn't been able to save Ronon. The Satedan was back down there, miles away now in the forest clearing, maybe dead, maybe alive. Of all the men he had ever met, John Sheppard had never known any person to have a survival instinct as strong as Ronon Dex did, and he just hoped that he could get through this and go back for the brusque ex-soldier. But with each passing second they were getting further and further away from Ronon, not to mention Beckett and the others; and as for McKay... This whole mission was coming to pieces around his ears, and here was John, forced to play dial-a-ride for a Wraith raiding party.

Scar snapped out a guttural yowl at the other Wraiths in the back compartment of the Jumper. They were skittish and nervous, hissing and clawing at one another like cats in a cage two sizes too small. Scar's growls quieted them down for the moment, and he noticed Sheppard watching him.

"They obey me," he noted. "Despite all the ill-effects of the device, they still have enough intelligence to know that."

"Uh-huh," John pretended to be indifferent. "So how come you can chew gum and walk at the same time, but not them? Why aren't you doing the monkey?"

"Your idiom is peculiar." Scar sniffed. "I am a simply superior. My cadre is of a more intellectual vein than the common Wraith."

A humorless smile crossed Teyla's face. "You sound like Daus and the other nobles. The hunters. They also like to think they are superior."

"In my case, it is truth and not self-delusion."

Sheppard shrugged. "If you say so."

He turned the Jumper to avoid the peak of a snow-capped mountain and in the distance he saw a white patch among the foothills. The dolmen was just visible as a slate gray dot sitting on a broad arena of bare stone. Almost the instant the ship turned to face the distant obelisk, the feral Wraith in the rear compartment began to whine. The colonel saw Scar flinch. His hand crept toward a control on the console. Perhaps he could pull the same gag he had with the hitchhiker, dropping the hatch and turning off the gravity dampeners—

"Do not be foolish," Scar's voice was low and loaded with menace. He had Teyla's pistol in his hand. "We have come this far without incident. I would prefer not to kill you while we are still airborne."

"Just stretching my fingers," he lied.

The closer they approached, the more it was clear that the dolmen was causing the Wraith—Scar included—physical pain. Sheppard shot Teyla a look that said *be ready*, and she nodded back.

"I would think you would not wish to approach the dolmen," the woman began, "does it not hurt you to be so close to it?"

"The agony is intense." Scar bit out the words through gritted teeth. "But now the machine runs weak. After ten thousand years, we can tolerate it this much." He jerked Teyla's leash and the woman grabbed at her collar. "I know you will attempt to defy me at this moment, as you think I am distracted." He worked the controller and the collar contracted a little. "You are mistaken. Obey me, human."

The Jumper's on-board computer had recognized the dolmen as a piece of kindred Ancient technology and brought up a scan of the monument. Sheppard saw a cutaway of the interior. It was a maze of molecule-thin antennae broadcasting disruptive energy patterns on the Wraith's psychic wavelength.

"Destroy it," growled Scar. "Now."

"What? No way!" retorted the colonel. "That thing's got a ZPM powering its core. The detonation of something like that would blow the planet apart!"

"Wrong," spat the Wraith. He extended a finger and pointed to a section of the dolmen. "Target your weapons drones here. It will collapse the construct and discharge the energy safely."

"How can... You be sure?" gasped Teyla.

Scar grinned cruelly. "I have killed more of the Enemy than I can count. Destroyed hundreds of... Of their craft. I know how to defeat them!" He tightened the collar another notch on Teyla's neck. "Do it now!"

The sensing mechanisms in the pilot's chair had already read

Sheppard's train of thought and warmed a pair of drones for launch. The targeting cues on the head-up display framed the hit location on the dolmen, locking the weapons on. Every fiber in his being told him that this was not what he wanted to do, that this would be the absolute worst choice he could make; but there on the floor of the Puddle Jumper was Teyla Emmagan, dying by inches and gasping for one more breath of air. And John could not let her die.

"Firing," he grated, the word catching hard in his throat. Sheppard did not even need to touch a control. The two drones ejected from the Jumper's outrigger pods and spun away in brilliant corkscrews of yellow lightning. John brought the ship around hard, veering away at full throttle, making for the upper atmosphere. If the Wraith was wrong, they could quickly find themselves on the edge of a planet-sized fireball.

The watchful canopy display tracked the drones on their unerring course straight into the timeless gray stone of the obelisk. The matter-energy conversion matrix inside the complex Ancient missiles ignited and shattered the dolmen at the precise point Scar had indicated. Sheppard had been correct; a poorly aimed shot might have ruptured the contained bubble of space-time inside the crystalline Zero Point Module, allowing exotic particles of a kind never seen in this universe to shatter and release an apocalyptic storm of energy. Scar, however, had not lied. The impact point of the drones flattened a monument that had stood untouched for a hundred centuries, and the broadcast array collapsed in on itself. In a single, star-bright flash of power, the ZPM discharged the last of its potency into the sky. Even though the module was nearly drained, the force of the release sent lances of static discharge racing around the planet, warping tidal forces and whipping tornadoes and storms into instant fury. People in the cities and in the High Palace unlucky enough to be looking in its direction were blinded by the glare. A plume of glittering light punched out into space, and then dissipated.

On the ground, the dolmen and everything around it for a twenty mile radius was a pale wasteland of burnt soil. Airships and gyro-flyers too close to the shockwave were ripped apart or blown from the sky. In some regions, tall towers and tenement buildings were felled by earth tremors. Birds died in mid-air and fell to earth in flocks. Fallout made of burnt ash swirled into gray cloud masses. There were thunderstorms and hurricanes the like of which had never been seen on Halcyon before.

But all these consequences were forgotten as the pervasive energy of the dolmen ceased across the planet. Freed of the maddening mental interference of the Ancient device, every corralled Wraith, every Hound in every pen and street on Halcyon was released from psychic bondage. Some died from the shock, others as their kindred turned upon them; but all were wild with frenzy, their minds reduced to uncontrolled, brutal, animalistic madness.

The shockwave of charged air that radiated from the energy plume hit the Puddle Jumper's aft and flipped it end over end. Sheppard's controls refused to answer as he worked the steering yoke. The ground below raced past the cockpit canopy to be replaced by the azure sky, then repeated, green and blue, green and blue.

He was aware of Scar and Teyla there beside him, of the monstrous snarling cries coming from the other Wraith; but these were things he had to tune out of his mind, concentrating hard on the play of atmosphere across the blunt hull of the ship and the stuttering pulses of thrust from the gravity drives.

"No," he said under his breath, "no, don't... Don't do it..." Sheppard always talked to a bird whenever he flew it. Some pilots thought it was an eccentric quirk, others nodded sagely and agreed it was the thing to do, as if they were somehow communicating with the craft like it was a riding animal. There was no doubt in John's mind that the gene-linked Jumpers were the closest thing to a ship that actually *could* understand you; but that didn't stop this one from ignoring him now.

All the primary flight systems in the vessel went off-line at once. Forward thrust went instantly to nothing, and the gravity coils that held the un-aerodynamic Jumper fuselage in the air ceased as well. The ship stopped tumbling and started falling, like the big green brick it resembled. They still had normal gravity inside the cabin, thanks to the fact that the inertial dampeners were on a different circuit to the thrusters, but all that meant was that Sheppard, Teyla and their Wraith passengers would have a comfortable ride all the way down to the point the Jumper smashed into the landscape and crumpled like a beer can.

Teyla blurred in the corner of his vision and she heard a cry of anger from Scar as the Athosian woman barreled into him, knocking the alien out of his seat and on to the deck. "Great time for an escape attempt," he said, not daring to take his gaze away from the crippled, half-dead control console in front of him. Sheppard racked his brains for the sequence of manual start-up protocols that McKay had drawn from the Ancient databases on Atlantis, running his hands over the glassy buttons and feathering the g-drive throttle. He got a brief flicker of light from the head-up display before it died again. John ignored a crash and howl of pain as something heavy — probably an angry Wraith — collided with a box of gear clamped to the bulkhead. The Jumper rocked and threatened to nose over into another tumbling spin.

They were high when the shockwave struck, but now that altitude was being chewed up by Halcyon's unforgiving gravity. If he could just get this thing into a hover, if he could just get out of the chair and help Teyla...

"Come on!" Sheppard slapped the control panel with the flat of his hand, and held a breath, running through the re-start sequence from the top. *This panel, that button, then this switch, that one, that one, then here and the throttle.*

The display on the canopy blinked on, off, and then on again. Suddenly he was looking at an altimeter blinking red for danger and a string of collision warnings. John slammed the throttle forward and the Jumper bucked like a bronco, shifting and swinging. He reacted without thinking about it, throwing the ship into a static vertical hover mode, pushing off from his seat, turning in place, ready to vault over the console to Teyla's assistance.

The Athosian woman collided with him and slammed Sheppard back down into his chair, reeling away. Scar was behind her, his pale greenish-white face twisted in murderous fury. He had the end of the steel leash in his hand, dragging on it. In the other was the pistol, aimed at John. "Pathetic," it snarled.

Sheppard blew out a breath. "That's all the thanks I get for stopping you from becoming a greasy spot on the countryside?"

Scar shoved Teyla into the co-pilot's seat and sat behind her. Over his shoulder, the other Wraith were strangely quiet, cowed by the fury of their master.

Teyla's tawny complexion was waxy and dull. The Hound collar was taking its toll on her. "I tried," she husked, speaking through a bruised throat.

John grimaced, angry that he hadn't been able to come to her aid.

The Wraith holstered the Beretta again. "Show me a map. "

"Knock yourself out," grated Sheppard as a topographical display formed on the glass in front of them. "Where next, the beach? Want to get a little sun, huh?"

Scar showed him a location, miles to the northwest in a hilly, unpopulated area. "Take us there, or—"

"I know the drill," he retorted, and guided the Jumper away. "What's out in the middle of nowhere that you're so interested in?"

But the alien merely sneered at him and sat back in its seat. John grudgingly pushed the ship up to cruising speed and scrutinized the display in front of him. The Puddle Jumper's sensor suite was focusing on the point where Scar had ordered him to go, running a comparison through its database to a faint energy trace it had detected. After a moment, the Jumper's computer provided him with a report. There was something out there, all right, something large; a Wraith starship.

CHAPTER ELEVEN

Through the gyro-flyer's porthole, Carson saw the egg-shaped hot-air balloon drifting over the high barrier fence around the compound, watching blinks of light signal from the skeletal gondola tethered beneath it.

"We are over the hunting enclosure now," he heard Linnian say behind him. "Highness, the border guards are querying our approach."

"They see my seal upon this flyer's hull well enough," Lady Erony's reply was terse. "I do not need to justify my arrival to a mere guardsman."

"Nevertheless, they will be bound-bound to inform your father of your presence here," continued the adjutant, "and he will be displeased."

"Then let him be."

Dr. Beckett turned away from the oval window as the gyro-flyer descended and went low over the treetops. Linnian was already stalking back toward the flight deck, his posture tense and annoyed. Carson watched him pause to whisper orders to one of the riflemen standing at arms. Close to the soldier were two figures in heavy metal armor, so steady and unmoving that he might have thought they were statues had he not known better. The Hounds stood at attention, their stylized wolf-head helmets bowed in obedient submission. Beckett's fingers gripped the seat arms. It didn't matter how the Halcyons dressed them up, it still set his nerves on edge being this close to Wraiths.

"My mother always said they can smell fear, like a scent in the air."

He glanced at Erony and gave a weak smile. "I thought that was dogs."

"They killed her, you know," The admission fell from Erony's lips, out of nowhere, and Carson felt a sudden pang of sympathy for the young woman. "She took a splinter out on a sortie when I was a child, and I never saw her again. Just the withered husk of what she used to be." The proud and severe mask slipped, and Beckett found himself looking into the real Erony, the girl with fears and doubts and sorrows that she would never dare to show to her peers.

"I'm sorry," he told her, although the words were weak. In his line of work, Carson had often had the terrible duty of carrying news of a death to loved ones, and no matter how many times he said those platitudes, there was always a void inside him that went with them.

"Yes," Erony replied, "you are. So many say that they regret her passing, those who knew her and fought alongside her, but it is merely lip-service to her memory. You never even met my mother, and yet you keenly feel her death."

"I'm a doctor. If I didn't care about people I wouldn't be doing this job."

She looked away. "Halcyon has treated you Atlanteans poorly, and yet you still offer our commoners aid. You squander resources on people who cannot serve to strengthen your nation. You talk when you should fight. You fight when you should retreat. Why? I do not understand you."

"It's who we are, lass. Being strong does not automatically mean you have to become the bully in the playground. Strength is nothing without responsibility or conscience."

The mask moved back into place, her face hardening. "My father once told me that conscience and ethics are words that weak men hide behind when they cannot find the courage of their convictions."

"And what do you think, Your Highness?" Carson gave her a level stare. "Do you believe that compassion is a weakness?"

Whatever answer she might have given him was forestalled as Linnian returned to the cabin. There was a commotion visible in the compartment beyond and Beckett felt his stomach lurch as the flyer dropped toward the ground. "My Lady, one of our observers spotted the body of the Runner from the air. We are descending to make a closer inspection."

"The body?" Carson pushed out of his chair, aware of Staff Sergeant Mason coming up with him. "Is he alive?"

"That is not clear. You should remain on board until we—"

"Not bloody likely, mate," grated Mason, and shoved the adjutant aside as the aircraft's landing skis bumped against the ground.

Beckett grabbed the strap of his medical kit and hauled it after him, following Mason as the SAS soldier cut a wedge through the wary Halcyonite troopers.

The staff sergeant roared out orders to the riflemen with such force behind them that the conscripts jumped to obey him without even thinking, their years of unquestioning service to their superiors conditioning them for instant obedience. Mason led Beckett through a stand of knee-high grasses, a clearing that slanted down toward rocks and tall trees. The rattle of the gyro-flyer's rotor blades beat at his back in throbbing pulses of wind.

"Watch it!" snapped the sergeant, pulling the doctor to one side to avoid a headless corpse sprawled on the ground. "Clean kill," Mason noted dispassionately.

Carson grimaced at the decapitated Wraith and moved on, catching sight of a slumped shape in leather and buckskin. "There! Over there!"

Ronon Dex's complexion was sallow, and Beckett pressed a finger to the carotid artery in the man's neck. Something fluttered weakly against his fingertip and Carson blew out a breath. "He's alive."

"Been shot," noted Mason, pointing at the concentric rings of scorching on Dex's tunic. The soldier recovered something from the grass; Ronon's pistol. "With this, I reckon." Mason peered at the weapon. "Set for stun, looks like. Lucky for him."

The doctor stood and shouted at Linnian's men for help. Quickly, they had Ronon inside the flyer and Beckett jammed an injector full of stimulants into the meat of the Satedan's thigh.

Dex moaned and his eyes fluttered open. "Who...?"

"Ronon, it's Dr. Beckett. Take it easy, laddie, you've been

out for who knows how long."

The Runner growled and hauled himself up. "Give me room," he snarled. "Where... Where's the Wraith?"

"What Wraith?" said Erony.

"Scar!" he spat. "Wanted to kill me. Didn't see me switch modes on the gun. He has Sheppard and Teyla."

Mason frowned. "Where's Private Bishop?"

Ronon shook his head. "Dead."

"We came here as soon as we could," continued Carson. "Colonel Sheppard had a Puddle Jumper, do you have any idea where it is?"

"No." Dex leaned heavily against a seat and shook his head, fishing in his pocket. He produced the hand-held scanner that he had taken from the Jumper. "Track the ship with this."

Carson took the device. "Aye, that would work..." The doctor's words trailed off as he glanced down at the screen on the Ancient scanner. Trails of energetic waveforms like electroencephalograph patterns flexed across the panel, becoming more energetic by the second. The device gave out a warning chime and the readings went off the scale. At the same instant, Beckett heard a cry of alarm from one of the riflemen still outside the grounded flyer.

He turned in time to see a brilliant flash wash through the portholes on the starboard side of the aircraft. Linnian reeled backward, clutching at his eye.

"What the hell was that?" demanded Mason, "a nuke strike?"

Erony's face went deathly pale. "The... The dolmen..."

A thunderous wall of displaced air rolled over them from the tree line and suddenly the flyer was rocking on its skids, buffeted by a hurricane-force wind.

Carson fell hard against Erony and heard inhuman screams filling the flyer's cabin. His blood ran cold as he realized that it was the Hounds that were howling, the clawed nails of the armored Wraith tearing at their steel helmets and twitching in fury.

With a screech of bending metal, the Wraiths peeled back

the howling canine faces of their headgear and revealed their own terrible aspects. Carson had never seen such an expression of utter, animal hate on a Wraith as he did now; the vicious arrogance of the aliens he had witnessed before was absent, and it its place was something base and malignant. He felt as if he were seeing the black hate for all life at the heart of every Wraith, incarnate there in their eyes.

They exploded into violent motion. Moments earlier the cabin of the royal flyer had seemed wide and open; now it was a cramped killing floor, the two mad Wraiths eager to murder every human inside. Carson heard the sickening crack of a broken neck as the nearest of the Wraiths punched into the spine of a riflemen caught fleeing for the open hatchway. The other launched itself at Linnian's cowering form in the aisle beside the starboard seating. Heedless of his own injuries, Ronon Dex crashed into the Wraith and wrestled it away, smashing through ornate stained-glass lamps on the cabin walls.

The report from a long-lance rifle bellowed inside the flyer and Carson tasted acrid steam in the air. The nearer Wraith screeched and attacked the rifleman who had fired at it, ignoring the collection of needle-shot embedded in its chest. The discharge was horribly loud inside the cabin and Beckett's hearing rang with the echo.

He grabbed Erony's arm. "Is there another hatch?"

"This way!" she nodded, pulling him toward the back of the gyro-flyer.

Carson hazarded a glimpse over his shoulder, and immediately regretted it. The Wraith dispatched the rifleman with a ripping slash from its claws, but it did not stoop to feed upon the soldier. Instead, it came over the opulent velvet chairs like a raptor. Beckett swung his medical bag at it, but the Wraith was moving with insane speed, and it batted him away. Carson lost his footing and collided with a support stanchion. The alien punched Erony, knocking a push-dagger from her grip, and the woman skidded back against the curved inner walls of the compartment. Beckett heard the Wraith give out a shrieking hiss. Orange fire flashed at the periphery of his vision and brass cartridges glittered as someone discharged a weapon, but Carson's attention was locked on the angry Wraith as it made ready to claim the Halcyonite noble as another victim. Beckett reacted, all the frustration and annoyance of the past few days forming into fists. "Get off her, ya scunner!" he shouted, and punched the attacker hard in the rib. "Picking on girls, eh?"

He regretted the words the moment he said them. The Wraith yowled like a wildcat and spun about, pouncing on him. The air in Beckett's lungs came out of him in a whoosh as the alien slammed him against the carpeted decking, lighting sparks of pain behind his eyes. Foul, acidic breath caressed his face and the Wraith showed its teeth, hissing.

Carson was not an aggressive man, but he had grown up in a tough neighborhood, among those who liked to live up to a belligerent reputation, and he understood very well the principles of violence. Beckett brought his shoulders forward and butted the Wraith hard on the nose, with a satisfying crunch of bone. The alien reeled back, put off by such a sudden attack from its prey and hesitated a moment too long.

From behind him, staff sergeant Mason jerked the trigger of his L85 assault rifle and blew the creature off its feet with a stuttering discharge of bullets.

Carson rolled over and came face to face with the second Wraith, its neck twisted at an incorrect angle. Ronon Dex was hunched nearby, panting and sweating.

Erony came to him and helped Beckett into a chair as Mason and the riflemen dragged the dead Hounds out of the flyer. He looked up and found Ronon watching him. The Satedan had the ghost of a smile on his lips.

"Not bad, little man," said Dex. "I didn't think you had that much fight in you."

"I'm Scottish," he said glumly, "it's genetic."

"You attacked a Wraith bare-handed," added Erony, "you fought well."

"Only because I had no choice," Carson insisted, wincing at the building headache in his skull. "You want to understand us, lassie? That's it, right there. We don't fight because we want to.

It's our last choice."

"On my world, it is always the first," admitted the woman.

"Now you're getting it."

Mason climbed back into the cabin as Beckett moved to Linnian's side, examining the adjutant's injured eye. "Doc, I did a sweep of the clearing. Jumper put down here, like Ronon said it did, but it's long gone now. We got no rads in the air, but the weather's going mad out there."

"Wound's sake," breathed Erony as she peered out at the threatening, turbulent sky, "had we been airborne when the shockwave struck, we would have been thrown into the trees."

Dex gathered up the Ancient scanner from where it had fallen in the melee, working the device. "If I read this right, then it looks like Sheppard headed north."

"What about this Wraith, the one called Scar?"

Ronon frowned. "He had Teyla captive. My guess is he made the colonel fly them out of here."

"But where to?"

Erony's lips thinned to a line. "North, you say?" She sighed. "I know where they are going."

"Highness, do not speak further!" Linnian managed weakly. "These outworlders must not be party to such important matters!"

"Hush," insisted Carson. "Erony? Is there something we should know?"

The noblewoman threw a look to one of her riflemen. "Inform the pilots to raise the flyer and take us northwards. Our destination will be the protected lands of the Fourth Dynast." The soldier saluted and disappeared into the cockpit. "At best speed, we will reach them quickly, but I have no doubt your colonel's aircraft will be there before us."

"Mistake," whined the adjutant. "Do not speak of it!"

"There is a truth," she began, as the aircraft left the ground, "a hidden truth that my Dynast keep from the world, a truth that even I am not fully party to." Erony sagged, as if the weight of what she was about to reveal was dragging her down. "I gave my oath to hold this sacred, but now I fear more silence may doom my planet to extinction."

Beckett took a seat across from the young woman, and listened carefully as she told them the Lord Magnate's best-kept secret.

The ship had been constructed before any of the Wraith that now called it home had even been born; although 'constructed' might not have been the right way to describe it. Wraith vessels were not so much things of iron and steel, of plastic and glass, creations of artificial materials like the vessels built by the humans, the Goa'uld, the Asgard or the Ancients. Wraith craft were hatched; they were spun and carved into being, melded together out of matter more akin to bone and gristle than to titanium plate and silicon wafer. Electrochemical processes and nerve ganglions transmitted data and commands about the flesh of the Wraith Hive Ship. Organic bioluminescence and exothermal chemistry provided light, heat and breathing gasses. Skeletal matter formed the hull spaces and fuselage. The Wraith were parasites inside the gut of the craft, they probed and manipulated the simple brain to perform its flight tasks for them. And even, with a science now lost to all but a few castes of their kind, they found a way to warp the structure of reality so that rips into hyperspace could carry them from world to world, feeding, multiplying, *culling*.

This ship's mind had long since faded into docility, anything but the most basic cognitive functions still active, poked and prodded by the idiot flailings of the men-apes that discovered it. Once, at the heights of its prowess, the ship had been a living embodiment of fear. The vast shape of its insectile form, a giant mirror of the Iratus that had given birth to Wraithkind, it would drift above human worlds and strike terror into every prey that saw it. It had been glorious, then. To feed and feed, unfettered by everything except hunger. The Hive ate well and prospered; until the Enemy opposed them.

So began the long war, and along the way the Wraith lost something of themselves. The more they fought, the more they broke apart into factionalism, clan against clan, jockeying for the best feeding sites. In the end they had their victory, but the price was a high one. With the Enemy scattered, the galaxy was theirs—but food became scarce and the divisions of the war split wide. Wraith fought Wraith, and all the while the survivors of the great adversary sniped at them from every shadowed corner. Word of the Sleep began to spread. The Wraith were to embrace slumber and allow their feeding grounds to lie fallow and rebuild. Some would stay to stand sentinel; the rest would take the Sleep of millennia.

And so this Hive Ship came to this world for one final feast before venturing into hibernation; but the Enemy were waiting, and they had poisoned the prey, shielded them with their hateful technology. In the end, after many on both sides had fought and died, the vessel had fallen to earth and lay there, a wounded behemoth, its crew going insane with rage and hunger. Their only escape was to Sleep. The ship would wake them when it was time.

That time was now.

Inside the hibernation vault, the cells where Wraith still lay dormant took on a tepid white glow. First in ones and twos, then in clusters that faded into life, the neural links between the sleeping aliens and their vessel bringing both into gradual wakefulness.

Daus's elite corps of riflemen, his personal guard, had been deployed throughout the Hive Ship on his arrival. A contingent of them was stationed in the chamber, standing in a nervous ring on the bone walkway that extended across the open space. Their heads lifted to watch the patterns of light moving over the hexagonal hive cells. Sounds like eggshells cracking hissed and sputtered through the metallic air of the vast room. Wraiths, their minds shocked out of cold-sleep by the discharge from the shattered dolmen, reached out to peel back the fibrous sheaths that held them in stasis, spilling glutinous suspensor fluids out in a thick, cloying rain.

Naked, hateful and starving for the taste of their prey, the crew of the Hive Ship began to awaken. They had not fed in thousands of years, and the hunger they felt overwhelmed any reason they might have had. Pale and muscular bodies ripped themselves from the hibernation cells and scrambled across the walls, guttural screeches echoing as they spat out hunting calls.

The riflemen shone lamps into the darkness, casting pools of yellow sodium glare across the fluted curves of the bone walls. Shadows jumped and moved, drawing blares of nervous gunfire from fearful men. The Halcyons were used to being the hunters, the superiors in their dealings with the Wraith; but today those roles were reversed. The aliens swarmed upon the men in their black greatcoats, corpse-white forms rising up from beneath and falling upon them from above. In short order the crashes of gunfire were silenced and replaced with the howls and chatter of a feeding frenzy.

It was hard to make out details of exactly what was going on inside the hibernation vault. The screen in the Hive Ship's nexus chamber relayed visual data from one of hundreds of optical sensor orbs about the vessel's interior, and the images were attuned for Wraith eyes, not human ones; nevertheless, the shocked silence that hung in the room was proof enough that the Halcyon scientists were more than clear about the fate of the riflemen.

Rodney McKay's hand crept to his mouth. "We are so dead."

Kelfer was slumped beside him, the science minister now a paper-thin sketch of the man he had been. The scientist could not bear to watch the horrors unfolding on the screen. What he had witnessed in the past few days had finally broken him, as the facts he based his life around had come to pieces. McKay might have been able to spare a moment of pity for the guy, had he not been partially to blame for the danger that everyone on Halcyon was now facing.

Somewhere in the back of his mind, Rodney had been clinging on to the idea that he would, as he so often did, blossom under the pressure of the situation and come up with a brilliant solution that saved his life and those of everyone else around him; but as he watched the shadowy forms of the Wraith butchering those hapless soldiers, his heart felt like a fist of ice in his chest and the intellect he loved to trumpet was frozen with horror.

Everyone in the nexus chamber turned in fright as the hatch irised open, all of them expecting a flood of Wraith to boil in through the doorway; instead the Lord Magnate stalked in, followed by Vekken and a gaggle of panicked soldiers. All the men had their weapons out and Rodney saw smears of oily alien blood on their tunics.

Daus spied McKay and aimed a swordgun at the scientist. "You!" he thundered. "You did this to defy me, eh? You set them loose!" He advanced, fingering the trigger mechanism in the bowl hilt of the wicked blade.

Rodney recovered just enough to be incredulous. "What? No! That's insane! You think I'd wake up the Wraith just to get at you? I don't want them loose any more than you do!"

The Magnate's swordgun quivered. His fury was barely under his control and he wanted someone to take it out on, someone to blame no matter how undeserving they were. Daus roared wordlessly and dashed a trolley of equipment to the deck, stamping to his adjutant's side. "Vekken! Gather all the men and corral these alien abominations, force them back into their hives at blade point if you must, but do not let them run wild! This is my ship! *Mine!*"

McKay listened to the man's rantings and just like that, he had a solution. He crouched, speaking quietly into the First Scientist's ear. "Kelfer, listen to me. Vekken's troopers won't be able to stop the Wraith, we both know that. It's up to us to deal with this, you and me."

"How?" moaned the other man. "We are doomed."

"Help me with this." Rodney gestured to the control console. "You've been poking around in this derelict for years and you know the layout better than me. Help me access the main nerve cluster for the power systems."

Kelfer's eyes focused on him. "For what reason?"

"Hive Ships draw power from bio-reactors. If we alter the energy flow, unbalance the reaction, we could create a feedback loop."

McKay saw the light of understanding in the other man's expression. "A chain reaction. Yes. It could be done."

"Help me do it, Kelfer."

The scientist got shakily to his feet. "McKay," he husked, "this... This deed will be most destructive. It will destroy every living thing inside the vessel." Kelfer hesitated. "Us."

"Yes." Rodney blinked. *How odd.* His brain had been completely aware of that fact from the instant the idea had occurred to him, but at the same time it wasn't until Kelfer said it out loud that McKay realized that this course of action was a suicidal one. "Yes," he repeated, a peculiar kind of calm settling on him, "let's get to it, then."

Kelfer gave him a shaky nod and walked to one of the other control pedestals, quickly manipulating the organic switches and buttons.

"What are you doing?" Rodney turned to see Daus call out across the nexus chamber. "Kelfer? Those systems are not to be tampered with! Kelfer, answer me!"

"This must be done," said the scientist distractedly.

McKay's heart leapt as new data filtered in through the crude interface between the Wraith ship and his laptop computer. Complex new code strings and power distribution curve algorithms ticked across the screen. He saw at once how to make the overload happen; it would be a question of routing energy from the bio-reactors along dead and redundant ganglia, letting it rise to supercritical levels...

"First Scientist and Duke Kelfer, by my command you will step away from that mechanism!" Daus strode forward, Vekken and his men at arms all ready for imminent violence. "Stop this mutiny!"

"One moment more," Kelfer began.

There was a double detonation, twin barks of noise like a shotgun releasing both barrels, and Kelfer was jerked away from the console, struck by an invisible hammer of force. Smoke coiled from the gun muzzles concealed in the ornate scrollwork along the length of the Lord Magnate's sword.

McKay went to the man and felt his stomach knot at the ugly wound in Kelfer's torso. The Halcyonite scientist tried to push a word from his trembling lips, but there was only the hiss of bloody froth. There on the deck, Rodney watched the life fade from him.

Anger propelled McKay back to his feet and he whirled. Daus was close, the keen curve of the swordgun hanging at head height between them. "All those who disobey me are traitors," grated the Magnate, a mad glitter in his eyes, "and the reward for perfidy is murder!"

"You just shot that man in cold blood," Rodney retorted. "And you're not even remorseful, are you? Not one little bit. Is there anything that actually matters to you apart from power? Anything? *Anyone*?"

Daus's face softened and the sword dipped an inch. "Nothing I have done has been for myself. My every waking action is in service of my world, my people. *My family*." He nodded to one of his men, and the soldier moved Kelfer's body away. "Any man who defies me I will kill in the same manner."

"You have to let me destroy this vessel!" spat McKay.

"Never—"

The deck trembled and shuddered as something in the depths of the Hive Ship came to life. Fines of dust trickled from the ceiling overhead as the chamber's bone pillars creaked.

Rodney grabbed at his laptop as the readings displayed there spiked. "I think… This ship's alive."

Sheppard turned the Puddle Jumper in a tight banking maneuver and circled the encampment. At first glance it looked a like a mine head, just a couple of stone blockhouses, tents and some watchtowers; but second time around he saw the archway constructed into the face of the steep-sided hill that rose up over the compound, and like one of those weirdo dot pictures they always had at the mall, the shape of the landscape suddenly shifted in his perception and John saw it, as clear as day.

There was the edge of the broad, shield-shaped fuselage, buried under a carpet of grasses and younger trees. There were the bony spikes fanning out from the concealed hull, green with creepers and other plant growth. A Hive Ship, hiding in plain sight, camouflaged beneath centuries of mud and earth.

Scar clicked his amusement. "My craft. My home. At last."

"Might want to think about doing a little spring cleaning," sneered Sheppard, "looks a little overgrown from up here."

"Your mockery will not help you when your usefulness comes to an end, human," replied the Wraith. "And with regard to that... Land this craft." He pointed. "There. Close to the Hive."

Sheppard counted his blessings. The launch bays on most Hive Ships he'd encountered were on the ventral side of the hull, and in the case of this one that meant they were buried in the dirt. The last thing he wanted was to take the Jumper inside the alien vessel. Outside, there were still escape options. *I hope*, he told himself. He brought the Ancient shuttlecraft down easy, very much aware of Scar's tight grip on the controls for the choke collar around Teyla's neck. They were coming up to the point of no return here and the last thing he wanted to do was give the Wraith an excuse to kill the Athosian woman.

Through the trees he saw a silver object low to the ground and recognized the shape of a Fourth Dynast gyro-flyer. The helicopter was heavily decorated with golden detailing and bright heraldry across the gleaming chrome hull. *Only Daus would have a ride that pimped*, Sheppard thought, *and if his high-and-mighty Lordship is here, then maybe McKay's not far away either.* It made sense; if the man had a Hive Ship on his land, then why not kidnap the most qualified guy from Atlantis to take a look at it?

Sheppard gently turned the Jumper in a hundred-and-eighty degree yaw before settling the craft on the grass. *Here we go. Last chance we're gonna get to take these creeps.*

"The hatch," ordered Scar, and John obliged. But instead of letting the drawbridge drop slowly, he stabbed a key that let it fall open with a crashing slam of noise. The distraction provided the instant he needed, and he vaulted out of the pilot's chair and threw himself bodily at the Wraith commander.

"Teyla, run-!" he cried, but Scar's arm blurred and the colonel felt a punishing blow impact on his jaw, knocking him aside. He struck the Jumper's deck and rolled.

"Crude," said Scar, a mocking lilt to the word. "Is that the most sophisticated escape attempt you could concoct? If all your warriors are as obvious as you, your human militias will not survive for long against us." He gurgled a command to the other Wraith, and two of them grabbed at Teyla, dragging her out of the Jumper.

She spat and clawed at them, fighting to break free with no success. Scar watched the Wraith exit the ship, then turned to face Sheppard.

"Let the woman go," said John. "You don't need her."

"I disagree." Scar drew the gun from his belt. "A lure is always a valuable commodity when one is hunting."

"Take me instead, then."

Scar made that irritating clicking noise again. "You have proven yourself too wild to be trained. You would not make a decent Hound. So now you will gain the rewards for your disobedience." The Wraith's hand twitched and he recognized the feeding maw in its palm. Sheppard saw Colonel Sumner again in his mind's eye, the man's life draining away before him. Scar read the fear on John's face and grinned broadly. "No, human, I will not take my nourishment from you. I imagine a specimen as inferior as yourself would leave a poor taste." He threw back his head with a snort of laughter. "Besides, one of your soldiers already slaked my thirst. I am quite sated for the moment... And there is always the woman if I become hungry again."

That was enough to propel John Sheppard up from his feet, the combat knife he'd palmed during the scuffle flicking out.

Scar met him with the barrel of the Beretta and fired twice into his chest at close range. John felt burning hot rods of pain lance into his ribs and his sternum, the sudden impacts striking him back and away across the Jumper's forward compartment.

"Die slowly, human," grated the Wraith. "Know that you will

not be the last of your kind I kill today." Toying with the pistol, Scar wandered away, leaving the colonel in a heap on the decking.

Teyla ran for the Jumper and made it three steps before the collar began to bite. She dropped to her knees and kept pushing forward, her vision turning gray as the open hatch loomed in front of her. She blinked away tears of agony, holding herself up from the ground.

Scar's hateful smile appeared before her. "Where are you going, Hound? I did not release you from your leash."

She tried to call out Sheppard's name, but her voice was stolen away. Faint gasps of air came in choking rattles.

The alien grinned. "You will not defy me again, prey. You are the last one of your war band that lives, and you want more than anything to take revenge for the death of your comrades, yes?" He pulled her to her feet. "So you will not defy me again, because for every moment you live you may entertain a little longer the fantasy of killing me yourself." Scar leered over her. "And I know your kind, Tey-lah. I know you want that more than you want to die."

She didn't resist him; the Athosian let herself go slack, as if she were defeated, and after a moment the collar retracted.

Teyla looked up and spat into Scar's face. She tensed for a blow, but none came. Instead, the alien wiped the spittle away without expression and took the steel leash in his hand. With a jerk of his wrist, he pulled her away from the Jumper and toward the ragged entrance cut in the flanks of the Hive Ship.

Ronon. John. And now I am alone. She forced the thoughts away and concentrated on the cable connected to her heavy necklet. *The Wraith's arrogance will be its downfall*, she decided, her eyes flint-hard with determination. *I swear on my father's grave, Scar will not leave this ship alive.*

In basic training, recruit John Sheppard had been unfortunate enough to have a firearms instructor who went by the name of Master Sergeant Gunn. It seemed like a joke when he first

heard it, but after he'd stood in front of the man and weathered
the force five tirade of creative invective the training sergeant
poured on anyone who failed to be an outstanding marksman,
John had quickly leaned that 'Big' Gunn had a knowledge of
weapons and their destructive capacity greater than any man
he'd ever met. Gunn was a veteran, and would gladly display
the place where he had been hit by a 5.56 bullet from an AK-
47 to trainees who demonstrated any squeamishness about the
tools of the military's trade. He made Sheppard's squad use pig
carcasses for target practice so that they would understand the
lethal damage a bullet could do on a piece of unprotected flesh.
Never mind the fact that most of Gunn's charges would end up
shooting missiles at over-the-horizon targets from twenty thousand feet up; he wanted them to know the results of pulling a
trigger.

Eventually, someone in the squad was nominated to ask Gunn
what it felt like to get shot; and when Recruit Sheppard put the
question to the man, his answer was hard and to the point. *You
like bowling, Sheppard?* He had asked. *Ever drop a ball on your
foot? Well, kid, you think about lying on your back right there in
the number one lane, and you get your buddy to stand over you
with a twelve-pound ball in his sweaty grip. Then you let him
drop it on your chest. Take that and cross it with a red hot poker
being slammed through your gut and you got about a tenth of
what it feels like to take a round. You following me, Recruit?*

"Yes, sergeant," the colonel said thickly, his voice faint to
his own ears. He could taste blood on his lips and there was a
feeling like jagged glass in his torso each time he took a breath.
"Did I bust a rib…?"

Sheppard looked around, his vision swimming as the Jumper's
cabin gradually came into focus. With care he hauled himself
up to a sitting position and pulled open the front of his jacket.
Inside, the thick, high-impact Kevlar body armor was distorted
and tight across his chest. Two warped coins of metal—the
flattened heads of the bullets from Scar's shots—were embedded in the dense plastic weave, the surrounding fibers knitted
together where the heat from the rounds had melted them. John

moaned as he released the Velcro straps on the armor and let it fall away. He probed gingerly at the spots on his torso beneath the bullet impact points and got fresh hits of pain from both. Sheppard peered down the front of his undershirt and saw ugly bruises already turning yellowish-purple. "Ow," he declared, with feeling.

As quickly as he could manage, the colonel rooted through a medical kit for field dressings and an analgesic gel, then plundered the Jumper's weapons locker for a fresh P90 submachinegun and as many sticks of ammunition as he could carry. He took a swig of water from a canteen to wash the coppery taste of blood from his mouth and winced as he took a deep breath. "You're still alive, John," he said aloud, reflecting on the accuracy of Sergeant Gunn's description. "Even if it does hurt like hell."

Sheppard forced the pain to the back of his thoughts and slipped out of the Jumper, moving quickly toward the hull of the grounded Hive Ship.

The Halcyons had built a short stone tunnel up to the side of the Wraith vessel, hiding the place where their engineers had cut into the exterior ten generations ago. The slice through the alien fuselage was a rough-edged wound that had never been allowed to close, kept open with giant sutures and heavy clamps of rusty metal. Typically, two Fourth Dynast riflemen were permanently stationed in this antechamber, standing at arms around the clock under the light from chemical lamps. Scar's cohorts had made short work of them, and Sheppard's lip twisted as he came across the desiccated corpses of what had been young men only hours earlier.

He pulled himself into the vessel and a creeping chill settled on him. The same crawling spook house vibe he felt the last time he'd boarded a Wraith craft was there in an instant, the itch like spider webs on his skin. And the smell, that battery acid stink, hanging in the cold still air. Sheppard flicked the torch on his P90 on-off to test it, and then moved forward, the butt of the boxy weapon pressed into his shoulder. There was a dull vibration coming up through the floor, a sense of something powerful building up to speed. Now and then, a rumbling shudder would twitch through the walls.

As far as the Atlantis expedition had been able to discover, Wraith ships had little in the way of interior variation, structured inwardly like a spade-shaped ribcage with internal spaces. Previous jaunts on board these craft meant Sheppard knew some of the basic layout, like where to find the hibernation chamber or the holding areas; but he was working blind here, trying to second-guess Scar. If the alien was one of the Wraith 'officer class' then he was on board this tub because he had a goal in mind. *The bridge? Engineering? A weapons deck? Do these Hive Ships even have those things?* The gaps in Sheppard's knowledge were infuriating. He came to a fork in the corridor and hesitated.

"Okay," he said, after a moment. "Eeny, Meeny, Miny, Mo."

Above him, set in a socket on the curved ceiling, a ball of optic jelly watched the colonel making his choice.

"Sheppard, you idiot!" yelped McKay. "Are you...? Is he actually doing that stupid *eeny-meeny* thing to find his way around?" In a vain attempt to provide some sort of assistance to Vekken and his soldiers, Rodney had — at gunpoint — been made to tap back into the Hive Ship's internal sensor systems. The large glassy screens in the nexus chamber showed dozens of views through fish-eye lenses, some watching empty compartments of the vessel, others catching glimpses of Wraith as they moved about the starship, hunting and feeding. By sheer chance, McKay had caught the colonel on camera.

"Still alive," Vekken seemed surprised. "Your commander has more resilience than I would have credited him with." The adjutant threw a glance over his shoulder at the Lord Magnate, who was in heated discussion with the late Kelfer's subordinates.

"Behind you! Behind you!" snapped Rodney at the monitor display. A second optical feed from an area further down the same corridor showed a lone Wraith creeping toward the colonel, who seemed oblivious of the alien's stealthy approach. "This is like watching one of those idiotic slasher movies!" He slapped at the control console. "Sheppard! It's behind you!"

"Perhaps if you call out a little louder, he might hear," said Vekken archly.

McKay spun around, galvanized into action. "He might hear this!" The scientist snatched at the bag of equipment that the Halcyons had taken from him at the dolmen and tore it open, grabbing at the radio inside. He hesitated for a second, twisting the dials on the top of the walkie-talkie. He couldn't remember the frequency! That was the stupid bloody military for you, changing the channel setting for every bloody mission, and Rodney could never remember which was which. "Sheppard!" he barked into the pickup. *Nothing.* He fiddled with the dial again. "Sheppard, watch your back—"

Vekken plucked the radio from his grip. "You will desist, Dr. McKay." He handed the device to one of his soldiers. "If he attempts to use this communicator again, wound him."

"Yes sir."

"He'll be killed!" blurted McKay.

"Possibly," agreed Vekken, "but you should be more concerned about your own safety. The Magnate has given you an order. Fulfill it."

"*—eppard, watch...ack—*"

The sound from the radio was so quick and so distorted that for a moment it sounded like some random squawk of static and not actually a human voice at all. "Rodney?" Sheppard froze, straining to hear; and in that second he caught the sound of something else entirely. A bare footstep, claws ticking over chitinous deck plates.

John swung the P90 around and thumbed the switch. The compact torch blinked on and caught the newly awakened Wraith in a halo of harsh white light. The alien's skin was still wet with processing fluids from the hibernation process, and its skin was tight over gaunt muscle and bone. More than anything, the ghoulish creature looked *ravenous*.

It moved fast; Sheppard's first three-round burst went wide, the tongue of yellow fire from the P90's muzzle cutting the air where it had crouched a heartbeat earlier. He swept the gun back and forth, working the trigger, eschewing the method of short and controlled bursts for something closer to the spray-and-pray technique. The Wraith was almost on him when John's attack connected and the bullets marched across the killer's torso in a line of black impacts. It didn't go down straight away; the Wraith were tough like that. Before it could recover, Sheppard advanced a step and fired twice more, aiming for the collection of organs in the chest cavity that approximated a human heart. With a rattling gasp, the Wraith collapsed and John realized he'd been holding his breath the whole time. He puffed and checked the machinegun's clear plastic magazine. Third of a clip gone and he'd only taken out a single Wraith. He was going to have to find a solution to this situation that didn't involve bullets.

Sheppard moved forward down the tunnel, continuing on. He got ten steps before the vibration coming up through his boots changed tempo, becoming a resonating howl of motion and sound. The deck shifted beneath him in pulsed, shuddering tremors.

"We cannot land!" called the pilot from the cockpit compartment. "Your Highness, the ground is unstable!"

Ronon pushed Linnian aside and pressed his face to the glass oval of the gyro-flyer's porthole. Beneath them he could see low buildings, the green cylinder of a parked Puddle Jumper. As he watched the surrounding trees wafted back and forth as if a stiff wind was blowing. One of the watchtowers crumpled abruptly at the midpoint and fell away, collapsing in a heap. "It's an earthquake."

"This region is geologically inactive," Erony countered. "It's the vessel."

The doctor crowded in beside the Satedan. "Oh my. Do you see there?" He pointed to the hillside. "Landslide."

Dex followed his direction and saw great clods of earth falling away from the shallow hill, uprooting trees as they disintegrated. Pale, bluish-white rock was revealed underneath; but no, not rock. It glittered dully in the daylight, the color of oiled, beaten metal. "They're raising the ship," he said it aloud, unable to believe the evidence of his own eyes. Ronon shouted out a command down the length of the cabin. "Back us off, now! Get us away from the hill!"

The gyro-flyer's rotors buzzed and the aircraft retreated into a hover, just as coils of dust and earth boiled up from around the perimeter of the concealed craft. The ground cracked apart with a hoarse roar, and the Hive Ship's drives swelled to optimal power. Ronon watched the hill rise from its setting and tremble, shaking off the accumulated camouflage of countless years. Stone and wood, earth and grass fell away and flocks of birds were unseated from their roosts.

Erony's pilot kept them level with the craft as it slowly rose above the tops of the trees, a deluge of rendered soil raining down across the landscape. Torn free from its hiding place, the Wraith Hive Ship cast a monstrous arachnid shadow, the ponderous and deadly mass drifting upward into the sky in defiance of gravity.

"We are too late," breathed the woman.

CHAPTER TWELVE

Beckett blinked. "Well. It's not every day of your life that you get to see a hill take off and fly away."

"How long must've that ship been down here to get grown over like that?" demanded Mason. "Two hundred years? Five hundred? More?" He fixed Lady Erony with a hard, angry stare, daring her to answer him.

"The vessel has been here on our lands since before the Wars of Unification. I was never permitted to visit it." Her words caught in her throat. The noblewoman was like everyone else on the gyro-flyer, dwarfed by the horror of the reborn Hive Ship.

Ronon gave the Wraith vessel one last look and then ran his hands over his tunic, checking his gear. The drifting alien hulk hung like a storm front, moving against the wind, the throbbing hum of the gravity drives gradually increasing in pitch. The craft was elderly and still shaking off the throes of sleep, he reasoned, but it would not take long for the Hive Ship's systems to return to full capacity. Once that happened, it would outpace this flying machine in seconds, rise to orbit and be free to do whatever Scar commanded. Contact other Hive Fleets, launch bombardments or flights of Darts. The prospect chilled him, even if on some level Dex's sense of justice told him the Halcyons were fully deserving of such a fate.

There wasn't time to touch down and get to the Puddle Jumper; and even if he did, he only had the doctor to fly the craft for him. *No.* It was up to him to stop this.

Ronon pulled his way up the cabin to the cockpit hatch and summoned the flyer pilot's attention. "You. Get us closer."

The aviator's jaw dropped open. "Closer? Are you mad?"

The Satedan made a show of checking the power cell on his particle magnum. "Take us over the dorsal hull, close to the spinal ridge. Hurry, before the autonomic cannons wake up and start shooting."

The pilot nodded woodenly and pushed the steering yoke forward. The flyer pitched and the leviathan starship loomed to fill the glass canopy.

Ronon met Mason at the main hatch. "What do you think you're up to, son?" snapped the soldier. "I'm the ranking—"

"Get out of my way." Dex yanked on a control lever and the steel hatch yawned open, letting wind and the unearthly drone of the Hive Ship's engines fill the cabin. He pulled two keen battle daggers from a concealed holster.

"You're gonna kill yourself," Mason told him.

"There's plenty of Wraith who will do that for me." Outside of the hatch, he saw the bony hull of the Wraith ship come into view as the flyer drifted into near-collision distance. He threw a quick look at Beckett. "Keep your distance from the ship. I'm going inside."

"And just how are you going to do that?"

Ronon felt the kick of adrenaline rush into him and he couldn't stop the flicker of a grin as he stepped up. "Watch."

The knives raised, Dex threw himself out of the gyro-flyer and into the bitter air, the tree tops fluttering a thousand feet below.

"We are airborne." At first Teyla had thought the tremors passing through the Hive Ship were something else, perhaps an attack of some kind. She half-hoped that were the case, wishing that the Halcyons had seen sense and brought their air-battleships to smash the dormant vessel into wreckage; but the shift in gravity told her otherwise, as the decking seemed to become softer beneath her feet, the g-force lessening as the mammoth vessel discarded its cover. The corridors of the Wraith craft were taking on a different hue, the dead and ashen white of fleshy processing conduits along the walls changing to a cold blue-green. They pulsed like veins as life returned to the alien ship.

Scar's retinue of Wraiths had become muted ever since they boarded the hive. Teyla saw some of them sniffing at the walls or licking at scent-traces that only they could detect. The anxiety the aliens had demonstrated before the dolmen and inside the Jumper was completely gone. These beings were in their own element now, moment by moment regaining the poise that their leader demonstrated. She had no doubt that in days, perhaps even hours, the Wraith once tormented and made feral by the Ancient device would become their former selves; and when that happened she pitied the people of Halcyon. The Wraith were frightening enough when they preyed upon you just to fulfill their needs for sustenance; Teyla shuddered beneath her choke collar as she contemplated of the depths of cruelty they would show to a people who had made them slaves. She swallowed, trying to soothe her bruised throat. Breathing was difficult, even with the heavy Hound collar's cogs in a relaxed mode. "Ah," she gasped. "Gods protect me…"

Scar heard her whisper and cocked his head. "Your deities will not hear you in this place, Tey-lah. Of that, you must have no doubt." He sniffed the air. "Only my wishes will be answered today."

Teyla had never considered that Wraiths might have gods of their own. *What kind of creator would they worship?* she wondered; but it was more likely that Scar was simply mocking her. She was reduced to this, a pet for her most hated foe's amusement. Teyla caught the spark of revulsion that thought kindled inside her and held on to it, letting it warm her.

A warning yowl from one of the other Wraith brought them all to a halt. The alien dropped to a crouch and lapped at the chilly air, glancing back over its shoulder with a wary grimace. Scar became very still, and his cohorts followed suit. "Listen," he murmured, "can you hear them? Can you feel them, Tey-lah?"

She didn't want to. She did not want to acknowledge the swarming presence in the corners of her mind, the insect crawl of alien thought scratching at the insides of her skull; but they were there, the fierce colors of other Wraith psyches pushing in on her, tight and constricting. They were so very close now, in the walls, the floor, crowding out the sound of her heartbeat.

Man-shapes moved at the far end of the corridor, things that loped and hissed shifting away from bone alcoves in the walls. Some wore scraps of armor, some even carried weapons aglow with lethal power.

Scar made cracking, spitting sounds that were returned by the newcomers. Her heart pounding against the inside of her ribs, Teyla shrank back against a skeletal pillar as the newly awakened Wraiths came to walk among their brethren. Scar moved close to a female with blood-red hair that came to her knees. In the sallow glow of the corridor's bioluminescence, she could pick out black curves and loops of tribal tattoos on the female's bare shoulders. Scar had the same patterns about his neck and cheeks.

The female caught sight of Teyla and her nostrils flared. She jerked and spat, angry and hungry at the sight of a live human. The Athosian woman tensed, ready to fight off the Wraith, but Scar made a grumbling sound and the female demurred, backing off. One of the female's group presented its weapon to Scar, cementing his place as the alpha in the newly enlarged pack. Teyla recognized the shape of a Wraith stunner rifle, the long gun fat and rounded like a huge silver maggot, the emerald glow of energy cells along its flanks and the wicked barb at the end. Scar accepted it and tugged on the cable leash connected to her collar. Teyla moved with them as the pack pressed deeper into the ship.

It was difficult to do anything other than put one foot in front of the other, hard for her to keep herself held strongly in the grip of her own will. From all sides, the boiling invisible hate of the Wraiths pressed down on her. Teyla knew that with one single moment of weakness from her, the pressure would overwhelm her mind with raw, inchoate fear.

There was a moment when Ronon thought he was going to miss it; but then the wind caught him and the Satedan saw the glistening flank of the Hive Ship there in front of him. He struck hard and found no purchase on the slippery fuselage. The curved hull plates were broad and interlocked, lapping over one another in the same fashion as the carapace of an armored beetle. Instantly he was sliding away, down toward the lip of the fuselage and the sheer drop into the Halcyon woodlands. Ronon lashed out with the battle daggers with all his might and felt the blade tips bite into the hull. Bone squealed at the impact points and threatened to tear the knives from his hands, but he hung on grimly, snarling with effort. The wind pulled at him, whipping his hair about his face. His slide slowed and he felt air beneath his feet; Dex was almost off the edge of the drifting Hive Ship.

With a savage grunt of effort, Ronon used the daggers as pitons, advancing up and away from the brink in a march of cutting wounds across the organic hull. He knew from past experience that Wraith craft were sheathed not with rigid and inflexible matter, but with fleshy material that could bend and deform under impacts from micrometeorites or ballistic weapons. He found a shallow duct and scrambled into it, breathing hard. The wind was rushing over the hull now, as the Hive Ship began to pick up speed. Ronon cast around and saw the gyro-flyer, below and to the starboard side, the rotor blades chopping through the air as it raced to keep up.

Sheathing the daggers, Dex swallowed down his tense adrenalin aftershock and fired his pistol point-blank into the skeletal duct. Bone and cartilage shattered around the intake, and almost as quickly a thick gel began to ooze over the new wound, hardening to scab it closed. Ronon drew his short sword, took a deep breath, and plunged himself into the cut, forcing his way through the exterior hull.

Sheppard found himself wishing for a ball of string or a piece of chalk. "A bag of bread crumbs, even," he said to the air, "or better yet, a deck plan." He had a pack of chemical glow-sticks, but nowhere near enough that he would have been able to mark the path. At what seemed like the hundredth T-junction he'd passed in the past ten minutes, the colonel halted and flashed the P90's torch down the branching corridors. He found himself thinking of the adventure games he used to play as a kid on his cousin's computer. "You are in a maze of tunnels, all alike," he grimaced. "Huh. I always liked first-person shooters better, anyhow."

In answer, a pulse of sound echoed down the corridor to his right, followed by a faint crash of impact noise. It sounded suspiciously like gunfire. "I was just kidding," added Sheppard, training his weapon. The sounds repeated, this time in rapid succession. The colonel strained to hear. He couldn't be sure, but one of the noises sounded a lot like a Wraith blaster, and the other some kind of energy weapon.

It came again, and with it an angry snarl. An angry *human* snarl.

"Ronon?" Sheppard flicked the P90's fire select switch to fully automatic and set off at a swift pace, homing in on the sounds of the firefight.

The passageway opened out into an inverted bone bowl, a strange colonnade where other corridors fed away like threads from the center of a web. There were glistening lens-screens on some of the walls and Scar moved to them, manipulating controls with quick, deft motions. Liquid sounds came from some of the doorways as irises made from leaves of razor-edged chitin worked shut, closing off avenues of approach behind them. Teyla watched Scar working the controls. That he knew this ship intimately was obvious, and she had no doubt he had been fully aware of how the vessel would be affected by the destruction of the dolmen. *He was waiting,* she realized, *biding his time out in that enclosure, looking for the tools he needed to reanimate his ship, his crew. And Daus gave them to him without knowing it. He gave him us.* The cruel irony of it was heavy in her chest. The arrival of the Atlanteans had merely allowed the Wraith commander to advance his plans, instead of waiting for the return of his kindred. Teyla tried to imagine the depths of hate it would take to live for so long, to hold out against the animal madness broadcast by the dolmen. There could be no other feeling inside that being but the need for revenge.

Scar noticed Teyla watching him and paused. "Speak," he told her.

"Where are you taking me?"

He ran a finger over a spot on the screen. "To my rightful place. To my *throne*," Scar smiled, the word entertaining him. "These prey rule their world through force of arms, and so by that measure I will soon be the new Lord Magnate of Halcyon." He clicked with soft laughter, but beneath the studied amusement was a dark streak of lethal antipathy, surfacing in his eyes. "I'll take the title just before I raze this planet to ashes."

Teyla saw a glimmer of imagery flash past on the screen, a display of the Hive Ship's internal spaces. Green glows surrounded a section several compartments away, nestled in the dense core of the vessel's meat. She felt an abrupt stab of understanding. They were moving toward the heart of the Hive Ship, toward what could only be the vessel's command center.

A pattern of blinking dots overlaid itself across the image and Scar gave an annoyed growl. He waved his hand over the console and it went dark. He spat out more commands in the Wraith language, and suddenly the pack were melting away, falling into shadowed corners or pressing themselves into alcoves where the corridor's gloomy illumination did not fall. In moments, it was almost as if Teyla and Scar were the only two in the room. She sensed their anticipation, stinging at her mind as the charged air before a thunderstorm might prickle her bare skin.

Now there were new sounds filtering up through the corridors that remained open to the chamber. Voices and footsteps, the sound of heavy boots against the deck plates. She looked at Scar and with theatrical indolence, the Wraith placed a hand to his lips in a gesture of silence.

The moment snapped and Teyla realized that the alien was laying an ambush for whomever it was that approached them. She bolted forward, opening her mouth to cry out, and the choke collar reacted instantly. The rings around her neck contracted to half their diameter, turning her shout into a wordless yap of noise, no more human than the bark of a graywolf. Furious, Teyla spun about, digging her fingers into the flesh of her throat, her nails scratching at her tawny skin as she pulled at the strangling necklet. Every noise she tried to make was incoherent, and the agony of the device was terrible.

Her vision fogged. Scar was gone, hidden away like his kindred, leaving Teyla wheezing like an elderly woman. She sagged against the curved wall as the first of the men came into the circular room. They had gas lanterns that popped and fizzed in the half-light.

"There!" A voice cried out and yellow glows hovered toward her. "Don't fire, she's not one of them…"

Another person spoke, a stiff voice used to wielding authority and being obeyed. "What in wound's sake is going on here? Get her over here."

Teyla held up her hands to warn them off, shaking her head and mouthing 'No,' over and over. She backed away but they followed her in, unaware.

"It's all right, girl, we won't hurt you," said the first voice, and now she could make out the silhouettes of Halcyon riflemen, their high hats, brocade coats and their long-lance rifles.

"Stay away," she forced the words to her lips but the sound that emerged was a rattling hiss; and then it was too late to stop it.

Shapes moved in the deep shade of the chamber, fast and deadly. Men cried out and screamed. Teyla dropped to the floor as gunshots rang out, ripping swarms of needle-rounds cutting past her and white sheens of stunner fire answering them back. Blood glistened as a lantern was tossed into the air, the pool of yellow light whipping around and catching frozen images of the Wraith attack before it shattered against the deck. A heavy form crumpled into a heap close to her and she came face to face with a dead man, the papery skin of his cheeks hollow against the bones of his skull. The Wraith had fallen on the trooper in an instant, a dozen of them ripping the years from his life before his body could hit the ground.

He had something held in the death-grip of his fingers; a curved fighting knife with a serrated edge. Blocking out the terrible melee around her, Teyla pushed forward and grabbed the weapon, taking it and folding it to her chest. Hope flared inside her. If she could get away while they were still feeding, perhaps the blade might be enough to work open the collar's locks.

She came up into a crouch, tensing her muscles for flight, as the last of the riflemen perished with a scream, his lantern dying with him. *Too late*. Bodies lay about the chamber, spindly with sudden rigor.

The Wraith chittered with post-kill excitement, but Scar was not among them. He crossed to Teyla and found the end of the steel leash where it trailed upon the floor. "What do you have, Tey-lah?" he demanded, holding out his hand. "Show me." Scar manipulated the leash's control and the collar relaxed again.

The Athosian woman spat out acidic bile and shot him a murderous stare. "You used me! You left me there to distract them! You made me your bait!"

"Give it to me," he said, ignoring her fury.

Teyla knew instantly that if she did not give him something, Scar would take it by force, perhaps even break a limb or draw off a few years of her life as punishment. In the same moment, she hated herself for falling into the trap of thinking like a slave, letting fear of the Wraith's reprimand rule her before he had even committed it. She held tight to herself, hands in the folds of her torn and dirty jacket, shivering with anger and near panic.

"Tey-lah," Scar warned, reaching for her.

She thrust out her hand and showed him the object there. The Wraith allowed himself a smile and took it, turning it over in his grip. Teyla looked away, and slowly drew herself back up.

"A transmitter unit." Scar weighed the Atlantis-issue radio in his hand, studying it. With a long-nailed thumb he toyed with the dials. "You were attempting to call your friends for help, yes?" He absently pocketed the compact walkie-talkie. "How quickly you forget, my little Hound. Remember what I told you; only my wishes will be answered today."

Teyla did her best to look contrite and afraid of him. It wasn't difficult to do, the leering face with its maw of jagged fangs there before her and a dozen others all the same around it, all ready to rip her to shreds; but she had the knife now, hidden and ready. Her fingers curved around it, the metal hilt solid in her grip. There would be a moment, very soon, when she would use it exactly as the dead soldier had intended to.

Sheppard emerged from a low tunnel on to a catwalk several meters up, running parallel to a long corridor overlooking a dozen clawed cradles, each one grasping a dormant Dart fighter and heavy with webs from a million generations of spiders. *Observation gallery*, he decided. When the Hive Ship was fully active, anyone standing down there would be able to direct the launches of multiple Dart flights, something akin to the catapult officer on a naval aircraft carrier. Right now though, the corridor was alight with pulses of deadly energy as a group of armored Wraith enforcers traded fire with a single figure at the far end of the gallery. From his high vantage point, the colonel saw their target moving and firing, and recognized the tall warrior instantly. He went through a bunch of emotions in quick succession; *pleased* to see that Ronon Dex was still alive; *confused* about how it was the Satedan had got on board the Hive Ship; and then *worried* by the overwhelming enemy opposition that Dex was trying to hold off.

Sheppard sighted down the barrel of his P90 and looked for a good angle to give Ronon some covering fire. He had to make it count. The moment he squeezed the trigger, he'd lose the element of surprise. The colonel had to get as many of those Wraiths in the kill zone as possible. "If I had a SAW, I'd be able to take them all in one burst," he said under his breath; but they had left the heavy M249 support weapons back on Atlantis. Sheppard waited, the seconds ticking by, anticipating the moment for the perfect shot. From up here, the whole confrontation was visible, and he had his choice of targets.

There was a noise behind him. The same noise as before, the same click of Wraith feet on Wraith decks, the faintest rasp of a hungry predator's breath as it closed in for the kill. One of the aliens had clearly had the same idea as Sheppard, slipping away from the firefight to clamber up here and take out Ronon from the catwalk. This time, however, John didn't have a shouted call over the radio to warn him. The Wraith slammed into him with all the force of a linebacker, the impact making the bone gantry clatter and rock from side to side. The alien's body check knocked Sheppard's gun from his grip and it swung away from him like a pendulum, still connected to his gear vest by a lanyard, although at this moment it might as well have been on Mars. They traded hard and rapid blows, Wraith and human punching at places where nerve bundles and soft tissues could be damaged. The colonel fell into the combat training he'd learnt from Teyla, remembering the Athosian two-strike combo that always hurt like hell whenever the woman used it on him.

The Wraith lashed out at him with its claws, screeching at him from a frenzied face framed by a storm of stringy white hair. The razor-tipped nails raked over his vest, ripping open pockets and spilling their contents, tearing a rent in his blue jacket. *That's two of them I've ruined on this mission.* He feinted and threw another punch, but the Wraith anticipated and hit him hard in the head. John stumbled and fell among the mess of ration packs, field dressings and other gear on the catwalk. By now the two fighters were attracting fire from the other Wraith down in the gallery, streaks of white lightning spitting past them.

By sheer reflex, he grabbed at a black plastic cylinder near his hand and smashed it into the face of the alien as it came down to feed on him. The ferocity of the blow staggered the Wraith back a step and Sheppard hit him again, suddenly aware of what he was holding in his grip. The colonel jammed the object into the folds of the Wraith's body armor and snatched back his hand, clutching a metal pull-ring. He brought his palms up to his face and spun away just as the flash-bang grenade went off.

An ululating scream tore from the lips of the Wraith as the burning phosphorus elements and explosive charge burnt into its chest. Flash-bangs were supposed to be an indirect, non-lethal weapon; but stuffed down a guy's shirt it would still do a horrific amount of burn damage. Dazzled by the glare from the grenade, the Wraith staggered over the lip of the catwalk and fell into the midst of its comrades.

Sheppard shook off the ringing in his ears to see Ronon race out from behind his cover, taking advantage of the mayhem. John grabbed his dangling P90 and after a moment of applied lethality, the two men had the gallery to themselves. Ronon blew out a breath and saluted Sheppard with his short sword. "Messy," he called out, with a hint of gallows humor, nodding at the Wraiths.

John hauled himself over the edge of the catwalk and half-climbed, half-slid down one of the bone support stanchions. "I prefer to think of it as improvised." Sheppard tried to force his usual smile to the surface but it was hard to find. This day had turned into one long and painful ordeal, and he still couldn't be sure if there was an end in sight. He glanced at Dex and for the first time Sheppard saw that the Satedan was streaked with dark blood. "Whoa, Ronon! You're hit, you're bleeding, man!"

The ex-soldier shrugged. "It's not mine."

"Then whose blood is it?"

He nodded at the walls. "The ship's. I cut my way in. It got a little..."

"Messy?" offered Sheppard.

"Yeah. You find Teyla or McKay?"

John shook his head. "Not yet. But they gotta be on board. There's nowhere else on this planet they could be." He quickly reloaded the P90. "I'm thinking we need to find the control center for this tub and bring it to heel, if Lord Daus's boys haven't already snafu'ed the whole damn thing."

Dex nodded. "Scar will do the same. I was on my way there when I got pinned down."

"You know where to go?"

He pointed. "Wraith held me on board one of these ships for weeks after Sateda fell. I got away from them a couple of times. I have an idea about the layout."

Sheppard gestured with his gun. "Great, you can play tour guide —"

A rasping crackle of static from his radio cut him off in mid-speech. "*Colonel Sheppard? Ronon? I hope you can hear this...*"

"Beckett?" John toggled the mike. "Carson, we read you, what's your situation, over?"

"My situation?" Beckett repeated into his headset. "Never mind me, what about you? We thought you were dead in there!"

"*Doctor,*" Sheppard said firmly, "*are you all right? Is the medical team safe?*"

Carson glanced up at Erony's worried expression in the seat across from his inside the flyer cabin. She was gripping another walkie-talkie, listening in, her knuckles white around the radio. "Aye, I think so. Corporal Clarke's back in the city. I'm here with Mason and Lady Erony."

"*Where the hell is 'here', Carson? You were told to stay in the capital!*"

"Ah, well. We came out looking for you in the lass's flyer. We found Ronon... Although he's since got another lift... We're going to head back and pick up the Jumper where you left it."

Beckett heard the exasperation in the colonel's tone. "*Listen to me, if you're anywhere near this Hive Ship, you have to back off right now! We don't know who's in charge of this thing, and you could get your asses shot out of the sky!*"

The doctor craned his neck to peer through the flyer's porthole. "That's just it, John, we can't keep up with it!" The Wraith craft was now the size of a dollar coin, the beetle-like shape no different from a garden insect clinging to the outside of the window. With every passing moment it grew smaller as it gained altitude. "The Hive Ship is picking up speed and climbing. It's heading for orbit."

In the nexus chamber, Daus's rifleman stared at the radio in his hand in stunned silence as Sheppard and Beckett's conversation went back and forth. McKay made a sour face. "Thank you, Carson," he said to the air, knowing full well that the doctor wouldn't be able to hear him, "thank you for confirming the completely obvious level of trouble we are now in." Before him, the control center's eye-like view ports showed nothing but blue sky, the color deepening toward dark magenta with every passing second. Consoles all across the chamber that had been dark and dormant were now alive with color, alien displays casting strange light over the fearful faces of the Halcyon scientists.

"The Lieutenant Colonel and the Runner," said Vekken, "they are on board this vessel."

"It matters not!" snapped the Magnate, jabbing a finger at the air. "The Wraith will kill them. Our survival is the issue here. Without me, Halcyon will be lost, rudderless!" He glared at Rodney, the light of mad fury in his watery eyes. "I order you to stop this ship! Do it now!"

McKay threw up his hands. "Make up your mind! The hibernation systems or the flight brain, I can't work on both at the same time!"

"Who is controlling this craft?" roared Daus. "Is this your doing? Have you made this happen, outworlder?" He advanced menacingly.

Rodney blanched, the memory of Kelfer's murder still very fresh in his mind. "As far as I can ascertain, these ships are autonomic," he managed, "they're like trained animals. Give them a command, they execute it. Only a Wraith can make a Hive Ship obey."

"Scar!" Daus spat out the word like a curse. "He did this."

And like the secret name of a demon conjuring the very beast it described, the next voice they heard was the rasping purr of the Wraith commander.

The Wraith played with the radio, caressing it and examining the device at eye level, in the way that an artisan might appraise a gemstone for flaws. Scar had quickly deduced the functioning of the communicator. "Human," he husked, a vein of anger audible under the words. "You prove more resilient than I expected."

Teyla smiled coldly at the sneer in Sheppard's reply, inwardly elated that her friends were still alive. "*You know, for a superior kinda Wraith, you're not as smart as you like folks to think.*"

"I killed you," growled the alien.

"*Beg to differ with you, eyeball. That's what happens when you mess with weapons you don't understand,*" the colonel retorted. "*Why don't you tell us where you are? We'd be happy to swing by and show you how they're supposed to work.*"

With an expression of loathing on his face, Scar reached into his tunic and removed the Beretta pistol he had taken from Teyla, holding it as if the gun filled him with disgust, as if it had somehow betrayed him. With an angry flick of his wrist he tossed it away, over the edge of the walkway where they stood. It clattered away into the darkness below. "I will not make that mistake again,"

"*Too late for that. We've got explosive charges planted all over this ship. One command from me and ka-boom. Game over. You're finished.*"

A cruel smile appeared on Scar's face. "A lie. If you had the power to destroy this vessel, you would have done so before now. You are not like the natives, you have no desire to keep it intact, like some wretched breedery." He threw a wicked glance at Teyla and kept speaking. "Let me tell you how this will end, prey. Once we achieve orbital parity, my ship's guns will carve Halcyon's settlements into rubble. I will sow panic and fear in the prey that swarm on this world. Calls have already been sent, Hive Fleets are already on their way. My kindred are coming to Halcyon, of that you may be certain. When they arrive here, I will lead them in a culling so brutal, so total, that it will become legendary in the annals of the Wraith. We will harvest everything that lives on this world, spare nothing but one single survivor..." He chuckled, and the sound was chilling. "Yes. I will spare the woman Tey-lah, so that when your species see her broken by the horrors she has witnessed, they will know that the dominion of the Wraith is total."

When Sheppard replied, his words were curt and clipped. "*Atlantis team, switch to alternate channel delta. Scarface can talk to himself for a while.*"

The Wraith commander gave a guttural laugh and turned

back to face the Athosian; he was quite unprepared for her to spring at him and bury a curved dagger in his chest.

"Delta!" Rodney shouted. "I know that one!" Without thinking, he snatched at the radio in the rifleman's hands and twisted the frequency dial to the right setting. "Sheppard!" he called. "It's me, I'm alive! I'm here, on the control deck! I think we can—"

The sudden impact came from nowhere and without any apparent intervening movement McKay found himself sprawled on the floor, clutching at his shoulder. The radio spun away, out of his reach.

"Do not dare to speak without my permission!" Daus raged, towering over him with his fists balled. His face was flushed with color. "I warned you!"

He could hear Sheppard calling out to him, but the thudding of his pulse in his ears made McKay giddy. "They can help us! I can't do this alone!"

"Are you as much a liar as you are a coward?" thundered the Magnate.

"I'm not a coward!" Rodney retorted. "I just have a heightened level of self-preservation!"

"You told my daughter you were the font of knowledge regarding the Wraith," he continued, "but you are not! You pathetic weakling! I would have killed you out of hand had I known how useless you are, instead of bringing you here!"

McKay felt sick inside. "You brought me here... Because of Erony?"

The rifleman's knife went into Scar's torso, through the ragged leather jerkin he wore, into corpse-colored flesh to the jeweled hilt. Oily blood flowed as the Wraith howled and beat at Teyla. Scar had released the control leash for her collar, and was clawing at her face with both hands, frantic as he tried to force her away.

The Athosian woman had her grip on the blade and she worked, trying to turn it. Wraith were incredibly resilient, their cellular structure and monstrous physiology capable of repairing wounds that would be instantly fatal to a human. A cut like this one would be only a memory in a day or so, unless she could render so much damage that Scar's body would not be able to save him. Blaster fire, decapitation, a salvo of hollow point bullets — all these things would have finished Scar off in an instant, but Teyla Emmagan had only the tools at hand to work with.

She tried to let herself slip into a cool, steady battle-mind state, a point of focus without anger or fury; but her years of training failed her. She had too much rage for this creature, a towering hate built from his cruelty to her and the brutality he had shown to those riflemen, to John and Ronon, to poor Bishop. Teyla realized that she did not just want Scar to die. She wanted to make him suffer first.

That chink in her psyche was enough, and Scar fought back with rage of his own, striking her mentally even as he clawed at her flesh.

Other hands grabbed at her, tore her away from him. Teyla went wild, turning and grabbing the neck of one Wraith under her arm, twisting it until it broke. She let the corpse fall and flew at the next pale-faced alien, her hands finding flesh to gouge. The thick spike of a stunner came at her and Teyla sank her fist into the owner's sternum, hearing ribs snap. She disarmed him with a crippling kick to the knee and spun the Wraith rifle about, using the spike to impale the alien to the deck.

Fingers flicked at Teyla's auburn hair and she felt a wave of pain as an unseen attacker dragged her backward with a savage jerk. She stumbled and her footing fled, the deck rising up to meet her. The woman cried out with the impact, the metal torc of the choke collar vibrating where it hit the ground.

Teyla spat out blood and tried to right herself. A heavy boot pressed into her chest and held her down there. Through a haze of agony she saw Scar hunched over her, the dagger still in his chest, his tunic dark with alien fluids.

"Bad little Hound," he said thickly, pain rattling his words. "I... I am disappointed in you. I thought we had.... An understanding."

Scar gurgled with distress as he used one hand to ease the curved knife out of his chest. He let it drop to the floor with a clatter. Teyla bared her teeth in a fierce grin. She had injured the Wraith severely, if not enough to kill him.

"You are no more use to me. Your purpose is served." Scar threw a nod to one of the other Wraiths, and the alien disconnected the steel leash from the choke collar. Without a controller to govern it, the collar's mechanism slowly began to tighten, the cogs and cables inside it ticking like clockwork.

Once again, Teyla felt the pain biting into her, the bruised flesh of her throat giving under the implacable metal device. She forced air into her lungs, filling them before the collar grew too tight.

The Wraith left her there to die. Scar glanced over his shoulder as he walked away. "It will not be quick," he smiled, his teeth discolored with blood.

Rodney gaped, for once almost lost for words. Erony... He had thought that they had, well, *something*. The beginnings of a friendship, maybe, a moment or two of shared interest in things bigger than Halcyon's petty wars and games of empire. He felt foolish. *You're just some guy from another planet, McKay,* said a voice in his head, *did you think you were going to bowl over some alien princess with your rapier wit and brilliant intellect? Of course she was going to be loyal to her homeworld first. Of course she would!*

"Erony told you about me?"

Daus's eyes flared with annoyance. "She was quite impressed with you, Doctor. 'He can help us', she said. 'He is a good man'." The Magnate spat. "Such pitiful sentiment! To think, my own daughter would have the temerity to suggest that Halcyon's supreme ruler place himself in the debt of another?"

Perversely, McKay felt a surge of gladness. "Then... You're saying she *didn't* tell you to kidnap me?"

If anything, it seemed that every word Rodney spoke made Daus even angrier than before. "Of course not! It is my greatest disappointment. Erony is weak, you fool, weak like her mother. So beautiful and perfect, so sharp and intelligent, but where is her killer instinct?" He raged on, eyes unfocussed, caught in the whirlwind of his own tirade. "A ruler must be heartless to truly lead a nation. Pity is not for the strong. I could never trust her to take the throne. Erony cannot wield the sword with dispassion, she feels the death of each lesser as if it actually mattered... And you!" Daus's fist hovered an inch from McKay's face, and he flinched back. "You have brought it all to the surface, with your ridiculous talk and your interference. She should have left you to die on the ice moon. You made my daughter *weak*!"

"You're her father and you don't even know her," Rodney managed, but the Magnate didn't hear him, too deep in fury.

"My world... My world and my precious child are ruined!" he said in a wounded snarl.

"*And who is to blame?*" The voice cut through the air, laden with static. McKay and every other person in the room turned to hear the retort that emerged from the discarded radio. "*You are, father!*" cried Erony's voice. "*You and you alone!*"

Daus picked up the device as if it were a poisonous animal, and Rodney saw clearly the indicator light showing that the channel had been open all along. For the first time, McKay saw real fear in the eyes of the Lord Magnate.

The tension inside the flyer's cabin was as thick as smoke. Beckett reached a gentle hand out to touch the young woman's arm, but she shook it off, gripping the radio handset and fixing all her energy upon it. Anger and sadness made her eyes shine brightly.

"*Daughter...?*" came a voice, whispers of interference beneath it.

"'The Magnate is Halcyon; Halcyon is the Magnate.' Do you remember those words, father? The first line of the Ceremony of the Throne, the words my grandfather spoke to you when he abdicated? We are not the masters of our world, we are its servants! You have turned our noble clans into a pack of squabbling beasts, fighting each other and living off the backs of the commoners. Your cruelty has become our people's... Halcyon is a mirror for the worst facets of your nature."

"*I did what I had to do to keep us strong!*" insisted Daus. "*There was no choice!*"

"There's always a choice," murmured Beckett. "It's just not always the easiest one."

Tears ran in streaks down Erony's face, lines of black forming as the formal make-up she wore smudged. "You pit the nobles against themselves to secure your power. You opened that wound-cursed Hive and let our greatest enemy walk among us, masked and leashed as if that excused it!"

"*Halcyon would be ashes if not for me!*" retorted the Magnate. "*Ashes and prey, dead and forgotten!*"

Not a single person dared to speak as Daus roared and thundered into the radio. His lips trembled and his words came out in strident barks, but Rodney saw the conflict crossing his face. The man was still, in his heart, the doting father of his daughter, even if the way he showed it was twisted and harsh to McKay's eyes. "I did this for our people, for your mother, for you!" he insisted, shouting to the ghostly voice of his daughter. "I did it out of love, do you not understand?"

"*Love?*" The sheer bitterness of the word aged Erony's father in a heartbeat, the color draining from his florid cheeks. "*Love was left behind when you created this society for us, father. It is a weakness you have expunged. Halcyon has nothing now but hate and anger.*"

The radio fell silent, the static hiss dying away to nothing as Erony ceased her transmission. McKay watched the man standing before him, the way he cradled the radio in his hands as if it might still give him some answer, some respite from the emotions churning inside him.

McKay watched the man and felt nothing but sadness and pity for him.

Her vision tunneled, the black shadows of the chamber encroaching on Teyla's sight, thickening, leaching the color from her world. The buzzing pain in her skull blotted out everything, all rational thought. She had sparks of memory burst before her, flaring and then gone as quick as the harvest festival fireworks on Athos. Dr. Weir had once told her how Earthers had a belief that a person's life would pass before their eyes in the moments prior to death; Teyla rebelled against the notion, trying to pull the last molecules of air into her lungs, but there was nothing but acid there now.

She saw the fields of rikka-wheat outside the village where she ran and played as a girl; a smile on the face of little Jinto as he offered her a cup of water; the rain on the day her father died; Sheppard speaking of his 'Ferris Wheels'; Elizabeth's friendly smile; and more.

Teyla thought of her friends, of John and Ronon, of how she would never see them again, and that cut more deeply than anything. The tunnel closed in over her, blood-warm and enveloping —

— and brought fire and agony. New pain ripped into her neck and she choked, a fierce blow as hard as a blacksmith's hammer resonating through her bones. Teyla felt a pressure against her lips, and a rush of aches from her battered throat as air was forced down it. Her chest rose in stutters as hot breath flooded in to fill the void. She gasped and the shock that came with it made her eyes prickle with tears.

"Teyla?" She felt the words on her cheeks. "Teyla, come on! Talk to me!"

"John." It hurt to speak, but she managed it. Her eyes fluttered open and a face faded into view, a hand's span away. "John?"

"Easy," he replied, his face drawn with concern. "Take it slow. You'd stopped breathing." He gestured to the side and Teyla saw the metal collar broken open on the floor, a bullet hole in the mechanism. "Had to risk it."

Teyla touched her lips. "You gave me your breath?"

Sheppard colored a little. "Uh. Yeah. Sorry. It was for the, uh, CPR."

She picked out Ronon standing nearby, arms folded and a discontented look on his face. "Are you two going to exchange bonding vows, or are we going to move on?"

"Right." The colonel pulled her to her feet and Teyla took a moment to get her bearings. "It's blind luck we found you. Another minute more, and…"

"Thank you," she said with a nod, "both of you. Have you located Rodney?"

Sheppard nodded. "Command center. Scar's probably there already, though."

"Good," Teyla said. "I have a debt to repay him."

The ascent program was almost complete.

Bio-reactors running at optimum power, the crystal-organic components of the gravity drive swelling with energy, the Hive Ship flexed and stretched as a waking beast would shake off the last vestiges of sleep. The engineered neural matrices of the flight brain and the nerve ganglia were alight with flurries of commands, new growths of bone sprouting to cover centuries of decrepitude and inactivity. Wounds in the hull were knitting closed and healing, the gash carved by the Fourth Dynast so long ago now a pale white dash of scar tissue, the gouge cut by Ronon Dex already a dark, shiny scab.

The rush of atmosphere over the blunt hull became thinner by the second, Halcyon's grip on the Wraith vessel diminishing as the drives pressed the craft up toward orbital velocity and away from the hand of gravity. The Hive Ship's hull embraced the icy kiss of space and silence flooded over it, the rumble of air fading away to nothing. The planet that had once held it prisoner turned beneath the twitching maws of energy cannons, optic sensors opening to study the sprawl of prey-life below, calculating and planning.

The ship had returned to its natural environment, the heavy and threatening mass that seemed so wrong trapped in Halcyon's watery skies suddenly free. It became the predator it once was, a lethal arrowhead of edges and spines, ready for the hunt. For the kill. For the culling to begin anew.

CHAPTER THIRTEEN

As one, every monitor screen tied into the Hive Ship's internal optical sensor went blank, the views of the corridors and shadowed chambers hazing over into milky gray nothingness.

McKay saw it happen and his chest tightened. "Oh, that is not a good thing," he breathed, and his hand clutched at the empty holster on his thigh in reflex, grasping for a pistol that wasn't there.

The Lord Magnate's eyes were still distant and unfocussed, the harsh words of his daughter still echoing in his mind. Vekken flashed him a look and then grabbed Rodney by the shoulder. "The screens," he said urgently, "what is the meaning of that?"

"A Wraith who was the former commander of this ship is on board, a Wraith who knows more about how this ship operates than every person in this room." McKay shook off the man's grip. "You figure it out."

"He's going to attack."

"If we're lucky. If we're not, he'll switch off the gravity in here, or vent all the air to space or something equally nasty." Rodney thought it through. "Unless... Unless he needs access to this chamber to fully take control of the ship..."

But Vekken was already moving across the nexus chamber's atrium, calling out orders to his riflemen. "Close all the entry points to this room! Set up firing positions! Prepare for enemy incursion!"

The scientist cast around the chamber, watching Kelfer's people milling in an anxious knot. *Those idiots have no idea what they're up against.* Halcyon troopers were quickly falling into kneeling stances, aiming their steaming long-lance rifles at the iris doors leading out to the ship's other decks. On the upper levels he noticed more figures moving, carefully taking up positions. They were difficult to see because of the asymmetrical way the Hive Ship's bio-lumes threw chilly blue light about the walls.

"I failed her." The whisper came from Daus's lips.

"What did you say?"

"I failed... Her. Both of them." The Magnate did not look at him. He seemed smaller somehow, all of a sudden the bluster and fury gone from his body. "I wanted... Wanted strength."

"Now is not the time for a crisis of confidence," grated Rodney. He dithered over his laptop. The control protocols where still displayed there, the setting to unbalance the bio-reactor and complete the sequence Kelfer had died trying to input. He looked again into the face of the man who had killed the Halcyon scientist and could hardly believe Daus was the same person; that such a man could be broken by something as simple as the words of his daughter.

Riflemen on the main level of the nexus chamber called out their readiness to Vekken, and the adjutant acknowledged them, pausing to load the heavy pistol in his gloved hand. "Steady, men. You will hold this line in the name of the Fourth Dynast, in death or victory!"

"Death or victory!" came the chorus of replies.

Rodney grimaced at the zealous sentiment. "Please! All the gung-ho crap in the world won't keep those things out." His words died off, as it occurred to him that the men up there in the shadows on the highest levels of the chamber had not responded along with the others.

Among the scattered gear from his Atlantis kitbag was a compact flashlight and McKay snatched it up, turning the beam on the raised gantries. The halo of illumination caught a pale face hidden behind clawed hands, and behind it the yawning maw of an open vent shaft.

"They're already inside..." he gasped. "*They're already inside!*" The words became a shout as Scar's Wraith began their attack.

Stunner pulses rained down in bright streaks of white, knock-

ing riflemen from their cover by the hatches. Vekken was screaming out orders, firing blindly into the overhead walkways. His
men reacted quickly, but the Wraith were already pouring down,
some flinging themselves from the higher catwalks to pounce
on their victims.

Rodney did a rare thing; he reacted without thinking about
it, and dragged the bewildered Magnate out of the line of fire,
forcing him into the cover of a bank of sputtering electromatic
valves. He was at a loss to explain the sudden impulse that made
him save the life of a man who was a killer and a tyrant.

He thrust the uncomfortable thought away. "A weapon!
You've got a weapon, right? Use it!"

Daus drew his swordgun and looked at it as if he didn't recognize it. "How can I... So much. So much blood on my hands."
He made a stifled sound like a sob. "Erony was right. Great
blades, I did not hear her..."

McKay took the swordgun and gripped the gold-plated pommel, fingering the trigger mechanism. It was heavy and unwieldy
in his grip. Nervously, he dared a look around the valve rack and
saw the melee in full frenzy.

The Wraith moved through the nexus chamber like a tornado,
killing and feeding, some of them struck down by rattling chugs
of needle-shot and left by their fellows, others taking up the
guns of their fallen human prey and smashing them against the
consoles. Vekken fought with unchained violence, the curved
half-moon blade along the breech of his pistol cutting into his
foes, the gun howling with each shot he placed into the heart of
a Wraith; but he was just one man, and the Wraiths, the freed
Hounds, the newly awakened and the wild and untamed, they
fell upon him and he vanished under a dozen screeching attackers.

Rodney let the swordgun go. It was useless in his hands, he
realized. He had to run, get away from this carnage, find some
other way to strike back at these creatures. To stay and fight
would mean death, or worse.

He grabbed at Daus's thick, ornate tunic. "Time to go!" he
snapped. "Before they find us, we have to get out of here!"

"Where would you go, prey?" asked an oily, menacing voice. "On my ship, tell me, where would you run to?"

"S-Scar," murmured Daus.

The Wraith commander circled around Rodney and the Magnate, apparently uninterested in the hoots of pleasure from his pack. He had a pair of ex-Hounds with him, their pristine silver armor now dirty and fouled. Scar cocked his head as he examined McKay, looking him up and down. The alien tapped his ragged tunic, indicating Rodney's Atlantis uniform jacket. "Another one. Another not-native. Wherever I turn I come across your kind. How interesting."

"Yeah, there's a lot of us," McKay found his mouth running away, babbling before he could stop himself. "Hundreds, thousands even, a whole army of, uh, us. You better not kill me, because there would really be trouble."

The other Wraith became calmer as Scar snarled out new orders. "Agreed. A kill is a waste of good nourishment." His eye narrowed as his gaze settled on Daus, the scar across his face dark with anger. "A waste of good *vengeance*."

One of the Hounds gripped Daus firmly and presented him to Scar. "It is you," husked the Magnate. "Still alive. Haunting me for my failures."

Scar sneered. "That is as good an explanation as any other. You cannot know how much it pleases me to find you here, Lord Daus." The alien poured scorn on the nobleman's title. "I wonder if you can understand the depths of hatred you engendered in me. The agony of living day after day with that accursed dolmen screaming in my head, doomed to watch my kindred made into primitives, fighting every moment to hold my psyche intact!" The raw anger coming from Scar was a palpable force, and McKay watched as he forced it from himself, grimacing with each breath. Rodney became aware of a horrific wound in the Wraith's chest, although Scar seemed to revel in the pain of it.

"You should be dead a hundred times over," Daus whispered. "Dead and dead and dead and dead..."

"Not before this," replied the Wraith, and his arm lashed out like a striking snake, ripping into the soft flesh of Daus's face.

Sickened, Rodney flinched away as Scar meticulously blinded the Magnate's right eye, ruining his face in the same manner that Daus had ruined the Wraith's on a hunt long since past. McKay felt his stomach rebel and swallowed hard, fighting down the urge to throw up. He lurched to a console and hung on to it, his head swimming.

"Now we are in balance," said Scar, over a strangled whimper from the nobleman.

Rodney blinked and his gaze fell on the control screen directly in front of him. He recognized it as part of the Hive Ship's sensor mechanisms, a monitoring station tied into the vessels array of passive detection systems. It could detect perturbations in various energy fields—magnetic, thermal, and gravitational—through reactions along organic gossamer webs, which trailed from the Hive Ship's spines in molecule-thin strings.

The console was juddery and kept failing to maintain a coherent image; Rodney could see where Kelfer's blundering experimentation had damaged the device, making its display foggy and riddled with ghost readings. A glow of light puckered into being on the glassy screen and something large registered on the gravity curve. The shape was ill defined but it was big, and it was moving somewhere out beyond the orbit of Halcyon's second moon.

"A ship." His heart sank as the words left his mouth. "A ship just came out of hyperspace."

He smelled the acid breath of the Wraith as Scar approached. "You are correct, prey. It seems my call for the Hives was heard after all. My kindred are coming to join the cull." The smile behind the words was chilling. "The fate of this world is sealed."

"It's sealed," frowned Ronon, running the flat of his palm along the leaves of the iris hatch. "No way we're going to get this open from here."

"Oh ye of little faith," retorted Sheppard, dropping into a crouch. "I brought a party favor from the Jumper before I came on board." From a pocket on his gear vest he pulled a small brick sealed in plastic and waggled it in the air. "C4."

"I thought you were bluffing when you told the Wraith you had explosives."

"Yeah, kinda. I just got the one." The colonel fixed the charge to the point on the hatchway where the detonation would do the most damage, and pressed a compact digital timer into the soft clay-like block.

"The gunfire inside has stopped," said Teyla, her voice still rough from her experience with the choke collar. She hefted a long-lance rifle she had appropriated from a fallen trooper. "We cannot tarry, colonel. Every moment Scar is in there, Halcyon is in danger."

"Fire in the hole!" The timer beeped. "Thirty seconds and counting." Sheppard waved them away. "Into cover, quick!"

Ronon checked the charge on his pistol and John slipped a full clip of ammunition into the P90. He glanced at Teyla and got a curt nod in return. "Hey, anyone got any flash-bangs left?"

Ronon nodded, producing a couple of stun grenades. "Two."

"Good," said Sheppard. "Use 'em."

The Wraith began herding the survivors across the chamber to the starboard side, dragging injured riflemen from where they had fallen and shoving them together with the few panic-stricken scientists who had not been cut down in the earlier crossfire. Others picked at control panels, illuminated systems that had laid silent for hundreds of years. Long-dormant gun turrets and beam cannons along the Hive Ship's ventral hull twitched and came back to life, lifeblood flowing back into them as they began the first stages of preparation for a planetary bombardment. Scar watched the activity with callous smugness.

"Is it too cliché for me to ask what it is you're going to do with us?" said McKay, trying to keep a whine from his tone. "Or is that a question I would be better off not raising?"

"There are many mouths to feed on my ship." The Wraith said it almost as if he were bored with the whole experience. "The malign influence of the Enemy's device will have affected many of my kindred. They will need to replenish their strength in order to return to their former temperaments."

"Yeah, I guess you wouldn't want to appear sickly when your buddies arrive, right? They might get the pick of the cull, and that would make you look a little stupid."

"Indeed." Ice formed on the word.

"Sorry. Sorry," McKay gulped. "Sometimes I babble when I'm nervous. Like now."

Scar eyed Rodney's laptop and the crude splice into the Hive Ship's systems. "What were you doing to my vessel, prey? Answer me."

"We... Wanted to..." McKay blinked, trying to think of a convincing lie and failing miserably. "Phone home?"

The Wraith commander snarled and came at him; but in the next second a wall of sound blasted out across the chamber and knocked all of them off their feet.

The charge did its work. The petals of the iris hatchway were either blown completely away or bent back in burnt, tattered shreds. Ronon leapt into the coiling smoke instants after the blast occurred, hurling the flash-bangs through the ruined doorway.

Inside, Rodney saw the familiar black cylinders arc through the hazy air and clatter across the deck. He spun away and covered his face with his arms just as the stun grenades blew. Brilliant magnesium-white flashes of light strobed inside the nexus chamber, throwing stark, sharp-edged shadows across the walls.

Ronon came in first, red bolts of energy issuing from the barrel of his gun. Sheppard took the right, laying down bursts of machinegun fire, and Teyla moved left, firing the steam-rifle from the hip in blaring chugs of discharge.

The ex-Hounds at Scar's sides were downed by the first broadside of shots, but the rest of the aliens reacted faster than the Atlantis team expected, shooting back with stunner rifles and blasters liberated from the Hive Ship's weapons pods. The flash-bangs had done the trick, however, and all the human survivors were flat to the floor or behind cover as the firefight raged across the control deck.

All except Rodney McKay, pressed up against a bone pillar that was barely wide enough to hide him. He glimpsed Scar, a blaster pistol in each hand, fanning stunner bolts back and forth, trying to catch the Atlantis team with a glancing hit. His mind raced. John and the others were turning the tide, but if that *was* another Wraith ship inbound, it wouldn't matter if they did win the day here. He could make out the sensor console from where he crouched; the mystery contact was coming closer, on a direct intercept course.

And if he could complete the reactor overload sequence Kelfer had started, by the time the other Hive Ship knew what was happening, it would be too late. The blast would engulf the other vessel. Two birds with one big thermonuclear stone.

But something seemed wrong, out of place. The silhouette of the new contact didn't move like a Wraith craft. Back on Atlantis, Rodney had pored over hours of sensor log footage of Hive Ships in the aftermath of the siege, hoping to find something of use if they ever came back. He knew how the Wraith slipped through space, and this craft wasn't doing that. It was coming in hard and fast, clearly primed for battle. The shape was all wrong, too, blocky and angular. It almost looked like the—

"*Daedalus*?" McKay's face split in a manic grin. "It's the *Daedalus*! Ha! We're saved! Weir sent them to get us!" But as fast as the bolt of euphoria raced through him, it vanished. *No, we are not saved.* The sensor return from the SGC Deep Space Carrier didn't show a ship about to mount a boarding operation or a rescue; *Daedalus* was on an attack vector, her rail guns running hot. To Colonel Caldwell and his crew, what they saw on their scopes was a Hive Ship preparing to annihilate a slew of defenseless ground targets. They'd have no idea that the Atlantis team were on board. *Daedalus* was looking at a clear and present threat to the planet Halcyon; and McKay knew Steven Caldwell enough to know that he wouldn't hesitate to shoot first and ask questions later.

"Sheppard! Anyone!" He shouted. "Warn them off! Tell

Caldwell to hold his fire!" But the din inside the nexus chamber flattened his every word, the crash of gunfire blotting them out.

Then Rodney saw the radio where Daus had dropped it, sitting there in the middle of the deck as bullets and energy bolts criss-crossed in the air around it

It was mayhem in here. John moved from cover to cover, taking advantage of consoles or pillars where he could, squeezing off three-round bursts at anything that looked Wraith. He heard the thunder of a long-lance and the sound brought the madness of the bound battle back to his thoughts, the sudden recollection of the scream of shot and the blurry frenzy of one long firefight. This was worse, as if someone had taken that skirmish and rolled it up, stuffed in a can and shook it. Enemy fire was coming from everywhere and the colonel's mind screamed at him to just react, to protect himself; the primitive fight or flight reflex warred with the trained, expert solider part of his brain, the part that pushed him on, forward, that stopped him from being pinned down.

Teyla made an angry noise at the Halcyon steam-rifle in her hands, the breech hissing open as the last cluster of needle-shot fed from the ammunition hopper. Hot vapor and droplets of condensation coiled from the muzzle, and without hesitation she turned the long gun into a club, striking a Wraith attacker across the head with it. The barrel broke, but the alien fell and did not rise again. The woman swung low and scooped up a discarded swordgun and brought it back up in a battle stance.

Sheppard wasn't worried. Teyla Emmagan could have taken on a dozen Wraiths with just a butter knife and he still would have put his money on the Athosian; and today she had a fury in her eyes that he had only seen on rare occasions. Scar's abuse of her with that damned collar had brought Teyla's darkest anger to the surface.

The chamber was filling with a haze of acrid chemical smoke, flames licking from places where missed shots had shattered Wraith screens or caught banks of combustible Halcyon technology alight. There was a moment when John was sure he heard a voice crying out over the noise of gunfire — *McKay, maybe?* — but then a couple more ex-Hounds came snarling over the tops of the control panels at him, and Sheppard found himself side by side with Ronon, fighting to stay alive for another minute longer.

Each time Rodney dared to think about leaving his cover, energy bolts rained past him or Wraith in battle frenzy screeched by. *I'm so close!* He could almost reach out and touch the radio, just a few feet more, maybe.

"So near and yet so far," murmured Daus, cradling his bloody face in one palm. The Magnate sat slumped against a panel, watching McKay with his remaining good eye. "It will not save you." He shuddered through the words, morose and pained. "The truth only wounds."

"I have to get to the radio!" Rodney blurted. "No one has to die! If I can get to it, no one has to die, you understand?"

A shadow passed over Daus's face, and he dropped his hand, letting McKay see the ruin of his blinded eye. "No one has to die," he repeated, traces of the ruler's former iron will surging in his voice. "You are wrong." The Magnate propelled himself up from the deck with a hard shove and heaved his bulk across the chamber, falling through the crossfire toward Scar. The Wraith reacted a heartbeat too slowly and the two of them collided, spinning around in a vicious dance.

On all fours, Rodney scuttled out from behind the bone pillar and snatched up the military radio, his heart in his mouth as he dove back before the moment of misdirection was lost.

Daus's blood-slick hands clamped tight around the Wraith commander's throat and he pressed every last ounce of his weight into the alien. "This hunt ends here," he snarled, "for my world and my daughter!"

Scar choked and wheezed, his eye bulging as the Magnate strangled the air from him. His pistols lost, the Wraith flailed at the man's torso, ripping the elegant silks of his jacket to ribbons, slashing into the meat of his broad chest. Scar spat curses in his own language, fighting against the Halcyonite's strength.

"No more!" Daus roared. "No more death!"

"No more life!" the alien spat back, plunging the saw-edged feeding maw in his palm straight into the cuts above the Magnate's racing heart. Scar's muscles jerked in a spasm of ecstasy as the Wraith tore Daus's life violently from him. Normally, a single Wraith would take their time over a feeding, savor it and make it last, but now the alien wanted nothing more than to turn this arrogant human into a husk, a hollow sack of skin and bone.

Daus's death-grip about Scar's throat lessened as the muscle and flesh on his skeleton shriveled away, the flesh puckering and turning tissue-thin. His last breath carried one last word from his lips. "Erony,"

Scar threw the corpse off him and let loose a screeching roar. "We are the Wraith!" he bellowed. "We are the hunters and you are the prey! We—"

A figure emerged from the choking smoke. "You talk too much!" snarled Teyla, and lunged with the swordgun. Scar spun, tried to turn the blow, but the Athosian woman was too quick, fuelled by her fury, and she ran him through. Gasping, twitching, Scar fell hard against the control console, bleeding out his last.

Teyla spat. "That's an end to it."

Ronon and Sheppard came to her side. "Left any for me?" asked Dex, glancing around. The Atlanteans had survived, for the moment.

Sheppard pulled a face. "Let's not forget, there's still a belly-ful of Wraith in the hibernation cells on this ship." He gestured to the Halcyonite survivors. "You people, get over here. We're gonna find a way off this ship, right now."

"You have a plan?" said Teyla, turning away.

"Oh sure," lied the colonel. "I'll let you know as soon as I've ironed out all the details." He waved at Rodney. "McKay! Stop messing with that radio, this is a rescue."

McKay paused with the walkie-talkie in front of his lips for just long enough to shoot Sheppard a withering glare. "*Daeda-*

lus, this is Dr. Rodney McKay, do you read? We are on board the Hive Ship, do not engage! I repeat, do not fire on the Hive Ship!"

The other team members approached the front of the nexus chamber, and there through the wide oval view ports above them the sliver shape of the SGC starship was visible as a glittering barb, turning to aim straight at them. "*Daedalus*?" repeated Sheppard. "How about that." He grinned at Teyla. "I told you I had a plan."

"I'm not getting any reply!" Rodney's voice was a terse yelp. "Maybe the radio's damaged, maybe the Hive Ship's interfering with the signal..."

To his credit, Sheppard grasped the gravity of the situation immediately and spoke urgently into his own radio. "Colonel Caldwell, do you copy? Wave off!"

"What's wrong?" Teyla asked wearily.

"Our own people are about to blast this ship, that's what's wrong!" Rodney blurted.

"Hah." The voice was thick and oily, a gurgling death rattle. Scar hung there, clinging to the console, Daus's discarded sword still buried in his chest in some mad parody of murder. "How entertaining. You prey seem to excel in killing one another."

Ronon turned his pistol on the alien. "What does it take to put this creep down?"

The Wraith had his hands on Rodney's computer. "I understand this device. So we. Will die together. You and I. My ship..." He nodded at the *Daedalus* as it came into range. "And yours."

"Stop him!" shouted Rodney.

Sheppard and Ronon opened fire, too late to stop Scar's finger tracing across the *execute* control.

Master Scientist Kelfer had made many mistakes during his studies of the Wraith craft. It had been his error that released the ship's commander, his errors that led to the uncontrollable awakenings of the dormant crew; but what Kelfer had understood was the horrific power that the alien vessel represented, and the lethal potential it possessed if it raged out of control. His overload program, hammered into the Wraith command matrix like a steel spike through bone, worked just as he had hoped it would.

In the Hive Ship's bio-reactor cores, chemical bladders filled with fluids to moderate and control the energetic effects of the power plant abruptly closed themselves off. Regulator valves and sphincters sealed tightly and outputs spiked. The coruscating energy, normally metered and synchronized to the Wraith vessel's moods and conditions, churned like magma. Crystalline monitors cracked and shattered, conduits full of plasma-like processing fluids split open and gushed super-heated liquid across the chitin decks, warping the bone and cartilage forms that made up the structure of the starship.

Whole decks of the Hive Ship instantly vented to space, burnt through by hyper-acidic reactions. Oxygen and breathing gasses combusted, firestorms rushing up every corridor. Wraiths were boiled alive in the amniotic baths of their hibernation cells. Organic sense-gels and nerve ganglia crisped and disintegrated.

Then finally, some tiny, critical element inside the bio-reactor perished, unleashing all the pent-up power of the Hive Ship's core in one single, fatal eruption of heat and radiation.

Erony stood alone on the lip of the shattered hillside, staring down into the huge bowl-shaped depression where the Hive Ship had stood only hours earlier, her face gray with the drain of emotion. Carson hesitated to approach her, and stood a few meters away, not wanting to intrude on her introspection, but conflicted by his need to help someone he saw was in pain.

Static crackled in his headset. Ever since they had landed back at the encampment, he had been unable to reach Sheppard or the others on the alien vessel. The hand-held radios only had a limited range, and if the Hive Ship was in orbit it was unlikely he would be able to get a signal to John and the others. He hesitated; perhaps if he went back to the Puddle Jumper, the shuttle's more advanced communications might do the trick.

"Such a great wound." Erony spoke quietly, almost to herself. "How can we heal such an injury as this?"

The noblewoman was staring into the gouge in the ground, but Carson wondered to which 'wound' she referred. This one, or one more personal? "Healing's my specialty, love. I'd be glad to help." Beckett wanted to mean it, but in truth, he was already thinking of how to broach the subject of evacuation to the young lady. How was he going to frame it? There was no easy way to tell a princess that she might have to lead her people from their home planet to some other, alien place.

The doctor turned as he heard urgent footsteps approaching. Linnian, drawn and sweaty, scrambled across the scattered dirt toward them. "My... My Lady," he puffed, "the camp's telekrypter was intact... I contacted the capital and First Minister Muruw had news. A ship, Milady! The observatories spotted a second space vessel in orbit. He counsels your return to the city with all due alacrity."

Erony faced them both. "Another ship? Have the Wraith returned?"

Carson opened his mouth to speak, but he stopped before he could take a breath, and pointed. High in the sky, a piercing, brilliant pinpoint of light flared. A ripple of static joined it on the open radio channel, and Beckett's blood ran cold. *A nuclear explosion?* "Oh no," he managed.

"What is that?" said Linnian.

"They destroyed themselves," whispered Erony, "they did it to save our planet."

The doctor grabbed the noblewoman's arm, the shock of the flash racing through him, bringing fear in its wake. "Erony, listen to me! We have to get to safety!"

Her eyes met his. "Where might that be, Doctor? Tell me, what place is safe from the Wraith?"

Beckett tried to give her an answer, but he found he had nothing.

Then from the hissing static, a very different reply formed in his ear. *"Atlantis team, respond."* The voice was curt and

businesslike. "*Atlantis team, this Colonel Steven Caldwell.
What is your situation, over?*"

"*Colonel Caldwell.*" Beckett's voice was heavy with fatigue.
"*I was afraid the next voice I heard would be a Wraith one.
The locals spotted your approach and thought it was another
Hive...*"

"Sorry to disappoint you," Caldwell said dryly. "We got here
as soon as we could. Looks like we arrived in time for the fireworks, though." The colonel frowned as crewmen darted about
the *Daedalus*'s bridge with portable fire extinguishers and damage control equipment. The shockwave from the detonation of
the Hive Ship had flipped the carrier over and blown out the
energy shields in a single surge of lethal power. Systems were
down throughout the vessel and reports of injuries and hull
breaches were still coming in.

"*You blew up the Hive Ship?*"

"Negative, Doctor, that ship did a fine job of destroying itself.
Almost got us too into the bargain." Caldwell threw an aside to
his executive officer. "Remind me to thank General Landry for
insisting on those shield upgrades."

"*Colonel,*" began Beckett, "*we had people on that Wraith
ship,*"

"The operative word being 'had', Doctor. Hermiod pulled
every human bio-signature with the Asgard transporters before
the explosion."

"Yeah, he's our new hero," Sheppard walked on to the bridge
with McKay following behind. "I thought Rodney was gonna
hug the little guy."

The scientist made a face. "He just has that weird Roswell
vibe..."

Sheppard nodded to the *Daedalus* commander. "Great tim-
ing, as always, Colonel."

"Pulling your backside out of the fire is starting to get habit-
forming," replied Caldwell, turning his attention to a report
from a junior officer.

"Next time we'll call Pegasus 911 instead." Sheppard ignored the jibe and patched into the communications circuit. "Carson. Tell Lady Erony the crisis is over for now. Scar's gone and so is his boatload of buddies."

"*Did... Did we lose anyone?*"

"Teyla's in sickbay, but she'll heal."

There was a moment of silence before Beckett spoke again. "*Colonel, Lady Erony has asked me to inquire after Lord Daus.*"

McKay picked up a headset. "Let me, uh, talk to her."

"*Rodney?*" Erony's voice was brittle. "*I am glad you... I am sorry for what happened to you. It was my fault, my carelessness with my words.*"

"No," he shook his head. "It's all right. I... I'm sorry. Your father..."

The bridge suddenly seemed confined and claustrophobic. "*He is dead.*" The woman said the words flatly, any sentiment bled from them. A simple statement devoid of all weight and emotion.

"I'm sorry," repeated Rodney. "His death saved the rest of us."

When Erony spoke again, she was calm and proper, as befitted a high noble of the Fourth Dynast. "*Thank you, Dr. McKay. In the absence of the Lord Magnate I must assume his duties for the interim. I will take my leave of you.*"

"Erony?" But she was gone, the channel silent.

The streets were lined with people as far as Elizabeth Weir could see. The queues snaked around the derelict dockside warehouses, out on to the main streets of the capital. Fuming omnibuses were halting every now and then to deposit more of them. She saw men and women of every age and ethnicity, children and teenagers. The only commonality they shared was the shabbiness of their clothes, the drawn look of a people who had grown used to being hungry all the time. The nineteenth-century tone of the Halcyon capital was something new to Weir, a sight she'd only seen to date in history books and Victorian costume dramas; but the faces of the people were all too familiar. She had seen that more times than she wanted, in Darfur and Kosovo, in Rwanda and Tikrit.

But there was a kind of hope here as well. She could sense it in the air, a mixture of anticipation and a little fear for good measure. Halcyon's people seemed to understand that their world had changed a great deal in the last few days, and it made them excited and scared in equal measure.

A huge poster across the flank of an elderly tenement building caught her eye. She could make out the remains of a massive artwork depicting the face of a portly, lordly man, but there were new leaves of heavy paper pasted over it. The jigsaw of pieces showed a young woman in regal finery, cupping a rifle in one hand and a basket of fruit in the other. But the new poster had been abandoned halfway through, and there were still ladders pressed up to the walls, as if they were waiting for the work to be completed.

"She made them stop," said Carson as he emerged from near the head of the line. "Apparently, when one of the reigning nobles dies, the first thing they do is paint over all the murals of the last fella." He shook his head. "Erony told them that her father's memory wasn't something they should just forget."

Weir nodded. "That's not an easy road to follow, especially after what took place under his leadership. She's taking responsibility for it, and that's a sign of a good ruler."

"Aye," agreed the doctor. "I've already heard talk that she's going to announce elections in the coming year. Democracy instead of monarchy. The nobles are going to have a very steep learning curve."

Elizabeth smiled. "And to think I just expected you to come back with some new diplomatic and trading contacts. Instead, you've sparked off a cultural revolution that will change life on this planet forever."

"It would have happened sooner or later," he noted, "people won't stand for tyranny forever. Hopefully this way there's been a lot less bloodletting."

"And at least we've made ourselves another ally in the Pegasus Galaxy. After all our recent troubles, I think we were due for a win, don't you?"

"Aye, but a ZPM would nae have gone amiss too. Shame about the dolmen. Rodney fair hit the roof when he heard that John had been forced to blow it up."

"Dr. Zelenka calculated that the energy release from the dolmen would have left it nearly dead by now, anyway." Weir added. "If the power source was waning, that would explain how Scar was able to resist the dolmen's influence."

"Couldn't we dig it out of the rubble? Those modules are tough, aren't they? There might still be some juice in there."

She shook her head. "That discharge you reported was probably the last gasp. If there is an intact ZPM under all that wreckage, it will more than likely be useless now."

They moved on toward the makeshift medical center, passing two heavy steam trucks. Beckett threw a nod to the nurse standing at the rear of the vehicles, checking off items of cargo on an inventory pad. "Thank you for authorizing this, Elizabeth."

Weir watched the pallets of gear come off the lorries. "Most of this was aboard *Daedalus* and earmarked for Atlantis re-supply, but I think we can spare it for someone in need. We can always send out for more. Erony's people don't have that luxury."

He nodded. "And now the Stargate has been reopened for travel, I've got the medicines I needed through from Atlantis."

"Are you making a difference, Carson?"

"Yes," he said firmly. "At last, I really think we are. Linnian's taken up the role of First Minister and he fits it well. The man's already talked with some of Caldwell's engineering crew about new irrigation plans, water supplies, that sort of thing. Changes are going to come, and for the better. With Daus and the Hive Ship gone, it's like the war is over. Finally."

Elizabeth looked away. *If only it were that simple.* In reality, Halcyon would find it hard to make its way through the transition from a military-based culture to one more focused on civilian life; and there still might be more Wraith on the way. *But we're going to be here to help them.*

Outside the warehouse-clinic, they came across Mason and Clarke, the two soldiers crouched and laughing with a couple of locals, a man with a prematurely wizened face and a youth in a brown robe. They were playing some kind of gambling game with polyhedral dice.

The dice rattled off the stone wall and Clarke scowled. "Oh, you bloody little —" The corporal caught sight of Weir and fell into a guilty silence. "Uh. Ma'am."

Mason came to attention. "Dr. Weir."

"At ease, gentlemen," she smiled. "Don't stop on my account. Cultural exchange is always a good thing. Who's winning?"

"Not me," Clarke frowned, adjusting the sling on his injured arm. "I think I left all my luck back in the Milky Way." He produced a chocolate bar from his ration pack and grudgingly handed it over to the younger man, who grinned. "Here you go. Don't eat it all at once."

Mason relaxed a little. "I thought you ought to know, ma'am, that I was briefed by one of the senior riflemen. They're still in the process of rounding up the last few Hounds that went garrity after the business with the dolmen and all. Lot of 'em have gone to ground, though, so it might take a fair while to find the last few."

"Thank you, Staff Sergeant. I'd like you to liaise with Erony's men, give them whatever help we can to assist in the search."

"Thank you, ma'am. And about that other matter..."

"You can proceed at your own discretion. Carry on."

Weir and Beckett crossed the clinic, the doctor pausing now and then to check on the flow of patients moving through the program of booster shots. "What was that about?" he asked, indicating Mason with a jerk of his head.

"He requested permission to be the one to write the condolence letters to the families of Private Bishop and Private Hill."

"Ah. Of course." Beckett hesitated. "You know, every time we lose someone, I find myself asking the same questions. Is it worth it? Will we ever be able to tell the people back home what goes on out here? There's never going to be an answer for Bishop's mum and dad or Hill's wife and kids, is there? Just a Union flag on a coffin."

"Everyone who comes to Atlantis, who serves in the SGC, all of us know the risks we face." Elizabeth smiled at a small girl as she left the room, the bloom of a fresh inoculation on her pale shoulder. "We just have to hold on to the knowledge that what we do here really *does* make a difference."

The Ceremony of the Throne began before dawn, on board the Fourth Dynast's sumptuous air-yacht. In a break with protocol, Erony had closed the High Palace's grand audience chamber and ordered the rites to be performed on the wide-open decks of the airship's flyer bay. The broad space was cleared of aircraft, and now it echoed with the music of brass instruments and percussion. Banners hung from catwalks and gantries overhead, and stark flood lamps illuminated the temporary dais set up at the mouth of the launch bay. Beyond the yawning aperture, it was possible to see the distant hills of the Halcyon countryside, a soft yellow glow at the horizon heralding the oncoming sunrise.

Every noble house on Halcyon was represented here, from the highest in rank to those at the very bottom of the pecking order. By official decree as interim ruler of the planet, Lady Erony had declared that all honor engagements and wars of privilege were nulled. All hunt splinters had been recalled. Every rivalry, every long-standing enmity was made forfeit. Barons and dukes who before would never had stood in the same room without drawing blades upon one another were together here, side by side.

These rulings had sent a shock through every highborn court on the planet, but the reaction to them was weak compared to Erony's final demand on those who attended the ceremony. No weapons of any kind were allowed inside the hangar. Every knife, sword and pistol, every poisoned hatpin and derringer, push-dagger and dart, all of them were left behind.

"She may as well have asked us to attend naked!" said one noblewoman, a dowdy baroness whose stage whisper easily reached the ears of Dr. Weir.

To her right, spit-shined and handsome in his Air Force dress blues, Sheppard heard the comment and spoke out of the side of his mouth. "Let's be thankful that she didn't."

"Eyes front, Colonel," said Caldwell, also in full uniform.
"You've got us into enough trouble on this planet as it is. Don't
start making fun of the rich kids now."

As the official invite had stated, Doctors McKay and Beckett, Ronon Dex and Teyla Emmagan also joined the three of
them. Ronon shifted uncomfortably under his greatcoat. He had
promised Weir that he was unarmed, but she had her doubts that
the big Satedan would ever put himself in a situation that he
couldn't fight his way out of. For her part, Teyla was resplen-
dent in a gossamer gown that her people had sent through the
Gate for the occasion; she very much looked the part of an elegant leader, the dignity of the Athosian tribes strong in her eyes.
Only someone who knew her as well as Elizabeth did could
have seen the slight tensing in her jaw, the haunted glint in her
eyes. Weir had only spoken briefly to Teyla in the aftermath of
the *Daedalus*'s rescue, but it was clear to her that she had faced
a traumatic experience while on Halcyon. Beckett caught her
eye and threw Elizabeth a brief smile; it was only Rodney who
seemed distracted by all the pomp and circumstance. McKay
couldn't keep his eyes off the ceremonial dais and the figure
that now approached it, clad in a wide robe trimmed with dark
green fur.

In her youth, on vacation in England, Weir had watched the
Trooping of the Colour outside Buckingham Palace, and she had
half-expected something of similar ritual and display to go on
here; but Halcyon was a militaristic people at heart, and their
culture mimicked a wartime mentality of blunt, direct action.

Erony climbed the dais and shrugged off the green robe,
revealing an ornamental sword at her hip. A gasp rolled around
the assembled crowd as she touched a belt buckle and let the
weapon, scabbard and all, go clattering to the floor.

"I'm guessing that's not a part of the ceremony," murmured
Sheppard.

When she spoke, Erony's voice was clear and strong. "The
Magnate is Halcyon. Halcyon is the Magnate. So it is written in
the codes of ascension, so it has been said time after time when

one took this role. But in hundreds of years, those words have become meaningless. They are spoken and they have no weight. Today, this changes. Today, I become Lady Magnate of Halcyon and I declare it to be so." She stepped forward, advancing toward the ranks of assembled nobles. "From this dawn, there will be no more wars over petty words and trivial deeds." Erony crossed by the parties of Barons Palfrun and Noryn, sparing them an even look. "We will no longer support battles without honor or humanity. From this dawn, Halcyon will take up arms only in defense of herself, in defiance of the true enemy... The Wraith."

Weir caught her eye and offered her a supportive nod. Erony continued. "Many among us feel as I do, that for too long our people have been set upon a course of self-destruction, of violence for the sake of violence. Many of you have yearned for peace, but lacked the fortitude or influence to bring it to be. But now you have a voice. Now our people, noble and common, have a voice, in me." She looked away for a moment. "A learned man, an outworlder and my friend, told me of a truism from his home planet."

McKay shifted uncomfortably and looked at his shoes.

"*Those who live by the sword, die by the sword.* I say here and now that this will not be the fate of Halcyon! The currency of death no longer carries any coin in this realm." She walked back to the dais, to where a second, more ornate set of robes of office was waiting. "I take my father's mantle now, and I take from his memory his love for this world... But I leave behind his appetite for warfare and the callous brutality that it spawned." She carefully donned the robes of the Magnate. "Our society changes as this dawn rises. It will not be easy, but it will be for the better, and our new friends from Atlantis will help us find the way." The woman drew herself up to her full height, and she was the very picture of regal nobility. "I am the Lady Magnate Erony Daus, I stand without Dynast and for my people, as Magistrex of the Sovereign World of Halcyon and her dominions... And to any baron who might plan to use force of arms to usurp my place, know that my army is not of soldiers, of riflemen or accursed Hounds. My army are the commoners, and without them, our world will not turn."

Silence fell as the first rays of the sun drew honey colors over the landscape, the assembled barony reeling from the import of the speech. Elizabeth drew her hands together and applauded, quickly joined by each member of the Atlantis contingent; and soon the whole chamber resonated with an ovation as Lady Erony turned away and bowed before the new day.

The airship's course took it over the jubilant streets of the city, the rolling countryside and back to the Terminal, slowing to a droning hover over the massive hangar that housed the Halcyon Stargate.

Down on the deck, the Atlantis team were gathering themselves together next to Jumper Three, ready to take the ship back through the wormhole to their city. Caldwell was already up on board *Daedalus*, after finding a discreet corner from where to beam back to the starship. Quite rightly, Dr. Weir figured that the locals were edgy enough without seeing a man vanish to add to their misgivings. Knots of chattering nobles drifted around in their own little cliques, some perturbed by their new ruler's edicts, but many alight with the possibility they represented.

Sheppard fiddled with his collar and loosened his tie a little. "Ah. These formal gigs are just not my thing. Dress blues always make me feel like I'm going to the prom."

Weir eyed him. "And I was just going to say how well you scrub up." There was a hint of reproach in her voice.

He shrugged. "Plain and simple suits me better, y'know? I guess I fit better when it comes to seeing things in a more, uh, *uncomplicated* way."

She caught the inference. "Maybe I'll handle the diplomatic stuff from now," she smiled. "I'm not sure if inciting a radical restructure of a planetary monarchy was really what I had in mind when I gave you the green light."

"You have no idea how happy it makes me feel to hear that, Elizabeth. From now on, I'll just do all the point-and-shoot hero stuff." He shrugged. "Your job's too damn tough for a grunt like me."

Weir followed him into the Jumper. "Well, don't sell yourself short, John. You helped these people find a better way. That's something to be proud of."

"Yeah, I guess it is." He sighed and paused to think for a moment. "Hey, you think I'll get a statue or something?"

"Just don't expect a pay rise."

Ronon found Teyla at one of the portals along the side of the launch bay, the chill wind whipping at the folds of her dress. He coughed self-consciously and she turned, offering him a wan smile. "Ronon. Is it time for us to depart?"

"Sheppard's warming up the ship now. We should get aboard."

"Yes." She looked back out at the landscape. "It seems so peaceful down there. The countryside reminds me of Athos. It is hard for me to look out there and think of the horrors we saw. The fighting…" Her hand strayed to the faint line of bruising on her neck. "The Wraith."

"When I was a Runner, I passed through worlds that looked like this. Like you say, peaceful. Quiet. But the Wraith were always there in the shadows, poisoning it. Always just out of reach. I hate them for that, for taking that away from people." Dex frowned, his own feelings conflicted about their time on Halcyon. "After all that happened here, at least on this planet, we gave it back." He studied his friend for a moment, thinking on the scars that were visible on her, and those that were not. There was much they shared in common in that regard, thanks to the predations of the Wraith.

"For now," Teyla replied. "I hope they understand how much it costs to keep it." She turned away and tapped Ronon on the arm. "Time to go."

As the last members of the team ducked to enter the open hatch at the rear of the Puddle Jumper, a clatter of footsteps drew their attention. Beckett backed inside to allow Erony and her retinue to address everyone.

The Lady Magnate bowed to them. "My friends. We must

go our separate ways and tend to our own concerns, but I hope this will not be the last time we meet." She inclined her head to Elizabeth. "Dr. Weir, thank you once again for your generous donations. With the information supplied to us by Dr. Beckett, we will be able to initiate a program of public works to eradicate the bone-rot once and for all." In turn she nodded to Sheppard, Ronon and Teyla. "You three fought like stormhawks in defense of my planet, despite the manner in which you were treated by my father. Your honor and courage will be a matter of record, and each of you shall be welcomed as warriors of highest rank when you next return. Halcyon is in your debt."

Weir took Erony's proffered hand and shook it warmly. "I've given an IDC transmitter to First Minister Linnian. You may feel free to contact us whenever you wish."

"And please, rest assured that the secret of Atlantis will not be revealed." The woman hesitated, and for a moment she lost her queenly air. "I wonder if, I might speak with Dr. McKay alone?"

"Oh. Sure." Rodney's cheeks colored a little, and awkwardly he followed Erony out of the Jumper.

She dismissed her retinue and then it was just the two of them. "I, uh," McKay frowned, fumbling at the right thing to say. "You look magnificent. Really… Royal."

"You are a good people, you Atlanteans," she told him, "and you are a good man, Rodney McKay. Your honesty opened my eyes, made me question when before I remained silent." She moved closer, her voice dropping to a husky whisper. "I owe you more than I can say."

"I didn't do anything," he said, frowning. "You took the leap. You stood up for what was right. You're the good person, Erony."

She looked away. "I find myself wondering… If things might have gone differently here, what future there might have been for you and I. The chances we might have had." Erony gently touched his hand. "But the world changes. I am Lady Magnate, and the business of state never rests. My life is no longer my own."

Rodney managed a smile. "You're going to be great. Halcyon has a golden age ahead of it."

She sighed, and then by turns she became regal once again, falling into the role of ruler. "I have only one more thing to ask you, Dr. McKay. I beg you to be honest with me in this, show me the same truth you have in all our dealings." The Lady Magnate looked him in the eyes. "Will the Wraith return to my world?"

He wanted to lie to her, to tell her everything would be fine and that she would live out her rule in peace and prosperity; but instead the truth fell from his lips in a hollow rush. "We have no way of knowing if a signal got out to any other Hive Ships. There's nothing to indicate the Wraith are going to come here, but…"

Erony nodded. "Then we will fight them when they come."

She left him there on the deck, lost for words, and walked off to join her people.

The Puddle Jumper described a lengthy arc through the dawn sky and turned inbound toward the hangar that concealed the Halcyon Stargate. Sheppard had an easy smile on his lips as he worked the ship's throttle and yoke like they were second nature.

"Ladies and gentlemen, welcome aboard Atlantis Air flight three," he grinned, "please put your seat backs and tray tables in a fully upright and locked position, and keep your hands and feet inside the Jumper until it has come to a complete stop…" He had to admit it; as harsh as things got, there was always something liberating about taking to the air, and no matter how far he traveled, no matter where John Sheppard went, getting some sky beneath his wings brought the world into sharp perspective.

"How are we getting back?" said Teyla. "The Stargate is sealed inside their bunker."

"Not any more," Sheppard replied. "Erony decided the Gate's been hidden away long enough." He pointed out the window. "Check it out."

Below them, the roof of the hangar complex cracked open and the massive silo doors retracted, dust and steam curling up from the mechanisms as they worked. From inside, a glitter of sunlight danced over an arc of brushed metal, and with the grinding hiss of a hundred pistons, the wide stone platform beneath the Great Circlet of Halcyon rose up into the dawn for the first time in hundreds of years.

The Stargate shone like a precious ring upon a cushion of limestone, the steely color of the naquadah bright against the shadows cast by the doors. At Sheppard's command, the dialing console flared and the symbol code for the city of Atlantis fed into the device, the electric blue chevrons locking in shimmers of chained power. The wormhole formed with a thunder of sound, the funnel of energy whipping into being, punching a hole through light-years of interstellar distance.

"Take us home, colonel," said Elizabeth, and Sheppard threw the ship into the shimmering pool of light.

ABOUT THE AUTHOR

James Swallow has written several novels, including *Jade Dragon, Faith & Fire,* the *Blood Angels* books *Deus Encarmine* and *Deus Sanguinius,* the *Sundowners* series of 'steampunk' Westerns (*Ghost Town, Underworld, Iron Dragon* and *Showdown*), *Eclipse, Whiteout, Blood Relative,* and *The Butterfly Effect.* His short fiction has appeared in *Stargate: The Official Magazine, Inferno!* and the anthologies *Silent Night, What Price Victory, Something Changed, Collected Works* and *Distant Shores.*

His non-fiction features *Dark Eye: The Films of David Fincher* and books on scriptwriting, genre television and animation; Swallow's other credits include writing for *Star Trek Voyager, Doctor Who,* and scripts for videogames and audio dramas. He lives in London, and is currently working on his next book.